We must do everything to insure they never do return. The old will die and the young will forget.

David Ben-Gurion
18 July 1948
Michael Bar Zohar, *Ben-Gurion: the Armed Prophet*, Prentice-Hall, 1967.

Jewish villages were built in the place of Arab villages. You do not even know the names of these Arab villages, and I do not blame you because geography books no longer exist. Not only do the books not exist, the Arab villages are not there either. Nahlal arose in the place of Mahlul; Kibbutz Gvat in the place of Jibta; Kibbutz Sarid in the place of Huneifis; and Kefar Yehushua in the place of Tal al-Shuman. There is not a single place built in this country that did not have a former Arab population.

Moshe Dayan, *Haaretz*, 4 April 1969.

Return

Faysal Mikdadi

- Lulu.com -

First published in 2008

Printed and distributed through www.lulu.com
Cover design by www.dixiepress.com

ISBN 978-1-4092-2931-5

This novel is dedicated to my wife Susan Walpole and to my children Catherine, Richard, Ray, Keli and Katy. I shall always be grateful to them for their unstinting support, encouragement, patience and love.

I have recently acquired a new family: Fleur, Chloë, Charles; and through Chloë, her two sons Joshua and Caleb. I hope that you will share this little narrative with me.

I am also grateful to Bob Walker, author of *The Progress Chaser*, for his patience and kind help, advice and support.

Finally, I owe an eternal debt of gratitude to my homeland Palestine. It has made me, for better or for worse, what I am now, a Diasporan with my heart in Jerusalem. I will return.

Book 1

Father of the Man

I am not alone,
I bring with me a great train of troubles, fears, and torments.

To begin my life from the beginning would be impossible.
Mine is not an ordinary life.
It does not move as a novel does. It is not chronological.
It starts now and returns to my birth.

I was born right after the War.
It would matter very little which war, were it not for the fact that it was
not the Second World War.
But it was a war that had more to do with my life than that other one.

For a start, it was blamed on me.
As a boy my aunt constantly reminded me that to be born in the spring
of 1948 was a fatal error of judgement.
At school my birthday was celebrated with the refrain, "We will return!
We will return!"
And for years I was never sure to where it was that we were going to
return.
I recited poems about "The Return" and sang songs to its honour.
Every morning of my school life I prayed fervently for it.

One day I was told the secret of The Return.
It came as no surprise and simply made all these poems, songs, and
prayers easier to understand.

The Return was to Palestine.

1

1. The Call

"Has the call come through?"

The speaker was a handsome man in his mid-forties. As he walked up and down in the area where the telephone hung, he kept adjusting his glasses. His blue eyes seemed disproportionately large behind them. This gave him an air of bemusement as he squinted at his younger sister. A slight scar on his left cheek kept appearing and disappearing as he moved his hand across an unshaven jaw.

"No Hussein, it will take some time. Why not let me make you a glass of tea?"

"Tea? Yes! Yes!"

He had been present at every one of his children's births. Being away at his fourth's caused him strong anxiety. The news was that the British were withdrawing from Palestine and that the new state of Israel would be declared any day. This in itself did not worry him much. The Arab armies would soon put an end to everything. Glubb Pasha's men alone were capable of crushing the Zionist state in its infancy. But nonetheless, ugly scenes had already been reported through the unofficial news medium of the spoken word. Nablus is a safe enough region. They are a tough lot those Nabulsis. Their town forms part of the triangle of death. Why worry?

The telephone rang. The man picked up the earphone apprehensively. The operator inquired in a harassed voice if this was Baghdad 305. Nablus on the line.

"Well? What is it?" asked the sister.

"Nothing. Allo operator. I'm not getting anything from … What? Yes! Yes! I'll hold."

He stood motionless before the telephone and felt amused at having shouted so hard. Somehow shouting down the telephone was the thing to do. He remembered how his father had refused to use that infernal talking machine. He had picked it up and thrown it down almost instantly, shouting, *"Iblis! Iblis!"* They had to tell the caller to recite *The Holy Qur'an* in order to convince him that the machine possessed none of the demonic. The old man had shrugged his shoulders and walked off mumbling something about the devil's tricks being as infinite as God's wisdom.

"Yes. I am still here. All right. Thank you."

A new voice came on at the other end. It sounded faint and half hearted. It asked him to keep his courage up.

"Is that you brother? What is it?"

It was a boy.

"Is it a girl?"

It was a boy.

"Cannot hear you."

A boy. A BABY BOY.

"How is Leila?"

Well.

"Disappointed?"

It was a BOY. Another SWORD in the ARMIES of ISLAM.

"Is she very disappointed?"

A little, of course, as only a woman might. But a boy is better, BETTER. He must be registered. Shall we call him Hisham?

"What name?"

HISHAM. After the great Islamic......

"NO! NO! Call him ..."

The round pair of glasses made a tour of the room and found no answer apart from a steaming glass of tea obscuring his sister's face. The eyes wandered helplessly over the walls and stopped at a picture of the young Prince Faysal.

"Call him Faysal."

A good choice brother! A blade. Saif. A sharp blade to cut through the enemies of Islam. A sword. Saif.

The eyes stared at the picture on the wall.

"*Cha*!" piped a commiserating voice.

Another boy. Three boys. One girl.

2. The Journey

Hussein readjusted his glasses and walked over to the train. Baghdad was bathed in heat. Everything was white. The houses were brilliant white. The sky was white. The train and its passengers seemed to exist in a life of their own against a white theatrical canvas.

Hussein walked into the first class compartment, sat in the corner seat and pulled the blinds down. Even then the sun penetrated the very metal of the train seeking to grill everything in its way. Hussein settled himself in his seat and took in a deep breath. He wiped his handkerchief over his face pulling it through his strong, brush-like black bristles. The train started to move, penetrating the haze of sunrays.

A boy!

Hussein had probably said that to himself a thousand times in the last month. In letters to his wife he had tried to hide his disappointment. Luckily, this had been made easier by a mistake made in naming the new baby.

Issam, Hussein's younger brother, had registered the boy as Saif instead of Faysal. He had most probably been drinking. Alternatively, he may have been so preoccupied with the meaning of the original name that he had confused the two words. Still, Saif was a nice enough name

After the initial feeling of sadness, Leila had accepted the boy. It never struck Hussein as odd that she should not. The insistence on a girl had been his all along. He had somehow felt that if he thought during his wife's pregnancy that the unborn baby was sure to be a girl, then it was sure to be a girl. In his wish for a girl he had been very much unlike his countrymen. A boy was considered a real addition to the family in more ways than one. But Hussein had wished for a girl, another one like his adorable second-born, Selma. When Leila had told him that she was expecting, they had both been unhappy. Three children were enough.

Hussein had asked his wife if she would like to get rid of the baby. They discussed the whole question very seriously and decided the pregnancy was better terminated. Hussein made inquiries and was told that the place to go would be Beirut. That city had everything in it. The doctor, a personal friend of the family, gave the go-ahead and all arrangements were made.

Leila had strong misgivings about the whole thing. Neither she nor her husband was particularly religious. They were both university educated, he as an agricultural engineer and she as an English literature graduate. But, nonetheless, she had misgivings. This made her more determined than ever to terminate the pregnancy.

As the time for the trip to Beirut approached, Hussein and his wife went to visit his eldest sister Al-Haji, who, blinded in her childhood, had become the religious monitor to the entire family. Holding the hem of her dress between thumb and forefinger and rolling it incessantly, she informed her sister-in-law of her opinion. It was not to be. It was wrong to terminate pregnancies. It was against everything that Moslems stood for. Life was put there by God through the agency of her husband. It was His will. It was His and only His to take away.

This harangue seemed to move the couple very little. Leila made gentle fun of the ageing lady. Hussein acquiesced - as he always did - and when asked to make promises replied that he could not lie. In despair the old Haji cast a dreadful curse upon the family, a curse backed by her fifty-eight years of light and a Holy Pilgrimage:

"If you go ahead with this lunacy; may He, in His Wisdom and Mercy, take the life of your other little one, Marwan. A life for a life, brother. A life for a life, sister!"

The curse was delivered with such vehemence and conviction that Hussein felt uneasy enough not to laugh. He felt angered because Leila's face had turned pale. He rebuked his sister gently and told her that all the curses of a troupe of pilgrims would not stop him from doing what he had decided upon. He was determined but laughed nervously.

A week or so later they left for Beirut. The journey was rather unpleasant. Leila was tearful and Hussein was bored. He was beginning to think that maybe this was a rather unnecessary fuss.

The fuss was not lessened by the bustle of Beirut. Hussein shepherded his wife into the Hotel Palestine thinking that God's real Mercy lay in keeping him out of such a noisy and affected city. A week or so and they would be back in Tulkarm. But they did not even stay a day and were on their way back the very next morning. A telephone call had informed them that their little boy, Marwan, had been taken very ill during the night. The two parents said nothing about the curse but its words haunted them all the way home, "A life for a life."

When they arrived they found that the little boy was indeed very ill. The doctors attending were of the opinion he had typhoid fever. His face had red blotches indicating a high fever. He had been sick all day and the doctors feared he might choke. Taking Hussein aside the doctors informed him they had done all they could for the boy. Whether he would live or not was entirely in the hands of the All Merciful and All Beneficent. Medically speaking, however, his chances of survival were about equal. They left instructions and promised to call in the morning. One of them ventured to suggest hiring a nurse.

Leila sat by the cot watching her child in a quiet slumber punctuated by an occasional heart-rending moan. Now and then he would open his large eyes and stare at his mother. At other times he simply opened his eyes and wailed pitifully, got himself into a state, and was sick again. The room was full of the nauseating smell of excrement, medicine and vomit.

Hussein sat beside his wife. Leila wanted no nurse in the house. Hussein agreed. Neither of them would go to sleep. He felt very tired and wished that he could go to bed for a while. The idea of doing so put him to shame. He held his wife's hand and squeezed it whenever he felt sleep overcoming him.

As they sat there staring at the boy lying asleep with his tiny fists clenched as if in defiance of the intrusions into his security, they spoke softly of the elder sister's curse. Hussein ridiculed the whole thing as sheer coincidence. Leila agreed intellectually though her heart would have nothing to do with her reasoning.

"Hussein, what if ..." she faltered.

"Nonsense, dear! Nonsense" Hussein quickly replied.

"You're right, of course, but what if it were possible? What if our plans ..."

Again Hussein interrupted; warning her to be scientific and not to give way to superstition.

But the large imploring eyes of the sick child and its tiny hand burning dispelled any serious thoughts of science. Nothing makes a human being so religious as that pained look and uncomprehending cry. And with the sick child there was the fatigue, sleeplessness, and despair. Leila promised that if her youngest was spared by Him the new child would also be spared. The agreement made her feel better.

So He spared him, and, so did she.

The train continued to cut its way through the haze of the sun. Hussein lifted the side of the blind and looked out at the desert. The only life was the shadow painted by the smoking and steaming machine making its way through the wilderness. A few hours more and he would be able to see his wife and the new boy.

A boy! When Leila had made her promise to the sick child they had both consoled themselves with the thought that it might be a girl. That would make two boys and two girls. The eldest, Ali, was twelve. His sister, Selma, was six and Marwan ten months. A little girl would be just perfect. They could call her Tamima or Muna. Hussein had made the mistake of constantly telling his two older children of the little sister on the way. How they must have been disappointed when they discovered it was yet another boy.

As Hussein neared home he became apprehensive. He had not seen his family for over a month. During that period Israel was born. The Zionist infant seemed more hearty than the Arab political midwives had thought it would be. Hussein had lost much of his property. But the family was safe. They had all been carried away from Tulkarm by Nassim, Hussein's elder brother. The future remained uncertain and very unsettling.

The train arrived on time. Whatever else, the railway still retained British punctuality! He got into a taxi whose driver talked incessantly of the war. He could not understand what King Abdullah was up to. Jerusalem was as good as won by his army. A truce? That was a mockery! He talked of the fighting and almost shed tears of anger at Deir Yassin. How could the King let that go unavenged? They were busy making deals. But, not to worry, the Arab armies were above such political manoeuvres.

Hussein listened to nothing of this, his thoughts racing home ahead of the sluggish taxi.

He arrived to a jolly, though somewhat sombre, reception. Leila was carrying the ailing Marwan who never seemed to have recovered completely from his long illness. She led the way to the newborn's nursery. Hussein stood by the cot staring at the sleeping infant with its tiny fist covering its nose. He gently moved the hand to look at the little face. Its hand flopped by its side as if it were not connected to the rest of the tiny body. Hussein smiled at the small head, the imperceptible nose hard at work breathing.

The sickly boy uttered a few feeble syllables for attention but

Hussein carried on staring at the baby. Leila smiled at Marwan who had suddenly stopped talking and inclined his head to one side. He lifted an arm in the air and waved at his father. Then he bent his head to the other side, scratched his mother's cheek, and violently rubbed his sleepy eyes. He breathed fast and noisily and his round face seemed to wonder what all the fuss was about. He looked at the little red head with the jet-black hair that his father was stroking. Then he gently put his head on his mother's shoulder, gave a prolonged and pathetic cry then fell asleep.

3. The Exodus

Everything that a man believes in; his way of life, his attitude towards his property and savings, his love for his family, all these tend to increase or decrease in inverse proportion to any trouble arising in his life. Hussein was no exception. As the Arab armies fought a bitter war against the various Jewish forces, which ultimately became the Israeli army, men busied themselves in cushioning their families in safety. A war between leaders of nations or between armies (after all a very small part of an overall population) decides the ultimate fate of millions. These millions, however, move more according to the rumours and passions amongst them.

Rumour had it that the Jews were committing atrocities in all the regions they overcame. Declarations by the Israeli authorities to the civilian population not to panic were ignored. The massacre of Palestinian villagers at Deir Yassin was still ripe in people's memories. Rumours were circulated that the occupying Israeli forces put pressure on the local population to move out. Palestinian currency was declared acceptable but was accepted by no one. Stamps were ignored. Provisions became scarce. In short, organised panic had set in. A great exodus of Palestinian people was taking place. Refugees reported being shot at over their heads in order to make them move faster. Some twelve days after his return from Baghdad, Hussein had decided to take his family out of the country.

Earlier that morning he had gone to the nearest town to bring the necessary money for the journey. There was a perverse pleasure from a sense of security at having withdrawn cash from his sacred savings. He had left the car at a small garage to have it checked and filled for the journey.

Secure in the knowledge of enough cash in his pocket, Hussein walked across the Town Square to see his ageing aunt. The aunt, who was over eighty years old, had categorically refused to leave her home. A similar position had been taken by the other elders. A polite deception was put forward to protect the younger members of the family. It was silently agreed by all that the mass departure was only an early summer holiday. Those leaving were: Hussein, his elder brother Nassim, his younger Issam, and his sister, Haji.

Hussein walked into the garden with its silent fountain in the middle. A rather frightened maid stood on the stairs with a tray in her hands. She inquired in her peasant voice if it were true that the English were coming. Hussein quietly explained that the 'English' had left Palestine. The maid was sceptical. She pointed out that in her village, a few miles away, there were several 'English' soldiers to be seen. Hussein reassured her again and walked into his aunt's front room.

The old woman was at her prayers, sitting up in her chair; she had long ago given up prostrating herself on account of her age. Hussein sat down in that patronising way that seeks to say, 'I don't mind you praying despite the obvious futility of such an exercise.' He sat back impatiently listening to his aunt repeating her prayers. Having looked right and then left with an expression of submission mixed with resentment at having to submit, the grand old lady looked at her nephew.

"Ahlan wa sahlan! Welcome. Welcome, nephew. So, you have decided to leave today?"

"Yes. We are going to Damascus, aunt."

She looked at him for a while, then, lowering her head, seemed about to doze. Suddenly she looked up as though affronted at anyone suspecting her of having had a quick nap.

"And everybody has left, then?"

"Yes."

"And Issam?"

"Yes."

"Took Haji with him?"

"Yes."

Hussein was accustomed to his aunt's mode of conversation, the art of which lay in asking, discussing, propounding, and commenting on very obvious facts. At forty five he knew of the intense pleasure derived from the obvious trifles of everyday life. He knew that this pleasure was enjoyed particularly by old men and women who found in it a convenient way of remembering.

"How long will you be away?"

"About a month. Till all this has simmered down," Hussein replied diffidently.

"Speak up, child. Speak up."

Hussein repeated his reply louder. The silence that came afterwards was in conflict with Hussein's inner turmoil as he wanted to leave quickly. Turkish coffee was brought in. Aunt spoke of Ottoman rule. She spoke of British rule. She spoke of rules in general. It mattered little who the authorities were. When the English came …

Shouting and commotion were heard from the streets. The maid came running into the room. Her face flushed, she shouted "*Inglese! Inglese!* The English are coming." The aunt told her to calm down and clear the coffee things. Hussein stood up, trying hard not to seem in too much of a hurry. He walked up to his aunt and kissed her hand.

"Yes. What a good boy you are!" she said with a mischievous twinkle in her eyes. "See you in a month, of course."

Hussein fancied that he saw her chin quiver slightly, but there was nothing there when he looked again. The old eyes kept their mischief as the maid motioned Hussein away.

At the garage all was pandemonium. Among the shouting and excitement could be heard the word "*inglese*" repeated over and over again. Hussein paid his bill, which seemed to have more than doubled since the morning, and got into his car. As he drove out he could hear the men nearest to him arguing.

"The English are coming!"

"Stupid! The English are gone. It's the Yid."

"Oh!! The Yid is coming. The Yid is coming. Anyhow they're all English."

From the corner of his eye Hussein caught sight of the garage owner spreading out a clean white sheet on a stick. Behind him hung the framed picture of Clark Gable to mollify the intruders.

****

Leila had been too busy packing to be worried. Hussein had told her that morning of his decision to leave. Since then she had been busily working about the house. Not that there was a great deal to pack. Hussein said that he would try to see if he could lay his hands on a lorry to transport some of their valuables. Under the circumstances this seemed doubtful. Ali and Selma, thirteen and seven years old respectively, were kept busy packing their toys. Marwan toddled about the house with that vacant look that had become part of him since his serious illness, a look that seemed to say, "What is happening? What have I done wrong?" Selma picked him up now and then and tried to comfort him. Ali made faces at him trying to elicit a smile. Marwan would stare at his brother, shake his head, and toddle off in search of his mother.

Saif was peacefully asleep in his cot which stood beside the luggage waiting to be loaded into the car. He had proved himself a very melancholy baby who neither cried nor made any other noise. It was as if he felt that the occasion was a momentous one requiring a goodly measure of a 'wait and see' policy.

Hussein arrived home just before lunch. The meal had been completely forgotten in the fuss. Dry biscuits were distributed in lieu. The family sat for a quick consultation on the state of affairs as Hussein told his wife about the morning. Selma looked up from behind her biscuit and asked: "Baba, why are the English coming? What are they?"

Selma vaguely associated the English with her father's car, Austin of England which he had always proudly referred to as being an example of great English workmanship. He explained that the British had left Palestine and that the people coming to take their homes were the Jews.

"Are they Germans?" she asked remembering seeing a picture of several Jews in a British transit camp after Germany lost the war.

"Hush Selma!" Leila was getting nervous now that she had sat down for a break.

"Are they Germans?" whispered Selma to Ali.

"No silly. The Germans are dead. The English killed them. The Germans killed the Jews."

"But the Jews are coming and ..."

"Quiet Selma. Ali be silent" Hussein ordered.

With the wisdom of children, Selma settled the problem to her satisfaction by taking a big bite of her biscuit and looking at Ali inviting him to compare bites.

Hussein explained that he had managed to get a lorry that would be arriving that afternoon after they were gone. He said he had given the key to the driver who had instructions to take only what would be in the large front room. Leila had piled all their valuable possessions in there. The Persian carpets were rolled up neatly with a bag tied at either end to prevent damage. Neither Hussein nor Leila said what was foremost in their minds: that the lorry driver need never deliver anything anywhere. They were aware that in times of fear, suspicion was pushed behind a cloak of acceptance of whatever was inevitable. The necessity was assumed as a shield against pain or the possibility of pain.

In the family car were to be taken all Hussein's documents, papers, and other bits and pieces. His books were to be entrusted to the lorry driver. The older maid was to come with them. The younger maid would be packed off to Nablus where her parents had sent a message that the invaders had been stopped in their march. The conference was broken up and hasty last minute arrangements had commenced.

All the things were loaded. Ali, Selma, Marwan, and the maid, holding Saif in her arms, sat in the back. Leila embraced the younger maid and gave her some money. "See you in one month my dear." The little white lie of an early summer holiday, propounded despite all appearances to the contrary was used to avoid any excess of nationalistic fervour. The lie had become the truth in Leila's mind. In times of national disasters to believe was to protect.

"See you in one month."

"Bye."

"See you."

"Allah be with you", shouted the maid as the car moved off. Marwan in the back seat suddenly shouted after his month long silence. All through the journey he would often pipe out, his voice getting louder and stronger, "Dee oo im ome mont!".

****

The journey to Damascus was long and slow. The car was often stopped at checkpoints set up by the various armies, distinguishable not so much by their uniforms as by their different accents. Syrians, Egyptians, Jordanians, and even a few Lebanese. The roads were one mass of people fleeing with what little they possessed. Men could be seen carrying mattresses, children, and luggage. At one checkpoint Hussein saw one man carrying a child on one arm, a mattress on his shoulder, and a second child on his back securing it by holding its sleeve in his mouth. Silently, full of fear, and weighed down with objects and children, the mass moved towards the River Jordan. Here and there stragglers sat by the roadside too exhausted to walk.

The nearer they approached the River Jordan the noisier the crowds became. There were rumours that the Jordanians were sending them back. Several people had passed them saying they had been told to go to Nablus where they would be safe. The Jordanian army would protect them. Some believed this and turned back. Others surged ahead. The confusion resulting from two masses moving in opposite directions was terrifying to anyone who would stop and watch, though no one did.

At a small village, some distance from the river, the surging masses stopped. News of dangerous action ahead of them spread like fire through dry wood. Hussein decided to stop the night at the village

Villagers, seeing a big car among the herd of people, came gathering round for a closer look. Seeing a pair of large blue eyes behind glasses nervously negotiating an entry into the village, and observing the driver's Western dress, they kept a suspicious distance. Their suspicion changed to curiosity when the man stepped out of the car and inquired about a place for the night. Interest replaced idle curiosity when he informed them that he would pay for accommodation. Suspicion, curiosity, interest, sympathy and then to rivalry as the peasants smiled and chattered amongst themselves. A middle aged man came forward and asked Hussein to share his house for the night.

Several women came up to Leila. Some admired Marwan, some Selma; others spoke to the maid on equal terms. As befitting anyone travelling by car the maid retained her distance remaining aloof from the women.

The family settled themselves in what passed for a house. One of its two rooms was without a roof and served as a sitting-room. By early evening Marwan and Saif were put to bed while the rest, along with the peasant and his wife, sat in the sitting-room. They sat in a circle around a small grill on which stood a kettle ready to make strong black tea to drink after a meal of bread and olives with onions and pickled cucumbers. The peasant, with his strong arms gesticulating, was proudly telling the master (as he called Hussein) how his two sons had gone to join up to fight the English. Hussein listened quietly without correcting the peasant's misconception about the Jews being English.

"Ah yes sayyidi the English are done for this time."

"But," his wife started in a voice that showed that her pronouncements had equal weight with her husband, "they say that these are only the Jews. They say that the English are gone and aren't helping them anymore. They say that more Jews are ..."

"Ah!! They can say what they want. They're all the same. They are all foreign. They came from the dark continent."

To change the subject, the wife complimented Leila on her husband's looks, especially his blue eyes. "Just like an English gentleman." The peasant agreed staring with his brown eyes, full of admiration. Leila smiled inwardly at the peasant woman's simple-minded contradiction.

When everyone had retired to sleep in the only other room in the house and the peasant had gone with his wife to his brother's house, Hussein sat watching the few remaining embers in the grill. Outside, noises of people talking and laughing floated in on his thoughts. In the background he was aware of the monotonous and comforting noise made by the crickets. He looked up at the sky and was filled with a feeling of warmth. A feeling of security engulfed him as he looked round at the four walls. His only roof was the quiet, dark sky, clear with thousands of twinkling stars but no moon to be seen anywhere. He was suddenly seized with a warm feeling of inexhaustible happiness. He rose quietly, walked to where his family was sleeping peacefully, opened the door, and stepped out.

Outside as far as the eye could see were fires burning. What had been a fleeing mass during the day had become pockets of isolated and talkative human beings about to spend their first night in the open. There was a festive air as that of a picnic. Some children ran from group to group sitting down with each for a little while and then running off to join another. The women were busy pouring tea into small glasses. In most groups one or two led the discussion while the others listened.

Hussein walked with that tranquillity of mind found in a man who had discovered the secret of his inner life regardless of the outside world. Being a severely practical man this new feeling both frightened, and made him happy. He knew that in practical terms this was a false security. Every time he felt the sensation slipping away from within himself he looked up at the sky which seemed to replenish him immediately.

"They say that the king has ordered a camp set up outside Nablus with all amenities." The voice came from a black form silhouetted against a camp fire.

"I don't believe it. They've betrayed us," shouted a young and angry voice.

Various voices piped out "Ah! Shame! Shame! How could you speak like that George?"

"I'll tell you why," said the first voice. "It's because he's a Nazarene and so he won't believe that ..."

Hussein could hear no more as he walked on. He thought of his life so far. He thought of how he had run away from home to study in France, of how he had come back with a degree but physically so weak that his sister had mistakenly sent him away as a beggar. He thought of how he went to Beirut to marry Leila. Good, pretty, intelligent, and quiet Leila. A good match, everyone had said. One of the richest families in Lebanon. The younger sister was prettier, but never mind, Leila had qualities of character to compensate.

Hussein stopped at another group and listened to their chatter. A vehement argument was going on as to whether the Jews had all come with the English or not. Someone, possibly a city labourer, protested that the English were shooting the Jews on the beaches. He was roundly condemned for treasonable words. Another asked how anyone could account for the Jews speaking English. A third replied that many spoke German. A quiet voice said that there were some Russian and even Arabic speaking Jews.

"A right mess the English have made of things!" said a voice that sounded as if it belonged to an educated man.

"Tell us about it Jos-ay-ph." clamoured several of the men. The man cleared his throat and started to explain about Balfour. Hussein walked off.

He returned to the dilapidated house and lay down in the front room. He did not want to lose sight of the sky which had given him so much comfort. He stared at it incessantly as he half-listened to the chatter outside. He felt himself overcome by sleep. Again and again he would start up and look at the sky. He felt himself going slowly. He tried to fight it off by looking up at the sky. He slept.

****

He woke when he heard a scream but could not make out what it was. He first saw the sky with stars still twinkling joyously. He suddenly realised that what he thought to be crickets was the sound of shots interspersed by shouts of confusion and fear. He heard the shriek again. He jumped up and ran out of the house. With the corner of his eye he checked that his family was safe. The sight outside made him stand motionless. Before him was a semi-circle of soldiers with smiles on their faces as they all stared at one point. The object was a black heap which seemed to move. It was a woman dressed in the black robes of a peasant. Her black hair streamed across her shoulders

16

showing here and there her white skin. She had her arms crossed in the manner of a Christian martyr. Only then did Hussein realise that she was holding her torn dress over her heaving breasts. The men around her laughed and shouted to each other in Hebrew and English. Behind were gathered the men whom Hussein had listened to earlier. Their faces were lit up by the dwindling camp fires which gave them an air of spectres, motionless and solitary. No one spoke.

The woman looked from one soldier to another. She looked at the men behind the soldiers. Her face was ugly with fear and hatred. She shrieked and asked to be spared. Several shots were heard at a distance. Still no one moved. She saw Hussein and ran up towards him. One of the soldiers tripped her while another asked with a cockney accent if she had enjoyed her trip. She looked up at Hussein.

"Master! *Sayyidi*! Help me." She articulated with her lips, rather than said aloud. Hussein stood still, too petrified and shocked to move. He thought of his family inside the house. He turned round, opened the door, and walked in. There was no one there. He decided that they must be in the other room.

Suddenly he heard a woman's laughter, or rather a devilish cackle.

"You want me! Come and take me! God damn your fathers as you have damned me."

She shrieked again and again.

Hussein recognised a mass of movement as being that of his fellow countrymen coming forward. He tried to open the door but it was jammed. He pulled, scratched, and shouted. The door would not move. The murmur behind the door was getting louder and louder. He heard the woman's voice saying in a loud and aggressive way: "Ready lads! Come on ....Come....Come...."

He woke up.

Leila was urging the children to get ready and not to make too much noise as baba was tired. The sky was blue and all was quiet.

Hussein sat up slowly trying to retain his dream but it was slipping away too fast.

"Baba! Baba! Saif is exactly forty days old. Forty! That's a lot. How many days old am I?"

4. The Settlers

The family spent the first month in Damascus. A second and third month passed. It became clear that there would be no return to Palestine for a long time to come. The state of Israel was getting stronger every day thanks to two factors: world recognition and a massive amount of armaments from the Eastern Bloc.

Amazingly the lorry driver had kept his word and delivered most of the items. A few things had been taken at checkpoints by soldiers but most of the Ibrahim family's valuables were safe in a relation's warehouse.

Hussein lost everything else that he had. That part of the country taken over by the Jordanians contained a very small piece of land in Tulkarm, right on the armistice line. It was currently occupied by a company of soldiers who seemed to have little intention of moving. Hussein's land inside Israel could have been sold through an intermediary by the name of Najjar, a Palestinian busy making a considerable fortune through sales of land to new Israeli citizens. This was an agreeable policy to the Israeli authorities who could then claim legal ownership of what was taken by force of arms if a fuss was ever made. Hussein resolutely refused to enter into what he considered a treacherous negotiation. He consoled himself against his loss by being a Palestinian patriot.

"We may have lost our riches but we still have our family. Hundreds of them spread all over the world. Aye! The Family - ancient and noble" he explained to his wife.

So there he was, three months later, still in Damascus, with little money and fewer possessions. His employers in Palestine had also politely assumed the holiday lie. Now he waited for new instructions from the ICI Company in London and was unofficially told that he might be sent to Iraq. After consultation with Leila he had written to London asking for a position in Beirut, the only place familiar to him despite his dislike of its noisy streets.

Waiting for a reply, he busied himself by arranging his various papers brought out of Palestine. These included a file on each member of the family, a magnificent stamp collection, a rare post-card collection, and various collections of letters, documents and qualifications. Among the various papers were over twenty small pocket diaries dating from his first year with ICI.

Much of his time was occupied with reading his old diaries. As well as Arabic, entries were mainly in English, French, Hebrew or Turkish which he had tried to teach himself at various times of his life. Most entries were short and succinct and had little reflective content. Now and then there would be a small outburst of anger or self-congratulation. Otherwise, the entries were merely factual.

Few entries had been made since the birth of Saif: Hussein was too busy to write anything down. For the moment this worried him, since being a methodical man, he disliked gaps in his thoughts. To have some hundred days without entries annoyed him. Equally annoying was the fact that no photograph had been taken of Saif whose file had nothing in it but the birth certificate written in Arabic, English, and Hebrew. Hussein decided that a photograph should be taken which was soon done. It showed the baby propped up on an armchair, his parents standing on either side of him squinting at the sun. On the boy's face was a broad smile occasioned by something behind the cameraman - most probably the sun.

A few weeks later a letter arrived from ICI confirming Hussein's appointment to their Beirut office. Although this meant losing a managerial post in Iraq, Hussein accepted it. It was decided that Leila would take the children and the maid to her parents' house in Beirut. She could look for a house while Hussein arranged for the transportation of their valuables from the warehouse. Although Beirut was being flooded by Palestinian refugees it was not considered difficult to find a house since it was Leila's hometown. Hussein would have no problem working there as, being married to a Lebanese citizen, he was entitled to live and work in Lebanon.

But all was not to be so easy for the Ibrahim family. Two days before Leila's scheduled departure, Hussein was interrupted from his paperwork by a woman's screech and a commotion from the next room in their rented Damascus flat. He ran out and found Leila standing in the middle of the room with the baby in her arms. The boy's face was covered in blood.

On the way to the hospital it became clear to Hussein what had happened. The maid had left Saif sleeping on the sofa. In order to stop him turning over and falling off she had pushed the coffee table forward. What she did not notice was that in pushing it forward, she had also pushed the glass covering the table onto the sofa. When the child had woken up, he lifted himself on his arm and flopped down again. Saif's right cheek came into contact with the glass which had cut him deeply.

Luckily the cut had missed his eye. The doctor told the parents that there would be a scar although it should get smaller as the boy grew.

"Thank God it's not a girl," remarked many people when they heard of the incident.

The maid was dismissed.

Chapter 5

The strains produced by a musical chord resemble a man's memory of childhood. He remembers a great deal and may even be able to talk about it. But when he comes to hum the tune that so haunts him, he is always horrified at the result. This is why the novel within each man is never written. It comes out in his behaviour, his way of life, his thoughts, that is, everything except on paper. He can always enjoy his novel vicariously through what others have written.

He is also like many a man who fancies being a conductor. In the privacy of his home he conducts Beethoven's Fifth to the strains of the Berliner Philharmoniker much to his satisfaction. While the music is on he succeeds as a conductor. Switch it off and he cannot continue since he cannot remember the music. Switch off the inner strains of childhood and you have music without sound.

I am such a man but I am lucky enough to be able to talk about my childhood. I have often caused girlfriends to shed tears of sadness or to laugh uproariously at little incidents from my little life. This may say a great deal about the sort of man I am rather than about what women like.

I shall talk then.

Of course, although I do not lie in any story that I tell my friends or listeners, I find myself having to reconstruct, organise, and most of all to re-order the material in a way that is comprehensible. After all, I do not want to open myself to any accusations of exaggeration or falsehood.

I shall talk then.

****

The earliest memories I have of my childhood are those of my mother. I picture her as a woman with pinchable arms. I see her, a giant before me, dancing to loud music that I can no longer hear. Her hair is black. Her eyes are dark. She wears black. The surrounding blackness accentuates the pallor of her white face. As she dances her arms move wildly. I am aware of a sense of discomfort and wish she would stop. She does so and bends down to me. Her form blends with the frightening patterns on the carpet, a carpet covered in faces of old men with large noses and white eyes. My mother sits on a chair and opens little and attractive boxes. Naziha comes in with the coffee. They drink, talk, and smoke.

Naziha's face contrasts sharply with my mother's. It is rugged and red. Her hair is so rigid it looks like a hat with nothing beneath. Whenever she smiles at me she shows a set of straight white teeth with a shining golden one at either end of the smile. She is soft spoken and gentle. My mother seems to possess no voice; simply expressions. More coffee is brought in by someone.

Let me describe our house. It is immense, the largest that you have ever seen. Entirely surrounded by a garden and a wall to stop intruders, it stands majestically. From the pavement the gate opens on to steps that are few but steep. My pleasure is great as I experience the terror of sitting on the top step looking down into the distant gate below. Overcome by terror I run and hide in the kitchen where the women folk bustle producing a homely smell of food and soapy cleanliness.

From the top of the steps I walk precariously towards the large entrance of the house. In front is the double door while on the left, are stairs leading up to the neighbour's home upstairs. Inside is the hallway leading on the right to the utility room smelling of soap and unwashed linen. Facing it is the Arabic toilet which I dislike as I cannot crouch over it for fear of falling in and being devoured by the large black rats that Naziha has always told me do not exist.

A smell of cooking leads me to the kitchen with its L-shaped entrance. As I enter I am aware of steps on my right leading up into the attic through a black mouth where Naziha lives and tells me stories. It smells of feet, sweat, soap and must. The kitchen is large with cold stone surfaces everywhere. As I walk in I am greeted by the smell of onions, pepper, soap, uncooked meat, coffee, and cigarette smoke. A woman looks up with a smile then she resumes her vigorous pumping of a small primus with a noisy blue flame encircling its top.

Retracing my steps I go through the swinging doors into the sitting room with its dark furniture and the dark carpet with the old men sporting large noses and white eyes. There is also a large, dark photograph of a forbidding old man: my grandfather. Despite the presence of my mother and Naziha I hasten out of the room through large double doors into the dining-room. The large French windows make this room look very light and cheerful. My favourite cosy hole is under the large dining table with its cold metal bar in the centre which is my seat while hiding.

I return to the hallway where a coat-stand towers above me. Its mirror is always obscured by a host of umbrellas and walking sticks. How proud I would be to own a walking stick! The door on the left leads to a long corridor with a European bathroom and toilet at its end. I do not like this room either because the seat is too cold and the hole too large though there are no rats in there. There are two bedrooms on each side of the corridor. One is Selma's the other Ali's (at the corner end). My parents' room is opposite Ali's. The bedroom that I share with Marwan is opposite Selma's. It is so large that the window seems distant and unreachable. Beside my bed with its many bars and pictures is a blue book-case. A blue cupboard stands high against the wall. A table with four chairs (with straw seats), all blue, is covered with toys, papers, pencils, and books - though not many.

A garden surrounds the entire house. The area near the gate is my father's and contains multi-coloured flowers and roses. I fancy that a big beaming sunflower is always inviting me in to join her swaying dance. But woe to any little ones who step into that garden without an adult escort! And woe to any adult who takes children in without father's permission! When he is angry he looks over his glasses and you immediately deny knowing the very existence of his garden.

The house garden turns left and continues for a second side of the square surrounding the house. Most of this side, though, is taken up by the veranda with its four enormous pillars which also hold the neighbours' balcony above. I have often hidden behind one of these pillars and grazed my knee as I ran round them while trying to hold on. They are enormous. Turn left again and you are at the back of the house, the third side of the square which consists of a narrow corridor with the house backed by a high wall. The soil is sandy and under Ali's window are several boxes I like so much. Marwan is not allowed to climb Ali's window. The corridor of land is blocked at the end with a high wooden barrier to stop us coming into father's garden through this back way. Beyond the barrier is paradise.

****

The largest section of the garden was ours, Marwan's and mine, I mean. We spent our days there building and demolishing entire cities, fighting treacherous Red Indians who had done us no harm, digging for treasure; finding it and reburying it in another section of the garden.

One day Marwan suggested we dig a tunnel under the house, which was to emerge in father's garden. What the exact object of that exercise was I could not quite understand but Marwan was older (by a whole year and a half no less) and infinitely wiser. So I started digging. What heat! What sweating after a day's work! The hole was enormous and would have been even bigger had I not insisted on using a fork to dig with. As the sand piled up it kept sliding back in. But Marwan and I worked valiantly and continuously. As the moment of triumph arrived we were both carried off for our evening bath covered in sand, wildly protesting to an insensitive adult that we had the great project nearly completed. It rained that night. Next morning our tunnel was full of water. Marwan suggested we dig a canal rather than a tunnel and sail to father's garden like ancient Phoenicians. I never argued but luckily the project was abandoned when Marwan had to fish out a muddy mid-morning biscuit from the famous canal.

In our childish world, Marwan proposed and Marwan disposed. I silently obeyed, not out of fear but rather from a deeply felt respect for him as my older brother. But, his loud and strong voice dominated our partnership.

Our garden was shaped like a large and wide L with the lower part being the thickest. At the top of the letter L there stood an enormous tree on which Marwan often perched when he needed solitude. In the centre of the bottom stroke of the L stood a fig tree that never bore figs that I remember. The rest was sand - soft, warm, and plentiful. The area with the fig tree was mine. The rest was Marwan's. My section also had a corner where Marwan often dug a hole to answer the call of nature. Beyond his large tree was the roof of the garage on which we were not allowed and on which Marwan spent much of his time.

My memories of that garden go so far back that they are but a series of images. I am sitting in a large box with a circular window on either side. A head peeps in from the front section and laughs showing a long line of white teeth with a golden one at either end. It disappears. Noises are heard all around although nothing is seen but enormous leaves above me. Some menacingly float down and disturb my slumber. A podgy hand appears over the side and throws a biscuit at my feet. I can not reach it. An adult is pushing me around the garden. Marwan shouts, "Train! Train!" An adult responds as the pace gets faster: "oooOOOOOOooo!!"

Another time I am sitting surrounded by several laughing and talking legs. Suddenly, they are all gone. A big boy toddles up to me and takes my hand. "Would you like to go for walkies?" I am picked up forcefully. Steps slide awkwardly below me. A gate opens above me. A Screech! A scream! I am on the ground staring at a huge face with a very wide smile and two enormous silver teeth on either side. Two round glass eyes stare back at me. My mother, pale and trembling, is shouting at somebody. A man is shouting back and Naziha is carrying Marwan who is crying. I cry. The man goes on shouting till my father comes and looks at him over his glasses. He goes away.

****

I can still see my father sitting in his garden. Sometimes he carries a book which he never seems to be reading for longer than a few minutes at a time. Now and then he lifts his head and stares at a few flowers swaying gently before him. Once in a while I see him busily writing in a small book - or at least it looks small, his hands are so large. When he writes in this book he never lifts his bowed head once. When he finishes he disappears into the house only to return a few minutes later with another book under his arm. I know that he has been inside the house to put the small book in the enormous desk in his bedroom and on which are all those enviable trinkets in wood and metal. Father seems to play with them a lot. But he looks so serious when he does so. Sometimes mother lets me play with them on her lap but only if father is out: there is a bow-shaped wooden piece with a handle on its flat surface. When you turn the handle it disengages and bits of thick fluffy paper fall out. Mother calls it "the blotter". I have seen father playing see-saw on it with a look of intense concentration on his face as the thing is swung back and forth. Its soft noise mingles with father's hard and loud mysterious sounds coming from the lower parts of the chair he sits on.

I remember one occasion when mother and I sat on the floor in the front room looking through the biggest book I have ever seen and with the smallest squiggles that my mother could turn into sounds. The book was very attractive with sloping edges, when opened in the middle, which looked like an undulating hill with terraces descending from the top right hand corner. There were several illustrations in the massive book. My mother was talking about some of the illustrations.

I wanted so much to touch the paper which was very fine and made an attractive rustling noise. I began to turn a page over but my mother put her hand down to prevent me from doing so. She was too quick: pushing the page down while I was pushing it up. What a catastrophe! Oh unspeakable calamity! I held the torn piece in my hand. I could feel the sobs rising. My mother's dark eyes looked at me. She smiled and gently took the torn piece and put it back in its original place saying, "Hush! We'll keep it a little secret between us." I must say that the piece was put back in place so neatly that father would have never been able to discover the offence - unless he tried to turn the page.

During supper that night my father was particularly solicitous about my welfare as he piled food on my plate. Pile it as he did, I could not eat it with the same joy with which he gave it. Miserable sinner that I was I felt worse when he made such a show of affection. I wanted so much to tell. I could not do so as his kindness made my sin much worse. Now and then he and mother spoke in a way that I could not understand. Marwan said that it was English and French and was bad because it came from a dark place with nasty people. I did not mind it because it sounded funny. My mother winked at me now and then. Marwan offered to eat my sweets: 'to stop father getting angry if you did not eat them', he explained.

After supper father took a cigarette from a round tin with a sailor on it and while smoking, talked to mother in English or French. He suddenly got up and walked towards the cabinet on which his newspaper lay. He held the paper for a while and then opened the glass cabinet. My heart sunk. I edged towards my mother. He touched the large book as if to take it out. I died. Suddenly, he laughed as he closed the cabinet. My mother laughed saying, "Stop it!" in a gentle drawl, her large dark eyes twinkling. Through a thick mist I saw a large strong hand come forward to stroke my head and heard a voice saying, "There's a brave lad."

One day stands out vividly in the confusion of images, tales and imaginings that make up my early childhood.

I woke up early, aware of that distinctive smell that goes with washing day. It was Monday. The air was full of a warm smell of soap. Windows had started to steam up. A long distance away, at the bedroom door, stood my father in his dressing gown and with dishevelled hair. In his hand he held up the stick used for prodding the washing in boiling water. He was waving it menacingly with a broad grin on his face. Above his head I could see a small cloud of steam coming from the stick. I closed my eyes and opened them again. In his place stood my mother. She walked up to my bed and knelt beside it. Gently, so very gently, she kissed my lips and asked me to get up for a very special breakfast. Excited, I jumped out of bed and started dressing.

"No rush. Take it easy, my love."

Mother's voice was very soft. Her eyes followed my movements, as I clumsily tried to dress. A few minutes later Naziha entered the room and began dressing me. I grabbed yesterday's trousers to put on but Naziha took them away and replaced them with a new white pair of shorts held round my waist with strong and rather uncomfortable elastic.

Breakfast was marvellous. All my favourite sweets followed: peanuts stuck together with melting sugar, peanuts crushed into a coating of fluffy pastry and fine sugar, and flat sweet pancakes covered in tasty sesame seeds. Mid-morning came and people started arriving. Aunts, uncles and cousins. Our garden reverberated with the sound of laughter and of bargains struck over the exchange of sweets with Marwan as master stockbroker. All the adults and children were very nice to me. Now and then I saw groups of people talking and looking at me. One child - a rather nasty cousin - was trying to pass off goats' droppings from his country home as chocolate drops in exchange for sugared peanuts. But he was put in his place when he tried the exchange on me. An uncle led him off with the promise of feeding him the aforementioned 'delicacy' one by one!

As the party continued we were promised a picnic lunch in the garden. Orders were taken from everybody except me. Naziha explained that I was to eat with the big ones.

All noise, games, and eating stopped a few minutes after the picnic was promised. This was caused by the arrival of a surly-looking man with a black bag containing, the older children said, all kinds of genies and ghouls. My father received him politely just outside our garden. As they talked I fancied that the black-eyed and black-haired man threw a glance towards me. Some of the very big children - my sister and two female cousins of her age - whispered to each other. "That's the man." "In a minute... Saif ..."

I went back to my game. Marwan walked up to where I was

crouching above a little hole I had dug. He emptied his pockets of all that they contained and put the lot into the hole then turned round and walked off. The assortment contained some biscuit crumbs, sugared peanuts covered in fluff, a used cotton reel, and a small curved piece of wood very adaptable to becoming anything from a pistol to a small sabre.

As I crouched there in amazement at such an invaluable gift, Naziha came into the garden and picked me up and took me into the house. I was given a very thorough and - as I then thought - unnecessarily proficient bath. New clothes were produced except for the elasticated shorts that were shaken out of the window to remove the sand.

Once ready, Naziha led me by the hand into our bedroom. There stood the surly looking man. I was led up to him. I smiled feebly. Without much ceremony he picked me up and put me on the table. Adults flocked into the room with grave looks on their faces. I could not see my parents. One woman, an aunt I believe, was entirely in black. I could only see her eyes. They stared at me severely. I tried to smile. I heard childish whispers coming from the window on my left. I looked round and saw my sister and her cousin-friends looking in with big smiling and curious eyes. Little hands appeared and disappeared on the window bars that squiggled and turned. Little heads bobbed up and down. Surly made a hissing sound and motioned towards the window. All faces disappeared immediately.

I looked at Surly's face. He had a determined and severe expression on it. Small particles of sweat stood on his brow. I stared at the black stubble covering the lower half of his badly shaven face. Above were two very large and very black nostrils.

Powerful hands took hold of my shorts and pulled them down sharply. I looked to my right. The black figure there nodded its head and said something. I caught a glimpse of Surly and heard him say something in a slow and loud voice. His hands disappeared between my legs. On my left a girl's head bobbed up and down. In front of me Surly's hand yanked back. Several adults' voices hummed louder and louder. But loudest of all was the scream that echoed over and over again and that I suddenly recognised as my own.

6. The Diary

Hussein's entry for the first of January 1951 read as follows:

Important facts carried forward from 1950:
1. Saif still does not talk. A visit to the specialist must be arranged.
IMPORTANT.
2. Promotion likely ICI - PURSUE.
*3. Ali's schooling unsuccessful. Advice on English schooling should
be sought. Certainly university. Decide on England or not.*
4. Sort out, rewrite, and arrange all diaries.

The final entry was made at the beginning of every year. Like the stamp collector whose ardent dream is to sort out his collection, Hussein never seemed to find time to sort out his diaries. Rewriting some of them was also another wish, as if in rewriting with hindsight he could make some kind of ordered sense out of a life otherwise bedevilled with seemingly unconnected coincidences and unfathomable events. Such desire for order was vicariously fulfilled in making endless lists of tasks with the accompanying pleasure of ticking those completed and transferring the rest to a new list. Hussein found a refreshing release from a periodic review of his lists.

Saif had been a major worry during the first few months of the New Year. Still unable to talk, he spent most of his time crouching in the garden, digging holes and filling them in. He obviously understood all that was said as he always did what he was told. He also enjoyed being told stories. In fact, that was the only time that his face showed animation. One got the impression that he could talk if he really wanted to. His silence seemed wilful.

Saif's parents tried everything they could to bring him out of himself. Hussein, in his despair, was forced to look up and study his most detested writer in an attempt at understanding his son's psychological make up. To read such an author implied a recognition of an insidious subject: psychiatry. Furthermore, the author in question was a Jew. To cap it all Saif seemed obsessively reliant on his mother.

Leila and Hussein sat in the sitting-room quietly discussing the matter. Saif stood beside his mother with his little arm entwined round her larger one. He looked from one parent to the other with a look of bewilderment at their gibberish since they both spoke in English.

Hussein was arguing against seeing a psychiatrist.

"Such people are charlatans living off other people's weaknesses. If you have a problem you should have the will-power to conquer it yourself. If you are weak enough to require assistance then nothing can help you anyhow."

Hussein argued quietly but firmly. Leila, whose main aim was to have her son seen to quickly, tried to argue against Hussein but knew the futility of such an exercise.

"If Sousie (as she called Saif) fell down and broke an arm you would see nothing wrong with taking him to see a doctor."

"That's different." Hussein interrupted irritably.

"Why?" Her large dark eyes stared at him patiently.

"For the obvious reason that a doctor's job is to mend the body whereas those charlatans have but one view in mind."

"Which is to mend the mind!"

A deathly silence ensued in which Leila could see her husband's temper rising through the workings of his cheek-bones. She had touched a very tender chord in her husband's pride in even suggesting that his son's mind was in the slightest need of examination.

The boy looked from one parent to another sensing their heavy silence which made him anxious. Slowly, his bottom lip started to quiver as he squeezed his mother's arm. Leila drew her husband's attention to the boy's face. They smiled at each other and Hussein approached his son and said in Arabic, "What's that funny face for, young man?" This was said in an assumed tone of severity which made Saif smile at his mother as if to say, *"He's up to his silly tricks again."* Then the smile developed into a hesitant *"he is, isn't he?"*

Hussein turned to Leila and said in English, "The lad's delayed speech could be seen to perfectly adequately by any ordinary specialist in paediatrics." The subject was closed and an appointment was made for a week's time.

Now that a decision had been made Hussein felt more at ease. But both he and his wife continued to worry at Saif's inability to talk. As Hussein worked at his desk or drove round from farm to farm in his capacity as an agricultural engineer, he thought of the various possible reasons for his son's condition. Similarly with Leila while at work in the orphanage she had started for Palestinian refugees. She sometimes took Saif there while Marwan became more independent by remaining at home with Naziha. During these visits Saif quietly walked by his mother's side wherever she went. The orphaned girls tried to be nice to him in an attempt to impress his mother. He remained distant and aloof, however, as if he felt the girls in their institutional setting were of a different species.

The visit to the paediatrician coincided with Saif's third birthday. Afterwards they were to go to visit Haji who had rented a small apartment in Beirut. From there the entire family was going to lunch at Leila's sister's house.

While waiting at the surgery Saif sat on his mother's lap playing with one of his birthday gifts. Leila felt sorry for him as he played quietly. It reminded her of that time recently when he entered her room beaming with pride at his new clothes only to undergo the agony of circumcision. She had been against the whole thing but gave in to Hussein's argument that although he was not a religious man, circumcision had other merits - which he failed to expound. Furthermore, it was what society expected of its members.

After a few tests the paediatrician informed the relieved parents that there was nothing to worry about. The boy was normal in every way. Further he was of above average intelligence. On the way out he reassured them laughingly that once the boy started talking there would be no stopping him.

****

"Ah, brother of mine! May this day be black for ever more!" This was the way Haji greeted Hussein as she sat there rolling the hem of her dress over and over again between her thumb and forefinger. Saif sat beside Leila staring at his aunt's white misty eyes.

"Nephew, come here! Ah, woe is me. You are a misfortune on all our heads. Your birthday is a black day for all of us. Black. Black" she repeated, striking her chest several times at each word. "Your birthday nephew? You celebrate? What for? We lost our land, our house. Oh brother, what a garden! Will the Jew look after it?" This last question was not directed at anyone and received no answer. "Nephew, nephew! Black! Here, take this. Some sugared almonds for you. Go! Go! What a day!"

Both Hussein and Leila knew better than to interrupt the old Haji in her soliloquy. They sat back, quietly exchanging smiles. Leila lit a cigarette.

"Sister, an evil habit. Evil, sister. Kindly sit by the window." The silence that ensued was only interrupted by Saif crunching and Haji sighing deeply.

"Brother! What is this I hear of Ali's school report?"

"It is not very good I'm afraid," replied Leila apologetically.

"Is the school telling me that my nephew lacks intelligence and needs to cheat! Abu Ali," she continued, bestowing on her brother the traditional Arab honour of fatherhood when she meant to be taken seriously. "Abu Ali. Give me the circumstances in which my nephew chose to consult a book."

Hussein explained that apparently Ali had not learned a passage by heart and had desperately resorted to cheating rather than owning up. Put this way, Haji took a serious view of the matter. This was a double sin of lying and cheating not to mention the paramount mistake, nay failing, of not preparing the passage in the first place. But surely there was a mitigating circumstance?

"None!" replied Hussein angrily.

"A headache, maybe?"

"No!"

"His brother's illness perhaps?"

"Cheating has no excuse!"

"Of course not. A sound thrashing."

"Yes."

"Not too sound."

"Very sound!"

"First offence, maybe a clean record is sufficient to ...."

"A first offence that we know about."

"Indeed. Severity is important but these are black days. Tell me, Abu Ali, what subject was he cheating at?"

After a short embarrassing silence Leila whispered, "Bible studies."

"Bible!" Haji echoed loudly in an assumed stentorian voice.

Saif stopped crunching and looked up. Leila lit another cigarette. Hussein resumed a comfortable attitude of not listening to any word.

"Bible, brother? Are there no Moslem schools? Has the Jew taken what the English left behind?"

"It is the best school available." Hussein replied half-heartedly.

"The boy would not have cheated had the passage come from *The Holy Qur'an*. He was wrong to consult the book during the test but God will forgive him and register his objection. Is it true that you will be sending him to the dark continent?"

"Yes. I am thinking of sending him to England."

"Well. Bible lessons will certainly equip him to join the infidel!" Haji snapped peremptorily.

The silence that followed was interrupted now and then by a strong sniff from Haji. Hussein stood up and said goodbye.

"God be with you, brother. Peace be on you."

As the three walked out they could hear Haji's feet shuffling down the corridor, her voice muttering bitterly "A black day. Bible! God is angry at me. Your will be done. It is written." Hussein closed the door on the strains of *The Opening*,

"Praise be to Allah, the Lord of the worlds,
The Beneficent, the Merciful,
Master of the day of Requital...."

On the way to Leila's sister, Hussein explained to his wife for the thousandth time, that Haji could not help being blunt and unhappy. Leila pointed out that Haji might after all, be right. Ali was being alienated from his heritage. Nonetheless, she agreed that under the circumstances and in the absence of good local Moslem education they had no option but to send Ali to England if they wanted him to have the best.

7. Chinese Whispers

The Lebanese had, and still have, two famous national games. One is a kind of Russian Roulette involving the production of an identity card instead of rolling the chambers. Depending on the other player's position it is then determined how his reaction to the religious information given on the first player's identity card should be. Such a reaction is usually dictated by the atmosphere surrounding the game. Like Russian Roulette, this game can be played by as many people as one wishes. It is mainly played by men.

The other game is popularly known as Chinese Whispers and is played much more often. The rules of the game are very simple. It is open to all ages and to both sexes although it is seemingly more popular with women. One woman whispers a fact or an opinion to another, this other to a third, the third to a fourth, fourth to fifth and so on. This leads to a position of reductio ad absurdum (the author is using the terms that go with the game). A loss is incurred if a person is caught in the actual act of whispering by one of the participants. The winning participant calls out "bitch!" and is consequently declared the winner.

Now, the loser may challenge the winning participant to disclose the whisper as she knows it. This is invariably different from anything that anyone had heard so far. But the argument is resolved by the whisper returning to the originator. If he or she cannot be found the player with the least score is chosen. The score is kept in a way not dissimilar to the keeping of balance sheets. The participants pitch into the loser and all whispers are turned into vocal substances to be thrown at the loser until such time as a new whisper is initiated.

The obvious advantage of the game is not only that it can go on for a long time but that it is self-perpetuating. Finally, an invariable rule of the game is that all participants address each other as *"mon cher"* and use expressions such as *"tu t'imagines"*, *"ça alors"*, *"tu exaggères"*, *"je m'en fou"*, the last being particularly popular among the losers, especially the sore ones.

Leila's younger sister was a recognised master-player. Her name was Muna Jbeili, though her husband's connection with the famous town whence the Bible got its name was, and remains, a mystery to all, even today. Equally mysterious was Hussein's choice of the elder sister for wife when the Samar family boasted such beauty in Muna.

The elder sister was twenty years old at the time of her marriage, whereas Muna was barely sixteen. Hussein found her sixteen years had made her terribly immature. Indeed, he believed her to have ceased to develop or grow up since around the age of twelve and, from all that he subsequently knew of her, for the rest of her life. It was also said that what Leila lacked in beauty she made up for in character and personality. Malicious persons called such gains as nothing but a sop to the riches and glory - now past - of the Samars. At the time of this narrative the elder Samar was a miserable bankrupt who seemed to do no more than await his death. He was reputed to have made a vast fortune in textiles during the Great War but lost it all on a venture that he was certain would double it. The old man now lived in a small house provided for him by his son-in-law, Jbeili, who had also made a handsome fortune in the distant past.

In contrast, Hussein was a careful and methodical man and disapproved of his wife's family. When he lost everything in Palestine he had recommenced through a slow but safe rebuilding process. He took no unnecessary risks but worked diligently and hard. Whenever he visited Leila's relations he adopted a polite but distant form of communication. In short he did his social duty but in a calculated manner, presenting a rather uneasy front.

When Hussein, Leila and Saif arrived at Muna's large house, Hussein's other children had already been picked up by her chauffeur in the Cadillac - always an exciting event. This was particularly so for Marwan who, having just started school, delighted in informing everyone that his aunt Muna's number plate, having a neat row of five ones, added up to five.

Mr. Jbeili received Hussein boisterously as all complacent men do.

"When are you going to change your horseless carriage for a new one, hey?" he asked and noisily laughed at his own joke.

Hussein winced and swallowed the rude reply. "Soon, soon, I hope."

"Hoping won't buy a new one. Hopping to your bank manager would! Ha ha ha!"

The joke was lost amongst the kissing and greetings. After the children were led to a play area and Saif was given an expensive birthday present, the adults sat down and socialised. Outside could be heard the voices of Marwan and an elder cousin fighting over Saif's present. Marwan was explaining that it belonged to him by right since

Saif left it on the floor. As Saif's brother he was only claiming his rights. Samir, the elder cousin, told him that he would pitch him into the swimming-pool and what's more that his parents bought the present. Marwan told him, in return, that giving them droppings from the farm goats for chocolate drops when they last met was nasty. Retorting, Samir said that his father had a big Cadillac, a Fiat and another car, and new suits and a big house.

"You've only got a lousy Austin!" Marwan was crushed.

Selma sat in another room with her two favourite cousins. Saif went into the kitchen with Naziha who, as a visiting maid, had the honour of supervision and endless coffee drinking while the resident maids gave her the latest gossip. A black cook from the Sudan absorbed much of Saif's attention. On either cheek he had three distinctive scars indicating his tribe. The black man was politely interested in the scar on Saif's right cheek.

****

"*Eh bien, mon cher*, what is this I hear about Ali?" asked Muna of her sister. Ali, now sixteen years old but small for his age, shuffled his feet with embarrassment. *"C'est vrai?"* Muna adopted French as being the language that the young were unable to speak, consequently it made Ali more uncomfortable.

"Yes, it is true." Leila's tone indicated her unwillingness to speak of the matter.

"And Selma? How's her school work?"

Leila gave a very good report on Selma's progress although it was not altogether without a tinge of harmless sarcasm at the girl's perfection in all that she did.

"All the same *tu exaggères*. She is still very young. Time enough to learn *les vices necessaires*."

Hussein stopped listening to Mr. Jbeili and directed what can only be described as a yellow noxious smile at Muna.

The conversation moved on to Marwan who Hussein declared too independent. Leila argued that this was not necessarily a bad thing. Mr. Jbeili gave himself as the perfect example of the result of independence. Hussein could not help but notice the look of utter contempt that Muna threw her husband. Leila and Muna then withdrew to another room.

36

As soon as they were alone Muna asked, "Have you been to the doctor about the little lump?"

"No. I am going tomorrow."

"Does Hussein know?"

"I haven't told him. He's got enough on his mind with Saif. Anyhow, it's most probably nothing serious. A small cyst or abscess or whatever they're called. By the way, talking of doctors, I visited Muhammad yesterday. He's getting worse. Hussein tried to convince him to go voluntarily into a sanatorium for a cure."

"Did he accept?"

"Not really. He swore and completely lost his temper. He accused us of wanting to get rid of him. It was awful but I think that he'll come round eventually. Muna darling, what's the matter?" Muna had started to sob quietly. Her bright blue eyes and soft skin gave her the look of a subject from Renaissance paintings: earthly but beautiful, illusory while real: a mystery of womanhood.

"What is it?" Leila repeated.

"Oh, Leila! What have we come to! Four of us happy and proud! Look at us now. Father is dying in poverty, mother absolutely senile. And now us, the four children. One an addict. Another a gambler. Me, I married the most ..."

"Muna. Don't!"

"Oh, God! I wish he were dead!"

"Mama! Mama! Lunch." Marwan ran into the room with his face red with excitement. Aunt Muna's lunches were famed for being delicious.

****

A few minutes later the sisters walked into the dining-room arm in arm. Marwan danced round them in his ecstasy. They all sat down to be served by the Sudanese cook who was now dressed for the occasion.

"Baba, can I see uncle Muhammad this afternoon?" asked Ali, who was very fond of his maternal uncle.

"No." Hussein tried not to sound disapproving.

Leila tried to save the situation. "He is ill."

"Pass the bread!" Marwan shouted.

Muna laughed. *"Mon cher, quel enfant terrible! By the way have you heard about Jacqui? Ça alors."*

"*Ça alors*." said Selma to one of her cousins.

"Hopping not hoping, my dear fellow."

Hussein switched off.

The children were happily whispering to each other. The national game had started in earnest.

Chapter 8

In the summer of 1952 I was over four years old. That summer was memorable because it was the first one during which we went up to the mountains. Although this meant a separation from my beloved garden, it had its compensations.

The house my parents rented was at the bottom of a long and steep descent from the high road above. As you came - or rather tumbled - down the stony and dusty hill, you could see a one storey building with green shutters. Imagine my delight on discovering a second floor below it hidden by the fact that the house was a split level built on a steep incline. Also the upper floor protruded out to create a shaded area where four columns of concrete were obscured by various climbing plants. This area extended right to the edge of the precipice with bars connected by circular shapes serving as banisters. In the afternoon, when the sun was on the front of the house, the family sat near the precipice edge chatting or quietly admiring the magnificent view below. Our bedroom was a kind of podium above this area. Looking out of the window, my arms around the bars and my legs dangling outside, I got the sensation of falling through endless space.

From that position I could see everything for miles around. Deep in the valley below was a small village. I could see the local people looking like tiny toy soldiers ambling from house to house. I felt I could put my hand out and pick a couple out for a special favour. I would give them three wishes like the genii in Naziha's stories. Then I could order them to do the impossible and when they failed I would put my huge arm out and push one of the enormous white rocks down on them. Then I would forgive them and make them pick some of the grapes growing to one side of the terraces. I could actually pick them by lying on the ground near the banister and putting an arm through the bars. Father had forbidden us to do so saying that the vines had been sprayed and that they would give us the bellyache. Marwan said that they were sour anyhow. Sometimes we would snatch a bunch and a handful of vine leaves. Then we would lick them clean of spray and roll the grapes in the vine leaves and eat them.

Where all was glaring white during the day, the night was pitch black. The white and brown houses of the village were turned into little sparkling stars. The thorny bushes that stood crisp and quiet under the sun swayed in the moonlight. Some of the pine trees became all kinds of things at night. Some were arms outstretched to the sky, some old men bent over with age, while others had long necks with big round heads on top. From all these trees came a pleasant chirping noise. Overlooking us was the huge mountain which was like a sleepy camel's hump, master of all it surveyed, including two little boys staring quietly at it from their windows. Very quietly as the grownups assumed them to be asleep!

One day, we were put to bed early for our afternoon siesta because the local mayor was coming to tea. Marwan was going to recite the Opening from *The Holy Qur'an*. We were too excited to sleep.

Sometime later my mother came and woke Marwan. Being the youngest I was to stay in bed a further half-hour. Having heard the clinking of cups and trays and having smelt the sweetness of cakes, I felt keenly the injustice of being the youngest. I tugged at my mother's skirt, and stared up at her twinkling eyes. She laughingly said, "Ooops! Out comes the bottom lip. Oooh! What a funny face!"

Such unsympathetic comments were not calculated to soothe. Determined not to sleep, I jumped out of bed and sat on the window with my legs dangling out. From my position I could see father's legs and the top of Ali's head as he sat politely answering the mayor's questions. I could also see the village below and the people who strangely seemed to get bigger and bigger. The heat was unbearable. Pine trees swayed and walked up to me.

I woke up with a burning sensation in my head. I was cross. I urgently wanted the toilet. Below I could hear Marwan's voice slowly chanting:

"In the name of Allah, the Beneficent."
I stood up.

"The Merciful.
Praise be to Allah, the lord of the worlds,
The Beneficent, the Merciful, Master..."

I struggled to push my tight shorts down.

"...of the day of the Requital.
Thee do we serve and Thee do we beseech for help.
Guide us on the right path."

I took aim between two bars

"The path of those upon whom
Thou hast bestowed favours,
Not those..."

I fancied I heard father join in loudly at this juncture.

"...upon whom wrath is brought down."

It was too late.

"Nor those who go astray."

Several adult voices echoed "Amen".
The mayor shouted "Bismillah, Bismillah, what a brave boy."
Several adults cheered and clapped.
"Allah! This tea is terribly weak. Mr. Mayor let me get you another cup."
As I jumped off the window. I could see my father looking up with glowering eyes. A few minutes later the door opened and he stood there, belt in hand. Below, the mayor was loudly asking Marwan if he knew the meaning of *The Opening* from *The Holy Qur'an*. Mother walked in. She was so cross that her eyebrows became one, but her dark eyes never looked ominous.
I stood terrified. They looked down. Suddenly mother started to laugh.
Father looked even angrier for a moment, then smiled. I laughed. The belt landed on the bed opposite making a swooshing sound followed by a sharp note.
Below the mayor was incanting:

"Bismillah
He will burn in fire giving rise to flames
Nay, he will certainly be hurled into the crushing disaster."

****

The incident was never mentioned again. Although Naziha had failed to see the funny side to it, Nassim, my eldest uncle, found it hilarious. When he next came to visit us he gave me a box of Turkish delights saying "I did it on the British. You do it on the French lackeys."

My uncle was described as an Arab Nationalist. Ali told us he had been to prison and that he was a very good and brave man. I too was determined to become an Arab Nationalist though how to go about becoming one was a mystery. Father said I had to work hard and study *The Holy Qur'an*. Uncle Nassim told me not to believe everything God said for He was a bit of a reactionary. Father said that it was wrong to talk like that even if I could not understand. I cried and got sent to bed. Uncle promised me a book if I would say "please".

Next morning, as he walked up the slope to leave, I ran after him.

"Yes son, what do you want?"

"…"

"You can tell me. Come on and I'll bring it back today."

"Alf Leila …"

"Arabian Nights!!!" shouted my uncle and suddenly picked me up and ran towards the house where my parents stood watching us.

"Hussein! Leila! *By Jupiter, he's done it at the* thousandth *shot. We shall make a* nationalist of him yet."

My mother hugged me and, laughing with her big eyes, said "*Now do you think you could possibly say tea?*" Both she and uncle started laughing. Father looked confused.

"Shaw!" A smile of delight came on his face.

I talked incessantly that day. Everyone was delighted at everything I said and laughed heartily. As to what I said, God forgive me, it could not have been much. Naziha gave me several apples. Father looked the other way as I bolted grapes. Ali patted me on the head. Marwan said that he could not quite see what the fuss was about: he had been talking for years and could I pick him a bunch or two of grapes.

Even during my siesta that afternoon I talked incessantly. Naziha had to adopt considerable measures to get me to sleep but to no avail. Nothing could stop me now, not even her awful threat of putting yoghurt on my ears and putting me in the cellar where the big rats who so loved yoghurt lived. To be honest it did silence me a little but I was determined to use my new-found ability to advantage before it became too late.

Chapter 9

When we returned from the mountain resort of Broumana at the end of the summer holidays I was admitted to school full-time having attended on and off during the previous year.

There I was, at just four and a half, standing by the front door waiting for Ali who was to take me there. I was fully dressed in grey shorts, navy blue blazer, white shirt, and a tie. Marwan stood beside me although he hadn't the sparkle: his uniform was at least a year old. He told me that if I thought I was going to play with him at school I should think again. He was in the top form.

Arriving at school I felt the sobs rising but suppressed them when Ali called me a baby. We parted at the gate and I went into my new classroom. I did not like it. There was a smell of stale food. The classroom was cold and the chairs hard.

But the worst was the teacher. She entered the room and started reading off names. Everyone whose name she called out replied, "Yes miss". I was determined to do exactly the same when my turn came. I prepared myself for the right response and shouted out "yes mama!" Some laughed. Others nudged me whispering urgently, "miss! miss!" A girl sitting beside me held my hand and I called out the right response. Then we all stood by our chairs and recited the Opening with our hands before our faces. I held mine up and mumbled. So far so good.

The first lesson was numbers and with the help of my neighbour I got through fairly well. But the alphabet! The chalk squiggled and screeched and the teacher shouted out: "A-lef, Beh, Teh."

I saw no connection between the teacher's squiggles and the bizarre noises she made. I did, however, manage to write a few of them down. These were the ones to which I took an immediate liking. I found something easygoing and friendly in the well-rounded 'Ain' which is written similarly to the English 3 backwards. The 'Alef', a straight vertical line, had character and determination and reminded me of my father. The 'Beh', shaped like a frying pan with one dot beneath, was Naziha's smile. But most delightful of all was the letter L which is similar to its English counterpart but backwards and with its base rounded off like a pelican's lower bill: That, God knows why, reminded me of my mother. By break-time I was beginning to feel that there was nothing much to education. I had not as yet been utterly confused by being told that one apple and one orange do not make two apples and oranges despite having the evidence before my very eyes!

At break-time the class teacher called me to her desk and spoke severely. "You missed school because you were ill last year. You'll have to work hard." She stared at me and then said, "I'll help you". I fancied I saw a smile on her lips but when I looked again there was the same stern expression. It might have been my imagination.

I was taken out by the little girl who sat next to me. We walked up and down the playground talking. Marwan came up with a group of big boys. He was eating a round crunchy bread-like cake covered in sesame seeds with thyme inside its wider section. He took me aside and told me that I was a fool and a sissy to talk to girls. As he did this he eyed his friends nervously. He continued, loudly enough to be heard, saying that I could not play with his friends and himself. He hurriedly gave me half his cake and walked off. I returned to my friend and carried on walking silently.

Marwan's friends started singing:

"Little black boy with the white white teeth
Little black boy with the pink pink bum
A banana? A banana?"

Marwan shuffled his feet, looked up and then down, then looked at me. I stuck my tongue out. He joined the singing. I could feel the tears rising.

The little girl said, "Don't listen to them. Come, we'll go over there. Big boys aren't allowed in there. Anyhow, I think brown boys are prettier than pink ones." We laughed and walked away. I felt less hurt.

"What's your name?" she asked.

"Saif."

"Mine is Muna. Do you like it?"

"Yes."

"How old are you?"

"Four and a half."

"I am over five."

I looked at her in admiration as one who had long past left my infant world. Indeed she did seem very much older and so much wiser than I was.

44

"Do you have a mother?"

Although I thought the question very strange I knew she had a good reason for asking it.

"Yes I've got one at home."

She looked at me for a while. "I haven't got one. Mine has been dead for a year now."

"When will she come back?" I asked in order to do the right thing.

"Never!" came the reply. She said it very quietly. Her face remained calm.

"But she must come back sometime when she is finished." I thought death was some kind of long term employment, rather like my mother's work at the orphanage.

"No. She'll never come back. She has gone to paradise. All mothers go there."

"Does she like it there?" I asked.

"I expect so. Baba looks after us. My brother is eleven. His name is Nayer. That's a star. Do you like your mother?"

"Oh yes. She is the bestest in the whole world. She sings a lot but I don't mind. She is..." Heaven forgive me but I did not mean to be insensitive. Muna looked unhappy. Her lips quivered. "What's wrong?"

"Nothing."

I looked at her and burst out "You can come to our house and see my mother. If you like her you can share her with me."

"Good. I agree. Now you can kiss my hand."

I did so.

Returning home that evening Marwan was very distant but I didn't care much. I had found a good friend. As we approached home I started to feel a little guilty and tried to talk to him. But he made it abundantly clear he was in no mood for little girls.

A few weeks later, and amid great excitement, Ali left home to go to University. Aunt Haji broke a great rule by leaving her apartment in order to see him off.

"Black! Black!" She kept wailing. "My brother's boy goes to the land of the heathen. Nephew, come here. *Jesus, son of Mary, is only a messenger of Allah. So believe in Allah and His messengers. And say not, Three. To desist is better for you. Allah is only one God. Far be it from His glory to have a son. To him belongs whatever is in the heavens and whatever is in the earth. And sufficient is Allah as having charge of affairs"*. Thus recited our Holy Prophet, nephew, God's blessings be upon Him. Nephew, be tolerant with the English heathen for our Lord says, *"The Truth is from your Lord, so let him who wishes believe and let him who wishes disbelieve."* The Nazarene was a messenger of Allah. Be good to his followers. And don't you come back married to some heathen Christian slut. Go. Allah be with you. Here's an envelope for you."

****

Ali was away from home for about three years. I have not the vaguest memory of his name being mentioned to us children once during that absence. I assume that news of him (and indeed from him) must have been received. I remember that on the day of his departure I found him in my sister's room. They both cried bitterly. I saw Ali trying to give her the envelope Aunt had given him. She kept refusing it. Pushing him off she threw herself on her bed crying quietly but convulsively. Her shoulders were moving in a jerky and tormented way. I somehow sensed that I should not be there. As I turned to go away Ali walked out of the room looking pale and, I thought, angry. He shot me a very frightening look and walked away quickly. I ran off.

A few hours later he was gone and I seemed to forget that he ever existed.

My memory of the next three years is rather confused. Both mother and father were away from home for very long periods. Marwan and I spent most of our time in the garden. Naziha was kind but distant. At school I worked as diligently as any child could. Within these three years I learnt to recite several verses from *The Holy Qur'an*. With Muna's help I learnt my tables though I never really understood them.

Muna and I became very close friends and, since she only lived a few minutes' drive from our home, we spent our holidays together. Marwan tolerated our friendship although he withdrew into himself in a way that I had never seen in him before. He became obsessively dependent on Selma whom he followed wherever she went. Some children from the neighbourhood and from the tenants' flat above our home used to join us for games in the garden. None leaves an indelible memory of a relationship remotely similar to that which I had with Muna. We used to spend hours sitting under the fig tree in my garden telling each other stories.

She told me all about her mother with whom she used to do fantastic things - though I forget what they were. In return, I told her all the stories that Naziha used to recount to me in her attic bedroom. I didn't have as many ghouls and genies in mine as Naziha had in hers. We sat in the garden for hours wondering over Sinbad's adventures, deliberating over Scheherazade's fate (which, strangely enough, we never took the trouble to inquire about), frightening ourselves with Douban, the physician's revenge, and generally speculating as to what we would do with the three wishes. We had many an argument over this last matter but they were never prolonged. We were too jealous of our friendship to quarrel permanently.

It is impossible for me to describe the memories of this period of my life. Heaven knows we understood very little of the feelings each aroused in the other. Like the uninitiated listener to a serenade we enjoyed the softness of the music and felt the permanence of its string of notes. We understood little or nothing. When the music ended it remained in our imagination, feeding our childish innocence as the rain does the rose. Neither cared what the other said or thought. I like to think that we spoke with one voice, thought with one mind, felt with one soul, and lived with one heart. As to separation or growing up, that was as implausible as the permanent disappearance of our smiling sunflower. Its certain appearance every year verified our love forever more. Even now, as an older and wiser man, it brings tears to my eyes when I think of what the future held in store. But this is for later.

One day, while Muna and I were busily digging for gold in order to use it to go to Ali Baba's cave, Marwan came to announce that several branches of our trees were being cut down. He was going to build a house in his corner of the garden. Naziha apportioned the branches between Marwan and myself. With a dexterity that was her own she threw various branches against the wall each holding its brother up. The result was a most delightful small house of green leaves and thick sturdy branches. Inside the tree house, Muna and I arranged a living-room with cushions and a few personal belongings to give it an air of permanence. Muna insisted that I should have a little study where I could retire for manly contemplation and deliberation on important matters. A small box that previously contained oranges and a smaller one yet (this one had contained dates I believe) were found for the purpose. Because of the disproportionate sizes of the two boxes it was impossible to sit on the smaller one in order to write on the bigger.

But, since meditation was the object, I sat on the table and used the chair as a footrest. From that position I recounted several tales loosely based on Arabian Nights, supplemented by the illustrations in the book bought for me by my uncle.

Life continued in this manner for some three years. Most enjoyable were the hot sunny summer holidays spent almost entirely in our little garden house the outside of which Naziha maintained by further branches cut secretly on demand. During one such holiday I received two head injuries, once when Marwan carried on digging for gold as I bent over to pick it up having decided that I had found it. The second was in falling off Marwan's large tree while playing cowboys and Indians in Muna's absence - in itself as big a rarity as an injury to the same spot on the head.

During this period Marwan had grown more and more solitary and quarrelsome. His stubbornness often led to confrontations with our father. Such showdowns inevitably ended with Marwan receiving a beating with the belt and being sent to bed. He never cried and his stubbornness increased daily. Selma always took his side at the risk of incurring father's terrifying wrath. One such incident was when Marwan found a stray cat and decided it should be severely punished for daring to enter his garden without his permission. He placed the wretched cat in a large box covered with metal netting used for wiping mud off our feet. Then he sat on top and proceeded to fill the box with sand regardless of the cat's pitiful mewing. I watched in trepidation lest he should be found out.

Despite my better feelings I could not resist joining in the awful game of power. I can still hear our shouts as we poured sand on top of the defenceless animal. I can still feel the excitement of knowing that we were doing wrong. Suddenly a loud and painful contact on the back of my head made me turn around wincing. Father stood behind me glowering with fury. He picked me up by my hair and slapped me hard several time shouting: "You're bigger than it. I am bigger than you. Do you like this? Do you? Hey? A little more? And another? Hey?" I showed clearly that I did not like it and that indeed I did not want anymore and certainly not another, hey! And so I was dropped on the spot.

Marwan sat on the box truculently smiling. Ordered to get off he replied in Selma's coquettish fashion, "Nopsie". A second and third warning were to no avail. Father took off his thick belt and pitched into

Marwan and would have whipped him to within a millimetre of his life had it not been for Selma's intercession.

Through the mist in my eyes and with the feeling that I had got off very lightly I sat looking at Marwan. His face was very red but there were no tears in his eyes. All over his legs I could see the dreaded red stripes. He looked at me and smiled. He got up very deliberately and approached the box with the cat still in it. From inside the house I could hear Selma crying. Marwan removed the netting on top. There was now someone else crying apart from Selma. The crying was hoarse and ugly. Marwan swung the cat by its tail several times. The sobs inside reminded me of a donkey's braying.

Swearing and declaring his intention to show who is boss, Marwan flung the cat against the wall. It crashed with a frightening thud and loud mewing. The sobbing inside the house stopped for a minute. It resumed less loudly but more desperately. The cat walked off a little and then fell. Marwan ran towards it and picked it up gently, holding it in his arms. As he looked up I could see that he had been crying. He stroked the cat gently and said sorry. Suddenly it wriggled out of his arms with a hissing sound and its claws scratching out at Marwan's arms and face. He let go and it ran off. Inside the house the crying and sobbing had subsided and all was silent as Marwan walked away leaving me there wondering, regretting and wishing.

****

My grandfather died in 1955 when I was just over seven years old. By then I had become accustomed to my parents' (particularly my mother's) prolonged absences. Just before his death we children had been excitedly looking forward to celebrating the Prophet's birthday with the bonfires and colourful fireworks that were part of it. During this period, mother had been at home for some time. She was extremely kind and loving. Sometimes she was very funny such as when she played the radio very loudly out of her bedroom window. She did this in response to an army officer living next door who had shouted at us boys for making too much noise during his siesta (this was my first conscious introduction to obscene language.) As the loud music filled the entire neighbourhood I could see mother's eyes mischievously searching for the complaining neighbour. After a tour of the outside windows they landed on me. Both large eyes broke through the music and approached me.   One winked laughingly.   Mother switched the radio off.   Most of our time, though, was spent with Naziha or alone in the garden.

My section of the garden below mother's window was closed off. She had moved into Ali's room since his departure.   Father occupied the old parental room.   Beside my mother's bed stood a book-case also used to stand her interminable cups of coffee and cigarettes.   Inside the case stood a thick Modern Library edition of the *Complete Poems of Keats and Shelley*.   There were several glossy-covered Shakespeare plays.   She used to tell me the stories of several although I only remember *King Lear*.

I had pointed out that this story was like several told me by Naziha, of being dutiful if you did not want to go to Hell.   She had told me that to displease my parents would cause Allah to strangle me and throw me into Hell.   No matter how well tucked up in bed and no matter how deeply I covered my head, Allah had ways of getting beneath the eiderdown and doing His job.   Sometimes, He would send Gabriel who was an angel in comparison to Allah when angry.

Mother would laugh and say that this was rubbish, quoting *"But if they contend with thee to associate with Me, of which thou has no knowledge, obey them not."*   Seeing my confusion she would ruffle my hair and laughingly say something in English - which I could not understand.   In most cases Muna used to join us.   Mother would be very kind to her on such occasions.   But I fancied she gave us both a strange and distant look as we sat at the bottom of her bed.   Several people came to visit her everyday.

Marwan and I hardly ever talked but there existed between us that silent love that only brothers could know. A love tinged with fear and some envy of imagined something or another.   We both avoided father's company as much as possible.   I took refuge with my mother and Marwan took refuge with Naziha or in the garden.   The slightest provocation seemed to throw my father into uncontrollable urges to belt us, particularly Marwan.   As if by common consent we never complained to anyone and he never showed any anger before our mother.

A few days before the Prophet's birthday we went to my grandfather's house where he lived with his wife, his youngest son, and a pretty maid.   For some reason Marwan was not with us.   Only father, mother, and I went.   My parents went into grandfather's bedroom and left me with the maid and my grandmother. The house smelt of boiled cabbage and cleaning polish. The walls were covered in pictures of grandfather on a horse, grandfather beside an old black limousine, grandfather with a fez on, grandfather wearing a uniform, his right hand resting on a high stand and his left gripping a sword. That same beautiful and shiny sword now hung on the wall. It had lost its colour and had several spots on it. Everywhere; including the furniture and walls, was covered with threadbare carpets and rugs.

My grandmother wore a magnificent old dress and sat in a high backed armchair. Her shoulders were wrapped in a black shawl which had the remnants of what must have been golden lines. She gazed ahead of her. When the maid was called out by mother I sat quietly looking around me. Suddenly my grandmother grunted and looked at me.

"Come here boy!" she said imperiously.

I sat still. She held up a piece of chocolate.

"Here. You can have it."

I approached her.

"Do you like my dress, boy?"

I snatched the piece of chocolate and stepped back, but too late. She had got hold of my arm and slapped me twice. Immediately she set up a pitiful wail. My mother came in.

"What is it?" she said quietly but looked angry.

"He took my chocolate. The horrible, horrible boy. Little Sambo!"

She continued to wail. I gave the chocolate back.

"Hush now. There. There it is. You can have it now. Hush." My mother was very gentle. "Do you feel like having a glass of milk?"

"No! No! Call my maids! No!" And she sat gazing ahead of her again.

Mother took me into the garden and asked me to occupy myself quietly. I walked around looking for something to do. How I wished Muna were there. I approached my grandfather's window. I heard nothing but I saw my father standing solemnly with his back to the window. I thought it fit to leave that area of the garden and went to another window from where I knew my grandmother would be staring. Seeing me, she held up the piece of chocolate and pushed her tongue out at me. I retaliated, but only after I was out of her line of vision. Turning a corner I reached a small sitting area outside my uncle's room. I went to the window and looked in hoping to see him and receive the usual present of a small coin.

He lay on his bed smoking a cigarette with his eyes shut. He only had a pair of small shorts on. Beside the sink stood the pretty maid with nothing on. I thought that she looked so bright and beautiful. She looked across at my uncle with wide shining eyes. I did not look at her for too long because I saw that she was busy with something that terrified me as I had had experience of it at school. She held a huge syringe in her hand and a very small container in the other. She gasped and picked a dirty towel and vigorously wiped something off her breasts. I feared that since my uncle was ill, I was unlikely to get a present of the usual small shiny coin. Father called. We drove home very quietly. Mother was tearful but very silent. Her wide beautiful eyes seemed misty and distant.

****

The day was here! The Prophet's birthday had at last arrived. We were to drive over to my aunt's house from where we could see the fireworks from the army barracks near the airport road. The aunt was my mother's younger sister and a very rich one. She had a very nasty son and a very friendly husband who was always laughing at his own jokes.

Father was away on business till late that night. We were to go in a taxi - an event in itself. The time arrived and we crowded into the back of the car with mother. Naziha sat in front. Marwan and Selma sat beside mother while I stood behind the driver's seat looking out excitedly with the delightful knowledge that I would have been in bed by now had it not been the Prophet's birthday.

We drove out of the city and onto the wide airport road. As we came out of a roundabout we were stopped by the police. Before we had a chance to make inquiries we were deafened by sirens. Fire engines, police cars, and several ambulances raced by. More followed suit. On our left several men ran into the large pine forest from which came thick smoke. Several women and children ran towards the trees screaming. The police stopped some and sent them back. I saw one policeman slap a woman several times as she fought her way through. He carried her away very gently and she seemed to stop resisting. I looked at my mother. She smiled and asked the driver if he could turn round because of the children. More cars with sirens disappeared into the trees. Our driver seemed helpless. A few cars raced out of the wood with their lights flashing and horns going. Ambulances followed. A policeman ran from car to car asking if anybody could spare his car to help. Many did. My mother offered but he refused saying that there were children to be considered.

A car racing towards us skidded, spun round once or twice and came to a halt. Several people ran towards it. Some started shouting, "A puncture!" Two men opened the rear door and took a struggling and blackened form out. I could hear a kind of screaming similar to the noise people make when they want to indicate they are very cold. I recognised some words: "Allah, peace, help me, Allah keep you, please!" The form was half dragged half carried to a car offered by a driver behind us where it was thrown into the back. The screaming stopped.

"Is he dead?" shouted someone.

The driver jumped in shouting "How the hell should I know? I am not a doctor. The AUB or al-Maqasid?" he asked. A policeman shouted back "Hotel Dieu. Quick!"

All this took a few seconds but it is as vivid in my memory as if it were happening this very minute in my little study. There before me I can see a little boy staring with wide eyes with his mother's two large hands crossed around his little torso holding him close to her body.

What seemed a very long time later and after several ambulances had raced past us, the driver came back from talking to a policeman who had told him that the fire was under control. We were allowed to drive on. Thick smoke was still rising and passing over our heads.

Selma cried. Marwan, who seemed to take his cue from her, dissolved into tears. My mother held me in her arms and told me about the approaching festivities at my aunt's house. I looked into her eyes and felt more frightened despite her words. The driver sat there talking to the terrified Naziha and telling her that if the government persisted in allowing those stupid Moslems to have fireworks such disasters were bound to occur. Fires like these never happened when the Christians let off fireworks!

When we arrived at aunt's house we were received with tremendous uproar. Knowing that our way lay near the pine forest and hearing of the fire, aunt had became worried. She tried to telephone but there was no reply since we had left home to drive to hers. As it was getting very late she started to fret. From fretting to crying, then to hysteria and a step beyond when she ran out onto the roof to jump off as she became convinced that we had all expired in the tremendous glow which she could see in the not-too-far distance. Mother ran up to the roof and we followed. Aunt was standing near the edge shouting her intention to jump off. Her eldest daughter was pulling her back. The younger one held on to the eldest and all three looked as if they were going to go down together. My mother stood there staring at the three with a suppressed smile. She drew my aunt's attention to the fact that if she really wanted to jump it may be worth considering the rather trifling obstacle of the five foot bars before her. Aunt stopped shrieking and stared at my mother.

"Thanks to Allah you're unhurt. Oh! I feel faint. Rose-water, quickly!"

Mother started to laugh. Aunt's daughters also joined in. I laughed. We all laughed but none seemed genuine. We had a silent meal with mother trying to amuse us. No fireworks were let off that night.

On the way home I stroked my mother's large hands crossed on my chest and asked her what had happened to the man we saw earlier. She told me that he was in hospital. Was he dead? Maybe. What did that mean? Selma pinched me while mother quietly said that she did not know. I thought that I heard her whispering something about finding out soon. I smiled up at her and she laughed hugging me hard. As we approached home Marwan seemed worried. Selma kept whispering kindly to him. He looked quite pale by the time we arrived.

It was not the fire that worried him. Father's silent wrath as he helped mother out of the car gave the reason for Marwan's state of mind. In a retaliatory action he had led a 'seek and destroy' party into father's garden. News of the fire and laughter at my aunt's antics saved Marwan from what Ali used to call 'Madame la Ceinture' in an affectionate echo of France's other equally deadly 'Madame la Guillotine'.

In the morning I discovered several yellow petals on the ground. A long green stalk stood high with its smiling and swaying sunflower head cut off. The earth around its base showed a valiant but failed attempt at replanting the torn stalk.

Chapter 10

For the rest of the year's summer holiday, Marwan and I were sent to a boarding school in the mountains. It was there that Marwan's private genie appeared. Known as Jalambo, I believed implicitly in his all encompassing and terrifying powers.

The school house was on the top of a hill. Descending the steps to the bottom there was the playground and a small tuck shop from where Jalambo seemed to get all his provisions. Behind the shop was a dainty little cottage in which lived a young teacher who took a keen interest in a small kitchen garden. We were expressly forbidden to go in there. Marwan and I adopted a very small chubby boy as our protégé and - God forgive us - as our amusement. This boy believed everything that Marwan told him. We had regular entertainment in sending him into the teacher's garden with the firm belief that the spring onions he was pulling out contained a limitless supply of chocolate. We would sit on a wall and gleefully applaud when the furious teacher smacked him several times. Then Marwan, with the aid of Jalambo, whom he found it necessary to converse with near the tuck shop, would produce a handful of peanuts or sugared chickpeas for the boy.

Another boy, a very big one, used to steal food from our mouse-proof tins. He was told that Allah would punish him. Sure enough He did. A boil, expertly and rather painfully lanced by the old headmistress, developed into something very nasty and no less than a real doctor had to be called in. I have a strong memory of this boy whimpering at night and no longer being there in the morning. The headmistress said that he went on a journey. Marwan said that he was sent to jail for stealing food and that he would be hanged on Tuesday of next week. He gave us little ones a vivid description of how hanging took place with his face turning very red and his eyes growing very large in the process.

I had to work very hard on my arithmetic and I sorely missed Muna's help. These were unhappy days. My extreme loneliness was lessened by Marwan and his invisible companion. Life was regimented, cold and uncomfortable. Our headmistress, always dressed in black and with a large scar across her mouth and chin, terrified us. She had an uncanny habit of appearing everywhere when least expected. Marwan said that she could talk to Allah and that he had actually heard her doing so. He told me not to worry because Jalambo would keep her at bay because he too could speak to Allah but only on Thursdays. He must have done so the very next Thursday because the woman in black never came near us. What made me dislike her even more was that she bore a remarkable resemblance to our mother's old Nanny who was deaf and always shouted at us and gave us resounding smacks on our bottoms when we came out of the bath.

I say that she never came near us although she did, once. Before every meal she conducted prayers and then warned us that every single scrap that we left uneaten would mean years in Hell trying to scoop it up off burning wood with our eye-lashes which, when burnt, would be instantly replaced. We never left a dish that did not sparkle with cleanliness. The weaker boys were made to eat what the stronger ones could not. The stronger boys would eat your leftovers for the price of all your tuck shop money for that day or the next. As a result when Ramadan arrived, we all volunteered to fast, which pleased our lady in black very much.

At the end of Ramadan we celebrated the *Eid* feast in style. Lessons were cancelled for three days. With the prospect of no more arithmetic for a long time I sat up in readiness for the evening meal. We ate heartily, that is until the dessert arrived. Made up of bread, boiled chickpeas, and other things immersed in milk, I could not smell, let alone eat, the supposed delicacy. My resistance was very low having had a month of fasting, getting up at midnight for a snack, and at four in the morning for early morning prayers. After some negotiation Marwan accepted to eat my portion in return for my traditional bag of sugared almonds distributed during celebrated occasions. We managed to exchange dishes secretly and I sat before an empty dish looking as full and as satisfied as one is expected to look after such an occasion.

With the corner of my eye I could see a black figure floating towards our table.

"Good lad. You've finished all?"

"Yes ma'am. Praise be to Allah, ma'am."

"And you, my boy?"

It was only then that I noticed Marwan's face. His eyes were misty, his nose a little red, and his throat moved up and down convulsively. He made a sudden move, put his hand to his mouth, and ran out of the room. The black lady went after him. She reappeared a few minutes later leading him forcefully by the ear.

"You'll eat every little scrap up, my boy. Every little scrap like everybody else."

"I will not!" came the wilful reply.

"We shall see. I have all the time in the world. All the time that I need. You'll sit here until you've finished every little bit. Eat!" She pushed his head forward. "Eat! Eat now rather than in Hell! Eat! Eat! Eat!"

I was sent to bed early that night. Marwan was left sitting in front of the horrible dish. He was not to move until he had eaten every little scrap. He refused. Nothing, not even the supreme threat of calling father, would induce him to eat.

****

I went to sleep but my mind was fully aware of its surroundings. Now and then I could hear murmurs down the corridor away from the dormitory, like two people remonstrating with each other. I heard several footsteps urgently walking up and down the corridor. Suddenly I felt a hand touch my shoulder. I turned round in bed to find the silhouette of the black figure standing at the bottom of my little curtained cubicle. It stood there for a few minutes looking at me. I fancied that the shaded face smiled cruelly, though how I could possibly see in that darkness never occurred to me. The figure raised its arm and pulled the curtains back. It turned towards the door and pointed to another figure standing there. I sat up in bed with my heart beating loudly and fast. At the door stood my father. The black lady walked, or rather floated, towards the door and out of it. As my father stepped aside to let her through I heard her mumble something to him.

He stood motionless for a while. Suddenly he turned towards me and, uttering a scream that I shall never forget, ran towards my bed. He suddenly stopped still and looked at me, smiled and said something quietly. I looked round to see if the other boys had heard him screaming. All was still. He started to return towards the door where my mother stood beckoning. She walked away towards the dining-room where Marwan sat. Father turned around and, with the same terrible scream, he lunged forward and, lifting his arm up in the air, let his fist down into my stomach with such force as to be heard at the other end of the school. I felt a strong pain. I was surprised that the pain was not as strong as I thought it should be. Father hit me again and again. Every time he hit, a strange noise came from my stomach like a tyre being deflated.

Spurts of blood sprang out and hit father in the face, covering it with small red dots. Each time that father hit me he made a gurgling noise that was even more frightening than the fist landing in my stomach. I screamed and screamed. I could hear footsteps in the corridor. Father looked up. He stood up straight, turned round, and started to run. I screamed more. He ran out of the door as mother came in. She walked up to my bed. I screamed louder. She took me in her arms. I woke up. The black lady stood at the bottom of my bed saying, "Are you all right? You've had a nightmare, my boy."

This dream has haunted me all my life. I dreamt it several times after that night. I would wake up in a sweat and fancy that I could still see the black lady standing at the bottom of the bed. At such times my only consolation would be the thought of that time when, having had a rather similar dream, mother came into the room and told me that if father came into my dream again I could shoot him with my cowboy pistol. I remember asking if that were really all right. She smiled and said, "Yes, go ahead. The man in your dream is not really Baba. It's someone like him in appearance."

Naziha explained that it must have been the devil who was appearing to turn me against my father in order that I may be disobedient and thus give him - the devil - another inhabitant in his domain.

Next morning I walked into the dining-room with a sick feeling in the pit of my stomach. I felt my whole body was a heavy burden supported on two weak and unsteady legs. Marwan was still sitting in his seat with his head resting on his folded arms. In front of him stood the hateful dish. Several of us offered to eat it for him but he refused, much to our relief. The young teacher was particularly kind to him but he remained sullen. Similarly at lunch-time.

I spent the afternoon walking outside the dining-room where I could see Marwan sitting there looking haggard and rather ill. Once I saw the black lady remonstrating with him. During one of those walks I saw father walking up the steps that led to the school. My heart sank and then jumped for joy. I started to run towards him then I stopped. I walked down the steps with the distracted air of one who saw much beauty to admire in the surrounding trees. He called out to me. "Ah!" I said distantly and ran jumping into the welcoming arms. A few minutes later I rushed into the dining-room. Inarticulate with excitement I told Marwan all that father had told me. We were going home. Father and mother had brought us a train set from London. We were going home. Home! Marwan walked away looking unhappy and tired. He turned round and came back towards me. He led me to the dormitory. On pain of the severest tortures from Jalambo he made me swear to say nothing of what had happened. I swore. Like Hamlet's ghost the offence was gone and Marwan assumed what antics he thought fit. We returned to the dining-room with our bags. Father shook hands with the black lady and thanked her for looking after us. He bade us make haste to the waiting car after we had said our good-byes. I approached the woman who embraced and kissed me. I smelt soap as I shut my eyes to avoid seeing the dreaded scar. She stood up and looked at Marwan.

"Come here, my boy. My dear boy, you must understand..."

Before she had time to finish, Marwan walked up to his place at the table, picked up the hateful dinner and threw it across the room with all his might. It missed her. She stood transfixed for a while. Marwan turned and ran shouting, "Bye old scar face." I stood still and in my embarrassment did not know what to do. I too blurted out "Scar face!" and ran as fast as my legs would carry me.

****

We soon returned to our normal winter school. The black lady was back in her capacity as matron in the boarding section of the school, but we were day boys. We delighted in leaving food uneaten after lunch. Our lunch lady did not seem to mind. But most delightful of all was the reunion with Muna to whom I had a lot of stories to tell. I never told her about Marwan's confrontation with old scar face.

Otherwise the first term at school passed off uneventfully except for my desperate struggles to master my numbers. To counter this weakness I was doing well in Arabic and English.

During our Christmas and New Year break mother spent most of her time in bed. Muna and I used to sit with her a great deal. I was not allowed to sleep in her bed anymore because she said that I fidgeted a lot. We had to keep very quiet most of the time. The slightest noise incurred a belting from father. He supervised my arithmetic homework, sometimes belt in hand, but more often without listening to me or paying any attention to my wrong sums.

New Year's Eve we went to the ICI office for the annual children's party. Selma stayed at home with mother. I received a fountain pen and Marwan a new satchel which didn't impress him. We returned home very late. Mother had been moved into father's room and away from our garden. My section of the garden remained a closed area though. I ran to mother's room to show her my new pen. Marwan ordered me to walk and not run. We walked in. The room was dimly lit by a bedside lamp. Mother lay quietly against the pillows. Selma knelt beside her bed. There was a smell of feet and stale cigarettes. On the wall above the bureau hung my father's degree and a few pictures of old people. Otherwise the room seemed very bare in the semi-darkness. I noticed that the furniture looked darker than usual.

Selma looked up and motioned us out. Mother opened her eyes and smiled. She asked us to come in. I ran up excitedly showing her my pen. Selma looked angry. Marwan stood beside Selma silently holding her hand. Mother looked at my pen and asked me to put it away because there was something important that she wanted to tell us. I asked if it were a surprise. She closed her eyes for a short while.

Mother winced with pain as she tried to move. She put her hand to her shoulder and sighed.

"Children." She spoke quietly, so very quietly. "Children. I think that I am going to die." Silence followed. Selma sobbed. Marwan looked at her and he too started crying. I bent my head and, looking at my new pen, turned it over and over again from hand to hand.

"Do you know what that means, Saif?" asked mother. Selma let out a sob. "Hush! *Tu vas leur faire peur.*"

"I know what that means. It's French" I declared looking into mother's eyes.

Mother smiled and looked back at me.

"Of course you do. You're a very clever boy."

I stood there for what felt like a long time. I could feel a lump in my throat.

"Soon I shall be going away. You'll have to look after Baba. You must be good, Marwan. You'll do what you are told, won't you? And you Saif ..." She became silent. I sensed rather than saw father's presence in the room. Mother looked at me and tried to smile. There were new lines under her large eyes.

"Take them away to bed. To bed!" She almost screamed. We were led out.

That night Marwan cried in bed. He would not tell me why he cried. When I persisted in asking him he made a motion to hit me.

"Sissy!" I retaliated. A short while later his crying ceased and we slept. Next day mother went away. We visited her in hospital once.

That was in the second week of January, 1956. The hospital impressed me with its cleanliness and brilliant whiteness. Mother was cheerful. She talked to us all the time we were there.

During our stay we drank orange juice and sat on the edge of mother's high bed. Marwan delighted in turning the handle that changed the position of the head rest. She smoked and smiled while she told us stories about the hospital. When it came for the time to leave, she stepped out of bed and walked both Marwan and me by the hand. At the bottom of the corridor I asked to be carried. Selma said no but mother picked me up. She said that I was ever so heavy. I kissed her on her cheek. She kissed me back and said that I was always a good boy and her favourite little prince. I laughed. She too laughed showing a row of white gleaming teeth. As she laughed one of her eyes closed a little, but both were still ever so large. She seemed to look through me at something beyond. She gave Marwan a kiss and told him that he was her big prince. He nodded and tried to smile but I thought that he wanted to cry. Selma took us down the stairs, holding Marwan's willing hand.

After a few steps down I turned round and ran up again. I walked through the door despite Selma's threats. At the other end of the corridor I saw mother walking away in her red dressing-gown. I called. She turned round. I waved. She waved back smiling. We did this for a long time till father emerged with a doctor and told me to wait downstairs in the car with the others.

Mother lit a cigarette and smiled encouragingly. She winked. I caught a glimpse of the much loved tassels of the belt around her dressing-gown. They reminded me of father's shaving-brush but they were softer and smelt of cigarettes and home.

During the third week in January and a few days after our visit to mother we were woken up earlier than usual and taken to school by Naziha. At school, lessons started with my usual miserable efforts at reciting my tables. To my delight the teacher did not get annoyed. In fact, she moved me to the front of the class to the seat of honour beside her desk. Privileged as I was I looked out of the window and ignored all her class teaching. Now and then she looked at me but when my eye caught hers she looked away. Halfway through the second lesson, our deputy-head (a close cousin of my mother's) walked into the room. We all stood up ready for a spot check on verses from *The Holy Qur'an* or on our tables. She asked us to sit down and resume work. Having mumbled a few words to our teacher, she asked me to go with her. With great deliberation and a heavy step I was led out into the corridor fully aware of the sixty or so eyes bent on me.

We walked down the corridor and turned right. There, Marwan stood beside another teacher. We walked downstairs together. I whispered asking him if he knew what all this was about. He told me to shut up. With a look of contempt I walked ahead of him. The deputy-head said softly, "No hurry. Take it easy love." This made me feel wretched but I soon ignored it. Below, at the end of another corridor stood our headmistress. She saw us coming and appeared to be remonstrating with someone. As we approached I recognised, through the frosted glass a dress that looked familiar. We got to the end of the corridor. Selma appeared holding a handkerchief in her hand. She had her hair in plaits on either side of her head. She smiled at us. The headmistress explained that we were going to spend the night at our uncle's house because father and Selma were going out for a while. Selma smiled again and explained that Uncle Issam had a very special supper prepared for us. We were also going to the cinema. She was in a hurry and walked away. The headmistress gave us each a chit to get whatever we wanted from the tuck shop. We were allowed out into the playground.

Marwan sat on a bench crying. I tried to explain that although we were going to uncle Issam's we were also going to the cinema. We did not like this uncle because he always asked us if we had said our prayers and flicked our fingers sharply, once for every dirty nail. Marwan got angry and said, "You're stupid. Don't you know what has happened?'

'Yes. We're going to uncle Issam's. And don't call me stupid, stupid!"

I felt triumphant as this seemed to hit the mark beautifully. He dissolved in bitter tears. A teacher took him away and sent me to the tuck shop. I bought a round cake covered in sesame seeds and sat on the steps eating it. Suddenly I was aware of several eyes looking at me out of class windows. I got up and walked up and down the playground with deliberate and slow steps. The bell rang. Boys and girls surrounded me. Muna was not one of them. She stood at a small distance away staring at me.

One of the boys surrounding me pushed his way forward and took me aside. Did I know that things were happening at home? What if I did? He saw some men carrying a big box in and out again. Were we moving? I thought not although I failed to see what concern it was of his. Some men were plastering stickers on the walls outside the house. I promised to investigate the whole thing as soon as possible. Muna walked up to us.

"Are you all right?" she asked.

"Of course."

"Why are you avoiding me then?"

"I have been rather occupied." I immediately regretted giving such an answer. She came forward and kissed me and ran off. I was furious. I turned to the boy and asked him to describe the box he had mentioned as having seen being carried in and out of our house.

We spent that night at uncle Issam's where we had a lovely meal after we had been to the cinema to see a black and white film about a boxer who kills his brother. It starred Paul Newman, was called *Somebody Up There Likes Me*. It was a very tortuous movie but it is burnt on my very soul to this day. Marwan was silent. So was I. Uncle said nothing about prayer and did not ask to see our finger-nails. That night I had terrible diarrhoea. We slept in the front room on two floor mattresses. Marwan told me that he too had the same complaint.

"They've poisoned us. They want to kill us" he whispered.

"What shall we do?"

"We'll phone home for help."

I agreed but the problem was how to go about doing such a thing. Marwan said that he knew the number and that I should make the call. I objected.

"You're younger. They'll believe you."

I got up and walked out into the dining-room where uncle sat talking quietly to his wife.

"Please. I would like to phone mum and dad."

Uncle stood up at the sound of my voice. My aunt explained that father would be coming in the morning to see us. She said that anyhow he would not be at home now. I went back to bed.

Marwan cried bitterly when I told him that I could not telephone. I cried with the stomach ache which I fancied was getting worse as the poison was working within. As sleep overcame me I tried to recite The Opening because I had been told that if I died reciting *The Holy Qur'an* I would go to Paradise. I covered my head so that Allah would not find me when He came looking, though I recognised the futility of this ploy. As I fell asleep I could feel Marwan's body shaking convulsively beside me.

****

We went to school the next day. Being Thursday it was a half day holiday before the Friday weekend. The day passed very much as before. At twelve thirty we emerged from classrooms to find a big man all dressed in black standing at the gates. It was Ali! I ran into his arms and he tossed me into the air. We walked home on either side of him. He told us that he had bought us extra bits for our train set. Before we got home he bought us each a handful of gob stoppers.

We arrived home and many people were there. In the sitting-room sat several women in black with white scarves on their heads. In the dining-room was a circle of men smoking and drinking coffee. They whispered to each other as we walked in. We were led to Selma's room. Father sat on her bed. He was all in black. So was Selma. I was very excited to see my aunt (father's youngest sister from Baghdad and a favourite aunt of ours) sitting in there. Ali stood by the door. Father kissed us both. He had a newspaper in his pocket. I took it out and found a picture of mother on the front page. She had a black gown and cap on and looked beautiful. When I looked up only aunt was in the room. Marwan stood by the window.

"You know, boys, that I have something to tell you..." she began.

"I know what you're going to say," I guessed excitedly. Marwan looked at me angrily.

"You know, boys, we all have to go back to Allah. You know that from school."

"Yes! Yes!" I could feel a sob rising.

"Mama has gone back to Him. That means that you won't see her for a very long time."

"Not till we die," blubbered Marwan.

"Yes."

I ran out of the room and into my own. The dining table had been moved in there. I stood staring at it. On it sat a Sheikh cross-legged drinking coffee. He started chanting. I ran out and into mother's new room. She was lying on her bed dressed in black with her face covered in white.

"Mama!" I whispered.

Selma sat up and grabbed me in her arms. She cried.

"She's gone. I'll be your mama. Yes. Yes. I shall be your mama little prince."

I tried to push her off. A loud commotion was heard outside and an old woman dressed all in black whom I had never seen before rushed in.

"My babies! Where are the little orphans? Give them to me. I'll have them. Oh Leila! Leila!"

My sister stood up and I clung to her to avoid this apparition. Father came in with Ali and tried to take the woman out.

"But look at him. Look at the poor baby. He is crying."

Selma let go of me and shouted "Let him cry! Get the hell out of here!"

I ran out at the moment that Selma collapsed. I walked from room to room. Various relations, both known and unknown, looked at me but no one came near me. I went to mother's old room. I looked at her books and cried. I thought of the time she beat me for stealing money in order to buy a cake. It was on that bed. I tried to think of the time that she refused me permission to go out until I had finished my sums - set by her - during one summer. I remembered her attempts at teaching me arithmetic. I looked at her books again. I heard a rustle by the door. I called out her name. Selma appeared and came towards me holding Marwan's hand. I ran out.

In the garden I went towards my fig tree hoping to find, I know not what. I walked back into the house and looked in the kitchen. Naziha embraced me and cried.

"Let him be," said a voice very gently. Mother! I looked around at Selma. She smiled and said that I could now go to my garden if I wanted to.

I walked out and toward my little house. By its entrance stood Muna. I walked past her and sat on my boxes. I cried bitterly but was aware that Muna was crouching in the corner staring at me.

Book 2

The Second Return

As I labour on towards another beginning, I bring with me what is left of my great train of troubles, fears, and torments.

Whether I shall turn out to be the hero of my own life, or whether that station will be held by anybody else, would be impossible to find out.

Since the novel became a serious art, people have been writing so well that real characters exist no more. Emotions are anathema. Personalities hide their faces in embarrassment. Details are boring.

In these dark ages of novel-writing, sentimental fools crave for a return to the enlightenment of a Thackeray, the humanity of a Dickens, the amused and gentle understanding of an Austen, the passion of an Emily Brontë.

Such persons skulk in dark rooms for fear of exposure. The return they wish for is acted out over and over again. But it is only a dream carried away by the great lapse. They are like a motherless child crawling in search of her remains in the rubble.

We were told that "Mama has gone back to Him".
We were told that we "won't see her for a very long time."
Meanwhile we children trod gently and softly amongst the rubble.

Awaiting The Second Return.

1. The Widower

During his wife's lifetime, Hussein was not in the habit of talking very much to her. They discussed the children, household affairs, and other practical matters that touched their daily lives. Now and then, but not often, Hussein would unexpectedly take her into his confidence, confiding in her of his endless lists, of entries carried forward, and other practical items in his pocket diaries. At such times Leila recognised his need to talk and would listen silently and apparently distractedly. Though not important to her, each entry carried an association in Hussein's mind with an emotion or a fleeting feeling which only he understood.

Since Leila's death, Hussein had felt a strong desire to confide to her his every inner secret. At night he lay sleepless but secure in the knowledge that she was there - somewhere. A feeling of warmth would engulf him as he hugged the covers around his ears. Silently and secretively, he would talk to her though no words were formed. Thousands of rushing little images raced before his eyes, crossed the dark room and entered the recesses of the near past, a past already becoming distant as new and renewed thoughts slowly obliterated little memories.

Like the child who wakes up in the morning to find its doll cold, silent, and distant; Hussein awoke with a heavy feeling of oppressive reality. The nightly satisfaction was but an insufficient dream.

Hussein, now aged fifty-four, had to find a way in which he could turn his solitary days to become as comfortably delusive as his nights. He worked harder at the office and increased his rounds of farms. After he had inspected a citrus grove he would willingly accept the coffee offered by the sociable farmer. A long walk in the countryside would follow. Being busy in every way possible brought temporary relief though nothing could match his nightly escapades.

During this period of dream-wish existence, Hussein's life felt very transitory. He seemed to be waiting for something to happen. At night part of his conscious self waited for the dawn to arrive so that it may anticipate the pleasures of the coming night. Unable to face the present moment, he floated irresistibly forward in routines that were agreeable to the bereaved side of his soul.

Amid this organised chaos Hussein discovered a change in one aspect of his life. The discovery, far from relieving his misery, seemed to frighten and yet excite him. One evening, sitting in his room looking over his diary as he half-listened to Selma getting the children ready for bed, he made the discovery of a new type of entry being made. During the period of Leila's illness his entries had remained strictly practical. Reading them now evoked memories and emotions that only he could recognise though not always understand. For a few weeks after her death the diary was empty. Some scattered entries were made after that period. Then, suddenly, about two months after Leila's death a reference was made to Hussein's sleepless nights. It was nothing in itself, simply a passing reference which he must have written as part of the usual list:

7. Sleepless night. Thoughts of Leila.

There was nothing practical in this statement yet it was repeated several times over the next few days. An additional note was made a week later in which Hussein admitted the comfort he derived from such nights. Hussein's fear subsided and his excitement increased as he read on. For the first time his diary had a purpose infinitely more satisfying than the simple release from the burdens of responsibility that he derived from daily lists. He felt conscious relief rather than the objective associations his practical lists evoked.

He stopped at a page written two or three days prior to that evening. In very small handwriting he had filled the entire four lines allocated to that day with the following entry:

5. Sleepless night again. Must live on. Such nights teach me the sweetness of life. I would rather suffer the pain of death hourly than die immediately.

He read the short passage over and over again. It was a quotation from Shakespeare's *King Lear*! He could not remember writing it. He assumed that this must have happened during the night. He tried hard to remember. When? Leila! He had been thinking of her reading and smoking quietly on the balcony; of her red dressing-gown and its tassels hanging from a knot around her waist. He wrote it then.

He got up to look among her books piled up in the corner. It was not there. He went into her bedroom to look for it. He must have her copy of *King Lear*.

The room was the same as it had been during Leila's last year of life except that her books had been removed to his room. Switching on the light he walked over to the bookcase beside her bed. Nothing was there. He looked in the cupboard which still contained Leila's clothes and which he would send to the orphanage started by her.

Overwhelmed by a strong desire to find the play, he started looking into drawers that could not possibly contain it. He sensed a presence behind him. Turning round he saw Selma standing at the door wearing her navy blue school uniform.

"Lost something, baba? Can I help?"

Selma spoke abruptly though with a gentleness in her quiet voice. She was now fifteen years old with an attractive face that seemed to show the pain of her newly acquired responsibilities. Her long auburn hair was spoilt by her recent neglect of it.

Hussein noticed how beautiful her hazel eyes looked. They seemed almost luminous. He carried on searching. Selma turned to walk out.

"*Lear*. Where's mama's copy of *King Lear*?"

"In your room. I put all the books in there."

"I cannot find it."

"I put them there."

He returned to his room. Selma quietly but hastily mumbled, "Good night, baba" and walked away towards her own room.

"What did you say?"

"Nothing."

He could not find *King Lear* anywhere. He looked through the books one by one. They were mainly Shakespeare plays with a few nineteenth century novels. He lined them up against the wall. A *Complete Keats and Shelley* was also missing. Hussein felt worried; there may be more missing. He must find these two. The whole matter took on an unexpected urgency.

He closed and locked his bedroom door for the day. The whole night was before him. He would study his diary. Still excited about his new discovery, he read the entry with the quotation from *King Lear* over and over again. He needed a larger diary if he were to write in this new vein. Endless comfort could be derived from frank entries. The small diary could be used to carry the endless lists.

****

69

The Lear entry brought a host of memories from his younger days. He had read the complete Dickens and Shakespeare in order to improve his English, a necessary task for his work with the ICI Company. He remembered how easy he had found Shakespeare to memorise. He had never realised he could memorise anything. His early schooling in *The Holy Qur'an* had proved arduous. He could not commit much of it to memory and, what he did remember he jumbled up and quoted verses out of context.

Now, almost thirty years later, his mind seemed to have opened up a Pandora's Box but a box containing no plagues or sorrows for mankind. Instead it contained Hussein's link with a new life, a new life to be lived in and through his diary. The outside could remain aloof.

That night, Hussein's conversation with Leila was constantly interrupted by a host of characters and remembered speeches.

The whole house was dark and silent. Doors and windows were closed and bolted.

Marwan and Saif dreamed of Jalambo and school activity. *Bismillah.* He took my chocolate. The horrible, horrible boy. *Ça alors.* Chocolate onions. *Bismillah.* She has gone back to Him.

Selma's sleep was restless. Her head rested on her arm as if to support its too early acquired responsibilities. I'll be your mama. Baba, Saif is forty days old today. Why England, Why?

Ali who slept in the sitting-room leaving his own room empty while his mother's things were there, also slept uneasily. Your mother is ill. I shall never leave England as long as I have you by me. The sitting-room was large and cold. What does the future hold? Failure?

Also that night, Hussein slept a deep sleep filled with dreams of the past and hopes for the future. His sleep was the calmest and happiest. Long overdue, he repaid the lost nights a hundredfold. The room, silenced by the night, reverberated and over-spilled with teeming characters pouring out of Hussein's dreams. In the corridor outside someone shouted to be *very careful o' vidders. I am a lone lorn creetur. Barkis is willin'. The course of true love never did run smooth. If the law supposes that, the law is a ass, a idiot. Ay, the bright day is done, and we are for the dark.*

An empty and motherless house, so quiet and cold, forces these creatures of the mind to shelter elsewhere.

Barkis is willin'.

Marwan and Saif breathed regularly. The clock ticked in time to Hussein's dreams.

They do not love that do not show their love. They do not love that do not show their love. No sweethearts, I believe? Sweetmeats did you say, Mr. Barkis? Is willin'.

****

"Tell me nephew, how does the heathen live?" Haji wiped off tears of laughter as she asked this question for the fifth time that evening. Ali had been talking about England during the evening meal. Apart from Haji there were Hussein's children, Hussein himself and his youngest brother Issam. Despite the jollity of the occasion and in spite of his laughter Hussein seemed uneasy. Selma looked tired although her brother's stories seemed to stir her admiration for him. The group sat around the dining table in Hussein's house. Since Leila's death Haji had become quite the peripatetic lady with a mission in life. She had decided that a jocular atmosphere over an evening meal would be the best preamble to fulfilling her momentous mission. She was laying the ground for an imminent attack on Hussein's state of widowhood. Laughter and a full stomach were, in her experience, the sharpest weapons for breaking down a man's resistance.

"Tell us, nephew. How do they live in that dark corner of the world? Hmm?"

Ali settled in his seat and prepared to tell further stories about England. Issam complacently fingered his glass of Scotch and sat back in his seat. His head shone brightly under the light as tiny beads of perspiration ran off it into a semi-circle of greying hair. Eight or nine hairs in the centre stood erect stubbornly resisting any attempt to be used as camouflage against the shiny bald patch. His cheeks radiated with redness while his eyes twinkled mischievously. He held an enormous cigar in his other hand.

"Why, they are a most strange lot!" Ali felt pleased to be the centre of attraction. "Everybody puts on a swimming suit in order to swim. It takes seconds and it's certainly more enjoyable. Now, the English don't do anything so mundane."

"What do they do? What do they do?" Marwan had heard all this several times before. Every time he laughed more.

"Well, you see, the English are quite lazy really. They cannot be

71

bothered to undress quickly and dive in. They first take their shoes off. Then they put their socks in them. After that they go through great torture trying to fold their trousers up to their knees. If it is sunny, they tie the smallest handkerchiefs around the biggest heads you've ever seen."

Ali paused to enjoy his uncle's loud guffaw. Selma smiled at him while Haji shook her head in amazement at his stories. Everybody laughed noisily.

"Then," Ali continued, "they gently and distractedly amble towards the water, stick a toe or two in and run backwards shouting..."

"Cor' it aint 'alf freezin'!" shouted Marwan whose English was improving dramatically. As everyone laughed, Haji inquired what the phrase meant in Arabic. Issam explained, destroying the point of the joke. Still, Haji joined in the laughter.

"Is it true, nephew, that they rarely wash?"

"No aunt. They wash often. They fill a bath with water, sit in it, wash themselves and then get out."

"Ugh!" shuddered Selma. "It's disgusting. In the same water?"

"This is very unfair, Ali." Hussein spoke irritably. "You generalise. I am led to believe that your education has been of no benefit to you. The British are a particularly clean race."

Ali fidgeted in embarrassment. Since his return nothing had been mentioned about his disastrous stay in England. Haji stepped in to save the situation.

"But they consume alcohol, brother!"

"They do indeed," said Issam with apparent disgust. "On our last visit we were most nauseated by that nation's apparent lack of morality. Most nauseated indeed!"

Both Ali and Selma tried hard not to laugh. Haji nodded her head in vigorous assent. Hussein smiled.

"More perfumed iced-tea, brother?" Hussein asked with such a straight face that both Ali and Selma burst out laughing. Issam seriously declined the offer while his mischievous eyes rested on Haji. The latter sat impassively as if she were completely deaf.

"You've changed a lot nephew," said Haji. "You've grown into a most worthy youth and magnificent sportsman, hey brother of mine?"

"Indeed!" Shouted Issam, jocularly.

"Yes, he has grown somewhat," said Hussein.

"Going bald, though!" Selma teasingly pointed to Ali's slightly receding hair line.

Issam immediately assumed an earnest look as he leant forward. "Fear not nephew. Fear not! We have the remedy. On our last voyage to Aleppo we met a most wise dervish whose austerity we found particularly purifying. We consulted the good man. He advised us on a sure method of restoring hair. It consists of a lotion that one rubs on one's head while remembering that *Allah made the sea subservient so that we may eat from it, the mountains firm lest the earth quake, the stars lest we be lost and so on.* We use it regularly. Here, look!" He pointed to his virtually bald head.

"And rivers and roads that you may go aright? And if you would count Allah's favours, you would not be able to number them." Haji's incantation was lost amongst the uproarious laughter from the diners. Issam sat erect angrily stroking his head. Saif laughed at Marwan who was on the ground with his legs in the air laughing uncontrollably.

Hussein joined in the laughter despite his feeling of annoyance at the children's apparent lack of respect for their uncle.

"Bed!" he ordered.

Selma led the children out amid outbursts of laughter that could not be controlled. Haji smiled at the children's merriment while Issam relit his cigar abstractedly and prepared to offer his hand to be kissed by the retiring boys. He shouted after them to clean their nails and say their prayers.

Naziha came in to clear up as the remaining four retired to the sitting-room. Glass in one hand and cigar in the other, Issam entered first, followed by Hussein on whose arm Haji rested hers. As they shuffled in she turned to Ali and said "Nephew, your sister requires your help." Ali, despite his twenty-two years, obeyed quietly though somewhat sulkily.

"Sit brother, sit." she said diplomatically. "Ah! I'm not long for this world. My legs. My legs are so bad. It won't be long before they carry me to my grave. Hey brother?"

"Nonsense!" whispered Hussein distractedly.

"O soul that art at rest" shouted Issam. *"Return to the Lord, well-pleased, well pleasing. Enter among My servants and enter My Garden.* Hey sister!"

"Kindly be quiet brother and drink your perfumed tea!"

Issam smiled mischievously as he settled in his seat. But for the occasional grunt of approval now and then, he remained silent during the conversation that followed.

"Brother, I say. I'm not long for this world. No. I'm not. I shall not live to see our land again. Let the damned Jew retain it. Brother, we have problems nearer home. No. May He forgive me for saying this. Palestine is our problem. Yes brother. Heed me."

Haji uneasily rolled the hem of her dress between forefinger and thumb. She rested an elbow on her knee as she bent slightly forward and directed her hazy eyes towards the area where her brother sat patiently waiting for the expected tirade.

"No, brother of mine. Allah keep you but I am not long for this world. So I have to speak. You'll not be angry with me. I am old and crotchety. I am blunt. My misfortune, brother. I never went to school. I am but a woman, my brother." She paused as if to feel her brother's reaction. He remained a distant blur sitting aloof and silent. She resumed. "Brother, heed me. Selma is a child. She can not be given such a responsibility. She is but a baby. She is tired. I note that she is short with the children. Oh brother, her kindness is most touching but her impatience in bringing them up is quite understandable. Brother, you must remarry. I'm blunt. Forgive me. Marry and give your children a mother."

Semi-blind as she may have been, Haji could feel Hussein's anger rising. This was going to be a very difficult mission.

"Tell me, Abu Ali, tell me. What is your objection?"

Hussein answered quietly keeping his rising anger under control. He did not want to hurt his sister.

"I have no desire to remarry, sister. Suffice to say, I think myself too old to remarry."

"But surely, brother, you realise the age of the holy Prophet (Allah's blessings be upon Him) when he married late in life?"

Issam grunted assent.

"These are different times" Hussein said thoughtlessly and regretted it almost immediately.

Another grunt came from Issam.

"Different? How different, Abu Ali? You talk of the Prophet Muhammad (Allah's blessings be upon Him). No difference here, brother."

"Haji, what I meant to say was that I feel it would be wrong for me to bring a young woman into my house. For a start Selma may resent having a young mother."

74

"But Abu Ali, you know of Abu Nayer's marriage to the young Fatima. What's wrong with that if I may inquire? I had no schooling."

Hussein was waiting for such an example to be brought up. He found this one particularly obnoxious. Abu Nayer's nuptials were a marriage engineered by his ever-scheming mother. Furthermore, that woman had had the temerity to hint that Selma would make an ideal wife in a year or so. Hussein tried to explain his objections to such marriages. He spoke sympathetically to his sister whom he felt was only trying to be kind. He suggested that the children had a good mother in Selma and in his two other sisters Yasmine and Melika. The former was moving to Beirut soon having been in Damascus since 1948, and there was also Naziha.

"Indeed Abu Ali. But the children need a regular mother. I can see your objection to a young wife. You've been to a university. But, brother, I know of a perfect widow-woman who would do just fine. Only one child who is married. A handsome dowry. Now, I have spoken to..."

"Enough! Enough!" Hussein stood up. "Listen Haji for I do not want to repeat this." He spoke quietly but his tone was firm and final. "I have no intention of getting remarried. Whatever reason you may have for making such a proposal may be very valid. But I do not believe that any woman can replace the void that Leila's death has created in my life. She is still my wife and I am still married. I want to hear no more of this." Hussein bade his sister good night and left the room.

The silence that ensued was interrupted only by Issam's occasional grunt and Haji's loud regretful sighs. "Brother," she said decisively. "Kindly escort me home."

****

Later that night Ali sat in Selma's room quietly smoking. Selma was busily preparing the children for bed. Their laughter could be heard all through the house. Hussein walked into their room and looked at them angrily. They stopped laughing. The lights were switched off and Selma went to her own bedroom to finish some schoolwork. Ali hastily threw the cigarette out of the window as he heard his father coming down the corridor. Hussein shot his son an angry glance.

"Come to the sitting-room." Hussein ordered, then hesitated before adding "if you please!"

Ali got up and looked at his sister who was busily arranging her books, but noticed that her chin was trembling. He followed his father out of the bedroom and into the sitting-room.

"Sit down." Hussein pushed an ash-tray towards Ali. Since his wife's death he had given up smoking and now despised the habit. Ali reluctantly lit up a cigarette.

"I have been waiting." Hussein started to speak but then stopped. He looked up at the light and winced. He got up and left the room. Ali inhaled deeply and avidly. When his father returned he nonchalantly stubbed out the cigarette. Hussein had his sunglasses on. He looked up at the light and sat down. Ali could see the reflection of the light in the glasses. Every time his father looked at him he saw his own reflection in duplicate. Uneasy, he fumbled for another cigarette.

"I have been wanting to speak to you on a matter of some urgency. I expect you know to what I am referring." He waited for an answer and received none. Ali preoccupied himself with staring at his elongated face reflected in the glasses. He wriggled his toes with a feeling of comfort at retaining that secret ability to reply. Hussein continued to speak quietly, but as the conversation progressed he continually adjusted and readjusted his dark glasses.

"I have several points that need to be discussed." As he said this he produced a piece of paper from his pocket. "This concerns your last year in England." He looked at his son as if expecting a reply. "Firstly, what have you to say about your results?"

Such a frontal attack took Ali completely by surprise. He continued to stare at his reflection and to wriggle his toes deep inside his shoes. He did not reply.

"Secondly, what explanation can you give for not writing home for over six months?" None could apparently be given.

"Thirdly, I have had reports on your conduct. Morally it is inexcusable. I am not a religious man. However, your drinking, smoking and whatever else are abhorrent to me. What have you to say? Finally, you may not know it, although you should, but I've had some heavy expenses lately. Some hospital bills are still outstanding. Your education in England cost a great deal. It was money that I could hardly spare. Regardless of this element I fail to see how you could explain the bills both for your college fees and for your board which I have recently received. I sent you the money for both payments at the beginning of the academic year."

Ali spoke timidly as he explained that he needed the expenses.

"Why didn't you write asking for more? What expenses?"

"A few debts..." Ali faltered. He could feel a lump rising in his throat as he said "debts".

"Debts?" Hussein spat out the word as if its very existence in his mouth soiled his body. He adjusted his glasses several times then got up and walked to one of the windows. Having assured himself that it was securely locked he sat down again. Ali saw the light reflected in his father's glasses. He tried to imagine what his eyes looked like behind them.

Staring upwards, Hussein recommenced speaking. "Before going to England we had a talk in this very room. Do you remember what I said to you?"

"Yes."

"I gave you the condition upon which you were being sent to England. I said that if you did not make the best of this opportunity it would be your last. You accepted this condition?"

"Yes."

"You thought it a fair one considering the expenses I was incurring?"

"Yes."

Hussein stared at the ceiling. He could feel Ali adjusting his sitting posture. He suddenly heard an ugly sob. He looked at Ali who sat holding his head in the palms of his hands, his finger digging deeply into his brow.

Hussein moved forward and stopped. "Take hold of yourself. You broke the condition upon which..."

"Please," Ali spoke inarticulately between heaving sobs, "Please. Can I have another chance?"

"No!" came the firm reply.

"It doesn't have to be England. I can go to the American University."

"Who said they'd accept you with your record. No! You've had your chance. The only worthy part of it is your sports record. I admit that it is brilliant. But I have other children's expensive education to think of."

"Please, baba. Allah keep you ..."

This personal reference to their relationship moved Hussein and he looked up at the light. He then stood up. Ali was crying in earnest now. Terror at an unprepared future and fear of the consequences of a misspent past welled up within him. He felt truly sorry for himself. Hussein stood towering over him.

"You have had your chance. I feel sorry for you, son, but..."

Ali jumped to his feet, his face distorted with rage, fear and hatred. "I do not want your sorrow!" he screamed. "You talk of morality." Ali became reckless, mad with the fury of those who regret being made to feel sorry for themselves. "You talk of morality, you damned hypocrite. You talk of uncle Muhammad's addiction but you, why, you are perfect, just bloody perfect!"

Hussein stood staring at his raging son.

"You have no weaknesses! None! None! None! Allah! We are so perfect, the Ibrahims are for paradise! We are something special." Ali walked to one end of the room and back. He wiped the sweat off his forehead. Hussein turned and walked out of the room. Ali lifted the long glass covering the side-board where Hussein kept some of his books. He hurled it across the room with a scream of rage. It crashed into the wall. Naziha ran into the room, looked at Ali, and ran out. He walked out and stood at the top of the corridor. The light went out in his father's room.

"The great Ibrahims! Ha! Uncle Issam the great swindler and thief! He finds it wrong to see women! Your saintly brother-in-law raped his miserable niece! Hush! Hush it up! Issam never drinks? Your symbol of respectability, old Jbeili's wife, does not gamble? You are all so good!"

Selma's hand was on his mouth begging him to stop. He pushed her aside and ran to his father's door, kicking it several times.

"I gave you a chance" he mimicked. "Keep your damned chance. Allah damn you and your forefathers."

During this last outburst Selma had been trying to pull the raging son away from the door. He kicked it several times more, suddenly stopped but trembled violently. Gently pushing Selma away, he walked off.

At the top of the corridor he stopped to turn around and spoke quietly and firmly. "You can keep your house. Keep your money. I'll look after myself you... you." He searched for a word as his anger started to rise again. When the word came he screamed it hysterically, fully realising its very impotence. "You lump of shit!"

As the house-door slammed behind him, Naziha stood where he had said his last farewell. She stared at Selma who stood at the other end of the corridor, trembling.

The children's bedroom door opened and Saif appeared. Naziha picked him up. He started crying. Marwan stood at the door looking at Selma. "Did Ali hit her?" he inquired manfully as his voice trembled for control.

Chapter 2

Very soon after my mother was said to have left us I returned to school as a boarder. The first day I tried to avoid the black lady. I knew that her vengeance would be swift and horrible. Towards the evening I went to my dormitory where I sat on my bed wanting to cry but unable to do so. I felt myself overcome with sleep. As it was becoming dark I stood up and walked towards the hateful dining-room. I felt a hand touch my shoulder. I looked back to find the black lady standing there with a smile across her face which was divided in two by the scar. I was very frightened.

"A visitor to see you my boy." I followed her into the office.

My father stood by the window. Without looking around he motioned the lady to leave the room. I stood by the closed door staring at his back. He turned. He looked at me hard and long, then uttering a scream that shook my very existence, he ran at me. I fell back as he lashed out with what seemed like one hundred hands. I tried to scream but could not. He mumbled something that I could not understand. He hit me hard on my stomach. I coughed and spurts of blood dotted his screaming face. I remembered mother telling me to defend myself against such attacks with my cowboy pistols, as the man was not really baba. Naziha had said that he was the devil. If I could only scream! I tried hard but suddenly realised that my father had disappeared. I woke up to find myself in my own bed at home. I got out of bed and walked sleepily towards the bedroom door. I opened it and Naziha caught me in her arms. Marwan followed me and stood at the door looking towards the bottom of the corridor. I looked too. Selma stood there. Marwan mumbled something that I could not hear. Selma smiled and walked towards us. She took Marwan by the hand.

Naziha put me back in bed and asked me why I could not sleep. I did not want to tell her my dream so I made up one about ghouls and genies. She laughed and said I was a good story-teller even in my dreams. I asked her to tell me a story. Marwan half-heartedly agreed to listen. Selma said that we could have a story for a few minutes. Afterwards she would wish us a good night.

Naziha told us the story of a man who is turned into stone in his lower half by a witch whose love he did not return. She kept him in a hall on an enchanted island. Every night she would visit him and ask if he loved her. He would say that he did not and receive a hundred lashes on the remaining fleshy part of his body. This went on for a thousand years. One day, as the man lay dying of old age, he remembered that he should leave no hatred behind him on earth. So he told the witch of his love for, and forgiveness of, her. No sooner had he said that than she turned into a beautiful princess. Apparently, she herself had been bewitched into her former state, not to be released until she received the love of the first man that she would meet. Alas, it was too late for the man who died soon afterwards. The princess turned into a beautiful statue which Naziha said she would take us to see very soon if we said our prayers regularly and behaved ourselves. She would do this as soon as she returned from her holidays.

Marwan could never be induced to say his prayers. Naziha had long ago despaired of saving him from the torments of Hell. She was always expecting Allah to come for his throat. So I prayed fervently. Naziha said I could pray to be granted five things, but these had to be in order of priority, should be asked for at the very end of my Qur'anic prayers, and said quickly as if they did not really matter (for Allah loathed selfish little boys).

Sometimes I had difficulties with my five items. When I found them, I could not decide on their order of priority. I spent ages rehearsing them for a quick delivery, but conscious that God must have known of all these preparations. Since He knew everything then the haste with which they were delivered did not matter much. One demand never changed although it sometimes dropped in the order of priorities as my desire for earthly things rose. At such times I underwent incalculable agonies of selfish guilt and would wake up and reorder the items in a less selfish way. I was assured that my mother would go to Paradise like all mothers, for the saying went that Heaven was under mothers' feet, but I had to make sure doubly sure. At such times I would quietly chat to a minute doll that I bought during the previous end of Ramadan Eid feast. She was no bigger than two fingers of mine but she held a very large place in my life at night. I hid her behind a few picture books on my small shelf. During the day she always lay on top of another little secret I had.

The doll lay on two books that had belonged to my mother. One was the story of Lear that she had told me several times. The other was a large volume that she used to look at a lot. I did not then know its title. I had quietly crept out one night soon after her books were taken to father's room and taken them both. I knew that I was doing wrong so I included a plea for forgiveness in my nightly items at the end of my prayers for several nights to come.

****

Marwan and I spent all our time in the garden during the spring of that year. We were beginning to drift apart as my friendship with Muna had always irritated him. Since our mother's departure he seemed more and more solitary. He remained very kind towards me although we had started to fight at times.

One spring day we were playing our favourite game of '*ballon chasseur*'. This was a game requiring at least ten people forming two teams of five each. The purpose was to hit one of the opposing team with a ball which, unless the player caught and retained it, meant that he would become the prisoner of the opposing team and would have to stand behind their lines. His only hope of release was to touch one of the opposing players with the ball when one of his team mates manages to throw it over the opposing team and behind their line where he was held prisoner. Once all the members of one team became prisoners; the other team was declared the winner. The ball should be kept on the move at all times, passing from one player to another until one decided to throw it at a player of the opposing team. Two members, one from each team, faced each other on the dividing line and played to decide who first had the ball. The referee threw it up into the air and each player tried to hit it into their respective courts.

It was the game's commencement rules that led to an argument between Marwan and me. The referee (Marwan) had thrown the ball up in the air. A member of the opposite team (Marwan) had knocked it into his court where another (Marwan) had caught it. I ran into my court, got hit by the ball and so became a prisoner. Since I was the only member of my team the referee declared the game over. I objected since the entire morning had been spent with Marwan hitting me with the ball and declaring himself the winner.

"It's not fair. Why can't I be the referee for once?"

"Because you're too little. You cannot control the players."

"But there are no players apart from us" I remonstrated.

"That's not the point. It's the principle that matters."

Marwan always won the arguments but this time I was determined. "Okay then, why don't I throw the ball?"

"Because you're not the referee, silly."

"Don't call me silly." I screeched impotently. Marwan looked at me for a moment then threw the ball at my head. I ducked and it missed me.

"I've won! I've won!" I danced around the garden. I had been hit so many times that morning that I had forgotten that I had to hit Marwan in order to take him prisoner and win.

"No you haven't. You haven't touched me yet."

I picked up the ball and stood on my side of the line. Marwan ran from side to side, a manoeuvre to which he was perfectly entitled.

"Stand still!" I shouted. He laughed and stood behind a tree. I threw the ball which hit the tree.

"You're out! You're out!" I jumped up and down.

"No, I'm not. You hit the tree, not me."

"But, you cannot stand behind the tree."

"Why not? It's in my court."

"You are not allowed to. Anyway if the tree hadn't been there then I would've hit you. So I've won."

"But the tree was there and as referee I declare the game still going." He quickly hit me with the ball. "Another game to me. Score: forty-two - nil."

I walked away towards my little house in the garden declaring that I had no intention of playing any more. Marwan started walking behind singing the score. I threw sand at him. He stood there stupefied.

"This calls for a word in Jalambo's ear, my little man," he said.

"I don't care. I don't believe in him anyhow. He doesn't really exist. You've made him up and Allah will stop him hurting me." I shouted all this with the loudest voice that I could muster.

Marwan looked bewildered for a while and then said "I can talk to Allah himself. I know his telephone number."

I trembled inwardly. "Go ahead. Call Him!"

"In my own time and when you least expect it," he replied and then added, "Go and play with Muna, you sissy." He walked off as she entered our garden and came towards me.

****

Muna seemed ever so grown-up to me, more like a young woman

83

than a little girl. She walked with confident steps and with an air of a person who brushed all problems aside and gave full expression to life. Physically she was tall and attractive. With her long fair hair that shone brightly in the sun, and her wide bright luminous eyes, she was, in my darker eyes, the perfect woman. I was very much in love with her though I never worried or fretted over this state of the heart. She reciprocated my affections with wise and kindly guidance.

Of course, Muna and I had long decided on a matrimonial conclusion to our youthful affair. We were to build a house, somewhat similar to my garden retreat, in a deserted area like the Cedars. There, we would live blissfully for a thousand and one years telling each other stories.

At that time we met regularly to discuss the necessary arrangements for our secret future. We had decided we could dispense with arithmetic and geography but were unable to decide on the type of stories to be told. I was for all kinds without the slightest omission. Muna counselled restraint and selectivity.

"You cannot have all kinds of stories," she explained.

"Why not?"

"Because your stories would have wars in them."

"Well, that's all right. I love war stories about cowboys and Indians."

"War is horrible. We don't want it in our stories. We can have ones like *The Arabian Nights.*"

"But," I interrupted, in what I thought was a clever argument, "War is not horrible. We are going to have one with Israel. And we shall beat them, they will all be killed and then we can all go home to Palestine."

This was a powerful argument which even Muna could not quite counter. She thought for a while before quietly replying "War is horrible. Always!"

This too seemed a powerful enough argument so we dropped the subject and talked about one of Naziha's latest stories which involved a princess who lost her hands for loving a pauper. Her father, the king, went mad and regretted what he had done when he saw her wail by the beautiful pond. Unable to feed herself she died of starvation and sorrow. The pauper went forward into the world to make his fortune. Although he eventually married a queen with immense riches he was never without a thought for his first love because, Naziha said, there was "no love like the first love" and "sometimes the last one was good too," she always added quietly.

Both Muna and I found this story so sad that we almost shed tears (not quite, because we were hardened by our vast experience of life in stories). We sat silently for a little while.

Suddenly, I said, "Why don't we change the story?"

Muna replied that we could not because otherwise the story would not be the same.

"But, why not? It's only a story."

"I know. But it's not right. You cannot change a story about what you did yesterday."

"Yes I could."

"You'd be lying."

I thought very hard. I wanted to explain that this was different. Also I felt hurt at the implication of Muna's statement.

"Anyhow," I continued, "If you change a story then you can make it do what you like.

"It's not the same but you can make up a new story that no one knows."

We decided to do just that. As it happened all our new stories were of the most criminally plagiaristic kind. Where they were not so, they never seemed to end. Every time we met from then onwards, I played Scheherazade to Muna's Shahriar. At the end of every story she would comment on various points and I got to know Muna's likes and told her these favourable stories. Sometimes, however, I recounted stories I knew she would hate. I found such perversity important in my position as the privileged story teller.

****

"Saif?"

"Uhuh."

"Do you miss your mama?"

The question took me so much by surprise that it was only after I whispered, "Yes! Yes, so very much," that I felt my tears rising.

Muna held my hand and said that she missed hers too.

"But you have a new one?" I replied questioning the validity of her feelings.

"Yes I do."

"Well?"

She looked at me with her large bright eyes and said nothing.

"She's very pretty" I said, rather encouragingly.

"Ali comes to visit baba a lot. Why doesn't he talk to his baba anymore?"

"I don't know. They argued about something. Ali failed at school. Marwan doesn't. He's so clever".

It was not long after this conversation that Ali returned home. I remember him coming back during our summer holidays. He came with uncle Nassim and had lunch. My father did not talk much during the meal but he kept piling chips on my plate. We ate on the veranda and it was very hot because baba and Ali had dark glasses on. I had a pair of plastic ones (pink I think) which I had bent inside out and so could not wear them properly. We had kebab, chips, and tabouli for lunch. I liked tabouli because you could taste the tomato after you sucked the bitter lemon dressing out of the mouthful.

Uncle Nassim and Ali were to return the next morning with Ali's things. He was going to the university where I wanted to go one day. Uncle Nassim was going to stay and listen to President Nasser making a speech. I liked my uncle Nassim: he was full of stories and gave us lots of toys, and many story books.

****

"Little nephew, sit! President Nasser shall speak. Niece you may sit by me. Elder brother, drink your tea. Ali, kindly smoke by the window. Nasser speaks."

We all sat around the radio waiting for the speech which was coming from the main square of Alexandria. Aunt Haji joined us and sat dressed all in black. I sat on uncle Nassim's lap. Father stood with his elbow resting on the radio. Military music filled the entire street. Uncle Nassim switched the radio off and laughed. We could hear the music coming from every house in the street.

"Big brother of mine, switch the wireless on. I want to hear the saviour speak." Uncle Nassim nudged me in the ribs. He said, "Don't listen to him when he speaks in colloquial Arabic. He is lying to the masses. The truth is in the classical sections."

"For shame, brother, for shame. He's not English, is he?"

Uncle Nassim laughed again.

"Pray silence everybody," commanded my aunt.

"This is the Voice of the Arabs. On this glorious and momentous day of our glorious history we take you to the main square of Alexandria where thousands..."

Uncle Nassim smiled and said "That means about two people."

"Shush! Can we please have some hush in here?" Aunt Haji leant forward on her seat. Her elbow rested on her knee with her hand around her ear. Her other hand was busy rolling the hem of her dress over and over again. She would drop the rolled hem now and then and recommence the ritual.

Silence filled the room.

President Nasser spoke in what I thought was a very ordinary voice and I felt terribly disappointed. I don't know what I had expected. Uncle Nassim handed me a bar of chocolate. Father looked cross. As the speech progressed he bent his head nearer and nearer to the radio yet turned the volume up and up.

"Whether these are Communist arms or not, in Egypt they are Egyptian arms."

We heard cheers and applause from the street below.

"How now? How now? The Communist is a heathen. A Kafir, an infidel." Aunt Haji collected the hem of her dress and rolled it angrily.

The monotonous voice went on endlessly. I felt my eyes get heavy and Uncle Nassim whispered "Wake up nephew. Nasser speaks."

My aunt looked angry. "Pray, brother of mine, who is this Lesseps he talks of?"

Uncle Nassim replied, "The man who built the Suez Canal. A Frenchman."

"An infidel." Aunt Haji dismissed him with a backward wave of her hand

"We shall build the High Dam and we shall gain our usurped rights. We shall build the High Dam. We shall build the High Dam. To hell with the Americans! We shall. We shall."

Aunt Haji accompanied every few words with a tap on my head which woke me to the shouting and applause from the street. I looked at uncle Nassim.

"The best dressed fool in Europe won't like this," he said, laughing.

"Won't he?" I asked, without the remotest idea of what he was talking about.

That was the last I heard before I fell asleep again.

****

We returned to school amid talk of war and of The Return to Palestine. One boy said that his family had packed all their things in preparation for the journey to Haifa, and asked if we were ready to go back. I explained that we had been ready for months.

Every morning at school assembly, V-day was proclaimed to be very near at hand. During our Arabic lessons we had endless speeches on the Promised Land. The teacher, Mr. Yafi, explained the intricacies and secrets of British betrayal and double-dealing. One day he came in waving a carbon paper in one hand and a small flag of Palestine in the other. He pointed to the black paper and asked us to read England's record of treachery. We read avidly and loudly while, during the rest of the lesson, he waved the flag at us.

It was at this time, towards the end of October, that Israel attacked Sinai. Mr. Yafi decided that we should make a contribution to the war effort. A competition was to be held. Each class was to memorise a poem. A representative from each group would go forward to the finals attended by the whole school. The winner would receive an anthology of Palestinian poetry. The poem to be memorised was entitled *"The Will to Live"* by the Tunisian poet Abu al-Kassim al-Shabi. It was a fiery poem recounting the strength of an oppressed people to rise and break their fetters. I can still remember its first few lines:

'If a nation wants life
Doubtless but that fate will stir
And night will become day
And the chain will break.
For he who loves not life
Will be submerged by it and be buried.
Woe to he who suffers not life
He who is defeated by its negation.
Thus spoke unto me the angel
And told me its infinite spirit.'

The poem contained nine pages of this fiery and occasionally moving verse. I spent hours trying to memorise it with Muna's help, for she too had to memorise it. But, Mr. Yafi said that only a boy could be a finalist as men were soldiers and girls were mothers of soldiers and did not need to perform – just to memorise so that they could teach the poems to their soldier sons.

Each day the entire lesson was spent busily memorising while Mr. Yafi walked up and down giving an incessant commentary on the conduct of the war.

"Now, Ruwafa Dam. Ha! The Zionists didn't bargain on that! One little infantry company. One! And the damned Jew has Super-Sherman tanks! But, oooh! Children! Children! Aren't you terrified? I quake with fear! Quake I tell you. Britain and France warned us! A bluff, boys. A bluff, girls. Read on. Read on!"

Two days later we prepared to recite the poem and to choose the best in our group. With a trembling heart I took my seat as I eyed Mr. Yafi walking up and down with a black-board rubber in his hand. We had had only four days to memorise nine pages. I was terrified. Muna had tried to reassure me before going into her own class.

"Tremble! Tremble! Boys, girls, you must quake and beg! The British have attacked. The Empire is here! Aren't you frightened? I am petrified! Where are we going to bury all those English Zionist soldiers? Sinai won't be enough? Hey little Muhammad? Recite! Recite!"

Muhammad, a little inoffensive boy with a large nose and flapping ears, stood up. In front of him was spread a piece of paper on which he had been drawing diagrams of a sailing ship that flies, a machine he was always planning to invent.

"Recite! Recite!" Mr. Yafi stood beside him. "Put your clenched fists out before you." My heart sank to my legs.

Muhammad started to recite:
"If a nation once wanted life…"

"WANTED!!" shouted Mr. Yafi as the black-board rubber hit Muhammad's knuckles.

"Wants. Wants, sir". Tears rose in the boy's eyes.
"If a nation once wants life
Doubtless but that fate would…"

"WOULD! WOULD!" Several sharp raps followed each one of the exclamations. Muhammad broke down and sat at his desk. Mr. Yafi came to me.

"Ibrahim! Show the long-eared Lebanese dunce how we

Palestinians work up a real fervour. Recite, my boy."

"If a nation once wants life
Doubtless but that fate will stir..."

"Well done! Well done, my boy! Keep your hands ready for the appropriate gesture. Recommence."

"If a nation once wants life
Doubtless but that fate will stir
And night will become day
And the chain will break
For him who..."

"Him! HIM!"

I put my hands out, but was too late: the rubber struck my head several times.

"HIM! BOY! You - can - not - re - cite. This - is - no - way! SIT!"

I sat down, looked at Muhammad, smiled weakly, then cried plentifully.

The competition was won by a very small boy with a very small nose and a very wide mouth. He went forward to lose the eventual finals held some weeks afterwards. I met him years later and he could still recite the whole poem. He had grown into a very big man with a very small nose and a very wide mouth.

Uncle Nassim consoled me when I returned home. Ali wanted to take care of the teacher for hitting me but father told him not to. Uncle Nassim and I used to listen to the radio together. He used to laugh a lot at the broadcasts, saying that even Goebbels with his infinite vulgarity did a better job than those crude fools in Cyprus. He wondered how the inhabitants of such a beautiful country could be so idiotic.

"Inhabitants of where?" I asked. "Cyprus?"

"No, England."

"England? Where? In Cyprus?"

"The most beautiful and green country. Are those fools in the radio station in Cyprus really related to Shakespeare? Milton? Churchill?"

I laughed because he laughed. He told me of how such vulgar tactics could be replied to with the honest Al-Azhar mosque like the early Caliphs of Islam. Nasser was the answer to Britain.

I was not sure whether it was Nasser in the Azhar or Al-Azhar in the Caliph playing Nasser. I became thoroughly confused which seemed to please my uncle even more.

Some weeks later I atoned for my failure in poetry, and amused uncle Nassim, while impressing aunt Haji into surrendering some half-kilo of sugared almonds, by reciting:

"Just as Egypt is determined to have political independence, so also Egypt is determined to have and to maintain ideological independence from all foreign ideologies such as Marxism, racism, colonialism, imperialism, and otherwise, all of which incidentally are European in origin."

I fed off this quotation for days!

During one such recitation, weeks later, Ali excused himself. Selma looked at him with fear in her eyes. It was uncle Nassim's last night with us before returning home to Kuwait where he was then living.

"Good-bye, then. I shall be sleeping when you return and I expect you'll be sleeping when I leave tomorrow." Uncle Nassim smiled as he said this. Ali looked embarrassed. Selma tried to busy herself by ordering me to sit still. I fancied that father looked angrily at Ali.

"Where are you going?" he asked.

"To uncle Muhammad's. Then we are going to visit Abu Nayer and Fatima." Ali spoke defiantly to father. He left the room. Selma got up.

"Stay here, Selma!" ordered father.

Selma put us to bed after what seemed an unnecessarily harsh washing session. When I said my prayers she pushed me into bed with a sharp slap on the back of my head.

While I lay in bed angry at the injustice of Selma's harshness I heard soft voices from the balcony outside. By climbing on to the window ledge I could see Ali talking quietly to both my uncles; Nassim and Issam. Beside him stood Maher, a cousin of mine as big as Ali. I thought that maybe he was bigger because he had a moustache.

"Tonight?" whispered my uncle Nassim.

"Yes," replied Maher.

"How much is involved?" asked uncle Nassim.

"Too much. The police have closed the shop. I must leave."

"Here. That should be enough. Damascus is your best bet. Go! Quiet! Can you hear something?"

I quickly got off the window ledge and returned to bed.

Next morning we were told that cousin Maher had gone to

Australia. I asked if they arrested people there. Ali looked cross.

"Not there!" laughed uncle Nassim. I wanted to ask what he meant but Ali looked at me crossly.

"How was Abu Nayer?" asked father.

"Well."

"And his wife?"

"Well, thank you," said Ali.

"Did you see Muna?" I asked.

"No. She was sleeping."

"Oh, God. Two brothers." Uncle Nassim started laughing.

Father looked annoyed.

****

As the summer holidays approached we celebrated with Mr. Yafi Britain's 'crushing humiliation' at Suez. Mr. Yafi used to ask us if our English Language teacher looked very much like Mr. Eden whom, he said, was desperately looking for a job. He laughed a lot when he said this. He always added that maybe the VSO would find him a teaching post in Upper Egypt! We laughed heartily, our eyes on the board-rubber.

At the beginning of our summer holidays Naziha returned from a very long absence a married woman. Selma said that she never liked her anyhow. She could go if she wanted to. You could get maids by the dozen. Father said he would fetch one from a refugee camp near Nablus. Selma told him that she did not particularly cherish having a refugee in the house. He said that that was what we were. Marwan said that we were not so, because we were Lebanese. Father got angry and dismissed us.

When Naziha left she hugged us children and cried. She said that she did not mean to leave like this and that she knew that we would understand. Marwan cried and said that he did not know about that. I cried.

A week later Naziha's replacement arrived. Her name was Amal. She wore the colourful dress of a Palestinian peasant. She had several scars on her face, the result of a bomb explosion in Israel, she said. Her forehead was tattooed in various shapes and odd arrangements. She smelt of sweat and I grew to love her dearly.

On her first day we retired to bed early only to be woken up while

92

it was very dark still. I could hear a clatter of buckets against stone and the slish-slosh of water. I felt uncomfortable and cold and suddenly realised what had woken me up. Someone had pulled the sheets off my bed. I got out of bed. Outside, the corridor was lit and its floor covered in water. Amal was on her knees scrubbing away and talking to herself. Selma stood in her bedroom door. Father was at the top end of the corridor where all the washing was piled up.

"It's three o'clock," said father.

Old Amal continued scrubbing the floor and talking to herself.

"Oh my God. She's mad. As mad as can be," said Selma, very angrily.

"They say that she's a very good cook," answered father in English.

They both laughed. I joined in.

Amal looked up, winked at me, and started laughing loudly.

Chapter 3

Very soon after Amal joined us, Mr. Yafi was promoted to become deputy head responsible for the boys' discipline. Although this made us happy because it meant that he would not be teaching us anymore, we soon found that he became more terrible as he supervised our playground. He was someone particularly to be avoided during the last few minutes of a break when he would walk around using a large silver bell in the same manner as he used the blackboard rubber.

One morning, just before our morning assembly, I was busy avoiding Mr. Yafi when Muhammad joined me. He told me that his father owned a cake-shop where he was going to work when he grew up. He spoke quietly and somewhat shyly. There was something about his gentle manner that I liked. We talked about each other's ambitions, but neither confided in the other his real boyish aspirations. Later I was to find out that Muhammad wanted to build boats and engines when he was not busy making cakes. Of course, I could not really tell him about my ambition to become a storyteller with Muna. That was a secret.

As we talked we heard the bell being rung in the girl's playground. Muna and I never met in school now as we had reached elementary class. We exchanged smiles in the dining hall or in the corridors.

Both Muhammad and I looked around for Mr. Yafi. We could not see him anywhere. We emerged from our corner and walked towards where the boys were already lining up. Suddenly, we heard the loud tones of the bell behind us. Descending from nowhere, Mr. Yafi stood ringing the bell right behind Muhammad's head. Muhammad froze.

"Move, you long-eared dunce. MOVE!" Mr. Yafi struck the bell on the motionless boy's head several times, each hit producing a different ringing tone to the one before. We both ran to our class groups and lined up. I looked at Muhammad. His eyes were distant. With one hand he alternately rubbed his head or violently shook his finger in either of his ears which seemed to flap with the motion. Meanwhile the bell rang its varying tones as Mr. Yafi ran up and down the playground gathering boys. The entire school was frozen.

"Silence!" screeched Mr. Yafi.

This produced a terrified murmur from all the boys. He dived down the steps violently waving his bell. Seconds later he re-emerged leading Marwan by the hair. All were silent: terror reigned amongst us. Marwan pushed him off in the despair of pain. Mr. Yafi tripped slightly and lost his balance, landing two or three steps below. Marwan stood behind him in absolute horror. Then he suddenly pointed to the sitting Mr. Yafi and started laughing. The entire school joined in.

Mr. Yafi jumped up, picked up his bell, and ran behind Marwan shaking it in the air. The entire episode took a few seconds but they were an instant to be remembered forever. As Marwan reached the top step we knew that he was lost. He cowered against the school-door as Mr. Yafi approached him with the bell raised. A few resonant sounds were made although whether they were from Marwan's throat or from the bell I could not tell. Suddenly the door opened and the headmistress appeared. Mr. Yafi rang the bell a few times, helped Marwan up and gently led him by the arm down the steps. Marwan winced several times.

We bowed our heads in preparation for morning prayers. Nothing happened. Our headmistress demanded our attention in a subdued voice.

"Silence!" shrieked her Deputy.

She spoke. "The Director of our school, Mr. Muhammad Salam, has died this morning."

We mourned quietly. Some asked who Muhammad Salam was. Muhammad told them he was the Premier's brother.

He had died peacefully in his sleep. I wondered why everyone always died peacefully in their sleep. We were to have an assembly in the hall for the entire school.

We bowed our heads and listened to a long list of things that the much lamented late Muhammad Salam was good at and how his goodness would earn Allah's eternal mercy. When we got to the part about him having been a complete angel, I wondered if he and my mother would be spending some time flying from cloud to cloud which must be great fun. Mother was always described as an angel. Regardless of context, whenever she was mentioned, which was a rarity in our household, somebody invariably shook their head and mumbled something about her having been an angel. Despite a lifetime of listening to endless hypocritical eulogies, I remain utterly confused by how good a deceased became on death regardless of the utter beast that he or she was in life.

After the assembly we were to go home. The school would be closed for three days.

We raised our heads with high expectations.

"Silence!" screamed Mr. Yafi.

We walked to the hall. In the corridor we joined the girls and formed two lines. I smiled at Muna and was immediately pulled out of the line. I looked up. My ear was being held by the Sheik who taught Religion and Qura'nic Studies. Soon the corridor was empty.

"Why were you smiling, son?" he asked.

"At a friend."

"What was that? I did not quite hear you." My ear smarted under the deep squeeze. I could not understand why the squeeze had to be accompanied by a wide grin showing thin lips and gritted teeth.

"I was smiling at a ......"

"I shall repeat my question" he said, very kindly whispering whilst his whole hand grasped the entire ear and turned it round rather like Uncle Nassim did the large knobs on our Philips wireless. "Why were you smiling?"

"I was smiling, sir, because I saw a friend among the crowd, sir."

"Well answered, my boy." He gave the ear one last twist and let go. He then tapped me on the head several times and walked around me slowly, tapping me again and again but a little harder at each circuit. I looked up at his face. His eyes were distant. He then slapped me across the cheek and other ear several times. My face stung as the tears rolled down it and a whistling sound entered my head.

"You must not smile, my boy. It is wrong to smile at girls." His whisper was accentuated by the sibilance of each word. He twisted my ear again. "Girls are dirty. They trap you. They are after one thing only." I wanted to ask him what it was that girls were after but thought better of engaging him in any lengthy conversation. I felt an urgent need to go to the toilet.

"No sidi. Yes sir. Yes sidi" I tried to reply.

"Horrible boy. Horrible. Horrible face. Horrible cheeks. Horrible nose." He continued to walk around me.

Finally, he shrieked, "You are a lump of black shit." He then paused before screaming: "Go!"

I ran all the way to the hall rubbing my ear vigorously and trying hard not to burst into tears.

****

Spring was always a special time for us. It heralded the beginning of the endless sunny Fridays, half-terms, and public holidays in the garden with Muna and sometimes with my new friend Muhammad. We had several public holidays that year: Port-Said evacuation, Director's death, Egyptian-Syrian Union, and several others.

Muhammad was very enthusiastic about the United Arab Republic. He told us that Lebanon would be joining soon and that Eisenhower would most probably go to Hell. Amal, our peasant maid, thought the whole thing was rubbish. The English would always win. She should know. Hadn't she been shot at? Bombed? That was why she became mad, you see. She lit another cigarette with the end of the previous one and left us to our games. Soon Muhammad became an avid listener to our stories. He contributed innumerable historical facts to our fairy tales.

During such a story-telling episode we were interrupted by a commotion from the streets. We ran out of our little garden retreat and jumped on the forbidden area: the garage roof. Amal came running out of the house with her hands by her side.

From the garage roof we looked down onto the street. There were several men standing there. A lorry stood below our position. A man on the back was prizing open some boxes. The men clamoured for their contents. We clapped our hands in excitement as gun after gun was thrown to the excited mob. Amal laughed.

"Now the English will see! We will teach them a lesson. And get off that ledge, potato eaters!"

"This one is for Chamoun," said a man holding a small metallic object in his hand. He loaded the gun. "This is for Malik. And this for Eisenhower." A burst of gunfire echoed down the street. I was a little disappointed. It was feeble. Not like the movies. Cowboys made a much louder din that this distant Rat-ta-ta-ta-ta. At the sound of gunfire the mob laughed.

"Chamoun wants another four years. Even two, he says." This came from the man on the back of the lorry. "We'll see to that, hey brothers? Long live Salam. Long live Jumblatt. Karami."

The whole street echoed with the refrain wishing all three politicians long life.

"Hey little brother! What about the Patriarch?"

Everybody laughed and shouted for long life to the Patriarch al-Meouchi.

"Fancy, even his own Christian brothers don't want him," shouted somebody.

"Who wants him - apart from himself!"

"Long live Salam!"

"Long live Karami!"

"Nasser! Nasser! Nasser!"

"Long live Chamoun our President!" I shouted, in order to join in. The whole street was silent. All eyes were on me. Amal stood in front of me.

"Who said that?" shouted an angry voice.

"He didn't mean it" Amal said. "He's a little mad, like me, you see."

Everybody burst out laughing.

"Get the little sperm inside!" shouted the man on the lorry. He bent forward. Rat-ta-ta-ta-ta. We looked towards the end of the street. I could see uniformed men running from one side of the street to the other. Below us the men scattered. Several jumped onto our garage roof. The air was filled with the smell of burning.

As Amal led us inside I saw a man run into a rose bush in father's garden with a gun in his hand. Father would not like that, I thought.

The fighting continued for a long time while we sat in the corridor with Amal. She amused us with stories about the Arab Revolt in Palestine.

"That was what made me mad, you see. But I'm not completely mad."

She winked at me and told us to stay there while she went to the kitchen to continue housekeeping. A few pellets were not going to stop her cooking the meal, she declared.

Soon, the shooting stopped and father arrived home. He looked relieved to see us playing in the corridor. Minutes later Selma and Ali arrived. We listened to the news as we had lunch. Our street was mentioned. Ali laughed when the speaker said that the President wanted to defend Lebanon against international Communism and international Arabism.

"That's why he wants to change the constitution to get re-elected. It won't work. The Basta lot would see to that."

The Basta men were in a quarter near our house. They were known for their strength and bravery - rather like Mr. Yafi. We asked whether we had to go to school the next day.

"Yes." said father. "You will continue to go to school."

Selma ordered us out as soon as we finished eating. Father was to take Muhammad and Muna home, and she wanted to talk to Ali.

****

"Hey wake up! Wake up! It's a bomb." Marwan shook me by the shoulder.

"Let him sleep," said Selma angrily. I heard father laughing when she told him I was still sleeping. Suddenly, I was aware of a strange smell, rather like burning. I woke up completely, remembering what Marwan had said.

It was dark outside except for a small light at the entrance. There was no door to the house. It lay flat on the floor. I stood near the gate to our garden watching some men carrying a white bundle. I saw blood trickling in a long line behind them as they walked off. Father was talking to a policeman while Selma held Marwan's hand beside him.

"No idea why. None." Father spoke quietly.

I felt a hand on my shoulder. I looked round at Amal. She told me to go back to bed. She held a bucket full of water. She walked towards the line of blood and threw the water. The red separated into the little lines floating on top and then all was pink. A policeman looked at her in amazement. She winked at him saying, "Messy business. Messy business. Need more than water. Coffee then?"

Father drove us to school the next morning. On the way he explained that the bomb was thrown at our house by mistake. The real target was an MP's house down the road. He told us to be careful what we said. We did not want to go to school but he said that we should. I asked why anybody wanted to throw bombs. He explained that a journalist called Matni had been shot and that people were angry.

At school, Muhammad explained that Matni was assassinated by friends of the President, and that he was a Christian who supported Nasser. He told us that we were going to have a civil war which meant Moslems against Christians. Marwan called him floppy ears and sent him off. I was frightened.

Mr. Yafi was particularly skilful with his bell that morning. We lined up excitedly and whispered about the imminent war: after all; it meant no school for the duration. I thought of the endless hours in the garden with Muna. Whispering continued as our headmistress came before us. Mr. Yafi's bell could be heard tinkling in several places amongst the crowd of boys. Suddenly a black cloud of smoke rose above the playground. Our headmistress looked up. The smoke became thicker. Mr. Yafi ran up the steps for a consultation. Several whispers went around.

"They're burning the United States Information Service building. The U.S.I.S. is burning!"

"No. It's the British Council!"

Mr. Yafi shouted for silence. No one listened. The headmistress made a hand motion that dismissed us. Some stones went flying from where the older boys stood. Several hit Mr. Yafi who first cowered and then ran up the stairs and into the school.

"Nasser! Nasser! Nasser!" chanted the older boys. The younger ones joined in. Marwan ran towards me. He took hold of my hand and dragged me towards the infant school, into one of the classes, and out of a window on to the street.

We ran down the road, past the burning library and stood watching. Some bookshelves were still standing. I wanted to ask Marwan why they were burning the books! Why the children's library?

"Take that sprout home!" shouted a man at Marwan.

"What do you think I'm doing, you fool!"

"Who're you calling a fool?" The man looked furious. He approached us.

"Let them be, Samir! Go home you two."

We ran as fast as our legs could carry us. As we ran, I remember wondering whether or not my membership of the burnt down library would remain valid.

****

About a week later father returned home very early. We had a speedy lunch after which he and Selma held a conference. I sat on the floor hugging my knees, listening. They decided that Amal should be packed off to Nablus until the troubles were over, and Selma suggested that this become permanent. Father disagreed as he felt that the children liked her. I nodded vigorously.

"You little creep," whispered Selma pinching my hand. Ali came in and ruffled my hair.

Sitting down, he said "I've been to the Basta. Saib Bey advises us to get out."

"Did you meet him?" Selma asked.

"Yes," replied Ali. "I know one of his nephews from university. There were several English journalists there who also thought it was going to hot up."

"Who was there?" asked father.

"David Holden of *The Times*. There were a couple of others. A fellow called Morris and another, a Kim Philby."

"Michael Adams?!" asked father.

"No. Who's he?"

"About the only honest journalist left around, apart from Nasib Matni."

"Well, he is not around now" said Selma irritably.

"What about the BBC World Service? Any news?"

"Nothing new. Just confirming the rumour that Beirut radio has denied. Sarraj pledges Syria's support. Nothing new."

Father looked at Ali and then at Selma. "We should move. We'll go to a flat in Ras Beirut. It's safer there. We could join uncle Nassim in the mountains when he arrives from Kuwait."

I was as happy to hear that uncle Nassim was moving into Lebanon as I was to hear that uncle Issam was taking his family to Damascus for good. Uncle Issam had said that he could no longer live in such a city as Beirut. Damascus was more to his taste. Aunt Haji was also to go there until the troubles stopped.

A day later we moved into a small flat on the top floor of a tall and ugly tower block. Most of our furniture was stored in the ICI warehouse. Father, Selma, Marwan, and I slept in one room - the only one. We had a kitchen and a bathroom. Marwan and I had a small balcony where we sat for quiet games and reading. Ali found a room at the university where he was a student.

We left our old home for the last time on a Sunday. Ali and Selma worked hard loading the lorry. Marwan helped. I hid mother's books in my small box of toys which Amal locked saying that she would retain its key until her return. We had a quick sandwich lunch which I ate in my garden retreat amid sobs and sighs. As I sat there quietly crying Selma came in and told me to stop being so childish. This made me cry even more. I got up to walk out when she pushed me back saying that I was a selfish little hypocrite. Ali called her away and I resumed crying. She was so big and I felt so little in my retreat.

Amal came in. "Woe! Woe! What are you crying for? A house?

A nice house we had before the English potato eaters came and a garden and a mama and baba all gone. You mustn't cry. Now. Now. I'm going to Nablus. You were born there and very, very sweet knafè they make so don't cry. Here, do you want a puff from my Egyptian cigarette ? She'd like to see me go because I embarrass her. Not because I'm mad - which I am not - but because of my peasant dress and because she speaks English like the English."

"But I like your dress" I shouted. "It has beautiful colours."

"Yes but the English is civilised so he thinks my dress a peasant one and he buys it for his wife and doesn't like it. You are clever. You can speak English. The English are very clever they can speak English. I cannot speak an alien language. Smile then. Must get you a gold tooth."

I laughed. Amal had a way of making everything seem so unimportant. But I was sad to leave my garden retreat. I regretted this very much at the time, very much. Yet another loss.

****

In order that the flat was not overcrowded during the day, father would take one of us boys to his office. There, we made ourselves useful fetching coffee, sticking stamps, folding circulars, and so on. I enjoyed going there because all father's colleagues, particularly the young ones, paid me a great deal of attention.

One morning Marwan declared his intention of not going down to work. Father said that it was his turn and that he should go because his duty cannot be avoided. Marwan replied that it could and made a lot of noise about it. I volunteered to go in his place. Selma called me a little creep. So I went.

The younger employees of the office were particularly kind. They let me play with the adding machines until father came out and said that this was a place of business and not a games room. I spent the rest of the morning folding circulars with pictures of mice, beetles and flies on them. The telephonist kept hugging me and calling me 'a poor little orphan'. She smelt funny. At twelve o'clock Ali arrived and joined me in my little corner. He told me that he had just seen Muna's stepmother. She told him that they were migrating to Australia.

"When will they come back?" I asked.

Ali explained that when you emigrated you usually never came back. He said that they might visit Beirut once in a while. This he added when my lips started quivering. He told me not to say anything to father because he had enough on his mind with the new flat. He made me promise. I did. He gave me fifty piasters and went into father's office.

Minutes later they emerged together. Father was wearing a white blazer with a little gold pin in its lapel. His grey trousers seemed baggy and his pockets deep. Ali had a short-sleeved shirt on. In its pocket, which bulged out comically, were his diary, a packet of Lucky Strike, a box of matches and several pens. He looked tall, strong and handsome. He smiled at everyone as he walked, launching his athletic body slightly forward. They beckoned me and I ran towards them.

As we walked down the stairs father stopped and said that we could not go the usual way. He had promised Selma to get her a book that she had ordered from the Librairie Antoine. Ali jovially replied that it would make a pleasant walk through the souk. We walked out, father and me on either side of Ali. I listened to their conversation as I looked at the busy crowds of people.

"Malik is lodging a complaint against the UAR at the Security Council," said Ali.

"So what?" father replied contemptuously. "The man is a little twisted upstairs."

"He was found walking on the ledge of the top storey of the Empire State Building." They both laughed. Ali continued. "They say that Ghaleb is allowing arms to be unloaded outside the Egyptian Embassy."

"They love exaggerating," replied father. "There are most probably more people being killed by our taxi-drivers than by the bullet! By the way, have you heard that David Holden of *The Times* has been asked to leave. I wonder what truth he told this time?"

As we reached the souk area we heard several people talking excitedly. Something had happened. Ali said that we had better inquire before going any further. We walked towards a shop-keeper.

"What's going on?" asked Ali.

"Haven't you heard? Everybody has. Haven't you? A bomb. A tram. Forty killed. Haven't you heard? Woman on balcony eating sugared peanuts. Happy. Minding own business. Several toes in peanuts. Haven't you heard? Here's a carpet. All the way from Iran. Going cheaply. For you. I'll let you in on a secret. You're an honest man. Smuggled. No tax. Perfect size for any front room."

We thanked him and walked off. He continued talking. "Good carpet, sir. Won't you negotiate. He won't. He hasn't heard! He hasn't heard! Doesn't want a carpet! Carpets. Carpets. Buy quick. Otherwise the police will be walking all over them at the station."

"Forty killed! More like four hairs singed." Father and Ali laughed; uneasily, I thought. We walked up the steps where the central fountain of the souk stood. It was octagon-shaped and on every one of its sides stood a man plying his trade. I was attracted by one side where stood a long block of ice. The vendor scraped the ice off it into a glass which he then filled with drink. It looked delicious with small pine seeds floating on top. I stood and watched the man who skilfully took a glass, ran it sideways on the surface of the ice, poured the drink, and threw in the seeds. He offered it to me. I shook my head. He mysteriously produced a little toy, stuck it on the ice, where it proceeded to beat a drum and clash a pair of cymbals. I motioned towards father and Ali. The man waved me off in despair. I ran towards the two and tugged at Ali's arm. He pushed me off and continued talking. I ran round him to father's side and took his hand. He squeezed mine - hard, I thought.

I saw a man lean against a bicycle. Another man, a policeman, was talking to him.

Two women walked in front of us and behind a parked car.

A window shop disclosed models neatly arranged in various postures and colourful dresses.

Some newspaper boy called out, "Bomb! Bomb! In tram. A hundred killed."

I remembered the fifty piasters. When we get to the book-shop, I could run back and get the drink.

Somebody or something pushed me back violently. I saw a flash and heard a tremendous crash. I could see nothing but black smoke. 'I wonder if they will still be serving drinks,' I thought. I felt in my pocket for the coin. It was not there. My pocket was wet.

I stood up and started walking with my arms before me. I fell on the parked car where the two women had been but were no longer there. I turned and walked on. In the shop window I saw the models on top of one another. One had a leg hanging loosely. Another had lost its hat and lay there bald and ugly.

"Get that boy away from the glass" shouted someone. I looked round for a boy. An arm pushed me forward and I ran a few yards. Ali called me. I ran and sat beside him on the pavement. He held his leg. I looked around at what seemed like a hundred people running in all directions.

Ali tore a sleeve of my shirt and tied it around my leg. I noticed blood spurting out, up and down, up and down. I cried. I tried not to.

"Go ahead and cry," said Ali. "Don't be frightened, you can cry!" I screamed. Ali smiled and tapped me on the head. I felt better. "What a brave lad, hey! Ha ha! The injuns are here! But don't worry, Roy Rogers." I tried to laugh, but couldn't.

"Where's baba?" I started to cry again.

"There he is!" shouted Ali excitedly. Father was walking down the middle of the road. His trousers were in shreds. He held his right arm. Blood flowed down his face and onto his white jacket. Ali got up and hopped towards him while holding up the other leg. A soldier came running towards me and picked me up.

"All right, my boy. It's all right. Take them to the junction. There's an ambulance there. All right, son. All right." He ran, bouncing me up and down. "We'll get the bastards!" he shrieked at the crowds lining the road.

Ali hopped after us while father walked sedately. The front of his white jacket was almost entirely red.

"Not Hotel Dieu," shouted Ali. "Get a taxi to the American Hospital." I was thrown in the back of the car. Ali helped father in.

"After you," said father with exceeding politeness to the soldier who had carried me. The soldier pushed him in and shut the door. Ali got into the front and offered the driver a cigarette.

"Drive slowly, my good man," said father imperiously.

"Father, wipe the blood off your face."

"Yes, it is hot today. I am sweating."

"It's going in your eyes."

"Yes, I left my handkerchief in my pocket."

"Take it out!"

"I left my pocket at home."

Ali wiped father's face. He looked at me.

"He's all right Saif. Just dazed. Don't be frightened." I felt a pain in my arm. I looked. "Take it out. It's only a piece of shrapnel. Take it out. Aye, a brave Roy Rogers you are!"

"Are we being followed?" asked father.

"Yes, it's someone from the ICI."

"Ask them to lunch."

I wriggled my toes and felt a pain in my leg. A sharp whistle went through my ears as the taxi screeched around the hospital entrance.

"We're here," said Ali, encouragingly.

"Have you asked them to lunch?"

Chapter 4

Ali was very seriously injured. Despite his pain and agony, he ordered the nurses to tend to me and father first. Later on, a doctor furiously demanded why he was not being cared for and he was taken into the operating theatre. He remained two months in hospital. Father was there three weeks. I was released after a week and taken to uncle Nassim's new house in the safety of the mountains.

The doctor, a man with very large blue eyes, ordered the nurse to take me to the operating theatre. As she rolled me down the corridor she told another nurse that I had lovely hair and eyes. I felt flattered, partly on account of the compliment and partly because I understood her English. She asked me if I understood English. I said that I did not.

I kept asking for my father. The double doors of an operating theatre were opened a little and a doctor whispered something to my father who lifted himself a little, smiled, and waved to me. I was wheeled to the other doctor, reassured.

Selma and Marwan came in, both crying. I felt so sorry for Marwan. I did not want him to cry. I gave him a piece of a biscuit a nurse had given me. He kindly refused the offer and continued crying.

A week later I said goodbye to father and Ali whose leg was in a plaster with a large red patch on it. He laughed with me and told father to give me a pound. He did. Ali winked at me and laughed but I could see he was in pain. I admired him for his bravery. As uncle Nassim wheeled my chair down the corridor I looked back and saw father bending over Ali's bed. I could see the brown tassels of the belt around his dressing gown.

I spent a very happy two summer months with uncle Nassim and his family. In the mornings he used to help me onto the enormous balcony overlooking the distant city. I stayed outside most of the day under the shadow of a huge umbrella, which Uncle Nassim used to shift around according to the movement of the sun. Marwan was sent to a boarding school (not with the black lady.) Selma occupied the flat with aunt Yasmine newly arrived from Damascus.

Sometimes, uncle Nassim went to the city and came back with news of the family and events in Beirut. But mostly he stayed at home and spent a lot of time with me. We talked and read together.

"Uncle Nassim," I asked one day, "What's the war about?"

"If those fighting knew it, there wouldn't be a war."

"How do you mean?"

"You know your *Arabian Nights*, don't you? Well, a man, an Englishman, translated the whole thing. He came to Lebanon for a visit. He expected to find a beautiful country full of romance, with winters like an early English summer and views to take your breath away. A place where he could be near people but also far away from them"

"Did he find that?" I asked, expecting a negative answer.

"Oh yes. Definitely. But he was also disillusioned."

"Why?"

"Let's see if you can understand. He said that the Lebanese would hide their guns and swords at the very mention of patriotism. But they would be very happy to die for their political party or their religion. Do you understand?"

"I don't think so."

"Allah worked extremely hard to create this country. He made it beautiful and bountiful. There is no other country like it. Then he called a couple of angels and asked them what they thought of his creation. They were in raptures about it. "But, Allah," one said, "I say, this is too much. It is a Paradise. What are you going to promise men if you give them heaven on earth?" Allah agreed. To redress the balance he sent a bit of hell down: Lebanon's population!"

I laughed at his irreverence in mimicking Allah and his angels. I then asked him if England was as beautiful.

He said it was but that its real beauty lay in its people and its system of government. He spoke seriously and slowly. "Its people leave you alone wherever you are or whatever you do. They respect your privacy."

"What if you're mad?" I teased.

"A good friend of mine, whose occupation is particularly called for in Beirut these days, said, ' *'Twill not be seen in him there; there the men are as mad as he…" Ils vous en fichent la paix*, the English."

I was a little confused. Everybody hated the English, I told him. They had put him in prison.

He laughed and said that this should not prevent us from admiring the good qualities of our enemies. He then gave me a book about Islamic history which he had written himself, and said that although the age of chivalry was gone, its spirit was there in great men like

Muhammad, Saladdin, and others.

"What about Nasser?" I asked.

"I'll tell you when he dies," he replied, sadly.

We talked a lot. He told me stories about Palestine and the life of the Prophet. Uncle Nassim had written a play about Him which he showed me. It was massive, too difficult for me to read, but he told me all about it.

"Don't you write stories at school?" he asked

"No. Only compositions. Describing ones."

I confided to him my secret about the plans I had with Muna. He did not laugh and asked me to write one of my stories for him to look at, which I did.

"Interesting," he said candidly, "but there are bits missing."

"What bits?" I asked, frightened at this early failure.

"I won't tell you. You must find out. I'll tell you what, why don't you write a story about your experience of the bomb?" I hesitated. "Try," he said. I did. When I gave it to him a few days later he looked at it, tossed it in my lap, saying, "Not enough detail. More detail."

For the rest of my stay in the mountains uncle Nassim made me write stories, read me ones, and lent me several books. On the days when he went down to Beirut he would rush out to the balcony and throw me a book. "Read this! We'll talk later." Or he would give me a pencil and paper. "A story. Say about a cigarette," or "that view in front of you," or "you see that building on the distant sea-front? What's going on inside it?"

Among the books he lent me that summer I remember *al-Ayam* by Taha Hussein, a translation of an abridged and simplified *David Copperfield*, over which I cried plentifully, and several historical novels by Zaydan.

In the second week of July I returned home to a new large apartment on the first floor of a building in Ras Beirut. This was felt to be a safe area away from the fighting and near the sea.

****

"No! No! I'll have none of that, brother. None of it!" Aunt Haji had just arrived in a taxi all the way from Damascus and had barged in on father and I as we sat in our new sitting-room. She dismissed Selma, ordering her to make a glass of lemonade. "No! I'll have none of it! You sent me to Damascus because it is safe there. Safe? Fie on you! Safe! I would rather be killed by a stray bullet than by the pontiff's tongue. Safe? Brother, our little nothing of a brother sits on his balcony pontificating all day! No, brother, give me the bullet any time. I cannot be bored to my grave, Arab unity or not." She tugged at her dress nervously.

Father calmed her down. She drank her lemonade and belched several times. "Forgive me, I'm an old woman. Cannot control my gizzards. I am old. I am old. Well nephew? How are your injuries? Are they well? Make a man of you, hey? A man. Hey?"

Selma always seemed embarrassed by aunt Haji's presence. She was polite but distant. Aunt also seemed to pay her little attention except when she reminded her of her duty to be married as quickly as possible. She talked to father who seemed to reply automatically and with little mental effort since aunt Haji rarely required any answers to her questions.

"And when does our hero come out of hospital?"

"Soon."

"When does Marwan return?"

"He is sorely missed."

"And Amal the mad maid?"

"Aye, but she cooks well."

"What is this I hear of Abu Nayer emigrating to Owst-Ast-Osterelli - over there? How now? Wife a bit of a handful, hey? Never liked old men marrying young girls. Why emigrate? Pray inform me, brother".

"There are several people in Abu Nayer's position. The troubles have driven them off. They cannot take it anymore. I don't really know Abu Nayer's specific reasons for wanting to leave."

"I shall discuss the matter with Ali when I see him next," concluded my aunt.

A long silence followed. Selma left the room and soon we could hear the radio from the study next door. Aunt broke the silence every now and then by exclaiming, "I am too old. I am an old woman. Ignorant too."

Then Selma burst into the room shouting excitedly. "Something has happened in Iraq. Something is going on!"

We all moved into the study. I gave my aunt my arm which she used rather like a control lever; squeezing it to make me stop, relaxing her grip for movement, twisting it for speed.

Baghdad radio kept interrupting marshal music to promise its listeners a great surprise. We sat and listened impatiently. Eventually, and after a long wait, the news arrived but was fragmented and vague. There was a revolution in Iraq. King Faysal and the entire royal family had been assassinated. A new republic was declared.

"*Le quatorze juillet*" said Selma, excitedly.

"Why were they shot?" I asked.

Father looked worried and thoughtful.

"Well nephew?" said my aunt. "Well nephew? Are you proud of yourself now? Hmm?" She dug me in the ribs several times. "Your birth was a black day. Your name isn't much better. Saif! Faysal! A sword. Are you happy? Hmm? A blade to chop our heads off with. And all this with your grandmother just gone! We are born, we become senile, and we die. We don't live long in between. You're born naked. You die naked. The cotton they shove up you is the bonus! I am old and therefore senile. You ought to be ashamed of yourself, nephew. Ashamed! Niece, make him a lemonade!"

The atmosphere in the house was very tense for the rest of the day. As more news trickled in, it became apparent that the Iraqi rebels had behaved with considerable savagery. Father said that although he had never approved of King Faysal's un-Arab activities, he did not particularly relish the thought of the new regime.

Aunt Haji was not so fearful. "Why, brother of mine, do you think that I fear a war? Let there be a third world war. I am old and ignorant. Yes, I'm an old woman. And ignorant. Escort me to my home. Woe! Woe! I'm such a burden on you brother. Maybe these events will relieve you. Yes."

That night, after he had taken aunt Haji home, father fetched Marwan from the boarding school

****

The next day Marwan and I went down to the sea front to watch the American marines land. We were very excited at the prospect of seeing a few thousand John Waynes. We arrived on a vast expanse of green by the sea-shore where several enormous tanks stood. Several boys were climbing over them. We each bought a corn on the cob and walked toward the tanks. Soldiers were waiting around in T-shirts and semi-combat uniforms. An immense soldier with very blond hair and a

111

minute nose smiled at us cheerfully.

"Hiya little fellas. You coming ta see mah jaloppy?"

Marwan and I giggled assent though we hardly understood what he was talking about. His smile broadened as he approached, then standing before us as a veritable tower of strength.

"Hey, little fella, watcha got there?"

"A corn on the cob, sir," I said timidly.

"A carn on the cub. Well I'll be. Didn't expect to see 'em in this here country. How about offeren' me some?"

"Give him your corn on the cob. He wants your corn on the cob," Marwan whispered urgently.

I handed it over. He put it to his mouth and rolled it several times. Distressed, I gaped at my cob as it disappeared. He returned what little was left and I thanked him.

"Well, I'll be darned. Come on little fella, jump aboard" he said and turned away, motioning us to follow.

I looked at Marwan. He looked at me as I threw my corn on the cob away with disgust. He then broke his in half, handed me the uneaten half, and we ran off.

Father said that the Americans landing was the best thing that could happen to the country. He explained that their enormous tanks were destroying our roads, and that they would compensate a million pounds worth of damage with a hundred million in aid. He added that the best way to make money was to declare war on America and then speedily surrender after a crushing defeat without loss of life!

I thought that the marines need only go through our supply of corn on the cob instead of shooting at us. I could picture them lined up and at the ready, working their powerful jaws.

We spent the next two months at home: our area was safe enough and the fighting had largely stopped. Various unconfirmed stories of atrocities committed by GIs, however, kept us inside. Now and then, we children would run to the window to watch the enormous American tanks pass below, leaving a trail of uprooted asphalt. A few explosions could be heard now and then in the distance. Most of our time, we either played or worked under father's supervision and had to write two compositions daily, one in Arabic and the other in English. We also had to converse in English for two hours each morning.

Father would mark the compositions very strictly. All were titles from previous Elementary Certificate Examination papers and were purely descriptive. Stories were not allowed. The descriptions had to be, what father called, "verifiable". In one composition that I remember well, I described the hunting of birds with shot-guns, a very popular sport in Lebanon. I described the injured bird as "bloodly writhing and battering its little body unto death." Father objected to the bad English and asked me to write it again. I argued that uncle Nassim had accepted sentences like that before. Father laughed and pointed out - somewhat sarcastically, I thought, - that unfortunately uncle Nassim was not one of the Elementary Certificate examiners. I refused to rewrite the composition and wrote another on a different topic which father accepted.

That summer also saw mine and Marwan's first literary venture. We produced a short news-magazine called 'Little Lebanon' which concerned itself mainly with family views, news, and jokes. It was a sell-out: its first and only copy being snapped up by the ever kind and helpful Ali at the exorbitant price of ten piasters.

****

Muna and I had not met since Ali had told me of her family's intention to emigrate. Every time I asked if I could visit her, father told me that the journey to her home would be too dangerous and that I had to be patient.

At last the day came. Muna and I were to spend the entire day together in our house. Since Marwan and I shared one of the four bedrooms, father gave permission for Muna and I to use the study next to the sitting-room. He was very kind and solicitous that day and instructed Selma to prepare a meal of tabbouli and kebbie, the latter being finely minced meat mixed with several ingredients and shaped flat in two round layers with pine seed in the middle. Selma grumbled saying that she had enough on her hands without preparing meals for little spoilt idiots like me or my friends. Father replied that she was preparing a meal because he had asked her to do so. She became silent.

During breakfast she accused me of scratching my head with a fork and sent me out to the kitchen. I was grateful for this as I was beginning to be aware of her injustice to me. I never really disliked her, but I never really could find it in myself to like her. I wanted to like her. I wanted to be obedient. I wanted her to become a second mother. But there was something about her abrupt manner that in time

I grew to hate. If only she showed her love. If only she assured me of her..... But this is out of place.

Muna arrived soon after breakfast. To start with, our meeting was awkward. I had so much to tell her about my accident, about uncle Nassim, and so many other things. Instead we greeted each other silently and shyly, withdrawing into our allotted room for the day where I waited for her to start talking.

"I like your new house," she declared.

"I don't. It has no garden and it's smaller. Selma likes it. She says that it's in a better class of neighbourhood."

"I suppose it is. You're near the American University."

A long silence followed which neither of us seemed able to break. I fetched 'Little Lebanon' and showed it to Muna. She became excited and from then onwards the conversation became animated and lasted for most of the day.

"Have you heard any new stories?" I asked.

"Not really. What about you? Have you made up any new ones?"

I showed her the compositions that father made us write and showed her the one that he had rejected for its bad English. She liked it. She said that her brother, Nayer, had told her that the story was more important than the language or the grammar. I agreed doubtfully as I thought of father's reaction to my description of the dying bird.

"I thought that Nayer was coming with you."

"No!" she replied in what I thought was a somewhat sharp tone. "He is busy preparing for our departure."

"When are you leaving?"

"Day after tomorrow."

I looked at her incredulously. Both of us had never thought of a permanent separation. We had our plans.

"Father wouldn't let me come here, but Nayer brought me. Father doesn't know."

"Why?"

"Because of a quarrel he's had with your brother Ali."

"What about?"

"I don't know." She spoke hesitantly as if she were hiding something. "I shall miss you," she added.

"Me too! Me too!" I replied eagerly. "But we'll write to each other."

"No, we cannot. Father said that I was to have nothing to do with your family."

"But why? You're Moslems like us." I could think of no other reason why people should fall out with each other.

"It's got nothing to do with that. It's Ali and my..." She fell silent.

"What about Ali?"

"Nothing. I don't know why it is." She looked at her feet for a while. I saw the top of her long fair hair which seemed dull. I thought very hard trying to find out what she was thinking. I felt uncomfortable.

"Saif?"

"Uhuh?"

"Promise me something?"

"Anything," I said eagerly, happy to hear the old familiar tone.

"Promise me not to forget our agreement."

"Agreement?" I asked. She looked hurt. "Ah, yes, of course," I lied.

"I told Nayer about it. He told me not to worry. He said that the same moon would look down on both of us. That the same sun would shine down on us. We'll always breathe the same air."

She stopped and looked at me. I was lost but smiled assent to encourage her.

"You will carry on with our plan to tell stories."

I now understood and listened eagerly.

"Nayer says that we could tell the stories at night when all is quiet. Sound travels, you see. You have to speak quietly, though, very quietly."

I felt a tinge of envy at her close relationship with her brother. He sounded so good.

Then Selma announced that lunch was ready.

We ate happily. Father told several funny jokes which made us both laugh. Marwan also laughed. Ali was not there and Selma, I thought, was more distant than usual. Father had his usual siesta and then went out. Selma took Marwan to the cinema.

In the afternoon I told Muna a new story about a man called Ahbal who worked for a caravan leader called Fatoush. Now, Ahbal liked his food and ate plentifully. One day, while relaxing after a meal, he met a most beautiful lioness and asked her to marry him. She told him that she could not because he did not have a tail. So he got one. She asked him for his mane so he got one. Then he sharpened his teeth. He also put on the skin of a lion. So they got married but when they got to the land of the lions all the other lions did not like Ahbal and wanted to throw him out. "He is not a real lion!" they roared. "He is now," argued his new wife. But all the other lions jumped on him and started tearing him to pieces. He screamed and screamed, "Oh! Let me go! Let me go!" Ahbal had eaten too much. Fatoush woke him up and told him that it was a nightmare.

Muna liked my story and said that it was sad. She said that I should write it down and maybe show it to father. I explained that he most probably would not like it. I also told Muna about the books that uncle Nassim had given me to read. We read parts of *David Copperfield* in Arabic and laughed at Micawber.

The moment that we had been putting off and hoping would never come arrived at last. Selma returned home and shortly afterwards the telephone rang. Muna's brother asked if his sister would wait downstairs because their father was on his way to pick her up and was in a hurry. Muna looked a little worried because her father did not know that she was staying with us. She seemed impatient to go downstairs. Selma left us alone for a while and we stood quietly facing each other. I looked at my feet and wriggled my toes. I stood on the side of my feet and almost stumbled.

"Good-bye Saif." I looked up. Muna was crying. She turned and ran out. I could hear the echo of her footsteps on the stairs outside.

I went out onto the sitting-room balcony and peeped over the banisters. Muna got into the car but never looked up. I could not bring myself to cry though I tried because I wanted to. An arm went round my shoulder. I shuddered and pushed the person off, looked and saw Selma smiling kindly at me. She gently pushed me inside the house.

"Go away! Leave me alone!" I ran into our bedroom. Selma followed and told Marwan to come with her. She closed the door. I cried quietly until I was tired. I fell asleep and had a vivid and horrifying dream.

****

I was in an arm-chair reading a Turkish newspaper. I seemed to understand every word I read. The paper was one of father's old collection from the first world war. In the centre page was an old-fashioned blurred picture of a very beautiful woman in a military

116

uniform standing on a pedestal and carrying a machine-gun. The picture reminded me of those of my grandfather which I used to stare at in his front-room. She looked beautiful, strikingly so. On either side of her stood a pretty girl in evening dress. One was Muna. The other I did not recognise. From several windows behind I could see Beirut with distant smoke and fire.

Suddenly, as I stared at the picture, the kind woman smiled and said in Classical Arabic, "What am I supposed to do?" I shouted back, "Anything! Anything!"

I jumped up and tried to get into the picture to see Muna but every time I tried the reality turned back into a newspaper picture which would then freeze for a while. I sat back and stared. The kind woman on the pedestal turned to the girl whom I did not recognise and spoke in French in a drawling and tired voice, which miraculously I understood perfectly and knew that my teacher would be proud of the fact.

"Mais, ma chère, ça ne te va pas, ça. C'est comme ça qu'on gagne une guèrre."

It was my sister, Selma. I tried again to get into the picture but could not. Then I drew a door on the picture and stepped in. Muna had disappeared. Selma stepped down and welcomed me. Someone began tearing up the paper and I ran to the corner of the picture which had not yet been torn up. I could hear the rustling and swishing of paper being crumpled up. I woke up in a sweat.

A woman was kneeling beside my bed. She was busy unwrapping a small parcel. By the faint light of the full moon I could see who it was. Amal was back!

"Ha! Awake hey? Well I'm back; cars and trains and donkeys you couldn't imagine. And the English again in Amman. Nasty, handsome young men on donkeys and trains and cars you couldn't imagine. Let me see your face. You've grown bombed and by the English. Yes you're like me now: mad but not really hey?"

Her face in the moonlight looked pale and tired. Her scar looked deeper and her tattoos darker. She opened a small box.

"Brought you some Knafè and Nablus. And cheese. You can have some friend you like Knafè girl-friend left you? Women are nothing but trouble. You can have my niece: she's stupid. You'll like donkeys too. Must do the washing." She winked at me and left the room.

I lay there listening to the clutter of buckets and to Amal's incessant monologue. The Knafè smelt beautiful. I ate some cold. I loved the taste of cheese followed by the sweet topping. I looked out of the window. The full moon seemed to be staring at me. Like Amal, it too had several faint blue tattoos.

I got up and as I entered the dining-room carrying my box of goodies, I heard Selma exclaim impatiently, "God! She's back. I shall feel ashamed to invite my friends here!"

"She cooks well." Father laughed, although I thought he looked disapprovingly at Selma.

We sat down to supper.

5. Alone

The house stood empty. Some of its walls had collapsed since its occupants had left. In an orgy of destruction, gunmen had blown up various sections. It still stood in many places, a grim reminder of months of feuding that destroyed years of childhood happiness. It stood quiet and majestic as if challenging anyone to forget the happy noises of children playing, noises that still reverberated in its innermost recesses and memories.

The pillars on its balcony overlooked the street and the houses opposite, and looked rather like the Roman pillars seen in Baalbeck, silent and distant. They gave a sense of history that seemed to say to passers by, "We know things that you don't!" Here and there were indentations of bullet holes, innumerable white eyes staring everywhere.

Inside the house some areas shone brightly with rays of light they had never seen before. All seemed brilliant and white as the sun penetrated the holes and spaces created by the explosives. If only these walls could bring forth their memories and their hidden thoughts! But they could not. They stood distant and immutable, destined not to be pulled down or replaced for years. Accustomed to the scene before them, the local inhabitants ceased to see the horror, not even as a memento of war and peace. It was there; reality.

For a while, and until the front entrance was blocked with concrete slabs, the neighbourhood children played within its grounds and, when the courage took them, inside the house. But now the garden was deserted and overgrown. There was something disquieting about a garden that continued to grow. Rose bushes pushed their way as if wildly trying to cover up the destruction. A large busy bougainvillea had climbed over the garden-wall and, becoming too heavy, had fallen towards the pavement below. Hundreds of almost concealed little red flowers dotted the large expanse of dangling green. The un-mowed grass danced from side to side, mournfully, repetitively.

In the children's garden small craters were dotted everywhere. The untrimmed fig tree stood stooped and unkempt.

Alone in the entire house and garden one thing stood intact. It was a little wooden structure clumsily built and standing against the house near the fig-tree. The twigs that covered it were bare of leaves. The rain had started to enter the little garden-house. Through its widening

119

crevices could be seen two boxes, one large and one small, crushed into each other.

Silence reigned. Even the music of birds had died out now that winter was approaching. But on a different plane, the wavelength that only children could inhabit, the noise was deafening. If you could hear it, you would hear childish laughter, genies, houris, fairies and a host of other impossible beings talking and laughing. If you were to listen very carefully you might have been able to hear the tones of a childish voice recounting endless stories, both probable and improbable.

A voice shouted to *be very careful of widders*. Another voice told you that *Barkis was willin'*. Listen more carefully and you would hear a clock's monotonous voice saying, *They-do-not-love-that-do-not-show-their-love*. Suddenly, you would be aware that all noises had blended into a recognisable serenade, mellifluous, slow and captivating, flowing into the unknown like never-ending circles on a gentle pond. All this you might have heard had you been on that different plane. As it was, silence reigned.

Outside, the streets had returned to normal. The short civil war had become something of the past. All had returned to what it had been before. The Lebanese, victims of their own follies, lived on, smiling, adaptable and strong. *Plus ça change, plus c'est la même chose.* And Lebanon, stony Lebanon, lofty black-eyed Lebanon, embraced her dead and sent the whistling wind of change to its majestic mountain-tops, which, white and tall, are like mighty swans afloat on heaven's pool.

But Lebanon, as became her Godlike role, despised the poet and the scribe. She gave them the tools and let them die without really understanding: loving but disloyal, learned but ignorant, living yet lifeless. In this, Lebanon signed her own death-warrant, for Sannin's ever lasting crown of snow was but snow and the crown its people; laughing, crying, exaggerating, and merchandising.

****

Hussein was proud of his youngest son's hard work. The eleven-year old Saif was working for his Elementary Certificate. He worked hard and long. Sometimes he seemed sick with worry and fear. During the two years that preceded the examination, the boy contracted a host of minor ailments. Doctors visited the Ibrahims' household regularly. They came, looked, prescribed and proscribed, and left the child to continue his hard work.

Since Muna's departure the boy seemed determined to distinguish himself. He wrote innumerable essays, read endless textbooks, solved insoluble problems, and drew maps of Lebanon with his eyes shut like an automaton. He became thin, wan, and lethargic. Hussein was beginning to get worried and had Saif moved into his own bedroom where he could keep an eye on him. Both Ali and Selma accused the boy of being a "sissy". Hussein protested that he was somewhat sensitive but that he was in no way spoilt.

Saif increasingly resented his sister. On one occasion, when the family were sitting having tea on the balcony, the boy started crying and complaining that he felt dizzy. His father was kind and solicitous. Selma and Ali told him not to be such a spoilt baby. Daily, Selma would snap at him, telling him not to drag his feet, to keep his head up, to stop sniffling, and many other orders.

When he once cried for fear of failing his examinations, she suddenly turned on him and shouted "It's only a lousy Elementary Certificate! Do you think that the whole world is in your debt for the little work that you're doing!"

Ali laughed and gently rumpled the boy's hair. Marwan stared uncomprehending at his tearful brother. Hussein was kind although he left matters of upbringing to his daughter.

Seeing no outlet for his fears and physical weakness, and daily growing more and more terrified of his sister, the boy withdrew into himself, becoming sullen, quiet, and distant. But this withdrawal did not save him from the scorn of his ever critical sister, whose very presence in the same room he was beginning to fear. In his limited vision he saw her as an unkind snob who refused to understand his inner fears and ambitions.

His only outlet was Amal to whom he paid regular visits in her dingy and ill-lit attic room over the kitchen. Sometimes he would sit silently on the floor staring at her while she worked: she was always working. At other times he would venture to tell her his fears and inner feelings to which she would reply with an endless babbling about the perfidious English and her life in Palestine. He found great security in listening to her nonsense. She, and only she, made him feel the triviality of his inner wretchedness and misery. She made everything - life itself - seem so transient and unimportant. All his gigantic fears and ambitions became what they really were in her presence; a minute drop in the ocean of humanity.

One day he gathered courage and showed his sister a short story that he had written, pretending it was a school essay. Would she correct it please? She did. She told him that it was stupid and childish. She made him rewrite it saying that it was filthy to talk about a woman giving birth. He did not understand and asked Marwan who told him to mind his own business. He paid Amal a visit and cried.

"Well, well, so it's tears. Save them for the English. They took our home and left us tents to sleep in. My nephew studies all night under the airport road lighting for free. He catches cold. I tell him why work so hard? It's not worth it just to be like the English. Ah Saif, such handsome blue eyes they had. Read me your story. Naughty is it? Read because I like it. And why show it to that cat; she'd scratch my eyes out because I embarrass her. Thinks I'm mad. You and I know better. Read on. Read."

And he would read his short stories and compositions. Amal would listen intently especially to those written in English, a language she could not understand. And then she always complimented him on his brilliance in knowing his letters. Saif sensed the falsity of the whole situation but chose to turn a blind eye to it.

In the last year of his Elementary School, Saif became more withdrawn and secretive. Half-way through his twelfth year he made a resolution not to confide to anyone his secret ambition of writing. He hid all his work in a file along with his mother's *Complete Keats and Shelley*, and *King Lear*. He locked them up in his side of the wardrobe that he now shared with his father.

****

Hussein, though proud of his son's hard work, was somewhat bemused by his reticence and secrecy. He consulted his two sisters Haji and Yasmine. Yasmine told him not to worry and leave the boy alone explaining that he was somewhat sensitive as any motherless boy was bound to be. Selma was looking after him well enough.

Hussein pointed out that the boy seemed to dislike his sister.

"A passing phase, brother. She is a little short with him, but she has had a very heavy responsibility thrust upon her, forced too young into the role of a mother, and Heaven knows she's right in resenting it." Yasmine understood early motherhood well, since she was made to marry a cousin when only fourteen. She bore him eight children. Her unhappy and unfulfilled hard life both before and after her husband's death seemed to have turned her into a kind, good, and gentle woman. There was no apparent bitterness about her, just the jolly, laughing, and somewhat corpulent woman that everyone grew up to love, and love sincerely. Further, all the men of the family adored her for her magnificent cooking.

Haji had different advice to offer her brother.

"Brother, the boy is weak, thin. No flesh on him. I recommend cod-liver oil twice daily, raw liver, plenty of yoghurt, and continual prayer. Yes. Clean the system out." What Hussein was reluctant to discuss was his youngest son's apparent fear of women. Was the boy a homosexual in the making? There was something ineffably feminine about him.

That Selma loved her two little brothers there was no doubt. She had sacrificed her young life to their upbringing. Young as she was she felt the bitter injustice of her position. She took shelter in an exaggerated social role to which her position hardly entitled her.

Marwan proved an easy and pliable child in her hands, full of laughter, joy, and alert intelligence. He seemed to grow up almost without effort. Saif, on the other hand, fought every minute that added its weight to his growing life. In Selma's eyes he was a pillar of complexities: shy, reticent, resentful, and spoilt by his gullible father. She saw him as a massive complicated knot that could not be untied but had to be ruthlessly and summarily cut through.

Marwan and Saif were drawing apart as they grew up. The elder seemed to understand the younger but there was a youthful difficulty in offering a helping hand. He could only be kind and this he was. He was also brutal in his joyous laughter which the younger misunderstood and resented. Sometimes an excess of emotion led to the most vicious fights, fights that seemed deadly. From every fight each child emerged hurt in body and soul. Saif felt himself weighed down with guilt and the irresponsibility of the inevitable.

Marwan found refuge in jokes. In young society he saved his brother from his own shyness by jokingly pointing to his temples and shaking a finger, saying, "A little mad. I hit him on the head twice when we were small. Shshsh, head injuries." People began to believe this and treat Saif kindly, leaving him alone.

Yet the two brothers retained a strong and silent love that only brothers knew and felt. They understood. They felt. Their most mundane conversations were full of meaningful looks, grunts, and secret language. Brotherly love *'c'est le plus muet des amours'*. What artist can describe it? What brother does not feel it?

****

The eldest Miss Jbeili was getting married. Immense preparations were being made for a wedding that would not be forgotten for a long time to come. Hussein charged his daughter to buy her cousin a most expensive wedding present which, it too, would not be forgotten for a long time. Selma busied herself with the necessary preparations for her own outfit, one that would put the bride to shame. Selma was indeed more beautiful than her cousin, or a lot of other women in Lebanese society for that matter. She also had the ability to switch on any of her various personalities. She was the defenceless pretty maiden, the dynamic and intelligent modern woman, the 'dumb' beauty, and a host of others. Her real kindly intelligent self remained in the background behind an aggressive and critical character. That is not to say that she was conscious of her acts. Rather she adapted as the chameleon would do. This made her a rising figure with a great future position in society. Her father proudly and innocently stretched his means to help her on her theatrical trail.

A few days before the wedding all the male folk of the family had to present themselves to Selma in their full wedding suits. The father was approved but was put on a stringent diet because of his 'corporation'. Ali cheerfully and laughingly accepted a change of tie and the necessity of a vigorous bath. Marwan put on what he was given. Selma was happy, that is, until Saif walked in with his new suit on. He was ordered to put on different socks. In itself a reasonable demand, but he refused. He would not go. Who wants to go to a wedding anyhow? He described the wedding in such profane language that Selma felt it necessary to slap him, which had her father's wholehearted approval.

Minutes later he presented himself again, was passed by his father but not by the rest of the family. Although dressed properly, he would not stand straight. He scratched his new shoes by performing a variety of absolutely impossible standing feats. His suit sat on him awkwardly making him a possible source of acute embarrassment to the rest of the family. He kept pulling at his elasticated tie.

Selma and Ali decided to give him a lesson in deportment. Much to Marwan's amusement, his younger brother was made to walk with one arm on his waist and a book on his head.

"The fool has splayed feet!" shouted Selma. Indeed, with a long stick in his free hand, Saif would have created a sensation in the court of Louis XIV! But in Beirut of 1959 he was an effete dolt. Ali and Selma joined in with Marwan's hilarity. Saif stopped, wavered, and dropped the book off his head, kicking it across the room with a string of obscenities flying behind it. He was sick of being treated like an unfeeling doll. At his father's insistence he was left alone.

But go to the wedding he did. Morose and quiet, Saif disappeared among the two thousand guests gathered at the Jbeilis' enormous villa. He walked in the garden, now looking at the high railings surrounding the solitary three storey villa, now looking at the adults and despising them.

Several groups of people stood dotted about the enormous garden. A black butler impassively served drinks. Several waiters and waitresses bustled busily amidst the crowds.

"*Eh bien, mon chère,*" said an old woman brilliant with jewellery. "What is this I hear about your stay in *la belle Paris*? Hmm? *Est-ce que c'est vrai* what you tell me of Jacqui?"

"Yes, *Ma chère, imagines-toi*, she came with a most vulgar man. And that tiara..."

The men stood aside talking politics and generally deciding the fate of the masses.

"Communism. I tell you, Communism. That is what you have to be wary of." The speaker was a man in his middle fifties who seemed to be enjoying himself. "Just look at Iraq. Look. Look." He continued pointing vaguely towards the airport road. As his hand came back he snatched a glass off a passing waiter's tray.

"I think that you're panicking. It's not as bad as all that," said a young man.

"What isn't?" asked the first speaker.

"Communism."

An uproar arose around the young man. His face reddened. He tried to say something about a welfare state like Britain. The entire group shouted at each other.

"*Ma chère,*" said a young woman reclining lazily on a long chair.

"*Ah ma chère, les hommes!*"

Her listener made a face that expressed contempt. A young man, sitting on his own near the arguing group, suddenly jumped from his seat and shouted, "I think..." Everyone turned to look at him intently. He smiled feebly and reclined back in his seat. He did this several times.

"Who is he?" whispered one woman whose dress may as well have remained at home, there was so little of it. She hugged herself against the chilly breeze.

"Lina's son. Fancies himself a bit of a poet! Back from England where he studied."

This was spoken in the utmost confidence and at very near proximity to her nose. "*L'enfant terrible.*" The listener turned to the woman on her other side and whispered confidentially so that everybody could hear. "*Pourquoi pas la France?* Why England? And where's the money in poetry?"

Saif walked on almost hugging the railings. He had walked around the garden several times without being noticed.

"Get us something, may Allah keep you."

He looked to where the voice had come from. Several children stood there clutching the rails and staring at him. Saif looked hard, with fear in his heart. The boys were dirty and haggard. They had very short hair and their heads had that look which he had seen on charity school children. They were covered in badly barbered patches where the skin showed through. Some had scabs instead of patches of skin. Their eyes were awful: large and deeply sunken. On their faces were several patches of dirt or peeling skin. Some had runny noses and broken teeth.

"Get us something, may Allah keep you," repeated the voice.

Saif hesitated then turned and ran. In the kitchen were several bags out of which the servant was removing roast chickens. He took two bags and ran out. At the railings the hungry children were waiting. He took out the hot chickens and handed them through the railings. Every time a chicken was passed through a few children disappeared as they jumped off the railing onto the ground below. Some stayed, a thin stick-like arm clutching on to the rails, while using the other to eat. Their manner of eating reminded Saif of a mad dog he had once watched from the safety of an upper floor window just before the police shot it. It had a piece of something that it tried to rip to pieces while at the same time trying to eat it. It kept dropping bits of it and getting angrier and angrier. Saif could hear the noises of fighting and munching. He handed the last chicken noticing that the children smelt. An older child took the chicken and held Saif's hand. Saif felt disgusted, pushed him off while jumping back but immediately said, "Must get some more."

As he ran out of the kitchen with two more bags he was met by Marwan.

"What are you doing?"

"Taking food to the Palestinian refugees outside." He looked embarrassed.

"My God! They'll kill you if you're caught."

"I don't care!" The blood rushed to Saif's face as he stood there heaving with defiance.

Marwan hesitated. "Neither do I!" He ran into the kitchen. This time both children ran round the back where there were fewer guests and were noticed stealthily speeding by with the bags, their delicious aroma of roast chicken rising as they passed. They looked like field mice as they ran between the several floodlights.

"Oh, how lovely. *Les enfants s'amusent.*" said a woman's voice.

The children changed direction. As they turned a corner they came to a full stop, face to face with their father. He looked cross.

"What do you think you're doing?" he demanded crossly.

Saif stood on the side of his feet. Suddenly he burst forth, "Look!" and pointed towards the railings. Hussein looked just in time to see several dirty childish heads disappear behind the wall on which the railings stood.

He looked at his children and said, "Listen. Get me all the very small children you can find. Quick! Leave the bags here!" They ran around collecting several very little ones and shepherding them towards Hussein.

"Who wants to play a game?" asked Hussein quietly. Several tiny voices clamoured for a part. "Shshsh! You have to be very, very quiet in order to play this." Everyone was silent while Hussein issued instructions for the game. "Now listen carefully. Let's see how much food you can collect and throw over that wall there. See, over there in between the railings. The one who gets the most food will win the game. Now, run. But you have to be very quiet or else I won't play."

He looked at Marwan and Saif and tapped them both on the head.

"Go!"

The game was a huge success as the children delighted in throwing large quantities of food over the railings. After a while fewer and fewer children returned until there were only Marwan and Saif left. They could hear several voices, both adult and childish, behind the wall: excited and happy voices. The two boys and their father listened intently. Hussein put an arm around each boy. He looked down at Saif who was beginning to cry. "That's all right son. All right." His own voice faltered as the three walked back towards the party.

"The chicken is going down well, what?" shouted Mr. Jbeili in his usual complacent way.

"*Ah mon cher Jbeili-eee. Les pooo-lets, C'est de-li-cieux!*"

****

19.6.59 Joseph has been caught. He admitted stealing the petty cash box after a lengthy interrogation. I refused to be present. The instrument they used on him was a wooden contraption with ropes that squeezed his ribs. His screams were horrible. At least he had done it or he would not have confessed. He wants his job back. I am advising against it.

The boys will be going to a new school soon. The International College is recognised as being the best in the Middle East. Saif does not seem to like it. What a strange boy. Seems all right if left alone with his stories. And he tells them by the dozen. I am rather worried despite Nassim's view of the matter. Not much for this artistic temperament business. Where is the stuff he writes? Is there any?

I walked in on him the other day. He had been crying. He would not say why but I assumed that it must be a quarrel with Selma. She had not seen him all evening. He had been reading a translation of Romeo and Juliet. Nobility of character? Sheer indulgence? Does he need to cry so any excuse would do?

His health is failing, though Dr. Amin reassures me that there is nothing to worry about. Propensity to colds and bad throats. I must consult Yasmine again.

Hussein read this last entry in his diary and sat back to think of what he wanted to write this time. His consultation with Yasmine had led to nothing. His real friend, the diary seemed the best and final solution to every problem he had.

28.6.59. Saif still a constant worry. He has passed his Elementary Certificate with distinction. Has certainly proved that hard work will pay in the end. "If it be boy's work, I'll do it" is written all over his face. He wants the original David Copperfield as a present. He does not seem particularly excited about succeeding. So secretive. Was I like that as a boy? Cannot remember, but I'm sure not.

I sorely miss Leila's help in this. She understood the children.

Here Hussein stopped writing and thought of his wife. He thought of her with a deep warmth engulfing his whole being. She understood.

Saif and Marwan are back together in one room. Yasmine thinks this better. It certainly saves Saif the torture of being called "baba's little baby".

Taking the family to see An American in Paris. I hope it is suitable for children. Most probably not, but Marwan likes all movies.

****

Yasmine accompanied her brother as he drove his four children to see *An American in Paris*. Leslie Caron was a particular favourite of his. The entire family was in high spirits, Ali, holding his sister's hand and joking about a new girl-friend, Samira, who was of Turkish origin.

"Is she now? You little *Pezevenk*!" said Selma laughing.

"Allah!" exclaimed the podgy Yasmine whose arms were being pinched by Marwan. "Do you know what that Turkish word means?"

"Don't know the girl that well, aunt."

Everyone laughed.

"*Sikttir ya deyyus!*" replied Hussein.

Yasmine laughed that deep laugh that seeks to tell everyone of knowing the meaning behind her brother's obscene Turkish.

"Shshsh!" she laughed, "the children."

"That's all right," shouted Marwan, "I know what it means. That first one means a pimp, and the ..." he proceeded to explain with the reckless hardihood of early teens.

"All right, that's enough!" ordered his father.

"And how's old misery guts?" asked Selma referring to Saif who quietly sat staring out of the car-window.

He had visited his new school that day and was feeling wretched. At least there was the summer holiday before that horrible, horrible school starts.

"Why don't you like it?" asked Ali, kindly.

"I cannot understand!" interrupted Selma. "The best people in society would love to send their children there."

How Saif hated the word 'society' in his sister's mouth. Every time she said it she puckered her lips in a way that reminded him of a mule defecating as it pulled a wagon. He had seen such sights while visiting farms with his father. Selma accompanied the word with a hand gesture that was meant to be graceful. It made Saif think of a dog standing by a lamp-post.

******

The film was a good one and everyone enjoyed it. All through it Saif had a thumping pain in his head. Now and then he would start as if from a deep sleep and look at the screen. He fancied he could see but not hear or that he could hear but not see. He recognised the film for what it was: a film. He could see it moving up on the screen frame by frame. He suddenly realised that he was blinking his eyes fast and regularly. He felt sick. A sensation of nausea climbed from the pit of his stomach up to his mouth. He groaned gently.

"All right, son?"

"Yes! Yes!" His tongue felt heavy and his voice distant.

"What does baba's little baby want? Hmmm?" asked Selma sarcastically.

"Shshsh!" whispered the aunt.

Saif felt determined to hide his feelings. He looked at his sister's face in the light reflected from the screen. He looked at Ali who was slumped beside her. Marwan looked intensely stupid. People's heads moved up and down the line of seats. He closed his eyes.

He jumped up at what sounded like a clash of cymbals. On the screen Leslie Caron was running up steep wide steps towards her beloved at the top. The music was deafening. The two danced gracefully on the screen and Saif wanted to join in. He tried to move his legs but could not. He waited. Maybe they had gone to sleep. He tried again.

As the lights came on Saif uttered a loud and piteous moan. Some spectators turned and looked at him. Selma stood up angrily.

"Get up. I've had enough of...." She stopped when she saw the boy's face. It was distorted with agony. He was pale with a shade of blue around his mouth. Ali jumped up and caught the boy as he slumped forward. He picked him up as if he were no more than a feather.

Saif saw the lights above fly back, fancying he had succeeded in joining the dance. He felt cold. He heard voices around him and quick steps. Then more angry voices.

"This is your new school, my boy!" said a voice with strong sibilant emphasis. "We concentrate on work here. Exercise. Mens sana in corpore sano, hey my little juvenile: Juvenal - ha ha ha."

"Please, sir, I don't like this school. Can I go back to my old one?"

"Why my son?" hissed the voice.

"It's cold and dark and unfriendly and please, sir, can I go back to my old school?"

Saif felt someone take hold of his legs and lift him up.

"We shall now bury you."

He lay in a coffin. Faces appeared and stared at him. First his father, then Marwan, Ali, Selma crying and saying something, and his aunt Yasmine.

"Can he see?" asked a strange voice. A hand passed before his face.

"No! He's dead. Let's bury him."

"Oh. Yes. Do let's," shouted Marwan gleefully.

Saif shouted that he was not dead. He moved his eyes. He sat up.

With terror in his heart, he realised he had not done any of these things. He thought he had. His father lent against his coffin and looked.

"He is dead, isn't he?" someone asked.

"Yes," his father answered. "But he can see us. You see when you die, your brain goes on working for a while. He can see us and understand us. But he's paralysed by death. Let's sing for him. That should cheer him up until he dies completely."

Saif tried desperately to say something. If only he could scream. That is it: scream. He hated the song. His father's face was pushed off and Selma's appeared. He screamed. He screamed hard and loud. He sat up and fell into Selma's arms.

"All right! All right, love. You've been ill, very ill. Lie down quietly. Lie down." He hung on to his sister. He wanted to push her off but he could not. He held on tightly and passionately.

Chapter 6

There was a fat bearded Englishman turned Moslem who used to pass below my window five times daily on his way to the mosque down the road. Back in father's room I used to lie propped up in bed looking out of the window. I could just see the pavement across the road and the wall surrounding a large villa. I used to watch out for the bearded man who had become the five most important events in my day as he shuffled down the sloping pavement towards the mosque.

Several papers stuck out of his jacket pockets and he wore slippers. Although his beard became him, I fancied he had a cruel and bitter look on his face. Unknown to him we became great friends during our five daily distant meetings. He always walked down to the mosque on the side of the road I could see. I could not see him coming back on the pavement directly below my window although I heard him dragging himself up the slope and muttering something or other.

While waiting for my friend to appear I used to stare outside at the wall opposite. On it were painted, in brilliant white, the slogans, "*Long live Kassim hero of the Arabs*" and, "*He and Nasser are brothers in arms*". I stared long at these words which sometimes seemed to jump out at me and perform a jig or two on the pavement. At such times they would be joined by the bearded Englishman who would dance around them as he tore papers out of his pocket. Throwing them up into the air, he would sing "Words! Words! Words for sale!" Then, angrily, he would take hold of the dancing slogans rather like a sailor takes hold of a length of rope, and rearrange them on the wall in the oddest arrangements. I decided to ask him what they meant and would float down to him for the purpose.

"You want to buy words, young chap? How many? Thrupence a word. How many?"

Then he would shuffle off towards the mosque and I would wake up at the sound of his steps to see him about to disappear from my line of vision just beyond the window ledge.

"Have you been dreaming?" asked a gentle voice in a whisper. I felt a cool hand on my brow. Father sat beside me on the edge of the bed.

"What time is it?" I asked.

"Just after eleven, little man," answered father, kindly.

"What day?"

"Tuesday."

"Aren't you working, baba?"

"No. I thought I would stay home with my little man. Would you like a drink?"

"No, thank you."

"Are you comfortable?"

"Yes. How long will I have to stay in bed? How much longer?"

"A very long time. You see, you've been very ill. Rheumatic Fever. Now you're on the mend. But you have to lie down very quietly and rest for a long time."

"How long?"

"Very long."

"Weeks?"

"Maybe. We'll see."

"Months?"

"Yes. But you'll be patient. That I know. Soon you'll feel better enough to resume reading and maybe you can write short stories."

"Short stories? Why?"

"Oh, just a suggestion. It might keep you amused."

"Can I have some books?"

"Yes, soon. Which ones do you want?"

"*David Copperfield* and *Don Quixote.*"

"In Arabic, of course."

"English. I don't care. No. In English, please."

"Go to sleep now. You're tired. Sleep well, little man."

I turned over slowly. I felt father's lips touch my cheek. His bristly face slid over my sweaty face. I thought that he too smelt sweaty. As I closed my eyes I heard him telling Marwan to be quiet. Selma came in. I pretended to be asleep. She felt my forehead, uttered a loud and echoing "humph", and walked out. I fell asleep.

****

I heard Selma storming into the bedroom, I shut my eyes tightly.

"Get up! There's nothing wrong with you. Get up!"

A hand wrenched the sheets backwards. My pyjamas were torn off.

"You smell!" she screamed. "Get washed."

I got up and moved precariously towards the door. I fell.

"Come. Here you are, Amal, come and sit on him. Raw liver. That's what he needs."

Someone sat on me. Selma forced my mouth open and tried to thrust little cubes of red meat, slithering, bloody, and glistening. I resisted. I saw Selma's long fingernails come forward to scratch me.

I woke up to the sound of the muezzin calling the faithful to prayers. My friend should be passing by soon. Someone was sitting on my bed.

"Hello!"

"Uncle Nassim. I'm glad you've come." I started to cry.

Selma entered the room. "What is it?" she asked kindly.

"I have a headache," I lied.

She looked at me from the bottom of the bed. Suddenly, she surged forward snappishly exclaiming, "Lie down properly then." I did. "Would you like anything?" she asked softly.

"No thank you."

"And you uncle Nassim?"

"Tea would greet the stomach rather nicely, my dear."

She left the room to prepare it and I breathed easier.

"What's the matter with our little author?" whispered uncle, confidentially.

"I have Romantic Fever," I replied quietly.

My uncle burst out laughing and continued to laugh for a long time.

"Yes, little author. That's exactly what you have. Too much of the Romanticky. Hey ticky tacky tacky Romantic Fever. Ha ha ha. Books! That's what you need. Eat yourself a few and digest them well and you'll be as new and as crisp as a new pound note. Hey, little author?"

I laughed for the first time in ages. Uncle Nassim had a lovely face. It was rubbery and he could do a lot with it. Selma came in with a tray which she put on the table beside the bed. On it stood six small glasses with handles and a large pot of tea. Selma stood by the bed.

"Well L.A., what about a glass for you? Settles your something or other. Hmmm?"

"He mustn't have stimulants," said Selma efficiently.

"Mustn't have stimulants" echoed my uncle.

I thought he eyed Selma and then the door. A long silence followed. Uncle Nassim ceremoniously poured the tea into the six glasses lined up before him. The steam rose in a gentle circular movement. Uncle stared at the glasses for some time, then, legs apart with one hand on his knee, he quickly lifted and swallowed the contents of every glass. Having done so, he proceeded to fill them again.

"What's L.A.?" asked Selma abruptly.

"L.A.?" answered uncle. "Confidential. Classified. Top secret." He made a circular movement with his eyes that took in the whole room and ended on my face. Accompanying this gesture was another where his index finger tapped the side of his nose several times. I laughed. Selma left the room.

"Now, what's wrong L.A.?"

"I told you. I have Romantic Fever."

"Yes! Yes! But," he pointed to his chest. "What's wrong in here?"

"Nothing!"

"And you cry for nothing?"

"Yes, nothing."

"Nothing will come of nothing. Speak again. Heave your heart into your mouth."

I started laughing at the way he spoke.

"Well, all right, all right. It sounds better in English. Shakespeare in Arabic is rather like a Bedouin pitching a tent in Trafalgar Square!"

"That should be all right," I said cleverly, "because Trafalgar comes from the Arabic taraful-aghar. The tempting corner of the cow's eye."

"I see. Education." Uncle Nassim laughed. "Talking about cows' eyes, what is really wrong?"

"She is."

"Thought so. Let's ship her off to the top of Nelson's column, hey, L.A.? What say you?"

I laughed and nodded vigorously.

Uncle Nassim became serious. "Listen L.A., she does care you know. You're old enough to recognise that she's under pressure. She is young. Efficient, hey?" he added, winking vigorously.

"She's a horrible snob. Never listens to anyone..." I stopped with excess of passion. Uncle Nassim turned to his six glasses and drank them off one after the other.

"That greeted the stomach rather nicely! The bladder too. Excuse me."

I turned over and fell asleep but not deeply, being aware where I really was. Now and then I started up with a sense of urgency then went back to sleep again.

I dreamt that I was standing on a ledge fifteen stories high. All was quiet. Below me stood the vast expanse of Beirut. The atmosphere was sombre and insecure. "No wonder it is," I thought as I looked below me. Father said "The bombs will start as soon as night comes. Get something to eat and draw the curtains. I cannot stand dust." He gave me ten piasters. I wanted to get out. I must get to Trafalgar Square. I had a house there. Explosions erupted everywhere around me. I could see beautifully luminous sparks flying towards me. "I shall die," I thought. An enormous spark like a gigantic star blinded me. "That's for me!" I fell on my knees and started crawling. The spark stopped and lit the room up. I was in the middle of a circle of seated people. A bee the size of a dog ran across the room. I jumped forward to crush it. My father, Selma, Marwan, and uncle Issam started laughing. "Can't you see it? There! There, behind the chair! Kill it!" They laughed. The bee came out and quivered its tail mockingly. "If I catch it, I can get its sting. Uncle Nassim would love that." I put my hand forward to crush it. "Its sting must be ten centimetres long." The bee became affectionate. I could not do it. Its sting came out and it flew off out of the window. I sat staring at the sting. Uncle Issam took it saying, "Lovely! Lovely!" He lit it and puffed away with great satisfaction. "I must get out," I thought. "I must. Beirut overwhelms me so. Beirut humiliates me so."

****

Selma left for England where she spent her summer holidays. My father looked after me very well. He was very kind and solicitous, providing me with an endless supply of books in English and Arabic. He also supplied me with several games that I could play with while quietly sitting up in bed. He must have had a great deal of patience to put up with the tremendous clattering clutter of plastic aeroplanes and boat models that I had stuck together and which I had displayed everywhere in the room.

But most of my time was spent reading. I would half-sit up in bed in the stifling summer heat listening to Marwan preparing to go swimming, and feeling a tinge of envy at his bouncy, healthy life. I would open my copy of *David Copperfield* with its red covers and read what I thought to be the true life of the author. I reread the sections on David's unjust punishment, on Salem House, and his mother's death. I cried and pretended that the pain in my knees had returned. I delighted in Micawber and hated Heep. I thoroughly enjoyed David's denunciation of Heep. I thought Dora a 'spoony' and had definite ideas of how I would deal with her. But Agnes! Everything that I was to hate in her as an adult, I thought then to be divine. Peggotty was a coward for not standing up for David by booting Murdstone into the adjoining graveyard. Steerforth reminded me of my patronising cousin who had once tried to give me goat-droppings telling me that they were chocolate drops. But I kept going back to the opening chapters and to my intense hatred of Murdstone.

I laughed with a heavy feeling in my heart at *Don Quixote*. I wished that I were with him in order to look after him and his library. A copy of *Othello* in Arabic inspired me to write a short story; changing its ending to a happy one.

My imagination was feverishly fired by a collection of historical novels by Zaydan and Scott. I had endless days and nights dreaming about alternative plots, alternative endings and so on. It was then that I discovered an ability to daydream that I had never thought I had. When tired of reading, or when father gently told me to have a rest, I would lay there staring at the enormous cupboard before me or at the sky through the window above me and transport myself into any place in the world. I saw Bois Guilbert bursting his very life for passion. I personally defeated Locksley in a friendly combat and, with the aid of the Arabic novels, I took great pains - in the person of Saladdin - to expose the heathen Richard the Lionheart for what he really was. As for Rebecca, little did anyone know that she disappeared out of Scott's novel right into my arms, nobler, stronger, and better than her secret love Ivanhoe.

I became as familiar with *Arabian Nights* as I was with slogans daubed on the wall opposite my window. The stories came in numerous little cheap volumes, each containing a story or two. I devoured them without discrimination. In time my mind was so full of fictitious characters that it over-spilled its very boundaries and lost control. Copperfield sat on the magic carpet while Sinbad married Dora. Don Quixote made several visits to various oases accompanied by Ivanhoe. And Sancho? Poor Sancho, he was married off to Rowena. Micawber lived in a Synagogue and Isaac the Jew sat hourly expecting something to turn up.

These happy times were only interrupted by a constant stream of visitors. Those who caught me with my eyes open stayed awhile. The majority walked off quietly seeing me in a deep peaceful sleep. But even with those who stayed I developed a method of passing the time in their unwelcome presence. I would imagine each to be in one of my stories or, if this proved impossible, I would impose one of my familiar characters on the visitor concerned and would sit back staring at him or her.

It was highly amusing to watch uncle Issam puffing at his cigar and drinking his 'tea' while hearing him pontificate in the Micawber style. Aunt Haji required little imagination to become a Betsy Trotwood or, if the mood took me, a Mrs. Crupp. Uncle Nassim was worthy of Saladdin. Aunt Muna had great difficulty keeping house and always pouted and said silly things. Uncle Muhammad and his pretty wife who used to be his maid were Othello and Desdemona in reverse. Father, I could never place. I fancied him as Mr. Dick but thought that cruel. To see Murdstone in him was unfair. Micawber never seemed to fit. Finally I decided to dispose of him as a kind of grown Traddles on account of the way his hair looked first thing in the morning.

And I?

I was like a god: inventing, manipulating, and changing the order of things. On my right hand sat uncle Nassim laughing uproariously at my inventions. He brought me other books and kept our secret.

It was very soon after that I found it impossible to separate the real world from the fictitious counterpart. I disinterestedly watched the rest of mankind go by. I saw none but myself, the omniscient god in the middle.

Thus I fought the loneliness and boredom of several months of illness.

****

As soon as I was well enough I went to my new school. I was very unhappy despite the pride I was told to feel at being accepted at such an important college. I could hardly wait for Friday night. This school being American we had Saturday and Sunday off instead of a half Thursday and Friday. All our subjects, with the exception of one or two, had to be studied in English. There was a friend from my old school there: Muhammad. Gentle and quiet, he worked diligently at his studies and at his diagrams of flying ships. I was excused physical training which made me happy as I hated undressing in front of others. This was a boys' school and I felt like a dwarf amongst giants. I withdrew into myself and did my best but with little success. I asked to go back into my old school. Father said that he would think about it and Selma stormed about for days calling me ungrateful and all sorts of other things. I stayed. After a term or so Marwan and I became virtual strangers as he moved up in his class. After a term or two, Muhammad and I became very close friends.

****

It was soon after I joined this new school that I experienced something that I did not understand then and that, despite my advanced years now giving me an understanding of the mechanics of the event, I still do not understand its meaning or awful provenance.

I received a message to report to my music teacher in the new music room. He had always been very kind to me in an alien and hateful environment. I enjoyed visiting his room, which was full of musical delights. He introduced me to classical music for which I quickly formed a lifelong love tinged with an inner fascinated terror. He often invited me into his room to listen to music especially Beethoven, Mozart and Prokofiev.

I walked into the room and found him sitting in the corner strumming a guitar. He motioned me to sit beside him. After a few minutes he hugged the guitar hard and stared at me. He then put the guitar aside and turned to face me. He spoke and his words were eventually burned into my consciousness and they still recur in sad dreams in my restless sleep and in raging wakeful day dreams even today. I can hear him now as I sit at my desk, an old man with so much irrevocable history propelling me towards some unknown.

"What would you like to listen to today? I thought that a little bit of old Ludwig would be nice. What about your favourite? *The Pastoral Symphony*. You fell in love with it from the very beginning. Here, listen to this wonderful opening. Doesn't it fill you with a real sense of awe? It is spectacular. Let's turn it up really loud. The door is locked now. Come here my boy. Don't be frightened. You have such silky hair. Just like a girl. Your cheeks are so soft. No. No. Stay. Here,

140

touch it if you want. Good boy. I will undo this. There. There.
You're all right. This is our secret. Turn around. Good boy. There.
The music is lovely and loud. There! There!"

The Pastoral Symphony drowned my initial screams slowly
subsiding to stifled moans as the music teacher held his huge hand over
my mouth.

"I love you. I love you. There! There! It's our little secret. You
mustn't tell anyone. They wouldn't understand and would be very
angry with you for doing this. Because what you did was wrong. But I
will take care of you. And you can come back tomorrow if you want. I
won't hurt you. Because you know that I love you so much. Here. I
bought you this book. Your favourite. There. It's for being such a
good darling boy. What is it? It's all right. Show me. Don't be
frightened. It will become easier soon. And you will always have me
to look after you. You are a sweetheart."

Even the passage of so many years, the experiences of a lifetime
and the repeated abuse in other ways – I say, even all this has not
accustomed me to the months of terror that went on from that day
onwards. So much so, that, sitting in my little study surrounded by my
beloved books, by my Beethoven, Mozart and Prokofiev, I can no
longer write of this episode and its descendants. So, guilty with the
dark secret and fearful of I know not what, I leave it and move on.

****

But momentous things were happening at home during my first
term at the new school: Ali was getting married. Visitors came and
went. There were incessant visits from, and to, Aunt Haji. Selma
neglected her first year university work as she ran all over the place but
doing little more than creating a fuss - at least that was how it seemed
to me.

The day arrived for Ali to introduce his bride to be to the rest of the
family, bringing her home to tea for the benefit of Aunt Haji and others.
Of course, our immediate family had seen her. Father and Selma had
met her with the greatest approbation. Never in the marital history of
mankind has such a great fuss been made over so small an event as the
presentation of Samira to Aunt Haji and other elders.

Selma had spent the entire morning preparing various delicacies to be served during the meeting. Marwan gave a helping hand. Selma kept sending me here and there in order to buy this and that: sweets, chocolates, cigarettes, serviettes, ash-trays. Every time I returned with the required purchase she would look at it, exclaim loudly while rolling her large at times hazel and at others blue eyes, and send me out to fetch more. As Amal was banished from the kitchen, she spent the day vigorously washing the floor. I was sure that if I had used a water-gauge the level of the water in which Amal waded all day would have exceeded the height of Selma's highest shoes. Occasionally, a cigarette was seen floating on the water as Amal took a rest and lit another one.

The flurry increased as time approached for the arrival of Samira and her panel of judges. As soon as I was allowed to, I ran and hid in the small bedroom which had now become mine. Ali was then living at university in order to prepare himself for his finals. I sat in my room very quietly for fear of discovery. I hated the fuss being made but for Ali's sake I tried to be cheerful. Selma's voice went right through my head as she shouted orders from room to room, orders for no one to carry out as Amal continued to scrub and I continued to hide in my room. Four o'clock arrived and with it came Haji whose prayers I could hear as the lift brought her up the one floor.

"Your arm nephew. Your arm." I presented my arm and my aunt steered me into the front-room. She was soon followed by aunt Yasmin, uncles Nassim and Issam, and several other relations. Marwan bounced into place and started pinching aunt Yasmin's podgy arms. Selma came in and welcomed the visitors with an air of one who tolerated society. My father sat in his usual corner seat and eyed everybody in a distant manner.

"Well! Woe is me, niece. The baby is getting married. Married. Fancy that. And only yesterday Hussein was born. Yes. Yesterday. I am an old woman. Ignorant too. Old! Old! Old!"

Aunt Haji slapped her chest violently at every one of these outbursts. "I am old. So, our hero marries a Turkish girl. Allah! Allah! Toooorkey! Pezevenk. Deyyus. Ya ah-man-y ll-ah. Hey brother. Turkish?" She laughed in sheer delight as the tears rolled down her face. "She speaks the language though?"

"Yes. She speaks Arabic," replied my father. "She has been at university here for three years."

"University, brother?" Screamed aunt Haji. "How now? Wherefore? Where to?" And, she added for emphasis, "If I may ask."

Since no one was sure what aunt's question was, silence reigned until uncle Isaam broke it.

"We are very happy," he spoke slowly and deliberately. "We are, that is, very happy. Happy we feel. That is, not to put too fine a point upon it, we feel matrimony to be a high state of bliss. State-of-bliss. Now we ourselves married twice, both women. That is to say, good women. We divorced the first after meeting with the second and ..."

Uncle Nassim started laughing and everyone joined in, even father and aunt Haji.

"Shshsh!" said uncle Nassim to his youngest brother. "The family elder speaks!" Father laughed.

"You may laugh" continued uncle Issam. "We are impervious. Our advice to the younger members of this family is: smoke not, drink not, emigrate to Damascus, and marry early. We ourselves personally have ten children." He was interrupted in his speech by a commotion outside announcing the arrival of Ali and his intended.

Father walked out and received them. I stood by the door. Samira was indeed attractive. Petite, she had a sweet face with long auburn hair. She smiled shyly. I noticed that she had very long well-manicured finger nails. Her lips struck me as being hard when she was not smiling, but she smiled most of the time. I heard father whisper something about Aunt Haji being almost blind. Samira nodded. Ali's face was very red. Selma whispered, "Oh! How embarrassing!" Father seemed totally at ease as he led her towards his eldest sister. Everybody stood up.

"Ah! Allah! Allah! Allah!" said aunt as she struck her chest several times. "Allah! Allah! Isn't it handsome? Brother! Look at its face. Let me feel you my dear. Let me. Let an old, blind, crippled, miserable woman feel you. And ignorant too. Allah! Allah! Lovely face. Hair so silky. Skin so soft. Good teeth too. Ah! May Allah protect me as you're a woman. Full. Full and good. May He send this tree fruits. For you know, my dear," she added jovially by way of a joke, "a tree that does not bear fruit will have to be cut down. Allah! Allah! It's crying, brother. I have embarrassed it. I am an old woman. And ignorant too. You'll soon be rid of me. I know that that's what you'd like."

Since no one offered any reassurance to the contrary, Aunt Haji sat down again and busied herself with rolling the hem of her dress vigorously.

143

Ali and father led the half laughing and half crying Samira to continue the introductions.

"We welcome you into the bosom of our ancient house."

Luckily Marwan was by the door and no one saw him as he fell out on his back laughing. Uncle Issam resumed his seat and his cigar.

Once all the introductions were made, we all sat down quietly except for the repressed laughter from Marwan. Selma served the tea and delicacies. Amal started scrubbing the kitchen floor and the stair up to the attic. The house was filled with the slobbering noise of tea drinking, the plonk-plonk-plonk of Amal's bucket going down the stairs, the shoogly sound of her brush-movement, and Aunt Haji's belching.

"Forgive me, I'm an old fff, woman. Cannot control my gizza-ff-s. I am old. I am old."

****

The wedding-day soon arrived. We had the afternoon off school. Selma was particularly bad-tempered that day. Even Marwan did not escape her fury.

The whole thing was to be a simple affair with only ourselves and a few of Ali's friends. Samira's family was not coming from Turkey.

In the afternoon Ali and Samira sat before the Sheikh who asked them if they would have each other. They said yes and signed. Witnesses followed and the two were married. The sheikh soon took his leave and Selma left the room crying. Father congratulated Ali and handed him several envelopes from various absent members of the family. Marwan and I received a large parcel of sugared almonds which we proceeded to barter in the corner.

Later I left the front room with what remained of my sugared almonds. As I entered my bedroom I heard sobbing coming from Selma's room. I went over and peeped through the half opened door and saw Selma in the middle of the room weeping convulsively. Ali stood behind her with his arms round her shoulders whispering something. She pushed him off. As she did so Samira came into my line of vision and took Ali by the hand as if to lead him out. Ali took one of his envelopes out and tried to push it to Selma. She refused. Samira said gently, "Oh do take it love. Do!" Selma refused saying that they needed it more than she did. I went to my room.

Ali and Samira were going to stay in a hotel for a few days before going off to Kuwait where Ali, who had just received his degree, had been offered a job. They left amid a shower of goodbyes and rice.

At dinner that night Selma was very cheerful. Father seemed a little sombre. As the four of us ate, Selma chatted away.

"I wonder where they are staying? I bet it's the St. George."

"Too expensive," said Father.

"Ali bet me that I could never find the place. I could. I have contacts," she added half-jokingly.

"Best to leave them alone. Ali may not like it" father said jokingly.

"Oh! He wouldn't mind. That would teach him not to lay bets with me."

After supper Selma sat in her room using her telephone extension phoning several hotels. Marwan enjoyed the detective game. I wanted to go to my room but she insisted on my staying for the great search. After several calls without success she suddenly shouted, "Of course. How stupid of me. The Plaza. He had a box of matches from there. He must have got it when he registered. Yes! Hey Saif, go and look."

I was reluctant.

"Come on. Don't be such a misery. I can't go. They would think I am being nosy. Come on. You're young. Don't let them see you" she pointed in that coquettish manner of hers that I disliked so much.

I walked to the Plaza Hotel and asked if Mr. and Mrs. Ibrahim were staying there. Yes, but they had just left instructions not to be disturbed.

As I walked out of the hotel I saw Ali and Samira coming in. I hid behind one of the tall pillars outside so that they would not see me. Ali looked very angry as he walked in followed by a frightened-looking Samira. I walked back home.

"Are they staying there? Are they? Are they?" shouted Selma excitedly from her room. I walked into her bedroom. She was reclining on her bed, relaxed. "Come here! Are they staying there?"

"No. No one is there."

"What do you mean 'no one is there'. The hotel isn't empty, is it?"

"No. I meant that they are not staying there."

"Ah! Well! I'm tired of this game. Tired. My legs ache. Marwan! Sit on my bottom, there's a good boy."

I went to my bedroom and shut myself in with a deep feeling of nausea and embarrassment.

7. Children

The move to the International College proved a disastrous failure for Saif but was a great success for Marwan whose academic work improved dramatically. Much to his father's amazement, not to say annoyance, Marwan seemed to do very little work, and, what little he did, he would do to the accompaniment of noisy modern music. His results, however, were excellent.

Saif, on the other hand, seemed to work conventionally, that is, in a quiet room and for long periods of time. Yet his results were appalling. Hussein tried all in his power to help the lad, particularly in mathematics. It became accepted that Saif would present his daily work to his sister who took enormous trouble to help him and who was utterly bewildered by his apparent stupidity. It also became a habit for the boy to fail in many subjects which, consequently, he had to study at a summer school. Such subjects excluded languages in which he performed extremely well. In this, his sister encouraged him in her usual abrupt way.

Hussein appointed Saif's music teacher to give the boy private lessons. Saif appeared reluctant to go – almost wilfully preferring to remain ignorant. Hussein was not going to stand any of it. He used to drive Saif to the music teacher's house and deliver him in person and pick him up an hour of so later. The boy was always morose and sat in the car softly repeating nursery rhymes to familiar tunes that Hussein could not quite place. It was becoming clear that the boy was going to be a handful in terms of his education.

Selma was beginning to realise how sensitive the growing boy was and became kind and careful in handling him. The relationship between the two should have improved. It did, but only a little. Saif saw his sister as being rather superficial, something that was apparent to everyone: a growing girl whose mannerisms and fussy behaviour indicated snobbishness.

With the temperament typical of a selfish artist he was growing into an intolerant youth who was unwilling to see beyond the roles people felt necessary to adopt in society. Instead of seeing such roles for the defence that they were, he grew to hate them for hypocrisy and unnecessary acting. Yet when his sister was herself, kind, generous, and affectionate, he grew embarrassed by what he saw as vulgar emotionalism. Thus Selma could never do anything right.

In his inability to understand the society around him, and where he did understand, in his inability to tolerate it, Saif became bitter and hateful. Silent and repressed, he transferred this bitterness to his sister who symbolised for him his very deep sense of imprisonment. His only escape was fiction. His mind became blurred as he clumsily and awkwardly weaved fiction into reality. Sitting alone in his room, reading or attempting to write, he neglected his school work completely. Where the adults assumed he was working hard on his mathematics or general science, he was avidly reading.

As soon as he had entered his new school he enrolled in the British Council where he used to go every evening to read. This move was encouraged by his father who assumed him to be working hard in the library. There he read various works by Lawrence, Joyce, and other modern authors that his father disapproved of. Once he was caught reading *Lady Chatterley's Lover* by Marwan who delighted in threatening to tell their father. Saif angrily replied that he himself would tell him. That evening, much to Marwan's discomfort, Saif declared suddenly and unexpectedly over dinner, "Father, I'm reading *Lady Chatterley's Lover*, an excellent book but one which is considered obscene by some."

Marwan reddened and became very busy with the contents of his plate.

"I have not read the work myself," replied Hussein after a short silence. "I understand that it has some very good points." Another silence followed. "Incidentally, you need not tell me that you are reading such and such a book in that defiant tone. You read what you like. I cannot stop you."

Inspired by this statement, Saif took the first opportunity to visit the Ouza'i market-place to buy a real pornographic work, one which would have made Lady Chatterley blush. He left it lying around as a test-case. When it disappeared he eventually found it in his father's room. Nothing was said about the matter. From then onwards Saif felt free to read whatever he wanted at home. This did not stop Hussein from giving his views on such modernistic filth as *Ulysses* and Sigmund Freud's works. Nevertheless, he felt it his duty to allow his children to choose whatever books they wanted to read. At the same time he encouraged them to read such 'giants' - as he called them - as Dickens, Churchill, Taha Hussein, and Shakespeare. A complete, leather-bound Dickens stood in his own library, a grand name for a glass-fronted bookcase containing some two hundred works, mainly on agricultural and farming matters.

Marwan became a member of the American counterpart of The British Council. This created an endless source of competitive friction between the two boys. The American Cultural Centre, or 'Center' as Marwan insisted it should be spelt, gave free membership. It had a glossy newness to everything it offered. Saif felt this to be superficial. Marwan saw the British Council as stodgy, unfriendly, and snobbish. Saif loved that musty smell of books, the old; generally sick-green colours of its walls, the dignity of its ancient years, and the depth of its learned atmosphere. The British Council, he felt, had no need to peddle itself to people. It had no need to advertise its free films and conferences. It did not require lots of glossy pictures in its magazines; that sort of thing was for the illiterate. One line from Shakespeare would submerge the entire American centre and turn it into a children's library! Marwan laughed at Saif's Anglophilic anger and dismissed him with a line or two from e.e. cummings. Saif despised the poet for not using capital letters.

"Ma Gud," Marwan would shout with an exaggerated American accent. "Little fella you're soooo stodgy. Yes sir, you is jest that." This would invariably be followed by a loud guffaw meant to imitate the English laugh. Marwan would then stroke an imaginary enormous moustache. "Ha ha, rather jolly that, what? Old chap? Ha ha. I say, I say."

Hussein encouraged both children in their separate ways, but reminded them of their duty to retain their Arab identity by working hard on their Arabic. Both children found Classical Arabic extremely arduous and slipped into English when writing letters or notes.

Such practice was encouraged by the fashion at the time. The Lebanese generally felt an innate embarrassment at recognising their mother tongue as Arabic, and tended to speak in French or English as an indication of their social standing. Being a nation of businessmen they lacked the true quality of patriotism. First and foremost they owed allegiance to themselves. Secondly, to some political party or other. Thirdly, they identified with the country whose language and institutions mostly affected their lives: France. And of course, being essentially mercantile they had a great admiration for all things American. They united in one thing, and that was their ability to laugh at themselves in an attempt to jolly things along as a small and deeply divided nation. They also had a deep love for their landscape though even then, a visitor always felt that this love stemmed from the tourist revenue that this magnificence attracted. This was unfair for, as both Saif and Marwan were beginning to realise, the real Lebanese, the non-cosmopolitan, had a deep attachment to the land that he tilled, the water that he used to feed his produce, and the sun that shone relentlessly on his labours.

Effectively, the Ibrahim family had necessarily become part of the country they lived in. Hussein loved its rich and beautiful land. Selma loved its seemingly rich and exclusive *haute société*. Ali integrated with its energy and will to survive. Marwan, in his intelligent and perceptive way, laughed at its triumphs and tragedies. Saif became its exile: sensitive to, and conscious of, its deep-rooted faults; alienated by the real and the imaginary alike.

****

News had been filtering in from Kuwait about difficulties in Ali's marriage. Apparently Ali had started drinking heavily and, although earning much more than his father, money seemed to disappear as quickly as it was earned. Rumour also had it that Ali had taken to gambling and womanising. Such reports were a constant source of worry to Hussein. Added to this was the lack of the news that everyone was expecting.

Aunt Haji repeatedly asked for news of Samira. "Is she well, brother? Any indication of a slight illness? A loss of appetite, perhaps? A little harmless morning sickness? Normal in such cases, brother, normal."

But alas no such news arrived, which increased Haji's impatience.

"Brother, I am old. You are an agricultural architect or is it engineer? If you had a tree that does not bear fruit, what would you do? Answer me not for even in my ignorance I know. Had I not a garden in Palestine? Mint, parsley, and herbs? You would cut its head off and plant a new one."

Saif felt disgusted at what his aunt was saying. He ventured to suggest that it may not be Samira's fault.

"How now, nephew? How now?" screeched Haji.

And even if it were her fault, he agreed, they loved each other.

"LOVE! LOVE! What pray is that? Inform me nephew. You go

to school."

He could not inform her.

"Love! How now? LOVE!" screamed Haji. "Do you see this old shoe I wear. Covered in holes and dirt. I am old. I have no money for fancy hoity-toity shoes. Do you see it?"

He saw it.

"But do you *see* it?"

He *saw* it.

"I would use it to stamp on your LOVE. Stamp! Stamp! Stamp! Love, indeed! In my days we had children!" She then proceeded to recite sections from *The Holy Qur'an* concerning divorce.

"Now nephew, you're going to Palestine, I see."

"Yes aunt."

"You'll drive through rebel country."

"Syria? Yes."

"When?"

"In a week's time when school has finished."

"Ooooooh! The U.A.R. is dead. Nasser, you've been too soft! Woe! Woe! My land, Palestine! My country, I cry for you. I cry for my home. I cry for my Palestine. Solid. Solid, it was not hoity-toity like this terrible place."

Although Saif could see the comical side of his aunt's mannerisms, he felt deeply sorry for her. Her hurt was deep and lasting but he could not fully empathise. Palestine to him was an incessant slogan and a host of Mr. Yafis beating him around the head with a bell.

Later on, he asked his father if he agreed with Haji's pronouncements concerning love.

"Yes." The reply shocked him. It sounded bitter and distant. Had his father had a disappointment sometime in his past? Did he really know - really know - what Love was? Saif thought of his mother. He must do. He must do.

"This love business, son, is a modern invention. Love? To love a woman may be delightful for a week or two but you have to eat, you have to work, you have to raise children, you have to live. Love is all very well in a poem but better to throw it out of the window."

Hussein made a backward motion with his hand that dismissed the whole subject.

"But you loved mama?" asked Saif with fear in his heart as he was entering an area that was taboo in the Ibrahim family.

"Of course I did!" Hussein answered viciously and impatiently. "That's different. She was an angel."

****

That summer of 1962 Saif did not have to attend summer-school. His English teacher, who had taken a particular interest in him since she read some of his short stories, interceded on his behalf with the teacher of mathematics. He, in turn, gave Saif a grade D in order to allow him to be promoted without having to attend summer school.

The school itself was a very good one, boasting the most modern methods of education. What those entailed was never absolutely clear to Saif. In his eyes, the children lacked discipline and the teachers lacked the ability to enforce it. He despised the presence of various American Peace Corps teachers whom he felt cared little or nothing about their pupils. He was embarrassed by the lack of uniforms and infuriated by having to sing a US style Alma Mater directed by a sonorous-voiced American. It was the Americanism of the whole place that repulsed him though he was not of an age to recognise this fact. He hated the school and that was that. Unlike his old school it lacked substance or depth. It felt transitory rather like a waiting-room at a railway station. One was always waiting for the train to arrive in order to leave the detested, dusty and dirty waiting-room.

Apart from a succession of English Language teachers who influenced the boy a great deal, the rest of the school passed by him deliberately unnoticed. He developed the ability to see nothing that he did not want to see, to feel nothing that he did not want to feel. He lived in his own little world and occasionally got wrenched out of it to experience what he did not want and rush back in again. But he was not destined to be left alone. He hated the school and, likewise, many of the school teachers disliked him for his seeming arrogance and adopted superiority.

At the end of his third year he was called up before his science teacher, a very tall Peace Corps American with crew-cut blond hair and an attractive smile called Mr. Dewey. He was relieved to hear that his overall average was a C plus which meant no summer-school. His relief was not destined to last.

"I don't like you, boy."

"Why, sir?

151

"I just don't!"

"Sorry, sir."

"I'm going to make that a C minus because of your attitude to work."

"But, sir, it is a C plus by right."

"Right, boy? What right?"

"You cannot change it."

"I'm not going to, boy. It's a D plus and it stays a D plus."

"Please. It's not fair."

"Fair, boy? D minus is fair enough for the work you do."

"But..."

"What? Are you going to beg, boy?"

"No. Certainly not. Never!"

"Good. You may be quiet, but you certainly have guts. You shouldn't feel too badly about your final result of E, should you, nigger boy?"

Saif had to take a summer-school in general sciences before being promoted.

****

But in the previous summer, when Saif was relieved of having to attend the habitual and much detested summer school, he went to Jordan with his father. From Jordan they crossed to Palestine and went to Nablus and Jerusalem. Saif's imagination was fired by the magnificent scenery on the journey there. Mountain ranges capped with a white crown were followed by fertile and colourful plains and then more mountains. In such scenery, and all through the Syrian-Jordanian desert, he fancied that he saw a host of hidden armies, caravans, and endless merriment. He imagined armies, refugees, traders, and travellers trudging the endless road to Damascus. Damascus! Damask silk and damask roses. Damascus. The very name was fraught with the whole magic of a great history, a great identity. Jerusalem: warm, heartfelt, and ancient. Saif turned a blind eye to the hustle and bustle of both noisy cities. He saw in them only what he wanted to see.

His most enjoyable time was spent in the refugee camp outside Nablus where they had gone to collect Amal after she had spent her annual holiday with her relations. There, for the first time, in a two-roomed hovel, he saw the real life of Palestinian refugees: honest, brave, suffering in silence, more sinned against than sinning. Like Amal, they lived from day to day, working, hoping and stoic. They looked to Nasser for their salvation and they trusted in Allah. They spoke of the old days in Palestine like a man speaks of his childhood; sentimentally embarrassed but glowing with the warmth of the child. Saif wondered why they were refugees in their own land. He asked Amal who told him that they expected to return to the other side soon and that was why they had accepted this temporary accommodation.

Saif spent two days with his new friends but felt confused. He liked their simplicity of life, their accommodation with the reality of the situation, and their open honesty. Yet he was saddened and repulsed by the squalor of their schools, the scantiness of their livelihood, and the utter indifference of outsiders to their existence. True to his secretive self, he did not ask an explanation from his elders. He pushed all confusions to the background and left them there.

Amal introduced him to a host of family members. But her favourite was her niece known as little Mary. She took Saif around the camp and out into the wilds where they explored aimlessly. Amal made a big fuss of both of them and told them that she would work on ensuring that they got married when they were older. When it was time to leave, she made them kiss good bye and laughed a lot at their innocent embarrassment. She came forward and, pushing Mary into Saif's arms, she told him to kiss her properly as a groom should his bride. He blushed and pecked her on the cheek as Amal roared with laughter at the two little ones. For the first time in his life, Saif saw a real broad smile appear on his father's face as the smile lit up his eyes and appeared sincere.

On his return home he wrote a short story, or rather a sketch, describing his experiences at the camp and his childish feelings for Mary. It was not much in itself, but it captured the essence of his people's position. In a simple style, he was able to portray the exiled, living in hope, fear, dejection, and somehow, happiness. Fearful of discovery, he secretly posted the story to a magazine in England. Some weeks later he received the manuscript back with a very kind personal letter encouraging him to work on maturing his style and explaining that this particular short story, though good, would not suit the magazine's readership. Suggested addresses were appended.

He showed the reply to Selma and Marwan. Marwan laughed but

was told to shut up by Selma. She asked to read the work. Saif looked embarrassed. She did not insist but she urged him to keep trying. Although he resented her manner of implying that he was somewhat of a dilettante, he was grateful for her encouragement. In his own way he was beginning to find some possible hidden love for the sister whom he disliked so much.

With Marwan's laughter cackling in his ears, he pushed his new short story in a drawer with all the others. He would try to publish only when he was ready, which was not now. The letter said as much.

****

After Saif returned to school in October, his studies went from bad to worse. Having become hopelessly entangled in mathematical work of any kind, he was relegated to a back seat where he secretly read poetry. As for sticking an H with an O and producing H_2O, that was as much beyond him as walking on water! And chemical Elements might well have been visitors from outer space! But his lack of progress was getting serious and Hussein had been contacted.

The headmaster, a short portly man with a strong loud whistling sibilance in his speech, told Hussein that his son may be reading *War and Peace* and *The Idiot,* but his performance in other subjects made the latter book seem but an autobiography of the child. Saif was furious at the analogy, not so much because he did not consider himself an idiot, but rather for the crass blasphemy that his headmaster had shown to literature in making such a comparison. He called him an ass and was instantly suspended for three days during which he read *The Magic Mountain.* Impressed, he read *Buddenbrooks* which he found somewhat slow but was delighted in how it mirrored his own family. Tony was Selma, Ida his aunt Yasmine, Consul Buddenbrook his father - what delight! They were all obnoxious wherever they may be, in Germany or in Lebanon! But Saif recognised the seriousness of his position and knew he had to try harder. He accepted the simple fact that to be without schooling meant to have no future, certainly not in writing. So he worked hard and long and for the first time at his new school his results improved; but many teachers continued to dislike him. His music teacher had tired of him and was soon having a new favourite musical prodigy visiting him regularly.

"And how is our poet today?" asked the mathematics teacher. A titter went round the class. Muhammad looked up at his friend in sympathy. "Can he solve this equation? No he cannot. Why cannot he solve this equation? Because he is an ass. Why is he an ass? Because he nods like one. Blackboard!"

Saif glanced at the open book before him and walked up to the blackboard. He quickly solved the problem but explain it, he could not.

"So. An ass! The son of an ass is usually also an ass! Been cheating. Let us see. Yes, there it is boys, in his book. Well, my dear Saif, how do you spell your name? A, double S? Thank you. Solve this one."

Saif tried hard and did it the long way.

"Ah! So you ask this ass where Damascus is and he goes West all around the world before he finds it! An ass!"

Similar incidents took place daily. Saif swallowed his annoyance and kept trying. With encouragement from his English teacher and from Muhammad, he managed to get through at the end of the year and was promoted to the fourth year conditional upon a repeat general science test in September, which he passed.

"You must work hard," Muhammad said to him one day. "There is no chance of doing anything without the Baccalaureate. I know your aspirations to become an author. And," he added with a look of intense embarrassment, "I believe that you'll succeed. In the name of Allah the Merciful and the Compassionate I know that you have something. I envy you."

Little did he know that Saif envied him: his steady progress, happy family life, the faith that his father showed in him, and his simple uncomplicated view of a future filled with the delights of making and serving delicious cakes whilst designing flying boats in his spare time.

****

During that year Saif's uncle and special friend fell seriously ill. It was apparent to everyone that Uncle Nassim was dying. His headaches became constant and deeply painful. He could only find relief by lying down. Saif visited him regularly at the American University Hospital, while he still retained his faculties. The whole situation was so sudden it seemed unbelievable. The uncle remained jovial and chatted with Saif. When Saif, somewhat selfishly, complained of his deep feelings of dissatisfaction, his uncle did not rebuke him. Calling him L.A., he seriously explained to him the essence of the artistic temperament.

"If you were satisfied and felt at home everywhere, why, you too would be a dolt like everybody else. Listen, L.A., you must work hard, you must read hard, you must become the unseen conscience of your people."

"But who are my people? I feel alien wherever I am. I don't feel Lebanese. I don't feel Palestinian, though they are the only people that make me feel something, though what; I don't know."

"Do you remember your short story, 'Refugees'?"

"Yes."

"As you said there, they make you feel the joy of life. That is enough. Life and the landscape. You will understand more fully later. Now listen to me. You are not alone in the world. You may sometimes wish that you were but you are not, NOT, alone. I'm not only talking about your family or your school-friends. I am talking about everyone before you and after you. You will go on to the end of the world and beyond. Collected in you is every scrap of anything from the past and from the future. Guard it. A father and mother before you, two fathers and two mothers before them, then eight, then sixteen. You are the eternal cell every time you're born: thirty-two, sixty-four. Leave me, now. I'm tired."

A few days later would be his last visit to uncle Nassim. Saif emerged from school at four o'clock and walked down the straight road towards the hospital, following the blackened university wall which entered into Bliss Street.

Bliss Street! There, in the tumult and noise of a closely-built city, was the university on one side and innumerable shops, cafés and cinemas on the other. There stood the university walls, impassive, impressive and secretive. Before them, men noisily plied their trade selling whatever could be sold and whatever would be bought. Students crouched by the vendors' illegal stalls and examined their wares while talking, laughing, and smoking. In front of the cinema, stood groups of people quietly smoking during the interval, knowing they were indeed in Beirut and not in some exotic world they had been staring at through celluloid eyes. Cafés burst with the noise and argument of students bent on changing their parent's lives. Their parents, huddled in red trams, snaked their way home with that desperate look that sought to understand the child and failed to accept the burning tongues of change. Taxis hooted their prospective passengers. Shoe-shine boys spat and polished and polished and spat. Like venomous snakes, their tongues hissed and their brushes rattled. Here and there a beggar sat leaning against the wall: tired, desperate and cold. A child, bandaged dirtily, lay on the lap of a begging woman. Inducted from birth, the child had grown to believe himself to be really injured. Injured from birth by poverty, the mother had grown to believe herself really sinning. And of the multitude walking noisily back and forth, not one eye - not one - fell on the child and its mother with any measure of compassion. A policeman, well-rounded and corpulent, strutted his daily act of duty like a cockerel upon a dung-heap. People: Lebanese, French, British, American, Armenian, and stateless talked at each other in a clattering and devilish cackle, bleating the mysterious tongues of Babel.

The sidewalk on which Saif went was empty. There stood the American University wall, impervious, high, and mocking. Saif arrived in the hospital with his mind full of his walk down Bliss Street but all images and thoughts disappeared when his nostrils were greeted by the nauseating smell of sterility. He walked down the long corridor and into his uncle's room. It was almost dark in there. Alert and somewhat frightened, Saif took in the whole room within the first few seconds of entering it.

It was a rectangular room with two windows at its long end. The blinds were drawn and shuttered. On the right of each blind dangled a thin rope doubled up on itself. Although there was not the slightest breeze in the air outside, the strings moved methodically from side to side. Near the door stood a deep basin looking like a man's face staring up: the taps were the eyes and through the wide open mouth Saif saw the tonsils in the plug-hole. The overflow was a wide flattened nose. Beside the basin, an arm went into the room with a towel covering it, reminding Saif of a busy waiter making his way amongst tables. Two chairs stood facing the bed as if ready to start a heated discussion on their respective uses. The bed, metallic and cold, stood white, its burden giving the impression of a series of snow-capped mountains. The room felt cold and unfriendly.

"Uncle!" whispered Saif as he approached the bed. No reply came. He could hear the heavy and loud breathing of the patient. He leant over and looked at his uncle's face which was turned towards Saif. Wide open, the eyes seemed to stare far away, glassy, uncomprehending, and silent. The mouth was open a little as the rapid breath moved in and out.

"Uncle Nassim?" Saif spoke quietly, afraid to wake his uncle. No reply came. The eyes stared on. Saif sat on one of the chairs and waited. Now and then he got up to look again but the eyes remained motionless and distant. Once, he fancied that the corner of the mouth twitched. He jumped up shouting, "Yes? Yes uncle?"

A nurse came into the room and put the light on.

"You must go now," she said efficiently. "You can wait outside if you want."

Saif did not reply. With the light on he saw his uncle's face properly. It had not changed. But it seemed naked, a stranger.

"Are you his son?" asked the nurse kindly. Saif seemed not to be listening.

"Yes ... No ..." he faltered.

The nurse commenced her work.

"Come. You wait outside. I won't be long."

Saif stood up and stared at the patient before him. That was not his uncle, so undignified, so ... Saif walked out of the room, looking back once. The nurse was gently lifting the patient forward and saying something to him. His shoulder twitched several times then he fell back still staring, rigid and misty. Saif could still hear him breathing hard as he walked away from the room.

He took a different exit as he knew that other members of the family would be arriving soon. As he emerged on Bliss Street he did not notice the crowds nor hear the noise.

'Collected in you is every scrap of anything from the past and from the future. Guard it. Guard it. A father and mother before you, two fathers and two mothers before them, eight before, sixteen. You are the eternal cell. The eternal cell!'

"*Ils vous en fichent la paix*, the English."

"Tell you what L.A., tell you what ..."

Saif walked along Bliss Street thinking and frightened.

"Shoes polished! Half price for gents, full price for the police. Shoes young man? Them shoes reflect your whole personality."

Saif ignored the appeal and walked on.

"The eternal cell."

That was not uncle but a statue, a dummy!

8. First Loves

Saif was woken by the sounds of a sandstorm. He got out of bed and roamed all over a vast empty desert of red sand - blood red. He felt as if he was walking on red hair. He was not so much frightened as lonely. It was the end of the world. He returned towards a solitary cottage that stood as a dot on the red horizon. Red sand blew against a gigantic red sunset, a sunset that covered the entire horizon with slowly moving and shifting redness.

He walked into the cottage and started to ascend the stairs but fell and lay there silently screaming, feeling the blood trickle onto his white shirt. Several teachers came in. Each walked right through him as he tried to touch them. "You're not coming out," said one of them and closed the glossy red door.

Saif wanted to stay in the sand, but only if he could have the cottage to live in with his wife. But which wife? He looked at a woman silhouetted against the sunset. She had a nose-bleed. All around her hovered little red glow-worms. He screamed again.

Saif woke up. He had dozed off sitting in the front-room. The blinding rays of the sun swept in through the large veranda doors. Drenched in sweat, he moved awkwardly on his seat. He tried to understand his dream as he felt its echoes slip away from him.

It was the height of the summer holidays. Hussein had decided that his children were now old enough to be left alone. He had therefore gone to Austria for a rest and a recommended treatment for his back which had never recovered from the bomb incident. Austria was said to have many excellent natural thermal baths for people with his complaint, though the exact nature of his complaint was never made really clear.

Marwan spent his days on the beach and his evenings at lively parties given by various friends. Selma spent the entire summer with the Jbeilis prior to her final year at university. Now and then she paid a flying visit to make sure that the boys were looking after themselves. At such times Saif climbed out of the window, down a drainpipe and waited for her to leave.

Poor Selma had not intentionally set out to annoy the growing boy. On the contrary, she had her moments of understanding; particularly of his adolescent sensitivity and of his aspirations to write. But she had her own life to live. Her ambitions and passions had to be fulfilled despite the necessity of mothering the two motherless boys. The truth of the matter was that Saif and his sister were very much alike. Beneath both outward appearances lay two lonely and seemingly different people: secretly hiding their feelings from all but themselves. Both sensitive and lonely, each built up a defensive cocoon. After a while, each thought of the other in the role they showed.

They had chosen different routes to fulfill their similar needs. Selma pursued social position ruthlessly, adopting various false outward gestures and manner of speaking but to Saif, she became aggressive and unfeeling.

Saif withdrew more and more into himself, seemingly secretive, intolerant and self engrossed. Saif's excuse may have been his youthful frustration, Selma's her early burden of responsibility.

With age on her side, Selma continued to sympathise with and tolerate her younger brother's behaviour. She released her feelings by discussing his secretive and sensitive character with others. Saif, on the other hand, bottled up his feelings of annoyance at what he saw to be interference from his insincere sister. Minor irritations and passing confrontations were secreted away into his hoard of passions and built up into intense hatred that fed on his very soul. In his prejudiced eyes his sister was no more than a snob who knew the price of everything and the value of nothing. To aggravate what might otherwise have been a normal and temporary brotherly dislike, Selma adopted the position of a mother, protecting her two brothers. Marwan responded well. With Saif the relationship was a disaster. He dreaded her very presence in the house.

In moments of truth Selma would tell Saif that she loved him but her declarations intensely embarrassed him, serving only to increase his feelings of hatred for what he saw as her insincerity and flagrant cheapness of character.

Such a view was bound to lead to a confrontation within the family. One afternoon Hussein called his youngest son into his bedroom. Saif entered and sat on the old bed that he had occupied during his illness. Hussein turned the key in the door and sat facing his son with that pained look on his face which sought to understand the intransigence of adolescent prejudice.

"Son, a man has little choice in the family into which he is born. To guard against this lack of choice, Nature has provided him with a fund of natural love to bestow upon that family. You see, when a man finds a wife then he is able to cultivate his love for her. He has time to do so. He also has the maturity. Wouldn't you agree? Of course, you need to think about it, don't you? Yes. Well, a child has a natural affection for the rest of his family. He has to, because he lacks the maturity to cultivate affection. When that child becomes older, he automatically overlooks any shortcomings his family might have. Indeed, he never sees these. Now, you would agree that a child had natural love for its family wouldn't you? Speak now. Let us discuss this freely."

"No."

"No what? No you do not wish to discuss this matter, or, no, a child has no natural love for his family?"

"It has a natural dependence upon its family."

"Dependence? Surely not, love?"

"Dependence."

"Don't be so idiotic. You don't understand as yet. You are too young."

"I'm glad we've discussed this freely, father."

"Don't be RUDE!"

Saif got off the bed and walked over to the window as if to keep a safe distance between himself and his angry father.

"Now, see, let me give you an example. Answer me this: do you love Marwan?"

"Yes."

"I don't see why you should be so embarrassed about such natural feelings. Let me see now. Ah, yes. Take this as an example: do you love your sister?"

"No."

"Now listen, my boy! You are intolerable and rude. What do you mean by this insult to your family? Hey?"

"I answer truthfully, father."

"Truthfully! Ha! The truth lies in the palm of my hand here. I could get the truth into you easily enough. No! Silence! Now, you listen to me and listen well. I will give you time to think this whole thing over. I shall withhold your pocket-money every Saturday until you think further. What? What are you laughing at? You laugh? You impudent rude fellow! Get out. Out! Look at you, skulking down a drain-pipe like a thief. Out!"

The matter was never raised again. Saif received his pocket-money as usual on Saturday.

****

The weather was stifling. Saif shook himself out of his stupor and went into the kitchen where Amal sat smoking and listening to the radio.

"Bored? Why bored? Find a girl. A healthy boy like you! What about that Frenchy upstairs, bazookas fit to burst in your face. Aye me, I'm ugly and mad and no man to top me, hey my boy. Go. Go find the Frenchy. Better than that English boy who is so good at music. Go. Go. Find the Frenchy and show her what you've got."

"No thank you."

"Why? Why, you so young and she so big, hey? Ha, you dirty little man, you're good enough aren't you? I've seen you in the bath."

Saif laughed. "Shshsh. Honestly, Amal!"

"Oh! Prudish aren't we and what's wrong with a bit of fun? She's French not an Arab. They're always on heat, those strange ones. All of them are sluts. Yours for the having." She laughed, loud and cackling. "I'm going out soon. Don't forget to leave me the key on the sideboard if you decide to get out of this furnace."

Amal always left the key inside the apartment when she went out just in case someone returned before her and wanted to get in.

Saif laughed, left the kitchen and went into the bathroom where he took a cold shower. The water was almost warm as it flowed through the sun-soaked pipes. He felt a little faint as he stood passively under the water, its droplets like hundreds of sharp pins. Wrapping a towel around himself, he decided to spend the afternoon reading a newly acquired translation of *War and Peace*. He sat on the edge of his bed unwilling to get dressed and feeling intensely embarrassed. He started to read and, expecting something complex and difficult, was immediately mesmerised by the simplicity of the work. The experience was similar to the time that he was first able to read and understand his mother's copy of *King Lear*. So simple and unpretentious; the simple genius. This amused him. He decided that 'simplistic' would be better. Only Tolstoy could write such a novel. Maybe Amal could too. She understood more about other people's inner secrets than anyone else in his so-called educated family.

He read on for a very long time, through most of the night.

Sometime during the night he was aware of Amal and Marwan returning. When he woke up in the morning he still had the damp towel around his waist. He showered again and returned to *War and Peace*. He was happy. His whole being felt content as he read through the day. Marwan and Amal left again. By mid-afternoon he had finished the first volume. He showered again and moved to the front-room with the second volume.

At four he stopped to have something to eat. The bell rang. He opened the door expecting Amal.

"Hello Saif." Andrew, a friend of Marwan's from the British Community School, stood on the mat. Andrew was regarded as a musical genius and had been made much of by everyone for his talents.

"Come in." Saif motioned him in. He held the towel round his waist. His body glistened with the heat in the air.

"Sorry I could not come yesterday."

"That's all right."

"What've you been doing? Reading?"

"Yes."

"What?"

"*War and Peace.*"

"God! You're a glutton for punishment."

The two boys stood facing each other in the hallway.

"Come into the sitting-room."

"Okay."

Andrew was a year older than Saif. He had long silky auburn hair and two large cheeky eyes. Taller than Saif, he stood with his head high and his spirit seemingly aloof. His mouth was set firmly in a beardless face which broke now and then into a cheeky smile. He came closer to Saif and took his hand.

"Are you angry?" asked Andrew.

"No."

"What's the matter?"

"Nothing."

The two stood facing each other for a little while. The sun's rays curved around Saif's body making him look a like a ghost. Andrew came even closer.

"Take that towel off!"

"No. We shouldn't."

"What is wrong?"

"Us. What we've been doing."

"Why?"

"It's wrong. It's gone beyond being just a phase. I can't explain it. We must stop. It's enough. I'm sorry."

Andrew looked at Saif closely. He took Saif's chin and gently raised his face.

"You want me?"

"No. No more."

"You want me. Do you remember that first time in the music room. And that time behind the stage at morning assembly."

"I was frightened. I didn't understand what was happening. No more. Please."

"You're just like a girl. Soft silky hair. Soft skin. You're as gentle as a girl. Do you know, your nanny should get a medal! That scar suits you. Gives you depth. Yes. Gentle. Gentle and soft. You need a man."

"No. Not anymore. I was wrong."

'Eh bien, mon prince, so Genoa and Lucca are now no more than private estates of the Bonaparte family.'

Natasha was so innocent, so pure. This was wrong, so very wrong.

Later that night Saif was disturbed by the noise of someone weeping in the next room. He sat up in bed and switched on the light. His copy of *War and Peace* was open at the title page. He read the inscription: "You were right. I am sorry. I do not even know how this happened. Music was my life. What has he done to us? Love, Andrew." The crying from the next room increased. He got up, put a pair of trousers on, and opened the door. In the corridor he met Selma carrying a bowl of water. They exchanged angry looks. Marwan emerged from his room. He was crying. When he saw Saif he laughed and cried. His mouth was full of blood.

"He's drunk," said Selma with disgust. "He jumped into an empty swimming-pool."

"Why?"

"It wash for a bet." Marwan laughed through his tears.

"Knocked his front teeth out." Selma spoke abruptly and angrily. "What's that smell? What is it?"

"Nothing," replied Saif as the two helped Marwan into bed.

In the faint light of the reading lamp, the two figures looked black as they bent over the white bed sheets. The atmosphere outside was dark hot, full of the hot air of a summer night.

"It wash for a bet, you shee. I didn't know there wash no water."

****

It was Hussein's first visit to Europe since his wife's death, his first visit on his own since his student days in France. Short holidays spent in France during the long summer days away from Montpellier crowded his head. He had determined for a long time to go to Montpellier before returning to Beirut.

But somehow, he could not get himself to go to France. It held too many memories for him that were both sad and happy, memories of surviving in a dark and icy Europe away from home. He had to work extremely hard to learn French, a language he did not speak. He remembered trying to make ends meet; getting up very early, breaking the top layer of ice in the bowl to wash his face; sitting down alone to memorise the endless lists of new French words. He thought of the lonely walking tours through Germany, France, Austria, Italy, and Switzerland.

The whole fortnight of thermal baths in Austria had allowed him the time to look back over his life, particularly as a student in France.

He was amused to remember leaving his landlady's house after being served the delicacy of jugged hare. Even now, some forty years later, his nostrils were filled with the nauseating smell of the 'rotting' meat. It was with a tinge of embarrassment that he recalled the injustice he had done Mme Bouvier in leaving her house when her intention was only to please him. His sense of the slight increased as he thought of her maternal goodness in looking after him during an illness which had caused him to soil himself. She had kept the whole thing a secret from the other tenants and thus avoided him great embarrassment.

The annual college dance! How vividly he remembered that great event. It was there that he had met Hélène: so delicate, quiet, and beautiful. It was there that his estrangement and loneliness temporarily ended. It almost brought bitter tears to his eyes to remember her parents' contemptuous treatment of his proposal of marriage. They were Catholics. In his youthful idealism he had respected their wishes and put an end to his relationship with their daughter. But to be called *"un sale musulman"* was the thing he could never bring himself to

165

forgive. His intense hatred of the Catholic Church dated from that one and only personal experience of it.

In order to forget this affair he had gone on a summer walking tour of Switzerland and Germany. He still felt a little embarrassed by his admiration for the emerging Nazi party. He admired the German quality of discipline and, in his limited experience, that supreme quality of Germanic honesty. His whole vision of Europe was contained and controlled by his loneliness. He well remembered the German landlady who had refused his offer of a Guinea after a month's residence because that Guinea was worth then a hundred times more Deutchmarks than it was at the beginning of his tenancy. She took exactly what she had agreed upon on his arrival. If inflation had made it worthless, she had explained, then that was not his fault. When he had insisted that he had put the Guinea aside for the rent anyhow, she had proudly replied "*Ich bin eine Deutsche!*"

He delighted in using the little German that he knew. During his stay in Austria, he used every opportunity of speaking German, which pleased his hosts. After every meal, a one sided conversation regularly took place as he shouted across to the waitress, with a half-eaten apple in his hand, "*Ich esse einen Apfel Er ist rot und schmeekt sehr gut.*" Invariably, the waitress always replied quietly, "*Gut! Danke schon Herr Abraham,*"

"*Nein! Nein! Herr Ibrahim!*"

Now, during his two week stay he had decided not to visit other European countries. Being in Austria he could enjoy again those memories of his youth which pleased him. France was still full of a distant numbness and gentle regret because of Hélène. Memories of Germany embarrassed him. Austria, however, seemed to occupy a special place in his memories. Its people spoke German without being German. They were delightfully cultured and gentle without being French, they were supremely civilised and organised without being Swiss. In short, the Austrians' presence around him seemed only to bring back happy memories without pain or regret.

Hussein was fascinated that such regret and pain could be felt after so many years. The greatest regret was felt when he thought of Switzerland. During his tour, after the disastrous and crushing affair with Hélène, he had met through a mutual friend an intelligent, independent, and tough Biology student named Anne Marie. They had become close friends overnight. Liberated and self-willed, Anne Marie accepted a teaching post in Lebanon despite her family's misgivings. With that typical Swiss pioneering spirit she had dauntlessly made her way to Lebanon after her graduation to serve a two-year contract within a Protestant school in Beirut.

By that time Hussein had also graduated and had started working for the ICI. He invited Anne Marie to spend a month with his family in Palestine. Against all traditional customs of both Swiss and Arabs she accepted the invitation eagerly and the two spent the entire month touring the area. Anne Marie voraciously devoured scenery, customs, traditions, and local history. Their friendship was entirely on a Platonic level. Memories of Hélène were still too ripe within Hussein to allow for any finer feelings than those of formal friendship to emerge. Anne Marie was an intelligent and alert companion. Her beauty was not entirely unseen by Hussein. Delicate of frame, her mildly Roman nose and large eyes contrasted strongly with her 'manly' intelligence and self-will. Hussein was somewhat awed by her qualities. He saw in her a strong companion on a long and tiring tour. Anne Marie thought him handsome and delighted in his Arab chauvinism both nationally and as a man. However, she thoroughly disliked his ridiculous toothbrush moustache.

When the day for her departure arrived Hussein found himself in turmoil. He did not feel a passionate love for her as he had felt for Hélène. Such feelings had ceased to be allowed to make themselves known to him. Love as such seemed fortuitous pain. Anne Marie was a fit companion, a solid partner, an equal thinker, in short, the perfect wife. Apparently Anne Marie did not feel the same way for upon completion of her contract she returned to Switzerland. A few years later all correspondence between the two stopped.

He wondered where Anne Marie was now. He decided that she was most probably dead or married. It would be interesting to meet her if he only knew where she was. His memories of her were not painful. However, a visit to Switzerland was not possible. In a day or two he had business meetings in London.

He decided to get his bags ready for the departure. Meticulously he checked everything: a valid visa for England; travellers' cheques were in order. He slipped his passport and cheques into a large envelope that the ICI had previously sent to him to Beirut from their offices in London. He took it downstairs, and in broken German, told the girl at the reception desk to put it away safely for him.

Two days later he returned to the receptionist and asked in German for his passport. There was no passport there. He panicked, and, slipping into English, made some unpleasant accusations to which the girl replied tearfully. The manager was called, and after a long discussion, it transpired that the girl had misunderstood Herr Ibrahim's instructions in German and had posted the envelope and its contents to the address on the front. Yes, she knew the envelope had already been used in the post, so she had done Herr Ibrahim a favour by transcribing the address on a new envelope and sending the contents of the used envelope to the Beirut address which she found on the old envelope.

That was how Herr Ibrahim found himself stranded in Austria for some ten days while awaiting the return of his passport. After having made the necessary telephone calls to make sure of the safe return of this essential document, he sat down to plan his extra week's holiday. The hotel management offered him a week's unpaid stay with their sincere apologies. He declined and contacted a friend in Geneva and arranged to spend a few days with him and his family. If the friend would meet him at the border and act as a guarantor, the Swiss authorities may allow him to enter with his Lebanese identity card instead of his passport.

An entire week was spent visiting Geneva, Lausanne, Zürich, and other towns. Hussein would travel to one of these centres by train and then return by boat when he could. Contrary to his first feelings of annoyance, this extra week of enforced relaxation rejuvenated him in a way that was unexpected. Maybe he would visit France after London if time allowed.

On his final day in Geneva, Hussein decided to make a journey partly by boat and partly by train, to Neuchâtel. Apart from being Anne Marie's university town during their student days, it was also a town where he had spent several stays before meeting her. As he got off the boat he was struck by how little the town had changed. A little bit more noisy and somewhat more crowded, it was still a clean, pleasant, well run, and civilised centre - in short it was beautifully and supremely Swiss.

He spent the day visiting the Musée des Beaux Arts, the Université de Neuchâtel, the old town and the market place. In the evening he walked, relaxed and complacent, along the lakeside and passed the barometer amid its floral arrangement. He tapped the barometer several times and looked at it knowingly and approvingly. He walked round the corner into the small harbour. His boat was not due for some time. He smiled to think of his complicated manner of travelling through Switzerland: boats, train, buses - all immaculately clean.

He walked towards the Touring Hotel which was very crowded. Normally, Hussein hated sharing a table at a café, but Switzerland was one place where such a practice did not matter. You could share a table with another person for hours and yet be as solitary as you liked. Alternatively, you could dive into an endless friendly chatter about anything, while your Swiss listener remained as solitary as he desired without making you feel stupid. He surveyed the tables in front of him. His eyes landed on a table occupied by one, somewhat matronly woman who was reading *Le Père Goriot* at very close proximity to her eyes as if she suffered from bad eyesight. Were it not for the book's title, Hussein would have taken her for a Swiss-German; she seemed so severe and self-willed.

"*Est-ce que vous permettez, madame?*" asked Hussein, pointing to the chair.

"*Mais bien sûr que oui monsieur,*" she answered abruptly as if Hussein had asked the most stupid question in the world. After all, the table was for public use. Hussein sat down.

"*Vous êtes d'ici, madame?*" Hussein asked conversationally.

"*Je suis Neuchâteloise, monsieur!*" Again Hussein had obviously asked a very stupid question. The lady, only a few years younger than Hussein, dived behind her book. Hussein stared at her. Her voice! Her abrupt impatient manner!

"Anne Marie !" he almost shouted. The woman stared at him as if he had lost his mind.

"*Mais, dites, monsieur, qui êtes vous?*" she asked.

"Hussein! Hussein!"

"*Ça alors! Impossible!*"

****

Saif was spending a few weeks in the mountains with his friend Muhammad. They had the house all to themselves as Muhammad's family had decided to spend the summer in the city.

The two boys spent their time walking and talking. During the chilly evenings they sat inside reading. Saif read some of his short stories to Muhammad who was a constant source of encouragement.

169

"I shall take down everything that you say and use it for my biography later on."

"Good man. An example, please, of your view of my genius, thank you."

"I knew Saif Ibrahim! Great fellow! Wise, brave, intelligent and an atrocious cook of spaghetti. The following is one of his sayings: 'All poetry can only be produced in the Winston Churchill. Only a true poet can enjoy its poetic fragrance'!"

The two smoked heavily, drank plentifully, and were thoroughly sick. Their days seemed spacious and sunny. Disastrous encounters with pretty neighbourhood girls accentuated their daily routine. Laughter was the order of the day and mock sobriety that of the night.

One evening they visited Beirut to see a film. They emerged from a rather bad movie about the life of Freud. They chanced on a taxi driver who lived near their mountain resort and who accepted to take them along for a fraction of the price. On the way up they sang and chatted irreverently about everything that came to mind. The taxi driver raced up the dangerous mountain road as if driving for dear life. Several cars took on the challenge and it was a most terrifyingly exciting drive. Little did the driver know that the other cars were speeding past him because of the rude signs that Saif was making with his hand out of the window!

The singing and laughter increased as the driver drove more and more dangerously. A thrill of fear went through the boys as the car screeched round corners very near deep chasms on the edge of the road while the driver gave them a lecture on Nasser's Pan Arabism.

They arrived home boisterous and happy, and tucked into a large meal consisting of everything they could find in the kitchen. Wine flowed, though mainly over the balcony edge as the two became merry with the sheer drunkenness of unspent youthful vitality.

Later that evening the two sat on the balcony smoking and staring at the stars.

"You know," said Saif aimlessly, "this is what literature should be about."

"What?" asked Muhammad. "Quick. Paper! Paper to Mr. Forster's Boswell. The master speaks."

"Shut up and sit down."

"Sorry. I thought you were joking. Cigarette?"

"Yes, just people. Incidents. Little vignettes of everyday life.

170

You know, that drive from Beirut tonight contained a great literary masterpiece."

"I told you that you had something. I could not see anything but a maniac at the wheel."

"No! No! A man. Passions, hatred, love - everything. Spacious, star-lit moments. Vast eternity. Everything. If only I could get it down on paper."

"How do you see all that?"

"Elementary my dear Watson, elementary. We could all do it if only we tried. Genius, my good long-eared Dr. Unsignifcantus, is the transcendent capacity for taking the trouble in the first place..."

".. being a corruption of?"

"Mr. Carlyle's scanty heavy-handed crapicisms!"

****

Spacious days denude a being of all connectivity. Unconscionably, life becomes a fiesta. So it was for Saif who found liberation in telling his English teacher about his experiences in the music room.

She listened and treated him in a gentle way that he had never experienced before. They spent hours chatting and holding hands.

Mrs. Fulbright seduced Saif. It was gentle, slow and loving. For the first time in his life, Saif felt the warmth of reciprocity.

The relationship lasted all summer and ended as abruptly as it had started. Not once did it occur to Saif to equate it to what had happened with his music teacher. Intellectually, he knew that there was little difference. Emotionally, he despised his musical interludes as strongly as he loved his literary ones.

****

Saif felt the blood fill his mouth. A sharp pain went cutting through his abdomen. He lay on the floor spitting and being sick. He had just returned from his stay in the mountains when he was stopped by three men who had asked his name. They pushed him against the wall and hit him several times. He kept asking why they were hitting him. "You Moslem bastard!" one of them kept shouting. Saif lay on the pavement recovering. He thought that the whole thing might be a dream. If only he could wake up. He closed his eyes but could taste the blood in his mouth. Had they broken a tooth? It must be a dream. He thought he was sleeping at home having one of his horrible nightmares. Soon Marwan would wake him up. Marwan. He remembered seeing some of Marwan's writings on his table. They were obscene. But he wrote well and evocatively. He felt sick. He opened his eyes. He must be at home. He could see the blurred street lights. He felt about for his glasses. One lens was broken. Why had they hit him? He tried to stand. He would wake up soon and find himself at home. It was another nightmare, vivid like all the others. He must be at home. Yes, of course, there was Marwan's voice. He opened his eyes.

"Come on brother. You'll be all right!"

Brother! Marwan never called him that.

"What has happened?"

"Beaten up. He's all right. Just shocked."

"He's petrified. Poor boy."

"Call the police."

It was not a dream. Saif stood up.

"No! Don't! I'm all right. Don't call the police."

"What is he?"

"A Moslem? Looks like one."

"Come on, brother, I'll take you home. Come on."

"Why? But why?"

"I don't know, brother. I don't know. Put your faith in Nasser."

Saif cried noisily. Pity, horror, and pain took hold of him. He still heard his assailants as they hit him.

"You Moslem bastard!"

9. Family

"Well nephews and others!"

Haji sat in her small front room, its walls covered with pictures of family members, some dating back to the turn of the century.

"Well nephews! So, my brother marries again! Well! Well! Well! And a Swiss woman! Hey? He tells me that I know her. By my blind eyes I don't. Ye ye ye ye ye! Marrying again! Hoooo yop! Wherefore? Whereto? Hey nephews? Your views, please?"

"We're very happy for baba" said Saif. "He seems so much younger."

"Nephew. Call it lamb but it's tough meat! No, nephew, my brother is wrong. What does he want to get himself hooked with a young woman at his age for? Hey?"

"But she is not young, aunt." Marwan replied.

"Isn't she a little spring chicken then? Hummmm-ma! I know my eyes. I don't know her. Stayed with us in Palestine? When? I am old-old-old. Don't ask me to the wedding. I might disgrace you before our civilised European friend. Pray inform me: Is she a Catholic?"

"No, aunt. A Protestant."

"A lesser evil, nephew. Yes. What does she look like? Have you a little daguerreotype?"

"What?"

"A likeness boy! A likeness that I can look at?"

"No. Sorry."

"No matter, youngest nephew, no matter. We shall soon see. Are you going to the airport with the reception committee?"

"Yes, we're all going. Selma too."

"Aunt," said Marwan, "I don't like that picture of me. Can I give you another?"

"Nephew! Don't blame the camera if it's your mug that is crooked. Ay! Marry at his age. Well, nephews, maybe I'll find me a man to marry. An Englishman. They're not too fussy about age and looks."

"Yes aunt," said Saif. "*We hope to see you one day fitted with a husband!*"

"Out! Impertinent youth! Out! Marry! Beauty is in the eye, ah yes, even an ape loves his love. *Were my lover an Ethiop, black as coal, I shall love him.* Yes."

As the two boys walked down the stairs from her small flat, Marwan was outraged.

"Hey, Saif, did you hear that? Racist old bag!"

****

As Anne-Marie stepped off the aeroplane she was aware of the warm air that hit her deep within. Breathing shallowly, nervous and unaware of what to expect, she walked to the customs stand. Her eyes travelled over the glass partition in an effort to spot Hussein, then saw him waving encouragingly and rather nervously. Beside him stood a pretty young woman who looked like her father. Where her father's face had mellowed with age into benign dignity the young woman seemed aloof. On the other side of Hussein stood a boy of about seventeen. Handsome, erect, and intelligent-looking, he stood there stroking his long curly hair. Talking to Selma was a young man with a devil-may-care expression on his attractive face. Anne-Marie decided that this must undoubtedly be Ali, the eldest. He was - must be - the little skeleton in the cupboard. Anne-Marie looked around for the baby of the family and felt rather like a shepherd counting his sheep. She could not find the baby when she noticed that Selma said something to a teenage boy behind her. He looked annoyed. That could not be Saif: that was not a baby! Anyway he did not look like any of the others. He had a brown complexion and long silky dark hair. He looked distant, thoughtful. Her eyes met his and he smiled. Yes. That must be the so-called baby. His smile was that of his father's. A scar on his right cheek gave him the look of someone well-versed in the vicissitudes of life.

Anne-Marie walked towards the double exit door completely unaware of the deafening noises that surrounded her. She was pushed once or twice but simply carried on. The family walked towards her. Selma was dressed in the latest fashion. The men all wore suits. The older three behaved with dignity. She laughed inwardly to see Saif come forward shuffling uneasily in his suit which seemed much too large in places and much too small in others. Selma seemed to nudge him. Hussein whispered something and the boy straightened his back.

Hussein approached his new wife and kissed her gently on both cheeks. Selma busied herself observing some emerging arrivals. Anne-Marie, firmly gripped at the elbow by Hussein, was led towards the rest of her new family.

"This is my daughter, Selma, *ma fille*."

"*Enchantée...*" said Anne-Marie, nervously.

"*Bonsoir madame. J'espère que vous avez eu bon voyage.*"

"*Merci*"

Selma was going to be difficult to handle. Anne-Marie felt herself being wheeled round towards the eldest.

"Ali," said Hussein. "He does not speak French."

"Hello! I do speak a little French. Oui. Jay parler une poo. Ha ha."

****

Fascinating! Fascinating to be born into a ready-made family when you are already sixty. She would have to turn the film backwards.

Anne-Marie was not listening but staring at the heavily tattooed woman standing by the sink. An original! Here was the eccentric to beat all eccentrics: Amal.

"*Bonsoir.*"

"Hey? Ah Bonsoor lady. I will TEACH you ARABIC. Do you understand me?"

"*Pardon?*"

"This is not going to be easy. Teee-ch you AR-a-BIC. No?"

The family left the kitchen amid Amal's monologue.

"Oh my God!" whispered Selma. "How embarrassing. She'll have to go."

****

Anne-Marie soon settled down in her new life but there was little doubt in her mind how she felt about Lebanon: she hated it. The people were pretentious and generally ashamed to admit their national heritage. How pathetic they sounded in their desperate attempt to sound and appear French. She was intensely embarrassed for them. Some, in fact the majority, sounded no more French than Mao-Tse-Tung would sound British. There was a lamentable lack of culture. All the people of her social standing seemed to do was visit each other and exchange meaningless gossip. At least Marwan and Saif seemed to have some culture. Looking at their reading material gave her a great sense of relief. But the rest of Society. Society! That was the word. 'Society' with the most abhorrent implication that that word gave: pretentious, ostentatious, but with no value whatever.

Had she made a mistake?

Was hers a precipitate marriage? Hussein was a decent and affectionate gentleman in the fullest meaning of the word. "*Il a des grandes qualités*" Anne-Marie kept thinking to herself. But Life was so different here: endless rounds of meaningless and enforced duty, society making idiotic demands. The demands that duty made on one was nothing less than the most awful form of social control. Similar, she felt, to Europe some two hundred years ago with the Church, the State and the Nobility running the show and the majority cow towing in the most cretinous and unthinking way.

Anne-Marie soon found three ways of making her life tolerable in this alien society. She joined *Le Cercle Suisse* which once a week brought some healthy Swiss sanity into her life. She also joined the British Council where she attended lessons in English and took part in every possible function which the Council organised. In this she had an interest in common with Saif who was also a keen member, and a special relationship soon sprung up between the two. In him she found an endless source of both amusing and distressing information on everything that she needed to know. In Anne-Marie, Saif found a confidante who not only understood his inner feelings but who also sympathised with them. She was the nearest to having a mother that he had ever experienced in his short lived memory.

Hussein and everybody else persisted in treating her as a very welcome tourist to whom only the best should be shown. Saif resented this attitude misunderstanding it for hypocrisy, so he took it upon himself to inform his newly acquired step-mother of everything that the others chose to hide. Being under no illusions about Lebanon he took her to the poor and miserable quarters of the city. Much to his father's annoyance, he told her all the family secrets that he knew. He was also the only one to talk about his mother, though there was very little that he could tell Anne-Marie.

As she had anticipated, her relationship with Selma was formal and restrained. The latter seemed to resent her father's new wife with ill-concealed venom. What did not help was Anne-Marie's mature dignity before all the aggravation that her new life brought. That she suffered in her new role was a fact that she and only she knew. At times she seriously thought of making use of her return ticket to Switzerland, a ticket given to her by Hussein as a sign of his acceptance - albeit silently - of a probationary period of one year. At such times Anne-Marie would go out on very long walks along the Beirut sea-front, allowing the magnificent blue seascape to heal her inner wounds - for a while at least.

And so Anne-Marie passed her first winter in Lebanon. Soon she was unashamedly happy preparing for her annual visit to Neuchâtel. This had been an agreement upon which she had accepted to marry Hussein. As for Hussein, marriage seemed to change him dramatically. He became youthful and adventurous, albeit in his circumspect manner. He renounced his diary which returned to its old use of being a convenient list which he carried around with him, the better to organise his life.

Now and then Hussein joined Anne-Marie and Saif in their numerous outings to the cinema. This in turn gave Saif a chance to understand his father better. He was pleasantly surprised, while intensely annoyed, at his father's understanding of, and sympathy with, the misunderstood hero of *Les 400 Coups*. He felt it annoying that Hussein should show such understanding of the misconceived and recalcitrant teenager in the film.

He explained his annoyance to Anne-Marie who tried to explain the difference between people's reactions to fiction and their attitude to reality. It was perfectly acceptable for Hussein to understand how the boy in the film felt and to feel the injustice of his parents' treatment of him. In fiction this did not demand an involved and active response from Hussein. However, in reality, Hussein would be too shy and reserved to respond to his young son's aspirations and problems as this demanded some kind of activity on his part. It was rather like Hussein feeling acutely sorry for Oliver Twist while he still pushed away the beggars in the streets of Beirut as being layabouts and parasites. Also, she added, Saif had the misfortune of having a father some forty five years older than himself, with two generations separating them.

Saif accepted this but argued that nonetheless it was a failure in Hussein's character.

"Not necessarily only in him", Anne-Marie explained, "but rather everybody's; for without this self-defensive quality, Art would cease to be needed in the way that it is now."

Such discussions became an invaluable part of Saif's life. His new stepmother seemed to become the restraining influence in his overflowing passions. Through her he began to channel his feelings.

"But *ma chère* Selma," said Muna Jbeili, "this brother of yours seems to have taken to his new *maman!*"

"*Qu'est ce que tu veux?* They are alike: both fools, *mon cher.*"

"Miaow! Miaow!"

"*Non! Non!* I couldn't be bothered to be bitchy about her. He likes her. Good luck to him. Maybe the fool will inherit something from her. I want nothing from her, thank you very much."

"*Eh bien?* When will you marry, *ma petite?*"

"The sooner the better!"

****

One day, late in the winter of that same year, Saif was invited by his sister to the University where she was doing her final year. She introduced him to a British lecturer who had shown interest in reading some of his writings. Being a teacher of drama she showed most interest in a surrealistic play that he had written. Entitled '*Enshkoopi*' (the nickname of its protagonist) it dealt with the problems of creating Art within an alien society. Saif's essential thought had been to show that the main business of Art was Art. This involved him in complexities that his youth did not enable him to sort out. He cut through the Gordian knot rather arbitrarily. Although immature in many respects, the lecturer thought his play showed some promise particularly because of its youthful honest idealism.

Soon a strong friendship emerged between Saif and the thirty year old Miss Eliot. Saif delighted in visiting her in her apartment which was no less than the dressing rooms and the stage of the old disused University theatre. They spent hours sitting on the stage chatting. Sometimes they sat in the main auditorium staring fixedly at the stage while imagining a production of a play.

The auditorium was very small, built a long time ago to seat some 150 spectators. The stage itself was small and fit only for those plays which required little or no scenery. Behind the stage were three small rooms. One served as a bedroom while another was Miss Eliot's study. The third contained a small gas cooker, a fridge, and a very small make-shift sink once used to wash off make-up. Above the cooker stood the old mirror surrounded by several lights. The stage itself served as Miss Eliot's dining cum reception room at which time she had the curtains closed. The entire auditorium still retained that theatrical smell of make-up and musty old clothes.

Although a new and much larger theatre had been built, Miss Eliot sometimes brought her small classes to the older one in order to act out short scenes from Shakespeare, Williams, O'Neil, and others. Saif joined her during the long winter evenings after school, warming themselves by the floodlights - most of which had blown a long time since, and chatting about various aspects of Art. Saif seemed eager to listen to long lectures on anything, from playwrights to the technical reasons why an actor should not turn his back to the audience. These meetings became less frequent as summer approached.

Anne-Marie left for Switzerland, followed by Hussein as business commitments allowed. Saif and Marwan both passed their final examinations although the school had written to Hussein explaining that his youngest son was suspected of cheating in some tests. Saif denied this and his father chose to believe him. A long hot summer holiday lay ahead of the two boys. Marwan soon disappeared on his endless social escapades in various friends' houses. He had recently taken to dyeing his hair green and wearing multi-coloured trousers. He was now part of the latest pop scene, much to Hussein's disgust and Saif's amusement. The two brothers still enjoyed that special relationship which was expressed in a quick confidential exchange of words then sank back into confident brotherly affection.

"Like the waters of the sea! The sea! The sea!" Ali was sitting in the front-room of his parent's house after saying good-bye to Hussein. He was due to fly back to Kuwait that evening. Selma sat laughing loudly. Saif asked what it was that was like the waters of the sea.

"Money! Money! The sea. The ocean. So much money I could wipe my ..."

"Ali! Stop it!" laughed Selma.

"Sorry sister. How about a little more invigorating libation?"

"You've had enough. Come on, you're travelling tonight."

"Ah! Just a teeny weeny drop of whisky, hey?" Ali poured himself a liberal measure from a half-empty bottle on the shelf. "Aye! Fu ... Fudge, sister, fudge. Ha ha. Just remembered. Problems."

"What problems?" asked Selma.

"Well, my dear sister. Hmm. No, this is serious. I've got a girl coming here tonight."

"What?"

"Now take it easy. My dear wife is going to kill me for being a week late anyhow. Ooops! I'm running out of lies."

"Who's the girl?"

Ali poured another drink. He looked at Selma and Saif abstractedly.

"Girl? What girl? Aiiee! I forgot. I invited an English girl while I was in London last week. Met her at my hotel."

"She won't come."

"She did! Ha ha ha. Ooops, sorry sister. Now, let's gather our thoughts. No, Selma, she did not. That was why I asked her to come here. Ha ha ha! Saif! Close your ears!"

"Did you pay for her to come?"

"Yes."

"Well, she won't. She'll keep the money and that's all."

"Hmm! Ticket. First class, of course."

"Oh, no! Ali. How could you be so stupid?"

"Selma. Selma. My little Salomi. Tell you what. I'm going home to my wife. You receive this girl, hey sister?"

"What is her name?"

"Ooops! Forgot."

"When does she arrive?"

"Tonight, I think. The sea! The sea! Like the sea. I have so much money. Money. La la la. Come little brother. Here's a big, big, bill. Spend it on what's her name. She's good." He whispered "Got such enormous...."

"Ali!" Selma almost screamed.

"...enormous ... enormous aeroplane I shall fly home tonight. What are you laughing at?" he screamed at Saif. "You think I'm drunk. Look. Look, you turd, my aim is excellent." Ali's shoe went flying across the room and hit the boy on the side of his head.

"Come on Ali. Time to go and catch your plane. Saif, I'm spending the night at Aunt Muna's. Will you be all right, my love?"

"Yes." Saif looked at the money his brother had given him through tearful eyes.

"I don't expect that girl will arrive," continued Selma. "If she does give her Marwan's room. I expect we shan't see him until next October."

"Yes," shouted Ali as he walked slowly down the stairs. "Yes.

180

Tell her that I died last night. The sea! The sea! One, two, three, four million smackers. And Saif is doing you know what with his English teacher. Takes after his stud of a brother. The sea! The sea!"

Selma ran back into the apartment and gave Saif an envelope from Ali. "Give her this," she said. "Ignore him. He doesn't mean it."

Saif felt angry and disgusted at his brother. Obviously Ali had noticed, otherwise why throw the shoe at him? He fingered the money, decided to go to Miss Eliot's and on the way brought chicken sandwiches with a lot of spice and garlic in them. He also bought several soft drinks and two enormous hamburgers, then walked over to Miss Eliot's theatre. She was in.

"Hello!"

"I thought we'd have a feast. A big nice smelly feast!"

"Lovely."

The two sat eating and talking. Saif told her about Ali's behaviour. He felt angry again. Very near to tears, he explained that he could not understand him.

"Nothing. Nothing is left of him. No joy. No understanding. How could he use his money so stupidly?"

"How do you know that he is not happy?"

"He must be miserable."

"You mean that you would be, in his place."

"Am I that intolerant?"

"Harmlessly and with cause, Saif."

A long silence followed.

"Elizabeth?"

"Yes?"

"I'm lonely."

"I know."

"I don't mean people. God knows there are enough of them. My entire family consists of over three hundred and fifty members scattered all over the world? No. I mean lonely in the middle of people. I cannot understand them. Everything they care about seems unimportant, transient. But what I see as important - life and death - they ignore. I have not seen Selma or father read one decent book."

"Be careful. You're being a little intolerant and a little too earnest. You only see those around you superficially..."

"But they are superficial!"

"No! No one is. They have all the complexities of passions and thoughts. They just do not choose to ponder over them as you do."

"Am I wrong? I want so much to understand. I feel like Pierre in *War and Peace* roaming aimlessly. I'm not going to find my salvation in some outdated belief in Christian goodness."

"You're not wrong. You are like Pierre. Very much so. But you're not a part of a novel. You're not clearly ordered, but confused."

"I wish I were," Saif said thoughtfully as he looked around the stage where they sat.

"What are you looking at?"

"Nothing. I love being here. It's safe. Not lonely. Outside, the solitude hurts."

"You should not be lonely. There is so much intelligence around you; both inside and outside your family."

"As if anyone cares!"

"I do. You do Saif. You are young. No, wait till I've finished. What I'm going to say may be wrong, but, Saif, if I were a few years younger and if you were a few older, I should find you the most attractive man ever. I would love you dearly."

Elizabeth jumped up and walked over to the left of the stage. Saif looked at her for a few minutes. He got up, walked across to her, and put his hands on her shoulders.

"But you are the most beautiful…"

She made a motion for him to go away.

"You mustn't give your back to the audience." He laughed feebly.

She turned round smiling. "You're sweet! Come on now. It's time for you to go. That girl might've arrived by now."

"Good night, Elizabeth."

Saif stood for a while looking at her round, old-fashioned glasses. He took her hand and kissed her gently but noisily on her cheek.

"Good night."

On his way out he stopped to look back. He saw the curtains move as if actors were busily changing scenes behind. His eye fell on several old posters hanging in the foyer.

The University Arts Faculty
Presents
Eugène Ionesco's Rhinoceros

****

Saif walked home with a feeling of depression gripping him so deeply that it became all the more acute for his inability to understand it. He arrived home to find a pretty young girl of about his age or a little older sitting on some suitcases outside the front door. She explained that she was waiting for Mr. Ibrahim who had given her this address while in London. Embarrassed, Saif invited her in and explained that Ali was suddenly called abroad on urgent business. To his surprise she did not seem unhappy, she appeared just a little inconvenienced. He gave her the envelope saying that his brother had asked him to look after her until she caught the London flight next morning. All she said to this was, "Oh!" and laughed. She was taken to Marwan's room while Amal prepared something to eat.

"Hoy! Hoy! A potato-eater and you're alone. Don't mind me. Eat, be merry, and - ha ha ha - I'm going into my attic and not a word. I'm not even here. Ah, crafty bugger Ali buys you an English one. Go. Go!" Amal climbed the stairs into her room and never emerged again that night. Now and then she could be heard shouting encouragingly, "Go to it my boy. To it. Show your metal. Show her what you've got!" Despite the fact that the girl could not understand Arabic, Saif felt intensely embarrassed.

During the meal the girl, whose name was Suzanne, monopolised the entire conversation. Saif felt depressed and a little sick. She asked him a hundred questions which he answered monosyllabically. Finally, when the meal ended she asked for a drink. Wine was all that was available.

"Fancy! I've never been a gift before." Suzanne spoke in a way that Saif found disgusting; it seemed rehearsed.

"A gift?"

"Yes. A gift to you."

"No. You don't understand. You see ..."

She got up and walked towards him "You are shy, aren't you? Come on." She led him towards Marwan's room. He could hear Amal shouting to him "to go to it." Suzanne pulled her dress over her head. "Come on. Sit down." Saif obeyed. She kissed him without getting any response from him. "Umm! You're good." She stood up and undressed completely and got into bed. Saif got up and awkwardly backed towards the door. "Where're you going? Come and get your present." He ran out slamming the door behind him. Amal was still haranguing him from within her attic room.

He walked the streets till very late at night. He moved fast and intensely. Hot and sweating he reached Hamra Street where he watched people going about their nightly business and felt an intense hatred for them all. They seemed like a seething, superfluous hot mass. He swore at a man who did not stop at traffic lights. He made a rude sign at an American who crossed the road when the sign was against him. He angrily asked a policeman why he had not stopped the American.

"More than my bloody job is worth trying to stop a tourist. A Dollar-carrying one at that."

As he walked back towards the apartment thinking of where to go for the night, he bumped into a man.

"Sorry," he said in English.

"What?" shouted the man.

"Sorry sir."

"Cannot you speak Arabic?" the man shouted angrily. Some people stopped to look.

"Of course I can."

"Then why speak in English? Arabic not good enough for you? No? Well son, I'm an Arab Moslem and proud of it! Nasser will see to people like you." He spat at Saif and walked off. Saif wiped his face with a feeling of nausea.

"Ignore him, brother. One in a thousand," shouted somebody after him.

Saif looked ahead as people and lights merged into one mass. The new shape danced before his eyes: luminous with its long pointed sides and dark moving centre. Suddenly everything burst into sharp focus as the tears rolled down his face. He turned a corner into a quiet empty street and was violently sick. He stood against the wall trying to gather his strength. A few minutes later he started to walk towards Elizabeth's place. When he arrived he found that the University gates were locked for the night. He headed for home.

He arrived home very late. Having sat down for a long time, he got up and washed his face several times. Every time the water touched his face on the spot where he was spat at he felt as if the water itself were turning gelatinous and nauseating. He looked in on Suzanne: she was sleeping. Her body lay disordered and heavy. He looked at her with a mixture of nausea and excitement.

On the balcony the air, though warm, felt somewhat fresher than it did inside. Saif stared at the ill-lit street and tried to think. His mind felt confused and restless. In the street below he saw both his father's and Selma's cars. Seized by a mad impulse to break all ordinary rules of conduct he ran downstairs with the key to Selma's car which he got from its usual place near the entrance.

Unable to drive properly he started off slowly. The Jaguar, powerful as it felt, was easy to handle. He headed for the airport road. Once on that road the Jaguar went at a great speed. There was a bizarre sensation of transience as lights and trees raced back in the opposite direction. At the airport roundabout the car screeched as it turned back onto the returning lane. A police whistle shot through the glaringly lit night. Saif drove faster.

He turned a corner and parked the car below the wall supporting the upper road on which the police-car raced by, unaware of Saif's hiding place. Saif sat looking at the wall and flicking the lights. He fancied seeing various people in the different shapes produced on the wall by the yellow rays of light. He thought confusedly of several things. He listened to voices coming in from all sides. Some voices he recognised while others he had never heard before. The voices crowded in from everywhere.

"I'm a gift to you. You Moslem bastard, cannot you speak Arabic. Hey, tell you what L.A. *Ça alors, mon cher.* You turd! You can kiss me if you like. Sshh! Let it be a secret between you and me. Baba will never know, There. There. That's nice, isn't it? Sshh...."

Saif reversed the car as far as it would go and, with a scream that seemed to rend his brain asunder, he drove it at the wall flashing his lights frantically.

As the sand and dust settled around the purring car Saif tried to get out. He fell, got up and tried to run towards a small opening in the wall. He leant against the wall and slid down slowly. He fancied that he was back in the old house again playing in the garden. He was not a child, but rather the same age as then. He saw himself, a teenager, sitting in the garden frantically digging a hole. He could smell, even taste, the sand. Someone called out to him. He looked up from his digging. He knew that he was not really in the garden but rather in some dirty little opening in the wall. He tried hard to play in the garden but could not. He saw himself, as a child now, sinking into the hole that he had been digging. He felt himself fall, fall, fall into an endless floating chasm. He heard voices. He opened his eyes and saw four police officers examining the car.

With courage that amazed him he got up and walked up to the officers. He spoke English - loudly and clearly.

"I say, chaps. Any chance of a tow?"

The officers looked at him and then at each other.

"American?" said one in Arabic.

"No!" replied another. "Must be British."

"Bizarre looking British. Looks Indian to me." They spoke in Arabic.

"What difference does it make? Damn foreigner."

"What does he want?"

"Ask him."

"What do you want?"

"Sorry. Don't speak the lingo, hey what?" Saif felt a little hot.

"Me speak. What - you - want?"

"A tow. A little pull of the old jalopy."

"What does he want?"

"Listen chaps. A garage."

"Ha! Garage. *Vous voulez? Vous voulez?*"

"Wee Wee and all that, what?"

"Come. We take. You car Jaguar."

"Yes. Took corner a bit sharpish, hey? Ha ha ha."

"Yes. You come. We take."

"I say, boys, steady on. Take where?"

"Garage. You want?"

"Hey! We've been off duty for half an hour. We've pushed his car out of the way. Leave him to deal with it. We're not in London."

"Okay .... Hey mistah! Garage up there. This hand turn ..."

"Left?"

"Yes. Left hand. Then other hand. We busy. We go."

"Good-night, lads. What?"

"Good to the night too mistah. What?"

"Okay. Okay. What?"

Saif stood watching as the police car drove off. He could feel himself starting to shake. He turned around and was sick. He surveyed the car. It was quite badly damaged. He threw the keys inside it and walked away.

As he walked he became aware of pain in his wrist. He wiped the sweat off his neck. It was mixed with a little blood. He ran home as fast as he could. When he arrived he examined himself in the mirror. There were several small cuts near his collar bone. He washed them and put a plaster on. His wrist was swelling a little. He bandaged it and went out on the balcony where he sat staring ahead of him and dreaming.

****

Selma was extremely kind to her brother when she found out the next day. She comforted him and told him not to worry about the car. He broke down and promised to pay for the repairs. As to what happened exactly and why it happened nobody asked and he volunteered no information. During the period immediately after the accident he felt strangely calm. He felt like someone who had accepted the fact that he would die in a few months and simply sat waiting for the inevitable.

He went to spend a week with Muhammad and his family in the mountains. Muhammad was very kind and offered Saif some money to help towards repairing the car. He listened to his thoughtful friend and let him talk. Otherwise, he accompanied him on long silent walks.

"Muhammad?"

"Yes."

"I want to return to Beirut."

"Do you think you should? You've been through a great deal."

"Yes. Listen, can you arrange for us to spend a couple of days at your town house. This way Selma would leave us alone."

"Of course. You leave it to me. I say? What is it that makes your life so sad?"

"I don't know. I wish I were you. You know where you are going."

"Hmm. Could be boring, you know."

Next morning the two went to Beirut, ostensibly to go to the cinema and spend a couple of quiet days on the beach.

Saif immediately went to the University. Elizabeth had a small group of students attending the summer school. She was explaining various terms used in the theatrical world. He sat at the back of the auditorium listening to her lecture.

After everybody left he sat there watching Elizabeth rearranging her sitting-room before she closed her curtain. She was fairly tall with long light brown hair, the front and side of which she collected in a small bundle at the back. The rest she let fall down over her neck and back. With a slightly podgy face, she had two rounded apple-cheeks that grew larger when she smiled or laughed. The two red cheeks shaded a small nose that twitched when she spoke. Her mouth seemed small but somehow deep with its full lips. What attracted him most were her hazel eyes which took on any expression that her heart assumed. She could not lie. Her honest face showed every scar within her - especially in her eyes. Her neck was long and white - maybe too white, thought Saif. She was the type of woman who would not attract much attention at first but seen at close quarters she was extremely beautiful in what Saif called a loveable way. She had a way of speaking that was quiet and wholesome. She looked at her listener with her head lowered a little and spoke in measured tones. She seemed to understand more than what was being said. Her eyes went beyond the words spoken. An action as simple as pouring coffee seemed to her to be worthy of special scrutiny. She had sheer delight in the trivia that made up the sum total of her daily life: simplistic and pleasant. Saif loved her without that intensity or urgency that he had experienced with girls of his age. He just liked being with her, listening to her, talking to her.

"Elizabeth?" He walked towards the stage.

"My God. What's happened to you?"

"Elizabeth?"

"Yes. Come up here." She closed the curtain. "Sit down. What's happened?"

"Nothing." Saif sat in the centre of the stage.

"But you're hurt." Elizabeth walked across to him. "Please tell me."

"Not now." In the silence that followed Elizabeth resumed her work of re-arranging things in an orderly fashion. Saif sat staring at the reflection of the stage lights on the curtains and on Elizabeth. Suddenly, he started talking and spoke at length into the night. He told her everything that had happened. She listened patiently and both laughed at the episode with the policemen.

"Elizabeth?"

"Yes."

Saif looked at her. She smiled.

"I love you."

They sat silently for a while.

"This is the same set that we had for Hedda Gabler. It's convenient with the dining table at the back. There's a curtain which Hedda pulls at the end when she shoots herself."

"Elizabeth. I love you."

"I know. I know I'm almost twice your age." She got up and walked over to the right of the stage.

Saif stood up and walked over to the back and leant against the dining table then crossed the stage and stood before her. He held her face in his hands and kissed her gently several times. With the back of her hand she stroked his face.

"I love you," he repeated.

"It sounds terrible."

"Yes. Ridiculous. I can always recite you a poem:
Come, Madame, come, all rest my powers defie,
Until I labour, I in labour lye."

"Don't be disgusting. Anyhow I don't like him."

"Ah! Well, what's done is done. All right here's another loving poem:
Vous serez au foyer une vieille accroupie,
Cueillez dès aujourd'hui les roses de la vie.
You haven't got long."

"Stop it. You're nothing to write home about, either!"

They laughed.

"I do love you, Elizabeth."

He kissed her and she held on to him.

"I love you too. I love your dimples. That scar makes one bigger than the other. I love you. I do. So much."

"Let's make this our secret hiding place. Our own private place."

The two walked away from the stage and into Elizabeth's bedroom. As they undressed in the dark Saif tried to think of what had just been said on stage. He could not order his thoughts properly. Everything seemed confused.

Elizabeth felt a mixture of guilt and excitement. She knew she was doing wrong. He was so young even if he did look and behave older than his age. She was also excited by this very fact. He was young and inexperienced. She felt embarrassed at her motives and desires, but she wanted him. She told herself that she did love him whatever the reasons may be. Something she needed was there. Something that a man her age could not give her: innocent and unspoilt.

With a feeling of guilt and excitement she got into bed and felt the warmth of his body against hers. He has haunted me for so long. He is like a ghost. He is my driving force, warm within me. Innocent. Every wild flower, the birds and their songs, horses and their grace, trees and their majesty. He is my burning youth but I no longer burn as I did then. It was youth that burnt within me. I cannot even remember it. But I could always remember him. He is in me. He is me. Yes. Yes. Yes!

****

The bill for the car was over fifteen hundred Lebanese pounds. Muhammad and Elizabeth paid Saif half of that sum. The other half he borrowed from an endless number of friends and acquaintances. Selma took his promise to pay seriously. Although forgiving, she never allowed him to forget his folly. It was not that Saif needed reminding. As far as he was concerned he cared little about the car but he felt extremely guilty at the sight of his sister. This feeling of guilt only served to increase his dislike for her. Quite unjustifiably he blamed her and Ali for what happened. He experienced moments of intense fear at the possibility of relapsing into that state of mind. In this his relationship with Elizabeth helped a great deal. In her company he was able to release his passions and fears. But the fact that he was unable to explore fully the events of that terrible night only increased his anxiety.

When Anne-Marie and Hussein returned from Switzerland his anxiety increased. He would have liked to confide in them. It was not so much the actual accident and its resulting expenses that worried him but rather the causes that led to it. Unable to face these causes squarely he tended to make the actual car accident take on a much greater significance than it really had. This state of affairs was furthered by the exaggerated role of keeping the whole thing a secret from his father. Of course, Hussein soon suspected something was amiss. With the intention of helping his son he pretended ignorance of the whole episode. His information was sketchy and half-imagined. But no one, except Saif and Elizabeth, knew what really led to the actual accident. That remained a universal secret - even the real knowledge eluded Saif.

Soon, this shared secret became a private sick joke. Ali would

190

invariably refer jovially and harmlessly to Saif's attempt at committing "suicide" over some secret love affair. Sadly, this was so near the truth that Ali's harmless joke caused Saif much pain. Further, Saif knew that Ali had contributed towards the cost of the car repairs. This meant that the repairs were paid for twice which meant that someone had pocketed the difference. Probably his father's driver who took charge of repairs. This did not particularly worry the boy. What really worried him was the awareness that no one knew what he was suffering in trying to atone for that night's behaviour. The assumption was that somebody else had paid the price, not Saif.

Matters came to a head in the second half of the school term. An acquaintance who had lent the boy a hundred pounds was putting pressure on him to repay. After stalling for some time Saif received a warning that unless the money was soon paid his father would hear everything. Although Saif knew that his father knew something, he was unable to make a clean breast of the whole matter. He could tell his father that he had 'borrowed' the car and wrecked it. At least, there would be a long speech and the matter would end there. But Saif did not trust his father to understand the real causes behind the event. He felt embarrassed and frightened, feelings he could not fully understand. Thus he compounded sin upon sin in order to alleviate the original lapse: mainly his lack of trust in his relationship with his father.

With a feeling of sickness and terror at being discovered, Saif walked into his parents' bedroom. He could hear the family talking and laughing in the front-room. He took a bunch of keys from a drawer and opened the main cupboard. From the housekeeping box he took one hundred pounds in two brown fifty pound notes. With an oppressive feeling of heat in his temples he replaced everything back in its place and walked out of the room.

As he sat listening to the rest of the family, he kept imagining that he had not replaced the keys properly. What if he had left the cupboard unlocked? Maybe the box was still open? He left the sitting-room and checked the cupboard. Fingerprints! He wiped everything clean. But he lived in the house so his prints would be expected there. What if he were to be accused? He could not deny it. He returned to his family as if seeking to disappear in a cloud of normality. Why not tell them now? What could he tell them? He did not know. How could he explain so much in so little: as an accident? Hussein would not understand. He looked at his father. No. He might dismiss the accident as a teenage prank but not whatever else went with it. Saif felt that his father had too simple and rigid a view of life to understand passions of the kind that he had. Ironically, he also knew that he was wrong in feeling this way. Next morning he paid the money off. He asked Muhammad for more cash. He borrowed another fifty which he rushed home and replaced in the box. When the discovery was made and the culprit never caught his guilt increased by the unexpected when he realised he had hurt Anne-Marie badly. Her entire life in this strange country had suddenly become insecure. He was unable to face her for several days. Yet again he compounded misfortune upon misfortune. He fabricated a quarrel with her in order that he may avoid her without a feeling of guilt!

Regular visits to Elizabeth continued, although Saif ceased to confide in her what seemed to him his dishonest and criminally devious behaviour. With her he was able to forget. The outside world ceased to exist. All the more so because they kept their relationship a very close secret. Neither wanted to imagine the horror that would be expressed if anyone was to find out. They, and they alone, understood!

Saif's school-work deteriorated dramatically. Only his excellent grades in English language and literature kept him from sinking beyond relief. He was caught cheating in several examinations. His teacher of English always saved him before the matter got to the headteacher. But matters were bound to become public soon.

They did so with the arrival of spring. Saif refused to go to school. He spent several days without attending. Eventually he went to tell his headteacher that he wanted to leave and was told to produce a parental letter to that effect. He swore obscenely at the old man and ran out. After a day spent sitting on rocks on the sea-front he made a pathetic attempt at cutting his wrists with a broken bottle. The school infirmary sent him to his family doctor.

After a very long talk, the doctor promised to keep the whole matter to himself. He recommended consultation with a psychiatrist in order to help Saif work out the confusion in his mind. When given the doctor's name, Hussein angrily telephoned the family practitioner telling him that the doctor he was recommending was a psychiatrist. Was he implying that Saif was in need of that kind of help? Could the family not help? What was wrong with the boy that conventional medicine would not solve?

Eventually the doctor's recommendation was put aside to make place for Hussein's agreement to allow Saif to leave school. After a long holiday the matter could be discussed anew. Saif confided, in part, some of his problems to Anne-Marie. She paid off all his debts, including – Saif naïvely assuming it to be without her knowledge - the fifty pounds which he replaced in the box after a decent interval.

In the late spring of that year Saif was on his way to Switzerland for a long holiday thanks to the kınd generosity of his ever-enigmatic eldest brother, Ali. Elizabeth was to join him there on her way back from a holiday in England. He left with a free mind, happy at the unknown prospects before him, and with Amal's incessant encouragement to "go to it."

Chapter 10

Switzerland! I have always felt that my love for that country was heavily influenced by the very happy time spent there with Elizabeth. I have visited La Belle Suisse numerous times since then, only to discover that, regardless of my associations between landscape and emotional tranquillity, the country has its own claim to beauty, sanity, and organisational goodness. It became my spiritual home.

I arrived in Switzerland amid an agitation of spirits as I had never experienced before. I felt that my hold on life was tenuous. In the last year I had died a thousand deaths, each more cowardly than that before it. My understanding of my life and its purposes was unfolding before me with all its accompaniment of frustrated desires and unfulfilled hopes. Refusing to face this understanding I tended to clutch at the nearest tangible disaster for a ready explanation. Thus I was overwhelmed by an exaggerated guilt for having destroyed my sister's car or stolen my step-mother's housekeeping money. All feelings of discomfort and lack of fulfilment found their origins in physical trivialities that should ordinarily mean nothing. Further, a grand illusion of life itself spread itself before me inexorably and defiantly.

Switzerland, like the child's toy town in which everything matters and from whence all life comes, rejuvenated my tired and mistaken view of my world. Nothing was explained. The ability to explain lay within me alone. But the Swiss landscape soothed and tamed a host of troubles, fears, and torments. The Swiss themselves added to this their delightful philosophy of life which based itself on the maxim that trivia is the sum-total of one's happiness or misery. Along with all that went the wonderful experiences of reading endless Swiss and French works. Camus, Gide, Piaget and Proust became lifelong loves. They also helped develop what became my wonderfully stilted and immaculate French just as Shakespeare and Dickens had formed my English similarly. Reading Piaget planted the first seed that eventually propelled me to a life in education.

Days were spent learning French in Neuchâtel. When not at school I wandered by the lake or took a trip on one of the small boats that regularly crossed from one side of the lake to the other. I also spent a few days in the magnificent mountains of Les Haudères where I could recollect my thoughts among the proud and hospitable Swiss with their keen appetite for good food and excellent conversation. Though I was too immersed in my own self to note much else, it did not escape my notice that Switzerland was run as a large family, each member of which worked for the others and therefore for himself. Democracy could be truly proud of her children: they lived according to its most ancient and wise precepts.

On the tired and confused mind of a youth, Switzerland had a balmy soothing effect both physically and culturally. Elizabeth and I spent hours of late summer evenings on board a small ferry-boat. Sometimes we talked quietly, but mainly we remained silent and thoughtful. We spent endless hours on the lake-side long after the last boat had ceased its silent and luminous journeying to and fro. We made love freely and without fear of discovery. Later on, when father joined Anne-Marie in Neuchâtel, I boldly introduced him to Elizabeth, who dressed as young as possible, and became known to him as Christina, a Swiss-German from Zurich. This deception was futile as I do not think that he ever believed it! I also furthered the deception by building up a reputation for myself as being a bit of a philanderer. This not so innocent deception I perpetuated by telling Anne-Marie endless humorous lies about my girlfriends. She, I think, never believed me either, though for a different reason.

I stayed another month or so after Elizabeth's return to Beirut. I would have liked to stay there forever but something - a secret or truth still undiscovered - seemed to pull me towards Lebanon again. So, at the age of seventeen, I returned home with a heavy heart but a free mind; for a time at least.

****

On my return to Beirut, father and I held a long conference during which we discussed my future. I asked to be sent to England to prepare for entry into a British university to study English literature. This was rejected on the basis of the lack of a prosperous future as a graduate of literature. Further, I suspect that father still had Ali's stay in England in the foreground of his reasoning against such an enterprise. Finally, it was decided that I should work for father while pursuing an evening course in business studies. In two years the matter could be reviewed and a final choice made. So I found myself encased into a routine of morning work in the office, afternoon preparation of lessons, and evening classes in an infamous school where no one really cared what happened. This routine lasted for some two years which, at the time, promised to be very boring and soul-destroying. As it turned out, they were very important years indeed.

No sooner had I started work for my father than I decided that business was not for me. Initially I worked as hard as I could. Soon, however, I started inventing excuses for not attending work. Eventually I ceased to go to the office altogether on the pretext that I wanted to use the mornings to study. My father proved a very unkind boss who insisted that I should learn the job from the bottom upwards. When, after a year, I found myself still sticking stamps on letters, I confronted father asking him for more responsibility. He was unable to delegate responsibility and try as he would I was getting angrier and angrier at what I thought to be his utter lack of faith in others. After one desperate attempt at proving myself capable, at the end of which he complimented me on my good typing and excellent coffee, I left.

This episode was rather sad as it not only meant that I had failed but also that from then onward I moved further away from my father. His opinion of me became worthless after it had been irritating for a long time. It was soul destroying to spend so much time in an office with an irascible, though very kind, accountant and a painfully shy engineer. The only delight was cavorting with the telephonist in the storeroom where, after a while, the smell of Phospherno 50 became strongly associated with exciting illicit sex with the publicly painfully shy but privately sexually very adventurous secretary. She taught me the inimitable art of wonderfully irreverent promiscuity made all the more enjoyable because father had asked me to stay out of her office adjoining his. He clumsily explained that if I as much as looked at her let alone tried anything, her people would probably make me marry her at gunpoint! For a while she became the only reason making my attendance at the office tolerable.

The pursuit of money, though necessary, struck me as soul-consuming and I determined that never again would I partake of that delicacy known as making more and more money. My year at the office did have one other great benefit: When I was not experimenting frantically and gleefully with Marie the secretary, I used to spend hours writing out little vignettes or character sketches about the people that I met. They filled an endless reservoir within my mind of characters that I could draw on later when I needed them. Being too young and too idealistic to see the necessity of those people's lives, I nonetheless saw their frustrations exaggerated into various delightful eccentricities both in behaviour and in thought. Eccentricities that were adopted as a means of survival in a hostile and uncertain world.

Soon, too, I stopped going to evening school when I realised that neither the director nor the lecturers cared much. I paid the fees which entitled me to enter the examination at the end of two years and that was all that was required of me. I remember how, at the end of the two years, I visited the school after sitting my examinations. The director produced a blank certificate and asked me to give a list of the courses that I had followed. I named all those in which I had been examined. He asked me what results I had got. I did not know. Had I done well? Of course, at least I thought so after all my hard work. He typed out the word 'Distinction' and rolled out the certificate on which he had misspelled my name. He stood up solemnly, and, approaching with heavy and deliberate steps, handed me the certificate. He immediately took it back and rolled it up. He looked around for a something. Not finding it he put an elastic band round the rolled certificate, handed it to me but retained hold of it. I gave him my hand which he shook with the utmost solemnity.

"It gives me great pleasure as Director of this ancient house to bestow upon you this Certificate in Business Studies!"

With an equal solemnity I threw the document in a drawer at home and soon lost it to eternity. Otherwise the entire two years were spent between the British Council and as a regular customer of Uncle Sam's, a café situated near the university in Bliss Street. I read incessantly. I devoured any book that I could get hold of. In the afternoons Elizabeth used to join me at Uncle Sam's where we sat drinking coffee and talking. Soon we were joined by various students from the university. After a while a little table in the corner was reserved for us by the ever friendly waiter who never seemed to mind the ridiculously low bills we ran up because we rarely ordered anything. In return we used to take turns in giving his two boys private lessons – allegedly in mathematics. What outrages we committed on those two boys' literary susceptibility by making them recite endless poems that we liked I shudder to think.

There were five of us: myself, Elizabeth, though she started to join us less and less as time went on, George, a Lebanese Christian, who was deep into Wittgenstein and to whom nobody listened, Walid, a fat lazy genius whose claim to fame was his outstanding photographic memory. He regularly recited the entire *Rape of the Lock* over lunch, and also spent hours reconstructing various famous battles with the aid of sugar lumps, coffee cups, and various cutlery. He was helped in this by our fifth member, Khalil, who insisted that Napoleon and Wellington should be represented by a cigarette each - Gauloise and Rothmans respectively.

Imagine the uproar when a customer asked for sugar and received none as every lump was taking part in the Battle of Waterloo or in some battle in the Spanish Civil War! Picture the complexities of turning history upside down by moving sugar lumps hither and thither. A cup of coffee consumed meant Nelson's death knell or the obliteration of the fifth column in Spain!

Sometimes we were joined by others but such characters tended to be transient especially if Walid held forth in recitation. Muhammad, now a student at the university, joined us now and then. He and Walid developed a venomous enmity after a particularly pitched battle (Waterloo) in which Muhammad (as Napoleon) emerged victorious!

In between battles fought and literary discussions wrought, I seemed to meet an endless array of short term girlfriends with whom I only shared one overwhelming urge: the desire for unrestrained and hidden sex. We did it in amongst the trees on the American University campus, behind rocks on the beach, in borrowed cars, on the sand dunes on the airport road and anywhere that opportunity took us to. We were once caught doing it on the beach and chased off with few clothes and less dignity. Another time, we were arrested and locked up together for a night – which initially frightened us until we realised what a wonderful opportunity this was. In another case, we were caught in a hotel room and locked in two separate rooms whilst the owner tried to interfere with both of us. Eventually, he received a terrified punch leading to my finding the key, escaping and unlocking the girl's room and running out amidst his pathetic moans coming from what used to be my room.

Endless such activity did not relate to my relationship with Elizabeth. A grand deception that suited me and seemed to teach me the art of fictionalising and dissociating on a grand scale. Dissociating was a wonderful drug that kept me going for years to come. Phospherno 50 was replaced by endless literary arguments that confused literature, especially story telling, with sheer sexual excitement.

****

In the spring of 1967 our illusionary lives exploded.

"Hey! Have you heard? Nasser's told U Thant to get out."

"What? My God! This means war."

So we were all thrown into continuous argument and nationalistic fervour that lasted some nineteen days until the outbreak of war.

George momentarily abandoned Wittgenstein. "What for? We don't stand a chance against Israel."

"Don't be so bloody stupid!" replied Walid. "We have over a quarter of a million men to their seventy thousand."

"And two hundred thousand reservists!"

"Ha! Reservists my backside! Fat, overfed civilians."

"That is the last thing that you can say about the Israelis. They are well trained and exceptionally well honed in the art of war. We will lose as sure as night follows day," argued George.

The argument continued for days afterwards during which every lump of sugar at Uncle Sam's was requisitioned to construct the various probabilities of the coming war.

"Hey Walid, breakfast in Tel Aviv?"

"Why not. I promised to bring my mum Dayan's balls pickled in a jar."

This last comment received uproarious applause from all sides.

"We could do with his other eye too!"

"What about us? We want to fight!"

"The bastards have got two billion dollars worth of American arms. Give us some."

Soon the outcry went from the entire university population. Hundreds of young men, myself included, marched towards the presidential palace chanting: "Arm us! Arm us! We want to fight!"

On the way there we were stopped by the police who politely advised us to go towards the UNESCO compound. The Prime Minister was going to address us there. A mass of humanity moved into the compound screaming and shouting hysterically.

"Brothers! Calm down. You will soon get what you want. Indeed, we will soon give you what you deserve!"

"Nasser! Nasser! Nasser!"

"Arm us!"

"We want to fight!"

"Speech! Speech!"

As the last few stragglers from the immense demonstration entered the large compound, an angry-looking young man appeared on the balcony above.

"Brothers! Silence! We want no speeches. No slogans. No talk. We've talked for twenty years. Let the gun talk! The gunnnn!!"

"Nasser! Nasser!'

"We've been tricked. They've closed the bloody gates."

The mass turned around and charged at the gates. Several people tried to climb them. Outside, the police hit them on the knuckles. They fell. I was frightened but furious.

"Open the gates!'

"Who do you get your orders from? Eshkol or Johnson?"

"Open the gates!"

"Nasser! Nasser! Nasser!"

"Nasser! Hey! They've got water canons!"

"Fresh from Washington! Let's inaugurate them!"

Several people stood in front of the jet of water undressing themselves. As the water hit them they flew backwards and tried to get up.

"Nasser! Nasser! Nasser!"

I took refuge behind a tree and looked out for my friends but could not see any of them. I heard shots.

"Someone's been killed. The bastards are shooting. Into the building! Into the building!"

Silence followed. An officer came forward to the gates.

"We shall open one gate. You can come out two at a time. Go home."

Walid joined me.

"Walid! For God's sake. We're supposed to fight Israel. What's going on?"

He and I walked towards the gate and stepped out. Several officers looked at us.

"Go home lads!"

At a small distance several officers were using their gun-butts to force some youths into a van.

"The so-called leaders. First to come out," said Walid.

"Walid. We'll lose this war. George is right. We are not ready for this. We are a nation of savages." I said as I felt my stomach turn. "The whole world is against us. Even ourselves."

"That's traitorous talk. I suppose you want us to recognise Israel next?"

"Why not?" I asked.

"And to hell with the one million miserable wretches in refugee camps! They can all become Lebanese citizens, hey? Just tell them. It's very easy."

With a sick feeling of fear rising within me, I remained silent and miserable. I knew that the coming war would be a disaster for us both as Arabs and, more importantly, as Palestinians. We had no chance against Israel's advanced technology and better trained and equipped army. It was going to be a massacre that would lose us any chance of ever returning to Palestine. I felt a deep and abiding sense of despair at my fellow Arabs' apparent gullibility. I was heart broken at what the future held. With all his economic successes, I felt that President Nasser was behaving irresponsibly and displaying criminal disregard for the masses that he allegedly so valued. I could not get the thought out of my mind of the tens of thousands of poor Arab soldiers who, walking free and alive then, would be dead within a very short period.

Yet another instance of Arab populism and self serving politicising relegating us to more years in the wilderness. Yet another Palestinian missed opportunity dooming us to an eternity of Diaspora with little chance of a homeland.

I went home and asked for permission to go to the Cedars with Muhammad. Only Anne-Marie knew my real intention. Muhammad and Elizabeth lent me the money needed. I went to Jerusalem. I had to see it once before its gates closed on me for the rest of my life. Little did I know then that my little dramatic gesture was in actuality such a prophetic event. I was never to see Jerusalem again. But I anticipate yet again.

Like a thief fearing discovery, I skulked from street to street in Palestinian Jerusalem. The receptionist at the St George's Hotel accompanied me to Nablus where we spent a day in the refugee camp. He talked about the whole uproar as nonsense. He felt disgusted at the Western press for their anti-Arab talk. How could they be so cruel? Let them support Israel if they wanted to, but this was unadulterated prejudice. I agreed saying that we need not expect such support from our so-called friends the Russians. Pity the Americans were not our friends!

At the American Colony I met a red haired girl on a tour of the

Middle East. She wanted to tell me about The Bible. I wanted sex. We both got our way on the hills outside Jerusalem on the night of Friday 2 June 1967 – just under three days before Israel launched its decisive blitzkrieg and set the trend for the several years to come. I kept dreaming of Little Mary as I watched the contorted face surrounded by a blaze of red hair.

After three days I bought a small box that had been hand-made and returned to Beirut with an ever-increasing confusion and fear in mind. The box sits on my desk to this day and I stop to gaze at it as I write this passage.

"Why did you go?" Elizabeth was sitting on the edge of the stage while I was in the auditorium.

"I don't know. I wanted to see it before the holocaust."

"Aren't you exaggerating a little?"

"Whatever happens, things won't be the same - ever again. And holocausts are not identified by numbers only. One death is one too many. We have well and truly lost our nation."

****

"If Israel wants to try war I would again say to it: Welcome."

"Ahlan ya Nasser. Ahlan. Welcome."

Several of us were crowded listening to President Nasser being interviewed by the world press.

"Now the sods will listen to him!"

"We accept no kind of co-existence with Israel. The rights of Palestinians should be given back to the...."

The rest disappeared in an uproar of applause.

"Come on Nasser. Give it to 'em!"

"Hey George. What do you think?"

"He is crude and vulgar. We will lose."

"Oh shut the fuck up, will you. Hey Walid, what do you think?"

"I love him! I love him!"

"Shshsh! Listen!"

"We, the Arabs, are an ancient people with an ancient civilisation going back seven thousand years. We can wait..."

"We can! One hundred million of us lads!"

"Shsh! Shut up, will you."

"When a child is born his mother tells him the whole story and all

that has happened. Thus he knows who are his friends and who are his foes. When the crusaders occupied our country we were under their rule for 70 years, but finally they were gone and only their castles remained behind as historical ruins."

"Walid relax. Israel can have another fifty years if they want it."

"As I said before, Arab people are not people who easily forget. They are a people who have a civilisation and a history and they must achieve their aim. That is the last question. Thank you for giving me you time."

"Any time, Nasser, any time my boy. Hey! Saif what's wrong with you?"

"They did not even thank him for the interview. They're supposed to. What's wrong with the West?"

"Shit on their thanks! How do you like the way he tore that rag to pieces: *'As for the Daily Express, I, again personally read this paper and when I find that you are not insulting me I feel worried.'* Beautiful!"

We all spent the next week meeting at the cafe and watching developments. I was still confused and frightened. I spent most nights with Elizabeth. One evening we went out together to see an old film about the Suez Invasion. We left the cinema early as we could not put up with the continuous applause every time Omar Sharif appeared as a guerrilla with a machine-gun. On the way back to the university we were hailed by Walid through the window of Uncle Sam's. We joined him.

"What battle have you been constructing this time?"

"The coming battle for Palestine."

Walid dived into a complex explanation of the pincer movement to be used by the combined Arab forces after a pre-emptive aerial attack, continuing his detailed exposé after ordering more sugar and several empty cups.

****

"What happened?"

"Walid! We've lost. It's impossible! Muhammad, I thought that God was on our side."

"Who told you that crap!? You were right George."

"I wish that I weren't."

"God on our side my arse! Where do you get that shit from?"
"Muhammad! You're supposed to be a good Moslem."
"Shit."
"Walid, for God's sake explain."
"You might as well fight Britain and the U.S."

****

"Brothers, at times of triumph and tribulation, in the sweet hours and bitter hours, we have become accustomed to sit together to discuss things, to speak frankly of facts, believing that only in this way can we always find the right path, however difficult the circumstances may be."
Walid, George, Khalil, Muhammad, Elizabeth and I sat or lounged on the roof of Muhammad's town house listening to President Nasser on Friday 9th June. Silence reigned amid quiet sobs that erupted here and there.
"I tell you truthfully and despite any factors on which I might have based my attitude during the crisis, that I am ready to bear the whole responsibility. I have taken a decision in which I want you all to help me. I have decided to give up completely and finally every official post and every political role and to return to the ranks of the masses and do my duty with them like every other citizen."
In the darkening evening it was difficult to see what people's faces were like. I heard several sobs as I felt a lump rising in my throat. In the streets below we could already hear crowds shouting and women wailing. Shotgun fire could be heard. The air was filled with the smell of burning and cordite. We all ran to the ledge and looked down. Below us, all over the city, still blacked out due to the war, we saw thousands of little lights coming from torch bearers. We could hear the shuffling of feet below us. A murmur started and got louder and louder. Suddenly, it burst forth into a huge uproar.
"NASSER! NASSER! Stay ya rayess! Stay ya rayess! NASSER! NASSER!"
We sat in the pitch darkness listening to the voices in the city below. The shouting increased and the smell of burning rubber became oppressive. We sat still, exhausted, shocked, frightened, pitiful.
Elizabeth squeezed up to me. She was half-crying.
"It's so cruel. So many killed. Horrible! Horrible!"
"I saw some Western papers today."

204

"Now they're telling us that Israel is not expansionist."

"How could they be so cruel? You'd think that they've won."

"Not won! Not won! Just a setback."

"Rubbish!"

"What do you mean Saif?"

"The Americans and the British weren't involved. We lost because we didn't really want to fight. We are no match for Israel and never will be. It was a bluff, just like this insulting resignation tonight."

"Saif, you never liked Nasser."

"I like the dignity that he stands for. I don't like his vulgar appeal. We're not idiots."

"Aren't we? Fifty thousand dead say we are."

"Not idiots. Cowards, maybe."

"But they're joking about it."

"I know. The New York Times ran a full-page advertisement for El Al."

"What's that?"

"Israel's airline. The advertisement said: Visit Israel and See the Pyramids!"

Everyone laughed.

"It's not funny!"

"Hey lads: what's very, very, very long and has a very black end? No? The Egyptian Army!"

"Don't laugh."

"Time magazine has the best: 'It's unfair,' said a UAR spokesman. 'They have 2,300,000 Jews on their side. And we have none!!'."

A clamour erupted from all sides to tell the best jokes.

"Hey, have you heard of the latest Egyptian invention. An Egyptian tank with one gear forward and four in reverse!"

"SHUT UP! People have died in this war."

"Not war. A little setback. Setback."

"God! I saw a jeep with three hurt by Napalm. Their faces..."

"Don't. Please!"

"Listen to those chaps downstairs. They're going to shout or burn Nasser back into power."

"Good. Come on lads! GET HIM BACK! Nasser! Nasser!"

"Oh shut up and sit down!"

****

We sat silently. I could see little red dots flaming up every time someone took a lungful of cigarette smoke. I tried to work out who was who by the method of smoking.

"We've sacrificed so that our children can live better."

"Crap!"

"Where were the other Arab countries?"

"Busy making deals. Just like our dear ancestors did in forty eight. Just as our loveable forefathers have done for hundreds of years. Selling us down the river."

"Why?"

"What sacrifice? What better life for our children? That idiot Chekhov spent his whole bloody life trying to write plays about sacrifice now for a better tomorrow."

"Look at the Russians now."

"Where were they? The bastards!"

"We've been let down."

"Let down? They're killing themselves laughing. Dayan's pickled balls, my foot!"

"I enjoyed that breakfast in Tel Aviv!"

"This man went up to a fellow and asked him the time. So he took his gun out and shot him. Shot him. Just like that. He lay there, twitched and died."

"And the point of the story is?"

"That life is meaningless and pointless... Kierkegaard was right."

"Have you seen pictures of the refugees? There is this man carrying a mattress, bags and a child in his arms and a baby in his mouth. It's horrible. Horrible sense of déja vue. I suppose some Western organisation will give the photographer concerned a prize. Ugh! And some smug American would bestow a cursory glance at it on his front page while he munches his morning toast – may he choke on it."

"Do you know that the American sonic receiver, Sosus, is still receiving echoes of North Atlantic battles from since the war: Unbelievable!"

"Nothing really ends .... Look at that sky."

"There is no husbandry in heaven tonight."

"Look at that moon."

"Yes. Yes. But us. Beirut. The Middle East."

"Asia and Africa."

"The world. The galaxy. The Universe."

"It's all one gigantic accident… And I had to be in it…"

"He's mad."

"Aye. But there's method in it."

"In what?"

"In night."

"But they're all dead… All."

"All?"

"All?"

"Shut up. Walid, sing."

"When this lousy war is over…"

"Yes?"

"No more fighting …"

"But there hasn't been any - It was a massacre."

"No! No! Only a little setback. Listen to Radio Cairo."

"It is the bewitching ..

"…hour of night ..

"No! *'Tis now the very witching time of night …*

"When churchyards yawn and hell itself breathes out ..

"Contagion to this land."

"World!"

"Poetic licence."

"Poor, sweet little Israel. Doesn't mean any harm."

"When churchyards open and let out their dead."

"Why Shakespeare all the time? Are there no Arab poets then?"

"They all died on the battle field."

"O O O O that Shakespeherian Rag –

It's so elegant

So intelligent

'What shall I do now? What shall I do?

I shall rush out as I am, and walk the street

With my hair down, so. What shall we do tomorrow?

What shall we ever do?'"

"T. S. Eliot had it all wrong. There are no tomorrows after this little debacle… This is the end. Tomorrow belongs to Israel as it did to the Nazis once before."

******

207

The gun-fire was dying down. I moved over to look out. The entire city was now lit by several fires. I sat down again. Now and then when a flame erupted I looked at the faces around me. Some seemed like ghosts returning from the dead, frightened and agonised.

"Why?"

"Oh! Shut up for God's sake. I don't know why!"

"Saif?"

"Yes."

"What are those two whispering about?"

"I don't know."

"Saif. Let's go home. Take me home."

"In a minute."

"Take me tonight. Deep and hard. Oh. Please!"

"Come on."

"Come ... Where?"

"Veni vidi vici..."

"It's more a case of veni veni veni with him!"

"Come on Elizabeth."

"Will you walk out of the air, my lord?"

"Into my grave?"

"Gentlemen. Excuse us. May we take leave of you?"

"My dear Saif, my dear Elizabeth, *you cannot take from* us *anything that* we *will more willingly part withal - except* our *life - except* our *life - except* our *life.*"

"Where're you going?"

"Home."

"And to England I. They cook and fornicate badly!"

"You should see their women with their stiff upper lip..."

"Japanese influence."

"Shut up!"

"Sorry Saif. Only a joke. Only a setback."

"Bye."

"Cheers old man. Ho ho ho."

As Elizabeth and I walked downstairs we could hear Walid talking and Muhammad laughing through the night. Their voices echoed a long way off as we walked hand in hand in the deepest darkness.

"There's an aunt in Dickens. Talks nonsense every time she appears in the book. But - ha! – observe and peripatize anon. String together her speeches separated by the few hundred pages and they make great sense."

"*It has been a turbulent and stormy night. I have been in many; but such a night as this, till now, I ne'er endur'd.*"

"Couldn't agree with you more. *The sun will not be seen to-day; the sky doth frown and lower upon our army.*"

"And that's why we've been thoroughly fucked... Victory certainly does not sit *on our helms*. A fuck! A fuck! *My kingdom for a fuck!*"

"*Rescue, my Lord of Norfolk, rescue, rescue!*"

"Agreed. I've been to Norfolk. They're all desperate to be rescued. Delightful hell hole! The buggers all look alike. "

"Let me recite you some T. S. Eliot to calm you down..."

"An anagram of toilets... And like toilets, T. S. Eliot is full of shit..."

We walked to the university through back streets in order to avoid the crowds. At the university entrance there was a crowd that seemed to be laughing at something. In their midst a man walked with an enormous paper-bag over his head.

"Shame! Shame! Don't look at me!"

"My God!" I shouted "It's Marwan." I ran forward and took the bag off his head.

"What the hell..."

"Shshsh...Come on. Join the fun."

He winked at me, replaced the bag on his head and walked off. He was obviously sober and in full command.

"Shame! Shame!" he shouted. "I am a paralogism! I am an Arab. Ergo an Arab is a paralogism: a contradiction in terms. Shame! Shame! *What's he that was not born of woman?* We've lost! Why? Nasser and one hundred million Arabs!"

He walked around in a circle.

"*...riverrun, past Eve and Adam's, from swerve of shore and bend of bay, brings us by a commodious vicus of recirculation back to Howth Castle and Environs...* Come my friends – my companions in ignominy, gather round and re-Joyce with me..."

We laughed uneasily and walked into the University grounds.

I went into the auditorium and had the curtains pulled back. Elizabeth joined me on the stage.

"He's potty!" she said referring to Marwan.

"Not really. As shocked as we all are. He just lets it overflow in an excess of rather idiotic humour."

"Has he always been like this?"

"Yes. But his jokes are always very meaningful. People laugh but only nervously."

"You like him, don't you?"

"No. I dislike him intensely. He is self engrossed and selfish beyond belief. He is inherently dishonest. But I love him very much. In his own way he is very sensitive and imaginative. I expect he'll be destroyed - like all of us. He has a selfish and callous streak in him."

I walked up to Elizabeth.

"I say, what say you to some *Hamlet? Country matters?*"

"Stop it."

"All right then. Recite Hamlet. You be Ophelia and I, Hamlet."

"No I'll be the lead player."

"You won't ."

"Shshsh... Sit down and listen." I sat in the front row. Elizabeth switched the lights off leaving only the few working stage floodlights on. She started to undress slowly as she spoke.

"*On the contrary, it's the only kind they do believe.*"

"That's not Hamlet!" I protested.

"Then shut up and watch ... *They're conditioned to it. I had an actor once who was condemned to hang for stealing a sheep - or a lamb, I forget which. So I got permission to have him hanged in the middle of a play. Had to change the plot a bit but I thought it would be effective, you know. And you wouldn't believe it, he just wasn't convincing! It was impossible to suspend one's belief. And what with the audience jeering and throwing peanuts, the whole thing was a disaster! He did nothing but cry all the time. Right out of character. Just stood there and cried. Never again!*"

"Is it Stoppard?" I guessed.

Elizabeth stood in the middle of the stage. The strong lights made her body glisten with whiteness.

I stood and approached the stage.

"Elizabeth. I don't want to be like them. Losing our homeland has turned us into being all the same. I want to strike off on my own. I feel like Berenger... I don't want to be like them. I don't want to be a monster either. I don't want to become a rhinoceros. *People who try to hang on to their individuality always come to a bad end! I'm the last*

man left, and I'm staying that way until the end. I'm not capitulating!"
"Do you like it?"
"What? The play? I believe in its message…"
"Do you like it?"
"What?" I asked again, feeling irritated at not being listened to.
"Us? You and I?"
I climbed on the stage and took her in my arms and kissed her as I had never done before.
"You promised?" she whispered.
"Yes. Leave the curtains open. Now! Now! Yes! Yes! Yes!"

****

"Muna!" I stood surprised as I held the door open. "My God! It's you." We hugged each other hard. "When did you get back? How long for? Come in. Come in and sit down."

Muna entered the sitting-room. She looked strikingly beautiful. Her eyes were still wide and luminous. Now tall and somewhat aloof, her long fair hair shone brightly in any light that hit it. After all those years she still seemed more grown up and appeared infinitely wiser than myself. She looked at me with a smile that seemed to say, 'You haven't changed much! Still the frightened little child that I knew!'

We talked for hours about everything except the war. She asked to see what I had written. Very kindly and gently she made various criticisms. We argued and she won. She told me that she was in Beirut for a few days only, on her way to the university in Paris. I made fun of her Australian accent. I told her that I was on my own as my parents were in Switzerland, and that Marwan and Selma were out as usual.

We went for a walk towards the university and I introduced her to friends at Uncle Sam's. From there we went to see Elizabeth.

"Muna! I've heard so much about you". Elizabeth seemed a little distant though friendly enough. She had recently decided to leave Beirut and return to England. Since that decision she had become very quiet and introverted. We never had a chance to talk about things as she refused to discuss her decision.

We sat on the stage chatting about Muna's and my childhood. As in all such cases Elizabeth found it difficult to enter into the spirit of the moment except on a second-hand basis. I suggested that we all had a meal together, maybe at Uncle Sam's. Elizabeth declined saying that she did not want to spoil our fun. We had lots to talk about. I promised to return later that night.

We continued our reminiscences during and after dinner. Muna listened as I did most of the talking. There was so much I wanted to tell her. We took a very long walk on the sea-front.

"What about you, Muna? What have you been doing?"

"Nothing special. I've been growing up!"

"Into a beautiful woman. Do you remember our plans to live together and spend the rest of our lives telling stories?"

She laughed. As she did so she threw her head backwards and opened her mouth wide. For a moment - for a moment only - she looked hideous. Somehow, her laugh seemed insincere and sinister. I turned away and looked out to sea. When I looked back she stood staring at the waters. The red sunset, turning into a bluish-grey evening, reflected against her face. She seemed almost enchanted. I could not believe that a minute before her whole beautiful face expressed such evil in that cackling laugh.

"Muna?"

"Yes?"

"What are you thinking of?"

"Nothing .... Sorry. I am tired. Take me to my hotel."

We returned to her hotel where we sat on the balcony looking out to sea. The evening was warm - too warm. From below us, crowds of people made their way to the numerous night-clubs down the road: a mass of bright lights.

"This is a time of night I hate. Beirut seems too seedy and violent." I looked at the people below.

"Are you happy?" she asked. Her voice seemed as if it were addressed to nothing and no one. I answered earnestly and excitedly.

"No. Something is missing. I feel like that first day at school, bewildered, frightened. I need something that I could do to explain my need - my want of that something somewhere. I am not really making sense."

"What's your name?" she interrupted.

"Sorry?"

"What's your name?"

I was surprised by her question and her strange tone of voice. True to my old faith in her I answered.

"Saif."

"Mine is Muna. Do you like it?"

"Yes."

"How old are you?"

"Nineteen and a half."

"I am over twenty. Do you have a Mother?"

"Muna! For God's sake, what are you getting at?"

She laughed and stood up leaning against the banister. "Have you forgotten?"

I had; up till the moment she laughed. This was a repeat of our very first conversation. "Why?" I asked, laughing.

"Felt like it. Do you have a mother?"

"Not now." I felt uneasy.

"I can be your mummy."

"And I yours since we are both orphans…"

"Do you have a lover?"

"Stop it."

"Can I share her with you if I like her?"

I did not answer. I felt angry and excited.

"Can I?"

"Stop it."

"Can I?"

"Yes!"

"Good. I agree. Now you can kiss my hand."

I laughed and did so.

"Do you want to kiss me?"

"Yes." And I did so. As I started undoing her dress I felt frightened and sick. I thought of Elizabeth and tried to push her out of my mind.

"Come inside." She spoke with authority, as if she expected to be obeyed.

We left the balcony. She whispered in a voice that did not seem to belong to her.

"Switch the lights off!"

I undressed in the dark overcome with excitement and apprehension. I could not think of Elizabeth. I did not care. I thought of nothing but Muna's full luscious body. She lay looking up at me. She held one breast as a suckling mother would do to help her child take the nipple.

"Come here. Let us do everything. Everything! Everything

tonight! Show mummy what you can do. Show mummy how much you've got."

Beirut did indeed seem to feel seedy and violent.

****

I was back in our old house. In the garden stood my little hut with its boxes inside. Muna sat listening to my story. Now and then she held my hand as if to encourage me in my narrative. I could not hear the content of the story. It did not matter. I talked and talked. Suddenly, at the entrance to the small hut, appeared my father's face: scowling and fierce. Beside it, his enormous hand stood motionless. Its long fingers started moving regularly and deliberately. It was then that I realised that he held strings. Below, a little puppet moved awkwardly. Father laughed. I started to laugh too. The puppet walked into the little hut and approached us. Though small, I recognised it as my mother. As it moved forward it made a snapping sound with its jaw as if to bite abruptly and viciously. I looked again. It was still my mother. I laughed. Behind me I could hear Muna laughing childishly. The laughter grew long and uproarious. It slowly became deeper until it turned into that cackle that had terrified me so. Still dwarfed on my boxes, I turned to look at Muna. There was no child there. Instead Muna, as a young women, stood there in the nude. She laughed, and as she did so her whole body shook and her hair fell backward luxuriously. She held a breast pulling it forward between thumb and index finger. The puppet was now very near her. She fell on her hands and knees with her back to me. I looked between her buttocks and legs with embarrassed fascination.

She laughed and barked pretending to be a dog. Seized with terror, I got down and kicked the puppet which stood before me still snapping its jaw. The harder I kicked it the bigger it grew, until, before me, stood my naked mother smiling kindly. Her white face with its two dark eyes twinkled at me. Behind her I could still see Muna, silent now, but still in the same position. Overcome with excitement I ran towards her. She laughed again.

I woke feeling very cold despite the hot night air. I expected to find Muna beside me. She was not. I realised that I had left her asleep in the hotel room and had gone over to Elizabeth's to explain.

To explain what? How could I explain anything? Elizabeth had not been there. I fell asleep waiting for her. I got up from the chair and walked off the stage and down into the auditorium. Suddenly, every light came on, sharply and viciously.

"Why?"

I looked around and saw no one.

"WHY?"

"Come out, love."

"Love? Yes, coming, LOVE!"

She appeared on the stage before me. I approached her.

"Stay off my stage! Stay off!"

I stood below her.

"Why?" she asked

"What do you mean?" I faltered stupidly.

"Why?"

"Elizabeth."

"Why?"

"Okay. Okay. I'll tell you."

"Why?"

"How did you...."

"Would you like the graphic details? Oh my God! How could you? With the balcony door open too..."

"Don't make an issue of what happened." I shouted defensively.

"You're a little bit sick! Both of you! I heard every word. What was it? The ride of the orphans?"

"Come on! Not much different from what we ..."

Before I could finish Elizabeth let out a horrible cry followed by an ugly guttural weeping noise. I ran up the steps and onto the stage. For a while I held her in my arms. I little knew what nonsense I was coming out with but I spoke for a long time. I could not bear listening to her cry. I felt utterly disgusted with myself for being so weak. I was sickened by the sudden realisation that Muna was not to blame for her feelings. I had wanted to do what we did. I had willed it. I had willed the utter destruction of my hopes and dreams. Any other woman would have served as well. It was just that what I had tried to control before in order to preserve my inner feelings from destroying themselves, could not be controlled in Muna's presence. It was somehow morally apposite that Muna should be the instrument of destroying while paradoxically magnifying my "want of that something somewhere".

Elizabeth and I spent the rest of the night together. She made me go through my previous encounter with Muna. I told her everything. She wanted to make love in the same way. I agreed and found a perverse pleasure in what we did and in watching her getting more and more deeply hurt. Like one possessed I hurt her again and again and again with every conceivable detail. I did not seek to understand my demoniac behaviour.

As I dressed in the morning I could hear Elizabeth moving on the stage. I stepped out from behind Hedda Gabler's curtain and walked towards the steps leading to the auditorium. I stepped down and approached the front row. Looking up, I saw Elizabeth staring down at me.

"Will you be back tonight?"

"No!"

"Seeing her?"

"No!"

"Saif....."

"Yes?"

I looked up too late. I felt a sharp and hard object hit my forehead. I reeled and turned round.

"Get out you bastard!"

I staggered a few steps then ran towards the exit. I looked back: Elizabeth was sitting on a chair with a pile of marking in front of her. She appeared oddly calm, as if nothing had happened. Outside, I heard several voices.

"Go," she said quietly. "Go. I have a class now. Sorry. I am, you know. Sorry for you. Go now."

I ran out, past the students coming in, and into the street. My forehead ached. I felt it with my fingers and it was sticky with blood. As I walked home I cried. I cried for myself: not in self-pity. Just for myself: misconceived, obscene, wretched, more sinning than sinned against.

I never saw Elizabeth again. Or Muna.

To England. With speed to England - to forge a stronger link with the past and a better bridge to the tortured future.

Book 3

O Sweet England

My great train of troubles, fears, and torments increases yet again as I
journey towards a last beginning and final ending.
*My lamp burns low, and I have written far into the night; but the dear
presence, without which I were nothing, bears me company.*

Beirut is now destroyed.
The 1967 war is forgotten.
Even Yom Kippur has lost its echoes. And so have the many wars that
succeeded it.
Only one echo reverberates still: death stalking my childhood
landscape.

But Beirut dies. Amidst its ruins echo the noises of happy children and
painted agony.
Rubble upon rubble, pain upon pain, death upon death.

The city trudges on towards a new life born of old.
It matters little what has happened. It matters even less what will
happen.
Nothing will change.
People will return to a past forgotten and a future uncertain.
Exiled, frightened, bewildered, and hateful they crawl towards another
childhood.
Children of a country that feeds on their jubilation and expectations.

And in the rubble lie mysteries and secrets that will never be known or
felt.
The rubble is cleared away.
Beneath it, above it, beside it, wandering eyes stare in search of more
rubble.
A child is dead; another is born.

I was told, as I packed for England, "No rush. Take it easy, my love."
But I crushed the coming rubble under my feet and all that went with it.
Awaiting The Third Return.

Chapter 1 The Portrait of the Artist as a Young Wog

Saif stepped out of his cottage with a sensation of disgust mixed with hope. He had just been listening to President Sadat's first speech before the Israeli Knesset and felt disgusted at what he sensed was a betrayal of Palestinian refugees. Further, President Sadat's long-awaited speech proved to be no more than a long chain of truisms held together by the importance of the occasion, not by the contents of the speech itself.

A soothing feeling of hope flowed through the turbulence of Saif's disgust. What if Sadat were to succeed? What if he were truly sincere in his references to the Palestinian problem? What if Palestine were to be reborn as a result of this brave action taken by yet another self seeking and dishonest Arab dictator? He felt a strong doubt and knew that there would not be a new Palestine reborn in fifty years if ever. How can this happen with every Arab government busily lining its own members' pockets with oil money and with every Arab citizen living in abject subjugation to heartless dictatorships? Even Lebanon, the so-called beacon of Arab democracy, was tearing itself apart in a most incomprehensible and mad way that no one in the world would have thought possible of a county with such glaring potential.

He decided not to think of the matter any further. He, like so many Palestinians, would have to wait and see. A tinge of nostalgia made him wish that the man speaking in Jerusalem had been the late Nasser who, despite his ineffable political stupidity, gave the Arabs some dignity and self respect before he took them too far to a humiliating defeat by Israel.

He walked down the long drive from his cottage. Before him stood a magnificent Essex view. Several fields undulated gently into the marshes but nowhere could he see the dividing line between the marshes and the sea. The entire landscape was spread out like a giant canvas. With great sensitivity, the artist had mixed his colours such that nowhere could one colour be distinguished from another. Several dead elms and a few massive birches spread their arms towards the sky in a supplication of prayers and humorous contortions of limbs. Here and there a few birds flew or hopped in search of food.

Saif entered the farmyard at the end of his lane. There, he stood for a short while watching two trees that stood at some distance bordering two fields. Depending on the position from which the onlooker admired them, they moved in the most enchanting tricks of perspective. Saif constantly referred to them as his own private Constable that changed every second of the day according to the light and the season. But the two trees never changed: they were dead elms.

They had two effects on Saif. Whenever depressed he would look between the two trees at the distant horizon and calmly drink in all the sensations and information that his clear-sighted vision fed him. He also felt a close affinity between his generally calm mood and the two dead elms before him.

The entire pastoral and sensuous silence that surrounded him seemed to contrast sharply with his daily life during the week. Comprehensive schools were oppressive and noisy. Everyone struggled to survive within the massive institution - just like the real world outside. Children, however, were still children and it struck Saif as the height of pathos that they struggled so hard yet had their innocence brutally extracted from them by an incompetent and uncaring education system.

As a writer, Saif despised teaching. He cut a rather uninspiring figure as he recited Shakespeare to a class that conceded no relevance between the great bard and Woolworth's Saturday job or the little sexual experiments in the local park accompanied by heavy drinking and drug taking learnt from immature and callous parents. Luckily for Saif, however, he had been working for over two years in a school with excellent staff and a very sensitive and maternal headteacher. He delighted in working with them and the children. Even his least intelligent pupil seemed to sense his sensitivity and to treat him gently.

The two elms moved fast towards Saif and towards each other. The one on the left seemed to move closer and closer until it merged with its brother nearest Saif. He sat beneath the one that shielded the other. Turning round he saw that the other tree had returned to its original distant position. Before him, across the field, he could see the upper floor of his tiny cottage. He wondered what his family was doing, surrounded by so much greenness that was slowly turning into an autumnal brown.

Colours always reminded him of his arrival in England. Everything was green and self-contained. The very first thing that he had done in London was to go to Hyde Park Corner, and had timed his arrival for a Sunday for that very purpose. It amused him now to recall his inexpressible happiness at seeing and listening to 'eccentric' people.

He eventually learnt that the English were not eccentric - they simply lived and let live. How delightful! If a heavily tattooed man dressed in a suit with white pearly buttons wanted to insult the Prime Minister, he did so. Saif's heart warmed to this island's two greatest possessions: liberty with individual dignity. He had set out to learn and acquire these greatest of qualities.

Ten years later he proudly swore allegiance to Her Most Gracious Majesty and became one of Her subjects. He smiled to think of how, like Micawber's colleague Captain Hopkins reading the petition to the House of Commons, he had given every word of the oath the same luscious roll whilst the solicitor, whose name of Mr. Powell oozed delightful irony, looked on impatiently and with palpable boredom. A long time later Saif met the real Enoch Powell at a political gathering and found him wonderfully articulate, logical and highly intelligent – but whose politics he continued to find pernicious.

Not that he could really understand his heavily tattooed friend at Hyde Park. Saif's English was immaculately and exclusively the property of Her Most Gracious Majesty. As a result, when his new friend had stepped off his box in Hyde Park after shouting, "'ow about a cuppa Rosy?" Saif was thoroughly confused. At Victoria station he approached a ticket collector and, in a tongue that would have made the compilers of the Oxford English Dictionary proud, he inquired for the Hastings train. He had to rely on his own resources when the official mumbled some indistinct noises at him.

He learnt fast, however, for he understood his landlord when he referred to his wife, "She can't arf rabbit!" Seeing no evidence of children he realised that he may have understood the words though not their meaning. After a few months at the hands of his patient landlady in Hastings, he recognised his mastery of the new tongue when he found himself asking for "them there bloody eggs"! Professor Higgins, in the person of his landlady, danced for joy at his successful education.

Mrs Lewis's laughter at this outburst still rang in his ears as he thought of this episode. Good old podgy comfortable Mrs Lewis! He had not seen her for years. She was so kind to him particularly during a series of minor illnesses brought on by the inclement British weather. He had not in fact returned to Hastings since a year after he had left it to attend Teachers' Training College. That had been a terrible waste of intellectual activity as had been teaching itself.

He had promised Vivienne never to return to that area in Sussex after they had parted for the last time. A year after that, he never returned. As for that year....

What, in Heaven's name, had prompted him to be so cruel in parting from her? What was behind that undying urge to hurt her? He still could not tell after all those years. She was a woman whose soul merged into his and, even after parting, they remained one for years.

They first met at the college where they were studying. It was just before Christmas. He had fallen ill yet again. During one of Mrs Lewis's numerous visits upstairs accompanied by her two dogs, three cats, and Joey, the moth-eaten parrot sitting on her shoulder, she had given him a letter delivered by Vivienne while he slept. Next morning, he returned to college and went with Vivienne for a long walk on the sea-front. He declared his undying love and was thrilled to find that it was fully requited.

Vivienne was a girl with a typical English beauty. Long auburn hair covered a high forehead and somewhat egg-shaped head. Her slightly aquiline nose gave her a rather haughty look that contrasted oddly with her soft skin and quiet voice. She had large brown eyes above two very red and rounded cheeks that reminded him of wonderful apples. A keen horse-rider, an artist, and a poet of nature, she opened before him an endless vista of natural beauty and sensuous delight in Nature in its minutest detail. For some two years they spent long days - and sometimes nights - walking softly, O so softly, on the hilly country where the famous Battle took place.

Some time after they had met they solemnised their relationship by promising eternal love: He, Lochinvar, and she his lady maiden, eternally young, eternally loved, eternally bound. Theirs was a beautiful relationship that could never be repeated except in *Paul et Virginie* and such wonderful epics.

Why? Why?

In a little hiding place where they fancied that William the Conqueror had stood with his Norman entourage, they regularly made passionate, innocent and hopeful love. Warm within their love, they lay in each other's arms amid flowers, grassy fields, and the endless wind-chatter of tall green trees, a language that Vivienne understood and that Saif wanted so much to learn. He learnt. He learnt to love selflessly and earnestly. They wrote poetry together shamelessly aping Wordsworth. Saif used to read Gray's *Elegy in a Country Church Yard* aloud under their favourite tree. He always finished the soft reading with the Stanza that was omitted after the first few editions:

"There scatter'd oft, the earliest of the year,
By hands unseen are showers of violets found;
The redbreast loves to build and warble there,
And little footstops lightly print the ground."

And as he finished whispering the last line, they would make love with heightened intensity and, looking in each other's eyes, declare their love over and over again until satiated.

Why?

Anne Guinivere Ashley was also training to become a teacher when Saif moved to Eastbourne. Saif felt bored and tired by the pettiness and insipidity of a trainee teacher's life and the utter stupidity of his lecturers whose little knowledge of education was surrounded by moth eaten second hand gibberish. He read avidly but had no one to discuss his work with. Anne made a willing and admiring listener. She loved selfishly and ardently. And duly worshipped at his pompous and oversized literary ego that could no longer tell fact from fiction. She took over the running of his life and played the role of a mother to his childish orphaned soul.

****

Feeling cold, Saif got up and started walking back to the cottage. As always he felt solemn when he thought of Vivienne. A drizzle fell gently down as a thin sheet that yet again transformed his Constable canvas. He removed his glasses to wipe them. Blurred, the canvas looked like some mad surrealistic blob.

Anne had unwittingly pushed him towards cruelly renouncing Vivienne. Passively, he had followed Anne into a whirlwind of misunderstood love and passion. Torn between honest desire and secret passion he swung back and forth between the two women.

It took three years of emotional torture, somehow wilfully wooed and intellectual frustration at college, before he left Anne - turbulent and tempestuous of spirit.

But by then he had lost Vivienne's poetry and natural love.

He clearly remembered that beautiful July morning with Vivienne on the Battle site. He had intended to ask her to marry him. They talked long and quietly. His guilt kept him away from the purpose of the meeting. Suddenly, as he gathered courage, Vivienne asked him to go away. She made him promise never to come back to that area again;

never to seek to see her. He promised. She left him seated where they had spent such long and happy hours.

He shuddered to think how he sat there for the whole day and late into the night hoping for her return. For a year after, he regularly went there or stood outside Vivienne's house hoping for a glimpse of her. But that was his sad and embarrassingly pathetic secret.

Must visit Mrs Lewis some day soon.

As he turned into his drive, he saw his young daughter running towards him. Behind her walked his wife. The child jumped into his open arms shouting, "Nanna Grandad here! Nanna Grandad here!" He carried her on one arm and held his wife with the other.

"Nice walk?" she asked gently.

No sooner had they entered the cottage and sat down than the little girl jumped on her grandmother's lap saying, "Oo read me a tory, pease!" Nanna started reading the child's favourite tale: "Booty and the Beat".

Within the bosom of his family and inside the little cottage, Saif always felt relaxed and easy. Not that those who saw him elsewhere ever noticed any but a quiet and apparently satisfied mood. Any conflicts or thoughts stayed inside him.

"Heard from Hussein recently?" asked his father-in-law by way of conversation.

"Nothing new. He's still in Beirut. Marwan is in London. Looks like finding a job for a while."

"Bad out there again?"

"Yes."

"How's school?"

"All right. I like it in so far as I could ever like teaching."

The same question and answer session took place between the two men every time that they met. There was something reassuring about the constant repetition of what had become a family ritual. It also seemed to put the two men at ease with each other. Eventually, as always, the conversation drifted into a discussion on political matters, money, or the history of union movements in Britain. Saif found it ironic that he should have married the daughter of an ex-docker from London. His own father, Hussein, used to refer disparagingly, and at times venomously, to the endless dockers' strikes which hindered the delivery of ICI material to Lebanon. He had tended to sympathise with his father's hardship. Now he was seeing the other side of the coin.

He was horrified by his father-in-law's stories of survival on the barges and at the docks, the arduous and long working hours, the ridiculously low pay and the freezing conditions in the winter. Also he was moved by the man's struggle to keep himself going, a struggle that showed in his face and in the glint in his eyes. The stories were never empty of their touches of humour: petty pilfering (particularly at Christmas), long conversations with foreign sailors who spoke little or no English, and minor antagonisms among union members.

The most exciting stories were those of the Socialist Sunday School. Saif was ever so excited to hear that his father in law had known George Orwell. He was constantly hoping for some nugget of a story about the great man. It never came. All that the old man could say was that Orwell did not say much and that he ate voraciously.

His wife's parents were simple folk who kept themselves to themselves and had worked hard. They were kind and generous, without pernicious intended prejudice or social consciousness. He felt a little saddened to note that his comparatively affluent upbringing had deprived him of a happy family life. The parents who sat before him had done so much to raise their daughter in an emotionally stable atmosphere. It seemed to him - presumptuous as it may appear - amazing that two virtually uneducated people could do so much to produce such a gentle, kind, and intelligently understanding daughter, his wife. Both her parents epitomised everything that he loved about England including their uuintentional and often quite hurtful racist remarks. As often in his life, he did not fully see beyond the façade. Little did he know that the woman he so loved and idolised then would eventually destroy him with unparalleled cruelty. She would leave him for another in a heartless and prolonged game of deserved as well as undeserved blame that eventually led to his life being destroyed. But then Saif compartmentalised his little life into what he wanted to know and what he preferred to pretend did not exist because it did not fit in with his ideals.

They drank tea amid the cheerful noises of a long conversation that no one seemed to listen to. The sounds were enough. Susan, his daughter, was, as always, the focus of attention.

"Where's your north and south?" shouted grandad. The little girl opened her mouth very wide in expectation of some reward.

"Tom!" shouted his wife in mock affectation. "Don't teach her that!"

"Eeya! Take a butcher's at this!" he shouted jocularly holding a bar of chocolate in his hand. Susan rushed towards him. "Hey mind me meats!"

Saif laughed and got up. "I am going to use the jellybone."

As always, this was said with such a correct accent that everybody laughed. Rhyming slang certainly did not fit the quiet and thoughtful voice, made more humorous coming from the rounded brown face and the Professor Higgins accent.

****

"Hello. Marwan, is that you?"

"Hello! What goes? Where to? How far?" asked Marwan in a loud welcoming voice.

"Nothing special. Nowhere special. No distance."

"Good. Glad to hear that life is as exciting as ever in bubbling Essex!"

"It isn't, thank God!"

"All right! Enough pleasantries."

"Okay."

"The wife?"

"Well."

"Despite having a little screw loose somewhere? Hmmm?"

"She is perfect."

"Salima?" This was Marwan's name for Susan to whom Saif had refused to give an Arabic name when his father insisted on one. Saif had refused to be instructed on what he felt to be his business, and his alone. The whole incident had been very unpleasant and Saif disliked being reminded of it. Like so much else his family constantly reminded him of his regrettable stand against his aged father. He felt strongly in his belief that he was right despite the discomfort hurting his father made him feel.

"She is well, thank you" he replied formally.

"Ooops! Sorry. Will you be writing another epistolary masterpiece?"

Saif thought that his humorous fool of a brother - as always - meant no apparent harm despite causing a great deal of it most of the time. The reference to a letter was to the time when Saif had written a sharp admonitory letter to his brothers and sister after a disastrous family

225

reunion in London during which they irritated him by their constant reference to his car accident, and Anne-Marie and everybody else's sexual and personal affairs. His response had been somewhat violent though under the circumstances probably justified. They meant no harm. His ever-irritating sensitivity gave him no defence against what he saw as their vulgarity and unbelievable stupidity. In effect the error was his; he should have never joined a family reunion, which he did out of a misplaced sense of duty.

"Ah shut up you rubbery faced old flabby-brain!" said Saif laughing, though a little nervously.

"Well! You shall soon be receiving a letter." Marwan laughed as he spoke. "How now nephew of mine. Why telephone? Wherefore? Where to? Haji has snuffed it!"

"You're joking?"

"Of course. I wouldn't be so serious if she had! Shame! Shame! Shame! She will live forever. Screamed all day. Took her to hospital. She sang for death to come. She named her coffin-bearers. She named you. Stomach in terrible pain. One little look, one big examination and one ginormous fart and they sent her home. She had bad wind. I always said that she's an old wind bag!"

Saif laughed as he imagined his rather corpulent aunt being carried to hospital singing and belching.

"By the way Marwan, I phoned concerning the shares. Can you sell them for me?"

"Worthless. War. Boom boom. You broke?"

"No. House buying."

"Hmm! I'm broke. Twenty thousand a year is a lot but shshsh! I'm spending forty - ha ha ha!" Beneath the laughter there was a distinct nervous culpability as Marwan knew that a British teacher's salary in the late seventies was barely a tenth of what he earned.

"Hmm! Sad about Muhammad. Hey?"

"What do you mean? What happened?"

"Oh! Haven't you heard?" There was a tinge of shamed excitement in Marwan's voice. "He's dead. Went back into the house. Forgotten his keys. Rocket. Nothing. Gone."

Saif felt his stomach fill with fear and bitterness.

"You there Saif old man? Yes. What the hell made him go back for the fucking key? His poor wife."

Saif said good-bye quickly and walked out of the cottage. He could hear the family still chatting and laughing.

****

Old big ears, dead! Muhammad, dead! A violent death by explosion and dismemberment. Impossible! Images raced through Saif's head as he walked towards his two trees.

Laughter on all sides. The little boy standing in front of the classroom, his lips trembling, tears glistening but not falling as he tried to defend the concept of a flying boat which he had been planning to build. An increase in laughter. Suddenly his voice seemed to be coming from somewhere else. He broke down crying but still managing to shout out as the tears fell onto his cheeks: "Why can't I build it? They always laugh at me and call me big ears."

"Since you've been in England I've met a girl. I'd like you to meet her."

Upstairs two girls were sitting on a divan. He introduced one as Leila and the other as his cousin. The latter had a husky voice and a trace of a moustache. Leila welcomed the two friends. They talked and drank. Muhammad drank incessantly as he sat by his girlfriend. His bravado resulted in his entire body, with the exception of his feet, being huddled up under the table. Leila asked Saif to take him home. The moustachioed cousin begged a lift. "Come on big ears!"

An hour later Saif and Leila sat holding hands. They kissed passionately. Leila refused to undress. "I shall preserve myself" she said, as her hand increased its motion causing Saif to whimper.

He was in Beirut for Selma's wedding. He spent hours with Muhammad, laughing at the ridiculous fuss being made of his sister's impending non event of a marriage and his father's repulsive social conformity, and regretted having ever accepted the invitation.

Eastbourne. "The radar is here!"

"Why do you call him that?" asked Anne.

"Good God! Haven't you seen his ears?"

"I'm only here for two days," declared big ears.

Five summer weeks passed by. Carol's bra was ripped off and he got a thicker big ear.

Since that visit, Saif had only seen Muhammad once during a brief visit to Beirut. Two years later big ears got married. *'My wife is almost as nice as yours,'* he had written. A photograph of the couple cutting a wedding cake. The ears had shrunk.

And now, married only a few months, his wife pregnant, Muhammad was dead. Killed by a stray rocket. God! Beirut had become a murderous Inferno. First poor George taking his own life and now Muhammad! What would Wittgenstein make of that?

****

Saif stood on the footpath staring at his two trees against the slowly darkening sky. He found a comfortable though cold seat on an old tree stump. The two dead elms seemed distant against the grey beyond, their limbs outstretched to the heavens, reminding Saif of women wailing at an Arab funeral. He tried not to think of Muhammad but it was impossible. He thought of their short time together in Eastbourne and their endless arguments about anything that came up. Saif had won an argument against what he kept calling the evils of Communism. Muhammad got the upper hand in a discussion about nationalism. Abhorrent to Saif's sensitive individuality, nationalism was lauded by his friend. They had also discussed Saif's college life. They spent endless nights talking about every subject that occurred to them. They both slept with the veterinary nurse who lived upstairs and spent hours talking about their experiences. They delighted in playing the game of each pretending not to know about the other when they were with her. They then spent hours after she left analysing her language for nuances of an admission that she had slept with both at different times.

No sooner had Muhammad departed than Saif quit his college while still in his final year. Disgusted and embittered by the lack of academic or any other challenge, Saif left Eastbourne for the University of Kent which he was to join in the next academic year. He, therefore, decided to spend a while in Beirut before returning to Canterbury to search for a place to live. During his final few weeks in Eastbourne he met Emily and became friends.

Emily was a little woman with a gentle and quiet spirit. They spent a week during which they saw each other every day. For the first time Saif could talk. For the only time in his life he confided in someone unreservedly. Emily was an excellent listener, questioning Saif on every detail of his life. He ran through it, from his boyhood days to the very moment that she sat by his side. She loved him for the suffering that his soul had known and he loved her for understanding him.

Desdemona to his Othello. Their love remained unspoken: it matured as they spoke and listened to each other. A week later the two friends said goodbye and Saif flew out to Beirut. This was his second visit since he had quitted that city some five years earlier.

He felt calm in a way that he had never done before. Emily now shared his burden, his want of something, somewhere, missing. They had parted good friends, ostensibly never to meet again. Within minutes of his arrival in Beirut his whole being raged with a desperate fire within. He missed England sorely.

"Will you marry me?"

Emily stared at the telegram for a long, long time. Only the day before the two had been talking about Nasser and how Saif had cried bitterly when he had heard of his death despite despising his vulgar politics. Emily had also cried to hear the story of this tragic and flawed fallen idol. She understood why Saif was so upset. She assumed no vulgar nationalist fever. Anne had always laughed at his tears.

During his five weeks stay in Beirut, Saif sensed the underlying violence of the city in a way that he had never done when he had lived there as a boy. In his letters to Emily he spoke of a raging fire that engulfed his every sense, a fire that was fed by the whole social and political existence of that country and its capital.

A short visit to Petra in Jordan alleviated some of the strains that he felt. Open, vast, and beautiful - he loved it. Petra was of another world: an older and nobler world. Crouching on top of a low mountain he watched the magnificent sunrise which turned the whole world into all shades of red. While sitting there he was approached by a little boy no older than four or five who seemed to appear from one of the numerous rocks that surrounded him.

"Hay mistah! Wanna buy?" He produced a little stone on which was engraved the picture of a woman straddling over a man lying on his back and holding his erection. Silhouetted in black both characters appeared upon a grey canvas. Behind the two stood one long object rather like an enormous foot.

Saif stared at the stone fascinated. "Where did you get this?" he asked in Arabic.

"Antique mistah. Antique."

"Come here." The boy approached suspiciously. "You can speak Arabic to me, all right?" Saif asked gently. The boy nodded slowly. "Where did you get this?"

"Found it, sir."

"Where?"

The boy pointed vaguely towards a range of hills in the distance.

"How much do you want for it?"

"Anything master."

"Tell you what," said Saif confidentially. "I will give you a whole pound for it."

"English?" asked the boy incredulously.

"Yes."

"American better master."

Saif laughed and the little boy joined in. "How does your father make them little one?" asked Saif suddenly.

"Easy master. He..." The boy stopped and stepped back.

"It's all right. Don't worry. I still want it. Here take this. It's all I've got. Twenty pounds. Take it to your father."

The boy stared at Saif as if he had gone a little mad. He was delighted. As he walked off a look of utter contempt passed over his face. He put the note in one of his shoes and ran down the side of the mountain like a wild goat, his little body soon disappearing amongst the rocks.

Saif smiled nostalgically as he thought of that boy. He wondered where he would be now. He must have become a young man of eight or nine. A cold chill went through his body as he looked around at the beginning of an early autumn evening. He sensed the tranquillity that he had felt at that time in Petra overcome his mind. Momentarily at least he had forgotten Muhammad's death.

****

As soon as he had returned from Petra he left Lebanon for England - and Emily. Being in her final year at college the two decided to wait until she received her degree before they married. They spent a quiet six months working, reading, and talking during long walks on the seafront.

Saif felt a tinge of embarrassment as he remembered his wedding day. The only member of his family present was Ali: he had brought one of his numerous girl friends along, a slender girl of great beauty but of lesser clothing. The poor thing was completely out of place. They had arrived in an enormous Rolls-Royce which Ali had hired for the

230

occasion. Seated in the small front room of Emily's humble parental home, Ali proceeded to drink. By the end of the small wedding reception he was completely drunk. Saif shuddered to think of how his eldest brother, like all very sympathetic drunkards, had proceeded to embrace Emily's father as he joined him in shedding tears. A picture of Ali persistently kissing Saif's new father-in-law on the neck rose before him. He could still hear Ali kissing loudly and saying frothily, "There! There! I love you too. You haven't lost a daughter. You have gained an idiot!" Saif laughed uneasily to think of the whole episode. Later on, several people had begged a lift of Saif and, when no place was found for yet another friend, it was suggested by someone that since the bride was so little maybe she would not mind sitting in the luggage compartment of the station-wagon. Saif rejected the suggestion impatiently.

Uneasily and with trembling spirits Saif took his new bride to Lebanon for a honeymoon. He could not bear to think of that visit. He got up and retraced his steps towards the cottage, looking behind once at the elm trees which were starting to disappear into a final blend with the coming night sky.

"Daddy! Daddy! We 'aving dith and dipth. Dum and dee."

"Oh! Isn't that exciting." Saif made a great effort. "Fish from Mersea."

"No daddy from da dop."

"Dilly!" mimicked Emily. "It's fresh fish from Mersea. Nanna bought it in da dop."

"Yet! Yet! I know," shouted little Susan excitedly.

During dinner Saif remained quiet and distant. No one paid him any attention. He was left alone as always when thoughtful. It was assumed that he was thinking of his PhD research which he was doing part-time while teaching. He stayed in the small dining room while Susan was made ready for bed. Sometime later she came in to give him a good night kiss.

"Ummm - ma! ood night. Dum and dee me in a minute."

A few minutes later he went upstairs where the two small bedrooms overlooked fields on either side of the cottage. He sat on Susan's bed for their nightly chat.

"What dall we do tomo'ow?" she asked wide-eyed in anticipation.

"What would you like to do, little one?"

"Do oo work tomo'ow?"

"No. It's Sunday."

"No. I mean in oo tuddy."

"No. No work in the study tomorrow. We will spend the day together. What would you like to do?"

"Shall we go to da doo and dee de monkeys. Yet. And bar-bee-oo out-tide. Yet. Yet. And nana grandad..." Susan spoke on at length as she always did during their nightly chats. When she had finished Saif kissed her good night and walked downstairs. As he did he went through their regular nightly ritual by shouting up the stairs and being echoed by the sleepy child's voice:

"Night night."

"Nat nat, daddy."

"Sleep well."

"Deep we'w."

"See you in the morning."

"Dee oo in da morn-ing."

"Love you."

"Lud oo."

After this interchange Susan settled into 'reading' one of her story books aloud until she fell asleep.

****

Emily waved her parents good-bye and returned to the cottage. She switched the outside light off, bolted and locked the door, and entered the tiny kitchen to prepare the coffee.

"Coffee?"

No reply came. She pushed open the sliding door and found Saif seated in his chair with his head held in his hands. He shook convulsively. No noise came from him. Emily gently shut the door and stayed out in the kitchen. He would tell her in his own good time.

Both she and Saif enjoyed a silent and undemonstrative love. They felt each other's moods and understood each other's gesture, tone of voice and movement. A silent agreement also enjoined them to leave each other alone in times of crises, or at any other time for that matter. Yet they shared everything of their quiet life, whether talked about or not.

"Muhammad is dead," said Saif calmly when Emily had sat down before his chair. She did not ask how and showed no particular

232

recognisable reaction. She just let Saif talk. He talked. He cried. He brought out every feeling of hate for the civil war in Lebanon. Soon he was beginning to feel cleansed but not clean.

"I don't understand. I cannot recognise myself anymore. I cannot recognise truth from fiction in my life. How much of my life has been a state of mind and not an event? I cannot...Bastards! Why?"

"Does it make any difference?" asked Emily.

"No. He's dead. That's all."

"I meant about your life. Reality or imagination, the result is the same. Events may be lunatic but the emotional reality is intact."

"Do you remember Muhammad in Beirut?"

"Yes. He always gave the punch line of a joke in Arabic."

Saif laughed to remember the circle of friends recounting jokes at Uncle Sam's. Muhammad had always insisted on translating Arabic jokes into English for Emily's benefit. Towards the end of every joke he would turn to Emily and say, "Sorry. Hmm. Untranslatable." Then he would proceed to continue in Arabic. Emily joined in the laughter because it was infectious.

"He wasn't at all affected like the others," she said in order to keep Saif talking.

"No. That's why they laughed at him so much."

They talked about their honeymoon in Beirut late into the night. At times they laughed, at other times spoke sadly as two old people might do when referring to a personal event of so long ago. Their memories were true to emotional realities even if their vision of the events was distorted by Saif's inner turmoil and passions when in Lebanon.

Summer 1973 had been Emily's first trip abroad. Both excited, the newly-weds had arrived at Beirut airport unaware of what to expect. Saif felt rather like a tourist who wanted to learn all he could about this beautiful country and its people. After some six years in England he had decided that his dislike of Lebanon was based on false assumptions of sensitivity of spirit and a misplaced sense of superiority that, intrinsically at least, had no validity. Armed with his love for Emily and with her inexhaustible supply of tolerance and patience, he had returned to his old home, from a loved exile, to try anew. Maybe this time he could understand better. Maybe England had taught him the supreme quality of patience.

But returning always tends to disappointment. The itinerant exile's view has usually changed by the time he returns. Where he expects to find everything exactly as he had left it, he finds that it too has changed. His attitude to it remains the same as when he had left it; therefore the change seems all the more oppressive. Paradoxically, those to whom he is returning see him with the same eyes as when he had left.

Saif and Emily had not anticipated this development when they arrived in Beirut for their honeymoon. Now, having moved as much as they had in their four years of marriage they had come to accept the heavy handed disappointment of returning, a disappointment that was amply balanced by their more pleasant aspects of a return to the past. Memories were aroused and emotions anticipated, especially when the changes seen or experienced were known to be on their side.

They were always amused to return to Faversham where they had spent a very happy first two years of their married life, while Saif was an undergraduate at Kent. They would regularly visit a shopkeeper by the name of Motley: a kind and honest elderly gentleman with whom they had often spent time chatting while making their purchases. The beauty of visiting Mr. Motley lay in the way that he managed to transport them right into the past, to the day when they had last met. As soon as they stepped into his shop after an absence of a year or so, he would turn around and continue the very same conversation that they had interrupted the last time they had met. They felt as if they had been absent for only a day or so. Good old Mr. Motley! A touch of solid companionable old England!

****

But the confusions of a return to the past had never been so disastrous as when the couple had gone back to Beirut. Emily, too, felt that she was "going back" as she had heard so much about Lebanon from her new husband.

No sooner had they stepped off the plane in Beirut than she noticed a change in Saif. The easy going, quiet, and somewhat reserved face was replaced with a very defensive attitude in everything he did or said. Suddenly, she was seeing another side to her husband, one she had never seen before. She realised that this required the utmost care in dealing with him, particularly if he was to dampen the burning fire that always raged within him at the very mention of his early life in Lebanon.

Emily saw her genial and somewhat old-fashioned husband ageing with suppressed and conflicting emotion. Externally, he made a grave show of exuberance. It was rather sad to watch him laugh inordinately at anything that was meant to amuse him. He never seemed to be himself. With his father, he seemed secretive, defiant, and almost rudely defensive. In the presence of his sister he remained polite and distant but obviously he disliked her intensely. He had no apparent reason to do so. Emily could see that his sister could be irritating. She was rather loud, insistent, and a little pretentious. She also seemed very spoilt. But beneath all these external qualities, Emily could see a kindly sister who loved her younger brother very much. Surely Saif had also seen her as intelligent and sensitive enough to avoid being taken in by external factors? He was usually so understanding particularly of other people's foibles. Why not with his own family?

Saif seemed to burn with contradictory passions. Within, he disliked all that he saw in Lebanon. The country did not seem to offer to him its real and undeniable beauty. In fact, it seemed to Emily as if Saif could not - and did not - see Lebanon as it was when they were there. He seemed to have made up his mind what everything should be and had to be. All evidence to the contrary he ignored. It was as if he were watching a film which he speeded up or slowed down as he wanted. He never watched it at the right speed.

Undeniably, Emily could see that there were things to dislike. The city of Beirut was overcrowded with people and with a tense atmosphere of underlying violence. It felt as if the whole place were about to blow up in one enormous cataclysm. True, the Lebanese were not as civilised as they liked to pretend. Indeed, the upper crust of society was pretty disgusting in its indifference to the suffering of the majority or to the impending and inevitable explosion. Though very well educated, the majority of Lebanese lacked culture, particularly a national culture. They seemed embarrassed by their education and offensively proud of their lack of culture. They came across as lacking a sense of nationhood. They owed their personal allegiance to their families or differing religions or tribal feudalism but never to an agreed shared national ideal or identity. All that Emily could see clearly.

The countryside's beauty was undoubtedly magnificent, which gave credence to the fact that man's first experience of written words must - and rightly should - have been born there. The majority of its people were genuinely hard-working and an exuberantly friendly lot.

Any failings that Lebanon may have had were due to an error of history and not to its people.

Emily knew and trusted her husband enough to realise that, distorted though his vision might be, his suffering during his childhood and youth must have been real and durably painful. What was it that distorted his view so? It was easy enough to talk about his mother's death. It was even easier to think of the childish eye resenting the good and valiant efforts of the surrogate mother, Selma. It was also somewhat comic to think that the corner in her husband's mind which concerned itself with his Lebanon experiences had never grown up. He seemed so childlike in his attitudes while in Beirut. He was so earnest, so vehement, so passionate, so defiant and stodgy. So English - and yet not so.

The two had gone to the Cedars to spend a few days. The landscape was outstanding and they spent five heavenly days just looking and feeding their inner selves with every conceivable beauty that the mind could take in. Emily began to understand the effect that the landscape had on her husband. Ironically, he yearned for England, even while at the Cedars. She jokingly called him a neophyte of the worst kind!

****

On their last night at the small mountain hotel, Emily was approached by the head waiter who tried to accost her. Naively, in the belief of tolerating different national customs, she allowed him to kiss her hand. Encouraged, he tried to go further. She repulsed his advances in no uncertain terms. Later on she told Saif what had happened. He quietly called the man to him and, in a gentle voice, admonished him for what he had tried. He did not seem angry or outraged. He spoke very quietly. The poor waiter stood there expecting to be shot in a classic *'crime passionnel'*. He apologised profusely and, as soon as he could, left the hotel and was not seen again while the couple were there. Later on, Saif's anger rose and he went out looking for the man. Luckily, Emily thought, he could not find him anywhere. But his anger was swift - belated pangs of manly pride that were suppressed almost as soon as they arose.

Emily's confusion was increased by this incident. She admired her husband for his apparent calmness. But where were the repressed passions and confusions? She had misjudged him in assuming an

236

explosion. She had hesitated in telling him but their frank and open relationship demanded that he be told, and now while he still had the option of reacting.

Saif had approached the man and politely accepted an apology. This, undoubtedly was a very civilised way of sorting out a problem. It was not without its humorous side. Emily laughed to see the face of the confused and terrified waiter. But decidedly two things seemed to act on her husband: the landscape and his memories. She was beginning to realise that Saif never lived in the present moment. He brooded over his memories and continually shaped and reshaped them. It was the attribute of the imaginative artist, she thought. Tired and unable to understand fully what she knew would take a lifetime to comprehend, she changed her point of view. She started to see her husband as the creative author she had known him to be. What made it difficult for her to see this before was the fact that he seemed to have two distinct characters.

Normally, he was a genial and extremely hard-working man. Dreaming, perhaps, but with a mental stamina that enabled him to perform seemingly impossible feats such as writing for four days with minimal food and no sleep.

As an author he was intolerable. He wrote for long hours at a time. Like a child he cried when it would not come right and danced when it did. He exaggerated his every emotion while writing. The normally quiet man turned into a volcanic tempered one: he would kick a chair continually for five minutes while screaming like a man demented. Suddenly, he would laugh, kiss his wife, and make prolonged and somewhat violent love to her. Once, writing a short detective story, he had cried noisily and long, after the murder was committed. For days, he sulked, then he burnt the manuscript and celebrated. She, and only she, understood his two predominant moods and knew how to deal with them. Rather like a mother with a spoilt child.

Horribly, he seemed to feel most creative when his emotions were aroused. He always wrote well and movingly after a visit from or to his family, or after they had made love. He would also work extremely hard at university or at school. Once utterly exhausted and consequently defenceless, he would write until he was physically sick for lack of sleep and food, and too much coffee and smoking.

Disastrous as their visit to Lebanon had been, Emily recognised, and took the chance to know better the man she loved so much. She came to understand him well. Kind, genial, and childishly romantic on the one hand; and emotional, sensual, and a little frightening on the other. On the surface the two aspects never seemed to meet. But, she learnt while in Lebanon, that the two were inseparable to those who knew him. The creative urge was always there and held in check. It was released only when needed, conversely when it became too much. That seemed to be the secret of the Lebanon experiences: to see him as an author. She so wanted to encourage him. She became a Dorothea to his Casaubon. Little did each know that some twenty years later, she would suddenly feel tired and walk out on him as he sat there with child like amazement at being deserted by the only person he ever truly trusted.

Emotions as well as events he seemed partially blind to, were collected and suppressed, then recollected in the tranquillity of his little study in England. In every recollection he relived the emotion and the partially seen event. He reacted then - and only then - as if he were a victim of a time lapse. It was this that made him so intolerant of his family and his country of origin. It was this that made him, ironically, so calm and collected during a crisis. His colleagues at school were continually asking her if he ever got angry. Publicly, he was quiet and gentle. The real experience was in reliving it in his small and overcrowded study. As a result his whole reality became distorted and therefore novelistic. He lived in a novel-like life in a fourth dimension.

He cried, for example, every time Juliet died, but appeared indifferent to the suffering of those around him.

****

"Isn't it strange" asked Emily, having sat silently for a while after chatting about their last visit to Lebanon. "Isn't it funny how for some quarter of a century we were going our own sweet ways without a thought of each other? Then, suddenly, we are married. Bizarre!"

"I expect that it was written," joked Saif.

"It must have been. Each was being formed for the other. We met and - poom!"

"Yes! Poom!"

"Stop it!" Emily laughed at the gesture that Saif had made.

"What were you doing on Monday 5th June 1967?" he asked

"Oh! Come on!"

"I woke up at seven-thirty. The Lebanese Air Force was making a show of force with its lousy two aircrafts! I went to Uncle Sam's café and in the afternoon slept at the Edison Cinema. At night I slept with Elizabeth. And you? Well, let me see. You went to an open air theatre in Regent's Park to see *Midsummer Night's Dream*. You were escorted home at the end of a warm evening by a fellow called Robert."

"You've been at my diaries!"

"Yet! Yet! I ha-ad!"

Emily laughed at his imitation of little Susan. She well remembered that theatre-outing. The evening newspaper headlines had caught her eye but had made no particular impression. She deplored all violence.

"Horrible!" she said. "While Arabs and Jews were massacring each other I was watching Shakespeare!"

"Why horrible! I wish we had been watching Shakespeare instead. So much to enjoy. I myself was listening to the radio and watching television."

Saif jumped up and assumed a supposedly belligerent attitude. *'To arms, Arabs! To the heart of occupied Palestine! Rendezvous in Tel Aviv, Arabs!'*

He laughed in that strange, almost hysterical way that he always did when he talked about the June 67 war.

"Hello Folks! This is Radio Jerusalem. Where is your airfield at Al-Arish now? Nothing but dust remains. We hope you managed to escape in time.'

"I was also being comforted by American reassurances of their desire for peace. Russian vows of friendship. My God! Never has there been a more horribly enjoyed war by everyone except the Arabs! A straight forward slaughter. Of course Israel does not really come into it. We did it."

"Like Lebanon now?" asked Emily who knew that the only way to deal with Saif in such cases was to pour more fuel on the fire so that it would burn itself out.

"Doesn't bear talking about," he said decisively.

"Right then. What was I doing on Thursday 18th October 1972? Bet you don't know."

"This." Saif kissed his wife gently and slowly.

"I thought that you wouldn't remember," she said.

"My dear lady, I live on the enormous fund of ridiculous dates in my head."

"Great! And you don't even know today's date." She laughed gently.

"'Nopdie! I don't! Oo dee, I had too much to doo', as little Susan would say."

The small door leading in from the kitchen slid open slowly. Both Saif and Emily jumped with the momentary fear of the unknown.

"Did oo call? I couldn't deep. Oo making too much noid. Oo two, three, door, dive, deben."

Susan waddled into the room with the air of someone who had given a good explanation for unreasonable behaviour. Unaware of anything else she dived into her pile of toys. Saif and Emily laughed.

"Bed for you young lady," laughed Emily.

"I'd had enough deep, dank oo mummy," Susan replied in a very matter of fact way.

"Come on, move!"

"I'm mooding! I'm mooding!" Susan ran up the cottage stairs with her excited laughter reverberating all over the little house.

****

Saif was fascinated by the inference of what Emily had said about their two respective lives. All was towards some purpose. If only the purpose could be reached by a painless short cut. He remembered how fascinated, though also a little irritated, he was by the inadequacy of fatalistic arguments.

Fate? Maybe. As a Moslem he should easily accept the inevitable. He did not. Whenever the inevitable happened he went back over it and rearranged it in a more readily manageable form.

"She's asleep now." Emily sat down with a sight of relief. "Peace at last!"

As so often, the two sat silently for a long time before the little fire in the centre wall of their sitting-room.

"Anything on television tonight?" asked Emily.

"No," replied Saif with a little of the usual contempt that he felt for television and other popular media. He was always too tired to watch anything of a serious nature.

"Isn't it nice having an evening together for a change?" asked Emily.

"Yes. Poor Muhammad. The great biography will never be."

"What?"

"Nothing. Just thinking of something Muhammad once jokingly said."

"I'm sorry," she whispered.

"So am I."

Saif became thoughtful. Emily could sense that a crisis was at hand. Soon he would get up and go into his cramped study in the garden shed to write. Something should be done or said or written to indicate Muhammad's futile death. Nothing. Maybe a few late night hours spent on the Ph.D. would help dispel any excess emotion.

For the last four years Saif had been working very hard, first on his BA degree, and later, on his Masters. He had first worked full-time as a teacher in an independent school. His routine was simple though very strenuous: when at home during the evenings and the week-ends he worked on his thesis. He had hated the school where the owner made enormous sums of money while his poor overseas students regularly failed miserably and lived wretchedly in damp and freezing classrooms. The whole set-up infuriated Saif beyond endurance. As always nothing showed. This repression caused him to work better on his M.Phil. thesis which was eventually accepted.

Now he was busy working on his Ph.D. after having applied to over two hundred universities and colleges for English literature jobs and been rejected. The main difference was that this time he was a little happier working in a state school despite the very hard work. Here, at least, teachers cared and the authorities tried to do their jobs to the best of their abilities. Ipswich had offered him an escape from the inefficiency and educational dishonesty of the independent school system that he had known. He was willing to put up with the long journey every day rather than experience the horrors and pretensions of his previous school.

****

Tired, sorrowful, and somewhat confused, Saif lay in bed beside Emily. They had made love happily and now Emily breathed gently by his side. He was struck by the difference in her face once she had closed her eyes. He picked up the book lying beside his bed for the usual quick nightly reading session. It was a large volume of the

Complete Keats and Shelley. He read absentmindedly for a while. Slowly, almost imperceptibly, words started to take shape and meanings. Pages moved gently swaying from side to side. Some words ran off the page and fell down off the edges. Thousands of others joined them and ran all over the bed. Saif jumped up. Words were approaching him menacingly and silently. Suddenly, they started humming and talking like a host of rebellious men. He crouched against the window but they kept coming towards him, their long spidery legs moving fast. The window opened and he fell out. The fall was long and persistent. Above him words fell like thousands of little lemmings driven to their death by a determined instinct. A line of words hand in hand passed him on the way down. *Beauty is truth, truth beauty, that is all ye know on earth, and all ye need to know.* The line twined itself round him. It felt tight. Oppressive.

Saif put the book aside and switched the light off. He turned over, frightened. What was the dream about. Poor big ears! As sleep started to overcome him he felt that oppressive feeling filling his chest, the same feeling of wanting something somewhere which had haunted him all his life.

Arriving at an airport he was met by his sister at the bottom of the escalator.

"Mama never died. You can see her now!"

In a room on top of a snowy mountain lay his mother dressed in black. He wondered what he should call her. Mother? Mama?

"Madame, I am pleased to meet you."

She smiled almost maliciously as if to leer at his assumed politeness.

"I am dying now." Her voice was the same as it had been when she told them that she was dying all those years ago.

He wanted to ask why she had hidden herself all these years.

"I have a wife and a daughter now" he bragged.

She smiled as she died a quiet death.

"Mother! Mother! Please don't. I have a wife and daughter. I want to show you my daughter. Mama!"

He looked at her through his tears. She had decayed like an exhumed skeleton. A worm crawled silently out of an eye socket.

Saif woke crying, and was enclosed in Emily's comforting arms.

Chapter 2

Handel's music for *The Royal Fireworks* solemnly and weightily ushered our arrival at Marwan's new country house in Surrey. Marwan himself stood at the top of the wide front steps. Gracefully, and somewhat regally, he descended the steps towards the three of us. Susan laughed to see her uncle walking in that way.

"He ooks ike a princess!" she shouted excitedly.

After our very long drive through Essex, London, and Surrey, I and my own family had come to spend the day at Marwan's. He was holding one of his ghastly family reunions.

Marwan held a large tome in his hand and recited from it in a Wagnerian voice.

"riverrun, past Eve and Adam's, from swerve of shore and bend of bay, brings us by a commodious vicus of recirculation back to Howth Castle and Environs."

I smiled and replied, "Wonderful opening to *Finnegan's Wake*."

"Oh my God. Our papa, affectionately but accurately known as 'the fool', was right. He said that you would recognise the quotation because, and I quote your most distinguished pater's very words, you liked the sort of excremental filth Joyce wrote."

Again I laughed – but this time somewhat nervously.

Emily and I did not do proper justice to Marwan's semi-humorous and semi-ironic comment on the grand family reunion. Father, Ali, Selma, and Marwan's family were all there for this long awaited reunion. I was rather apprehensive as memories of the last - and only – reunion's disastrous effects still burnt within me. That I disliked my family I had come to accept as a fact of life. Their world and mine were as far apart as they could ever be. I resented nothing that they did or said as long as it was done or said at a great distance from me. I tried hard not to show my intense dislike of their obsessive concern with other people's affairs. The result, sadly, was always of the worst kind. I ended up sitting among them more silent than usual; silent and bored. I felt conspicuous, rather like a non-smoker trying to look unaffected in the presence of a companion who smoked heavily. I dare say that, in their eyes, I must have seemed morose, critical, and, above all, a spoilsport.

Over the years I had developed a personal theory of existence that allowed me to jog along without having to be caused too much discomfort by that which could cause me to be unsettled. The theory was very simple.

The Universe was the result of a major accidental explosion which in itself accidentally caused the earth to cool sufficiently to accidentally support life which in turn accidentally produced various forms of accidental life. Two of these accidental lives accidentally met (my mother and father) and accidentally thought that they had fallen in love. They, therefore, decided to show the love that they accidentally fell into in the only way that they knew how. The result of these long lines of accidents was the final accident of my unplanned birth. If my father had loved the woman sitting to the left of my mother or the one sitting to her right, that accidental glance would have created a completely different me and this novel might have been a good detective story or an Homeric epic. If my mother had pleaded a headache instead of complying I would be nowhere. If my father had withdrawn at the moment of crisis instead of allowing his sperm to make contact with that solitary egg I should have been a mere little parental dream instead of becoming their nightmare. If Israel had lost and Palestinians continued their lives in Palestine, I might have been a farmer born of a Palestinian mother or maybe a Jewish emigrée so my father told me. The list of accidental ifs is endless. Consequently, being an accident, it did not really matter what I thought of my family or what they thought of me.

Years later, a good and kind psychiatrist diagnosed something called 'dissociation'. And by then, I, grown remarkably like my late father, thought her opinion excremental filth as I sat there wondering if she would have an affair with me. But I anticipate by several decades of quirky but easily foreseen maldevelopment.

Usually, I tried to make excuses for not being able to join such reunions. At that particular time, however, I felt that it would be wrong not to go especially as it was father who had asked us down. Also, Emily said that we should do and I never dreamt of not doing what Emily said. She was my soul, my centre, my everything. I knew that we were destined to a long and wonderful life of incessant happiness, love and comfort. Disliking the fuss that reunions of this kind caused, and infuriated by my family's usual indecision, lack of punctuality, and absence of intelligent conversation, I, nonetheless, felt it a cumbersome duty to answer father's summons. I never fully understood why I felt so obedient when I disliked everything that he stood for especially his

244

cold unemotional façade.

It is difficult to explain the seemingly contradictory feeling of excitement that I got every time I went to see the family. It was as if everything would be different. As always, I had arrived with the best of intentions of joining in and generally being pleasantly hypocritical. I had carefully built a strong external shell that would, I felt, please the family. I was, after all, in the minority.

Marwan's royal reception, albeit ironically though harmlessly intended, had the effect of putting me at ease during the initial meeting. His humour and, at times, trenchant sarcasm always alleviated some of the miseries of reunions.

"All the buggers are assembled above, milord!" he said mischievously. "Milord will find writing material in his chamber. Milord desires to indulge in the epistolary art, I presume?"

"Thank you Bunter. Thank you." I replied humorously.

"Milord will find her ladyship his sister much changed."

"To the better, I hope my good man."

Marwan's eyes rolled back and his arms went up in the air in an apparent expression of despair.

"Milord will also find Milord's elder's distillery much improved."

This reference was to Ali's drinking habits. In front of us Emily and little Susan were carefully negotiating the steps.

"Me! Me! I go up by mydelf!"

I asked Marwan how father was.

"Milord will..." I interrupted him.

"Milord will kick you in the posterior if you don't stop being stupid."

Marwan burst out laughing, happy with the effect his game was having on me.

"How is baba?" I asked.

"Mad as a hatter, but not to worry. It's nice to see one thing that hasn't changed in this family."

As we approached the large front-room I could hear several people talking loudly. Above the noise came the final strains of *The Royal Fireworks*. As the music stopped I heard father say, "I could swallow the price but, by God, I couldn't digest it!"

Marwan and I walked in.

"Ho ho! Ahlan! Ahlan! Welcome!" shouted father. We kissed reluctantly and I could smell the Brilliantine that I loved so much when a child being carried in his arms.

Selma drawled loudly. "Ah! I cannot be bothered to get up. I'm so tired."

The Lebanese civil war was telling in every line on her face. Dislike her as I did, I could not help but sense a deep and confusedly affectionate feeling for her strength and for the miseries she had recently endured.

"Hey! Where's Emily and Susan. I ain't gonna have you in ma house if they're not with you." Marwan's American wife had the misfortune of speaking with the loudest voice that her glorious continent could muster. Her apparent kindness, genial wide-eyed innocence and striking beauty did not, unfortunately, alleviate my irritation at her voice. Decidedly, this commencement of a family reunion was doomed to disaster. I felt angry with myself as I sensed my carefully built edifice of towering family tolerance crumbling at this frontal attack from across the Atlantic. Emily and Susan walked in. Thank heaven for little girls! Susan had saved the initial tension in the atmosphere by her entrance.

"Oh! Isn't she gor-rr-geous!" shouted Selma.

"Yet! Yet! I'm are!" responded little Susan. Everybody laughed.

"I see that she has Saif's modesty!" joked Selma.

Marwan changed the record and Tchaikovsky's 1812 filled the room.

"All right!" he shouted glibly. "I declare this family reunion open. You will, I am sure, appreciate the incidental music composed especially for this historic moment."

We all sat down. I could feel myself being irresistibly pulled down into an abysmal silence as the family settled down for the morning's chat.

****

"How's school?" asked father when we were left alone.

Outside, we could hear several people talking loudly and excitedly in the kitchen. They seemed to be arguing about the best place to have lunch. My heart sank. I hated going to restaurants, particularly expensive ones where the waiters watched over you in that irritatingly deferential manner. I heard Marwan shouting that he needed thousands to keep her royal highness happy. Selma laughed and told him that she would send him seven thousand pounds in a week. He jocularly thanked her and offered to do anything that she wanted for that price.

"How's school?" repeated father with a look of intense interest on his aged but rather stupid face.

"Quite well, thank you."

"Better than your old place at the private school?"

"Not private, father. Independent. Yes, it is. That other place was a nightmare! I'm happy at this school. An excellent head and a very friendly staff."

"Is the pay enough?"

"Rather. But teachers in England are paid a pittance. We're not in it for the money, that you can be sure of."

He looked thoughtful. "Yes," he mused. "Teachers are badly paid everywhere. I cannot understand how anyone could choose such an unrewarding profession. It is no different to domestic service."

"It's rewarding in other ways."

"Yes" he said doubtfully.

"I always felt as you obviously do. But you see, father, putting aside the feelings of disgust and bitterness one gets regularly at the end of every month because of the low salary, there are hours of challenge and enjoyment." I thought I spoke a little vehemently, and somewhat naively. "I felt very unhappy when I first joined the school, it was so massive. The headmistress was very good and she made life easier for me. So did everybody else. A gentle Head of Department, an earnest book stockist and others. Mind you, I was still unhappy."

"What happened to make you change your mind?" Father was beginning to lose interest as he always did when someone tried to confide in him. I suddenly sensed that I was embarrassing him but I liked doing so. I so wanted to shock him with details of rabid sex with the book stockist in the English stock cupboard. Of filthy notes passed on surreptitiously during staff meetings promising delights to come later on. Marwan came in.

"Ah! Milord speaks with the goodly pater. Incidental music coming up."

Within seconds Handel's *Messiah* echoed all over the house.

"Turn it down!" shouted father irritably. As Marwan did so he said quietly, "I shouldn't talk to the silly old fool myself."

"What did you say son?" asked father.

"I was saying that I shouldn't like to have a swimming pool

myself" he answered as he left the room

"Right you are my son. Too expensive."

I had a suspicion that father's alleged deafness was no more than a defence against the mild lunacy of his children. I continued talking earnestly about school.

"One day I sat in the staff-room, bored and dreamily composing my letter of resignation when I had an epiphany."

"A what?"

"An epiphany. A kind of vision or manifestation. As in Joyce's Stephen..."

"Joyce?"

"Joyce."

"James?"

"James."

"James Joyce?"

"James Joyce."

"Son! I can swallow a great deal but my stomach could never digest James Joyce, Freud, Lawrence. Filth. I leave you young ones to devour such intellectual excrement!"

"Norman Holland would love you father."

"Who is he?"

"A critic. Talks in Freudian terms of the oral and anal sensations of connections."

"Enough!"

I laughed nervously, remembering my father's vehement dislike of any post-Dickensian novel. And also because I was half inclined to agree with him.

"Anyway father, for want of a better word, I had an epiphany."

"And?"

"Well. I simply saw two teachers in an earnest conversation over some school work they were preparing. I was transformed. I felt happy."

"Why?" Father did not particularly take to my aesthetic or sensuous manner of expression. An argument should be bagged, weighed, and delivered. Feelings made him impatient. I must also add my slight sense of incompetence at not being able to explain myself better.

"The point. The point my boy. Take example from Churchill."

I tried to explain again. "The two teachers' earnestness and

248

selfless devotion had touched some dormant chord within me."

"My God! He's a musical instrument now!"

I laughed.

"The teachers' names?" asked father in true Lebanese tradition.

"Tricker and Pegnall."

"Odd names! English, are they?"

Father seemed to have a vague notion that all English names were divided into four equal parts: a quarter were hyphenated, another titled, a third were named Smith, and the remainder were Green, Brown, Black, White and other appropriate colourations. I amusingly watched his impassive face and affectionately wondered why an apparently intelligent and hard working man should feel so intimidated by the presence of his family as to adopt a false face.

"Your daughter is a little fat."

I swallowed my annoyance and mumbled something about keeping an eye on her. Marwan entered again, this time accompanied by Selma and Ali.

"I shall phone Anne-Marie."

Father got up and went to the telephone in Marwan's small study. As he sat down he shouted, "Great Art my boy. Great Art."

Marwan laughed. In his study hung an enormous picture of a woman's bottom.

"Take it down," joked Ali. "You'll kill him with the excitement."

"Ho ho!" cried Marwan. "I'll put a few more up. Money would come in handy."

Although a popular pleasantry within the family, I could not help but dislike that kind of joke. I laughed loudly and ostentatiously.

"Saif! Saif! Anne Marie wants to talk to you." I went into the study and took the telephone. Father left the room. Always a gentleman, I thought.

"*Allo! Anne-Marie. Salut ma biche!*" I shouted down the telephone. "How's *la belle belle belle Suisse*?"

"Fine. Are you coming next summer?"

"Of course. Without my annual visit to Switzerland to give me some civilisation I would go mad."

I heard a groan coming from the other room. The rest of the family did not particularly share my high opinion of Switzerland and its people.

"*Comment va la famille?*"

"Usual," I answered.

"Who is there?"

I told her.

"*Oh, mon Dieu, ça doit être affreux!*"

"Better than usual, but you're not missing anything" I shouted.

She joked about being able to stay away from family reunions. "Saif, I read your novel *Carol's Dream*."

"Oh good," I said excitedly. "What do you think of it?"

"*Je ne l'aime pas de tout.*"

Anne Marie always got to the point. Hurtful as it may sometimes be, I never really minded. I admired and valued her bluntness.

"It's not as good as your other novelette *The French Murders. C'était un roman intelligent.*"

"I agree."

"Have you tried publishers?"

"No. Only the definitive work will go out."

"*Et c'est quand que ce chef d'oeuvre sera écrit?*" There was not the slightest tinge of irony in her voice. I was grateful for her kind faith.

"*Je ne sais pas quand ça sera fini...*"

"Write it quickly. You must. I hear that *le Prix Nobel* is going begging".

I laughed and wished her good-bye. Father returned when I called him. As Anne-Marie wished me 'au-revoir' I thought that I heard a click as if someone had replaced the receiver of one of the extensions.

When I returned to the front-room Ali, Marwan, Selma, and Mary-Lou were noisily arguing about the rights and wrongs of something or other. I felt intensely irritated by their sweeping generalisations. Further, I was inhibited by the television being on too loudly.

"Yeah! Like I ain't saying nothing against Britain. But ma God! They pay all these taxes and get nothin' in return. Ma God! Some don't even have a bath in their house!"

Marwan looked at his wife with slight annoyance. Emily immersed herself further in a game she was playing with Susan.

"Ah mean! Sa-if, do yah think it's fair?"

"Yes," I answered curtly.

"Sa-if yah like it in England?"

"I love it. I'm British and proud of it," I declared pompously as I tried to suppress my anger.

"Well! See, I told you," said Ali triumphantly. He pointed to his head several times. My anger rose. 'For God's sake, do not be so earnest,' I thought to myself and smiled. Support came from an unexpected quarter.

"He's right!" Selma said, maternally. "Don't listen to them. You stay here in England."

"I intend to." I replied rudely. I followed this with a quick nervous laugh to make up for it. I realised that Emily was right. I get viciously different in the bosom of my family. I wondered how Ali, Selma, or Marwan acted outside the family circle. I felt sad that we could not be ourselves when together. We seemed to be in the grip of a controlled hysteria. If only we could discover the controller and kill him. We were all too damn dishonest, or alternatively wilfully stupid. I felt the sweat rising from every pore of my body. When the others dived into a discussion of the latest gossip, I left the room thankful for my one and only saving grace: My darling Emily.

As I made coffee in the kitchen, Marwan joined me.

"What a bore! A disastrous bore!" he shouted, enjoying every minute of it. I envied him his resilience. I admired him for his characteristic way of following me into the kitchen in order to make me feel better little knowing that he had done so to enjoy the sheer drama of my discomfort. But I knew that he was bound to say something to lessen my inexplicable annoyance. He started to pace up and down the kitchen in a very vigorous and determined manner. He always did this when he wanted to confide in his listener. Over the years I had grown to know and love him better for - I know not what as I was equally confused by my intense dislike of his ugly character. I sat at the table with my coffee and lit a cigarette. On the board beside me I saw a paper with a list of outstanding bills. He saw me looking.

"Ha! Yes, I'm broke. Thy brother is brothen. The more you have the poorer you are."

He spoke with the mock-wisdom of one who knew that he was being somewhat too smart. "Have you heard? No, wait a minute. This requires some incidental music. Vivaldi's *La Stravaganza*. Imagine you have it in the background because I don't feel like going into that room full of lunatics."

I promised that I would do so and laughingly hummed the opening allegro movement.

"No! No! Spiritoso please! Spiritosi - or arso as the case may be." He laughed at his own vulgarity.

"Proceed *mon cher Vautrin!*" I commanded jovially. It was like being back in our old garden again.

"Have you heard," he commenced in whispering confidence. "Have you heard that Samira and Ali are separated?"

"No."

He was delighted.

"What about their little boy?" I asked.

"Pray, my dear fellow, don't be such a bore. That side of things will provide endless gossip in twenty years."

"It's not funny!" I laughed.

"And," he continued ignoring me. "And - ha wait for it - wait for it. Selma and her good fellow are also in separatissimo."

I was a little taken aback. My conflicts with Selma have given her a very large place in my heart albeit not a sound one, the place I mean!

"Why?" I asked, horrified.

"I shall, my boy, adopt the Socratic manner with you. Observe and, pray, peripatize. Do you know your sister?"

"Yes."

"Can you see her?"

"No."

"Can you visualise her, you stupid ass."

"Yes, brother of mine."

"Can you hear her voice?"

"Yes."

"Does that answer your question?"

"Yes." We burst out laughing aware of the cruelty of our joke.

"It's sad," I said. "She deserves better from life."

"What?" screamed Marwan in mock horror. "Shall we make the circle a square? Shall we discover infinity? Shall we find Atlantis? Shall we make Hussein intelligent? Shall we regain Palestine? Yes! Yes! You are defending Selma?"

"Oh come on, Marwan. I may not particularly like her, but I recognise goodness and quality when I see them. My dislike of her is only due to some misconceived childish thoughts that I cannot help."

Marwan looked genuinely surprised. So was I.

"I cannot abide the serious dialogue, therefore I withdraw." He danced out of the room. Susan came running in shouting that she could have a biscuit. Emily came after her.

"Would oo like one, daddy?" she asked graciously. I gave the usual affirmative answer. She took two biscuits and walked out. Emily turned to me.

"Is it very bad?"

"Thank your stars that you don't speak Arabic."

"I understand enough to know what you mean. I'm afraid that I'll have to go to the restaurant with you. Mary-Lou insisted so much I couldn't refuse. I do wish she would take no for an answer," she added somewhat irritably.

"It's only once a year," I said jokingly. "Poor little Susan. She'll be exhausted."

"Yes. It takes her a week to recover afterwards."

"I suppose you couldn't put your foot down on this?" I asked hopefully.

"Not without being rude to Marwan's wife."

"Yes I know. If she tells me one more time to hire a maid to help you I shall pitch her out of the window, arse over apex!"

"Saif? What happens to you when you meet your family? What happens to everybody?"

"My dear lady if I knew I would make Shakespeare look like Pinocchio's puppet theatre."

She laughed.

"There are more things in families, *Horatio than are dreamt of in your philosophy."*

"But come: here, as before, never, so help you mercy,
How strange or odd soe'er I bear myself-
As I, perchance, hereafter shall think meet
To put an antick disposition on-"

I was interrupted by Susan walking in crying loudly and bitterly. In her hands she held a dozen or so Kit-Kat bars.

"What is it, love?" Emily asked.

"Uncle Marwan dave me choc-lade," she cried.

I laughed as I felt my initial annoyance at Marwan subside.

"Ooo! Daddy! I dan't eat dem all!" she cried.

Emily put the chocolate in her handbag, promising Susan to look after them. The latter cheered up and we prepared for our departure to the restaurant.

****

253

"Drive slowly son. We are in no great hurry. Marwan drives like a maniac. The alcohol in Ali's breath would be enough to power his car. Slowly now. Keep to the right. The RIGHT. Oh, of course. We're in England. Sorry my boy, it's my old age."

I drove at a steady speed of forty. Emily and Susan sat in the back. The little one had fallen asleep. I was thankful for that.

I could see Marwan's car disappearing ahead of us. Behind it, Ali's car persistently gripped the white line in the middle of the road. "He'll kill himself one of these days," I thought as I watched Selma waving her arms about in the passenger seat, being her usual voluble self. Since my disastrous letter to the family, Ali and I had exchanged very few formal words despite my offer of peace through Selma. I feared that his sensitivities of being the oldest child were bruised permanently. It mattered little to me since I despised him.

"Don't think, son. Concentrate on your driving. I'll talk to you in order to keep you awake. I had to do that once in 1927 to keep a driver awake during a night drive from Damascus to Baghdad."

I was amused to consider, rather rudely, that father's conversation was liable to have the opposite of its intended effect. I winked at Emily in the rear-view mirror. Father went forth.

"No good. Ali drinks too much. I've told him several times but to no avail. Watch those lights son! He drinks. Keep right - er - left - left now. You must remember that the English drive on the left. You know that of course. After ten years here. Yes. Too much money. They spend though. Do you know, son, if Ali or Marwan lost their jobs tomorrow they would be penniless. Penniless! I told them. Haji told them: '*O your white penny for your black day.*' That's an Arabic expression like saving for a rainy day. But, of course, I dare say that you know that. Change gear, my boy, you stay in third too long. So! You are British now. What's this nonsense I hear about you encountering racialism? Swore at you, did they? Carry a photograph of your sister or me to prove that you're of white stock. Ignore them. Pearls before swine. You are white. We'll have no insult to our family - er - not insult - I mean - er - well my boy. Your wife is a good one. I congratulate you on your choice. A good woman. Family, my boy, the family is all important. Alas, ours is not what it used to be. We have money now, but we've lost the family. And you're going to lose us if you light that cigarette while you're driving. The family is important...."

I stopped listening and thought back to the time when Anne and I had gone to the blue movie club in Soho. We spent an hour watching the filthiest film I had ever seen. The place was dirty and seedy. It smelt of smoke and heavy breathing. When we came out we made love in an alley behind a big theatre. I laughed to think of how I had insisted on carrying the tissues until I got to the rubbish-bin. That had been the height of civilisation in a permissive society.

"Yes! You may well smile my boy. But it is not correct that Marwan should behave like that. Someone will beat the living daylights out of him one of these days. Once, the fool shouted at the top of his voice in a Swiss restaurant in Lausanne: *'Est-ce que c'est vrai qu'il y en a beaucoup de Juifs en Suisse?'"* Father's imitation of Marwan was excellent and I laughed loudly.

"Not really very funny my boy is it? Such jokes are in bad taste."

"Oh, he doesn't mean any harm. He's full of exuberance," I said lamely. I detested racist jokes, but I knew Marwan.

"A fool!" shouted father irritably. "And your sister: what's this? Hey? A monster, a monster."

I always felt sad when father spoke disparagingly of Selma. He doted on her in every way. His anger sprang from an excess of love. "Overdose! What for?"

"She took an overdose?" I asked, really horrified.

"Nothing serious. Nothing. A little overdose of sleeping tablets. Nothing to worry about. Nonetheless, a thing of no little danger."

Father's habitual use of the meiosis allowed me to realise that the incident was somewhat serious.

"Why an overdose, son? Why? She had problems. I have little patience with this sort of thing. I believe in will-power. You have a problem. Crush it! Ali can stop drinking this very second. All he has to do is to decide to stop - and there you are."

Father's external firmness was only matched by his acquired extreme confidence in the powers of reason. This confidence would have bordered on the megalomania had it not been for my knowledge of his inner self through anecdotes. His all too human delusions were, to say the least, megascopic. This belief was confirmed when I read his diaries after he died. A true romantic at heart in every way.

"Love! That was her reason! LOVE! Love! Sentimental rubbish not worth a kilogramme of excrement!"

I wondered irreverently about father's past love affairs.   My disrespectful imagination tried to picture a young Hussein in bed with some German fraulein or Montpellier demoiselle smacking their lips after lengthy oral sex. I could not for now.

"Slow down! Slow down! There is no hurry, my boy."

I felt my affection increase for the irritating old man. If only I could see him in a more honest light. If only - what? Reverse our positions? We should soon do so.

"Are we dere, daddy." asked Susan's sleepy voice from behind.

"Almost," I answered.

"You mustn't speak to daddy while he is driving," said my father. Through the mirror I could see Susan's large eyes looking from father to me and from me to father.

I felt another surge of uncomfortable affection for the old man, tinged with increased irritation at his cold unemotional demeanour. I wondered if we would ever be really close – even this late in life. Little did I know that a few years later he, Marwan and Ali would be beyond the reach of any friendship. But I anticipate a future of isolation with that something missing permeating my little life.

****

"Wilkommen! Bienvenu! Welcome!"

Marwan stood outside the restaurant. *"I am your host,"* he shouted. "Selma, Mary-Lou, Emily, Susan, Hussein: *all and every one a virgin. You don't believe me? Here, ask old Hussein."*

He slapped father on the bottom.

"Marwan!" said father, laughing, "You are decidedly a lunatic."

We all walked into the spacious Lebanese restaurant where a table had been reserved for us.   The atmosphere felt somewhat false. Lebanese music cheerfully wound its way in and around the numerous tables. People chatted in English, Arabic, and French. The falsity arose from within me. I felt intensely uncomfortable in a setting that brought memories and, in addition, reflected none of the present Lebanon: bespattered in her prolonged and bloody agony.

We sat at the large table, Susan between Emily and me. Ali and father sat at each end.   Marwan and Selma sat on either side of Marwan's infant daughter. To my left perched Mary-Lou: she did not advise me to hire a maid. She did worse.

"Yah bad man!" she started. "Why don't yah take your wife to the country for a rest?"

I politely and doggedly pointed out that my wife and I lived in the country.

"Ah meen without Susan!"

I explained that we preferred to spend our holidays with our daughter. Further, I explained that my salary did not really allow for week-ends away from home.

"Yah bad man!" she drawled and immediately changed the subject.

Marwan looked at me and said, "You have my permission to kick her!" He laughed. "Or fuck her if you want. Everybody else does. She's not really like that - but you see money - ah.

Money

Money

MONEY makes her head go round and round."

The lunch was excellent. I ate it with the usual feelings of guilt at knowing the inevitable dyspeptic suffering to come. The entire conversation hinged around the latest gossip, with Marwan as master impersonator. Several people including aunt Haji, uncle Issam, and many others made their appearance in his chair. Now and then the conversation slipped from gossip to reminiscences. Unable to join for fear of seeming rude in expressing my thoughts, I confined myself to the occasional laugh or innocuous comment. I paid Emily, and particularly Susan, a great deal of attention. Susan and I chatted away about the various dishes that were put before her.

"You know that bitch had the audacity to say that she has suffered in Beirut. She was only there for a week. I spent the whole war in the middle of it all."

I thought it a strange thing for Selma to want to excel in. Her recent misfortunes and her experiences of the war had definitely affected her adversely. I wished that I could help. She remained externally impassively, a monster, as father would have it.

"But Selma," said father quietly, "that depends on the person. She most probably suffered enough in that one week to affect her like that."

"Rubbish!" shouted Selma.

"Nonsense!" echoed Ali.

"Bullshit!" stirred Marwan.

I looked around at the people in the restaurant. They seemed to be thoroughly enjoying the conversation at our table. To my left stood two little girls behind the trellis partition, their little fingers clutching the small bars as they strained to see the source of all the noise. Their large innocent eyes twinkled happily around our faces. I caught Marwan's eye. He nodded.

"Like the refugees at Jbeili's wedding. Do you remember?" he asked softly.

"Yes"

"Somewhat of a contrast. *Un peu vulgaire!*" He smiled at the two girls.

"*Oui. Très vul* - guèrre!" I answered with a motion of my hand.

"Ha? Oh, yes. Very good! Hey everybody drink up. Drink up. Saif cracked a joke!"

"Oh my!" shouted Ali. "We will regain Palestine yet!"

I laughed. The two girls' eyes behind the trellis laughed at our laughter. Their eyes reminded me of the time in Beirut when I had seen a man lying on the pavement with his throat cut. His eyes had rolled round and round. I had put my jacket under his head and given him all my pocket money to pay for the ambulance. I was only twelve. He was taken away and I never knew whether he had lived or died. Eyes. When mother died, someone had told me that she had one eye open and another closed. She had beautiful dark - very dark - eyes.

"No! I don't see why anyone should talk to me like that."

I listened to the family about to dive into another loud fuss over some insignificant incident. I switched off again and absently chatted to little Susan. The argument got louder and louder. I could still catch snippets of sentences from the various voices: "money", "the cheek", "our family", "not done", "when?" "how?", "damn it", "shit", "money", "pay", "how much". My mind slowly darkened in mad perpetuity. Escher's *Tower of Babel* darkened. I caught Marwan's eye.

Beside me Susan cried. Marwan pointed to his head and shook it. I looked from him to the others, from the others to the eyes behind the trellis, from there back to Marwan. He shook his head again and laughed. I looked from him to Susan, from Susan to him. I could no longer tell who was who.

Finale

25th December

My Dear Anne-Marie

Thank you for the lovely Christmas presents that we have just unwrapped. Poor Susan was so excited last night that she almost had convulsions! It was all my fault. I had inadvertently worked her imagination up to the pitch of hysteria. I really believe that the poor girl expected a man accompanied by four reindeers to walk into her room! She gave us a terrible fright and a sleepless night. But thank God she is all right now.

I have recovered from the slight depression brought upon by the unfortunate family reunion. It accurately represents our awful Palestinian Diaspora: unhinged, dislocated and depressed. I think that I now understand better what usually goes wrong during such meetings; but I shall not bother you with boring self and family analyses. To tell you the truth, I am having a rest from myself and my family. I utterly despise both.

School-work is going well and I am now happier than I have ever been before. Do you remember that feeling of want of something that I constantly referred to in my letters and in our conversations? It is disappearing for short periods but always comes back. I feel it now and then rather as the dregs in a sieve: a numb memory. Mostly, life is good for one reason: my little Emily.

Susan is fast asleep after the exertions of the day. Emily is having a relaxed read. Yes you have guessed it: another Dickens. She seems to be going through his works systematically. By the way, with the money you sent her, she has bought me his complete correspondence.

I know that I had not sent you the usual Christmas present. I had not forgotten. I enclose this letter with my new manuscript which I hope that you will like. Please give me your opinion of it; and under no circumstances should you allow father to read it. Not until it is corrected and revised.

While you read it, it will help you to remember our discussion of last summer in L'Ile de St. Pierre (Switzerland! How I miss its soothing effects). Do you remember what I tried to explain about writing 'novelistically' and 'presentifically' to show what the

Palestinian Diaspora has done to one growing artist? How it has created an apparently dysfunctional life? I have done so. I have acted as a fictor using both memories recollected within my little study here and 'presentific' observations. I have tried to create a kind of 'autobiographiction' if I may coin a rather attractive new word.

Well, I have just re-read all this and it sounds silly. Anyway I should not try to influence your point of view as a reader. If you are confused then the failure is mine.

But perhaps a few editorial notes would help. Peruse or ignore the following list as you desire.

To start with, the following comes from Kierkegaard:

"I am not alone, I bring with me a great train of troubles, fears, and torments."

Faysal Mikdadi was born in Nablus, Palestine in 1948, the youngest of four children. He was brought up in Beirut, Lebanon and moved to Britain in 1967 and has lived there ever since. His other works include two novels: *Chateaux en Palestine* (a French adaptation of *Return*) and *Tamra*; as well as a book of poetry *A Return: The Siege of Beirut* and two bibliographies *Gamal Abdel Nasser* and *Margaret Thatcher*. As well as his writing career, Faysal Mikdadi has worked in education all his life.